Voidrise

By

David Mills

authorHOUSE™

1663 LIBERTY DRIVE, SUITE 200
BLOOMINGTON, INDIANA 47403
(800) 839-8640
WWW.AUTHORHOUSE.COM

© 2005 David Mills. All Rights Reserved.

No part of this book may be reproduced, stored in a retrieval system, or transmitted by any means without the written permission of the author.

First published by AuthorHouse 06/20/05

ISBN: 1-4208-5826-2 (sc)
ISBN: 1-4208-5827-0 (dj)

Library of Congress Control Number: 2005904454

Printed in the United States of America
Bloomington, Indiana

This book is printed on acid-free paper.

Dear Reader,

    We shall create a universe, you and I.
    Step this way and I shall show you who the gods are...

                                                        D.M.

The voids make us!
The voids break us!
And, at the end, the voids take us!

These are the words of the Voidseer.

ONE: AWAKENING

I.

What must it be like inside the Void? Can the mind imagine it?

What would it be like to exist in nothing, in emptiness? To have vision and be surrounded by a darkness that sucks away even the memory of light? To be deafened by a silence louder than the singing of all the songs ever known and the blast of every trumpet? To have every sense starved of even the slightest stimulation?

For this is the Void, true emptiness. Not a single particle of matter or so much as a spark of energy to tickle the senses. Absolute absence.

This is no place for a living mind to be. A mind that remembers seeing, touching and tasting; a million microscopic sensations dancing across the nerves every instant. A mind that has known these things should not be here, must never come here.

And yet, once, in this Void a mind awoke.

That is to say, it became aware of itself again. To wake implies sleep. And from what sleep could it be waking? Here?

The mind awoke and asked "Where am I?"

A simple question, three basic concepts: where and I and to be. Enough for it to step over the threshold into consciousness. But that was all there was, the question. There were no answers.

"Darkness." All around, all enveloping. Thick and impenetrable darkness. No light.

"No light? Should there be light?"

No memory. Only shadows, silent motion in the darkness. Only the briefest flickers, unconnected facts. Yet it knew what light was.

"Have I.... been before? Yes. I was. I have been."

Not like this, though. Surely not like this. So empty, so basic. There had to be more.

"Light. Yes. There should be light."

Then the memory stirred, a brief flash dazzlingly bright in the absolute darkness. There had been light, once. More than ever before. And, then, nothing.

"Am I blind, then?"

Blind? So, it had known vision, once, or else how could it know what blindness was. The memory stirred again, recalling from the depths of instinct the wonder of a whole spectrum of colour and light, the palette that painted the universe for the mind to enjoy. A sterile memory only; no pictures just the raw fact that vision had existed and it had been a wonderful thing. But now it was gone. No vision, no light or colour, only the darkness. The pit from which every nightmare springs.

"What lies beyond?" It felt the fear, the ancient terror of the dark. What waited in the invisible shadows, ready to spring and devour?

"You cannot know," they seemed to whisper. "We might be here. We might not. Fear us, because you cannot know."

No way to see. No way to sense.

"No. Others. There were others."

Other senses. Check them. Check them all. The mind strained, pushed out with all the will it could muster, searching for any response. Anything, even the tiniest flicker.

"Nothing."

The fear jabbed; a spark of cold, bright flame, terribly tangible against the emptiness. The mind tried again, desperately struggling to reach out of the darkness.

"Nothing. Nothing. Nothing."

Darkness. Silence. Absence. Not a photon of light nor a whisper of sound. No warmth, no cold, no substance. Nothing.

"But I'm here!"

But there was no "here". There was nothing. Only the "I" existed, imprisoned in nothingness.

"Help me!"

There was no way out. No walls to beat on even if there had been fists to beat on them. The sparks of fear grew into a fire, an icy torrent of confusion. The only real thing in this emptiness other than the "I".

"Help me!"

The mind recoiled, retreated from the flames. It felt despair beckoning to it, inviting, offering the sanctuary of panic to cloak the danger from the perceptions, to envelop all in its dark folds.

"NO!"

A roar burst out of the shadows, a reverberating bellow before which the fear-fire seemed to cower and die.

"No. Think. You can think. You ARE here." The echoes faded, sucked away by the Void.

"Think. Reason. Yes. I reason. I think. I exist. I... I...."

But what? It existed as what?

"What am I?"

Something in nothing?

"Before, then. What before."

The shy shadows of the memory spoke too softly to be heard. Isolated words and glimpsed meanings. But, amongst the accumulation, the intangible ally, instinct, began to draw conclusions from the inadequate evidence as it, alone in all creation, knew how. Reaching out with unknown tendrils to sense that beyond the reach of the others. Churning every particle into a stream of possibilities, the likely, the doubtful, the nonsensical. Until one, the clone of the truth, darted out into the lurking memory and sought out its reluctant twin; seized, held, forced out into daylight.

"I had...a form. A solid form. A body. A body that could sense and touch. Hear... See."

Hopelessly, it strained the senses again for any impulse, any message. Not a flicker.

"No senses. Could it be that I live in a body with no senses? Blind, deaf, paralysed? That would explain it. Could it be so? There may be help for me, then."

But no, said the illogical reasoner. Would there not be the sensation of bodily warmth? Would there not be the swell of expanding lungs or the rhythmic vibration of a pounding heart? Would not the ceaseless flow of life-fluid be felt despite any paralysis? No body, I fear. No body.

"But, if no body, then...what?"

A mind from a body, now alone, detached. What did that mean? A sudden, terrible thought occurred to it.

"Could I be...dead?"

The ultimate inevitability. The ultimate fear. The point of ending or transition. The fear that lurks in every fibre of the being.

"Am I dead? Can all I knew be lost to me?"

"STOP!" Again the bellowing voice thundered out of the whispering shadows, seeming to sense the despair creeping back. "This will not help you," it growled.

"But if I'm dead..."

"Stop, I say! What if you are? You are here, existing. Keep your reason and you can find a way to cope with this, whatever it may be."

"With only...this?"

"Is it not enough? Besides, how do you know that this is all there is?"

"I can't remember. How can I know?"

"Search for yourself."

The echoes died and the mind was alone again. What had the voice said?

"Search. Explore every feeling."

Hadn't it done that already? It had fought with all its strength to reactivate the senses it knew it had lost. But, perhaps, there were other senses. Different information it could gather.

The mind relaxed, opened to embrace all. Any sensation that might remain.

"Such peace." Uncluttered void. The first basis, so simple and silent. Unsullied by the conflict life brings.

"Freedom." The instinct had been right. No body. For the first time, the mind knew what it felt like to be truly unhampered. No more demands to be satisfied. No more pain to be endured. No longer reliant on so clumsy an appendage. No longer locked in. Only careless drifting. Floating free.

"Heaven, perhaps."

But still there was the smothering darkness. A prison more terrible than ever the body could be. Shutting the mind away from all existence, starving the hunger for knowledge, taunting its captive with the threat of the unseen terror that may or may not lurk behind that darkest of all curtains.

"Any curtain can be drawn aside if you can but grasp its edge."

Where had that come from? A whispered sentence among the unconnected syllables. Meaningless. And yet seeming to hold so much meaning.

"Any curtain can be drawn aside if you can but grasp its edge." The riddle repeated. So familiar.

"What? What is the meaning? I know it. I'm sure I do."

"Its edge. ITS EDGE. HA...HA...HA...HA!" The very emptiness seemed to laugh at the ignorance. A mocking challenge. "Draw this aside if you can. If you dare."

Rage. Anger, wholly mental, bubbled up inside the substance of the mind. Was it not enough to be imprisoned? It would not stand to be taunted as well. From the frustration grew grim resolve.

"I will not stay here. Heaven or Hell, paradise or damnation, I care not. If a curtain it is, then open it I shall."

Every impulse bristled. Every particle tensed.

"I shall open it. I SHALL!"

It was a battle cry. Every thought, every iota of the being sprang into feverent life, working, searching, doing all that could be done. Anger gave it the fuel it needed, ransacking the shadows for the reserves of energy hidden there. Find the solution.

"Find the edge."

New impulses, undiscovered and unused, un-needed, stirred out of dormancy and reached out. All must search. Seek out the edge.

"The edge. The edge."

There! Was that something? A brief flash caught in mid sweep and passed beyond. Again, but slower. There. Yes. A split, a hair-thin sliver of light leaking into the nothingness.

"The EDGE!"

With no hands, the mind reached out. With no fingers, it grasped. Non-existent muscles flexed, contracted and threw the curtain aside. And eyeless vision saw.

"No!"

Light poured in. Thick, white light, heavy as mist, exploded into the Void, filling it from end to end.

"No. It should not be like this."

The core of the memory, the heart of the being, protested, betrayed itself.

"It cannot be."

What it saw was a vision of night. The punctuated vastness of outer space. The mind knew it well. It could be nothing else. There were no horizons to be seen so this could not be a night sky on some world. It was open space. But it was wrong.

"Space is dark."

Space should hold no light. It is a void.

"No. Space isn't a void. All Space has substance. The substance can't reflect light and has no illumination of its own, so it can't be seen." Another wild certainty, facts without foundation, plucked from nowhere, vanishing into nowhere as the echoes died. "It can't...be seen."

But the substance was being seen. The pale swirl of glowing mist. Parting before without resistance, closing softly over the wake. Space coloured white, not black.

"The stars?"

Oh, yes. There were stars. Minute pools of darkness scattered at random, each drawing the bright light into itself in eternal hunger but always remaining a point of blackness. Oh, yes. No detail had been omitted. A negative photograph of open space in wrap-around, three-dimensional reality.

"But this isn't Space as I know...knew it."

But the reality could not be denied.

"But I can't exist in Space."

A quandary.

"I do exist. I am here. In a visible Space I should not be able to see. That should have no light. That I should be unable to exist in. Yet I exist. I exist where I cannot exist."

The evidence looped, span. Questions lead to questions, cancelled questions. The whirl became a swarm, flashing across the vision and blurring out the false night.

"Help me. Will no-one help me?"

All that came before was lost, masked by the memory and hidden from the sense. All that came before was lost, those who came before were gone. And with them went the hope of deliverance.

"No hope. No help."

Contradictions swarmed. Hopes evaporated. Terror and panic flared beyond control. A terrible vortex of mind and soul and conflict. And at the eye, the core of the being, all that made the individual, stared into the lie-space vision that it had longed for. That, now, wouldn't go away. And every tortured particle cried out its anguish with all the strength that remained to it. A terrible cry without voice. A cry that none could hear.

2.

Yet someone did hear.

Te stood upon a small ledge, a short distance below the Peak. From here she could see her whole world stretching out beneath her. An immense sculpture in rock, moulded by a random hand and baked hard by the passage of eternity. Standing fast before all the forces that ravaging time could blast upon its surface, bearing them without a scratch.

It only changed for her, it seemed. Whenever she stood here, the panorama before her seemed subtly altered. Beyond reason, there were always details, small refinements that she was sure had not been there before. Shapes and forms, cracks dark with mystery, a thousand new inspirations for a young mind awash with dreams. The great Atlas, impervious to centuries, stirred in its sleep, yielded only to her. And she would look beyond the grey to the beauty that only her vision could perceive.

But today she was not looking at it. Though part of her mind ached at the missed opportunity, she confined her thoughts to the task that she had come to perform. She had been coming here less and less as approaching adulthood ordered her mind and the wondering child faded. Soon the day would come when her imago would stand here and see only the grey, only the Rock as it was, not as it could be. She should make the most of the magic while it lasted. But not today.

She turned her vision, instead, to the sky, a pale and endless sea of mist that, she felt, concealed too little for comfort. It could not conceal the voids, the ultimately dark pinpoints drawing, in their endless greed, on the very fabric of the universe. Absorbing everything. Even her, one day. Nonetheless, she gazed upwards.

And, though her vision probed the slow swirl in its limited fashion, it was her mind that truly reached out. The dead memories of the past and the intangible dreams for the future she left behind. The rest, all that was she, Te, in the present time, the motivation that made the memories and the soul that dreamed the dreams, detached itself from the physical shell of her body and soared spacewards. With the swiftness of thoughts she travelled, blissfully unfettered, save for a single thread, an invisible lifeline back to the cumbersome form that still stood, motionless, on the rock ledge. Parting the mists before her, seeing beyond physical vision, meticulously searching for something that, in all probability, did not exist.

Vo had known that when he'd set her this task. He must have. One of his lessons, no doubt. A test of discipline and method, to see if she would complete the search to the best of her ability though she felt it to be a pointless exercise and a waste of effort. It was his duty to her, after all.

And yet he had been curious. Genuine curiosity, she'd felt escape from him.

And anticipation. Reason proclaimed the search to be useless, and yet he was expecting it to yield positive results. Was there something more? Had he learned something from the Beyonder? Something he'd kept to himself?

The unanswered questions distracted her from the search and she was still turning them over in her thoughts when the cry was heard. It surged through the mists towards her, a vast wave of despair and fear, so powerful she could not possibly have missed it despite her lack of attention.

She snapped herself back to the alert but it was already too late. The wave was upon her; cold, insane terror, the ringing echoes of an agonised cry. There were words too, almost lost under the scream.

"All gone! Nothing left! No help! No help! No! No!"

She felt her own mind beginning to cry as the vortex tore at her reason. She heard herself echoing the words, "No help! No help!" Quickly she withdrew, fighting through the rushing torrent towards the sanctuary of her own body that waited, patiently, for her to return. She locked herself within it, abandoning the input from the senses, her mind raising barriers against the pain and a single impulse moving her body back from the brink of the ledge to lean against the rock wall behind. She had stared the insanity straight in the face and glimpsed the confusion, mind within mind.

She stood motionless, isolated within her own body, trying to order her disrupted thoughts. They sang in her mind like an angry mob, all shouting to be heard at once. Disfigured and disconnected ideas, shattered by the surge that had blasted against her mind. She had to reach deep down into her being to find... yes, a single thought, no more than a whim, locked in its rightful place, holding out in the turmoil all around it. She remembered what Vo had taught her.

"Begin with one ordered thought. A single block to be the keystone. Use that thought as a model for the others and they will soon conform to its dimensions."

The swarm of thoughts slowed. The softened shapes became focused, their perspective enhanced into extra dimension.

"Once that is done, to fit them into place becomes a simple logic problem. Every thought is linked to every other. Begin with the key and rebuild from within."

One by one, one on another, the pieces came together. Whims linked together to become thoughts, thoughts united to become ideas, ideas harmonised into beliefs. With each new union the puzzle became easier, each marriage pointing the way to a thousand others.

Slowly the structure of her mind took shape, a so familiar form that she had never seen before. Within it, two more forms. Herself, in duplicate. One a child, happily weaving its own private miracles. The other, grey and silent as the Rock, herself in time to come, the solemn reasoner, finding no pleasure in the youngster's games. She recognised them both, though she had never admitted to herself that they existed together. Now the blast had shattered the balance, scattering to the swarm the logic and experience of one, leaving the other exposed and afraid. Watching through the eyes of both, she saw the child sobbing as its form began to dwindle before the now dominant adult, reborn in the logical forge that now shaped her mind. Emphasis altered. The child shrank to infancy before the other. The adult reached down, enclosed the child in a protective embrace and lifted it gently. Then both turned to stare out at her. Both formed the silent words, "I am you."

The final piece clicked home and the whole picture lay before her. The impressions vanished, leaving only her mind, now healed, and her self, still shaken by the experience. She remained within herself for some minutes, allowing the ordered normality to calm her. She wanted to rid herself of the moment, forget the repulsive emotions, forget the pain. But the memory would not leave her, try as she did to expel it. The best she could do was to bury the poison deep within her soul and accept the lifelong struggle to contain it there.

She paused a moment longer, reluctant to expose herself to the outside lest the cry could still be heard, then slowly lowered the mind barriers and allowed all to enter. The cry had ceased.

The last to return to her was vision and, when it came, it revealed Vo standing, patiently, before her. She could tell, from his posture, that he'd long since settled into his watching vigil over her though he had offered her no help in her struggle. Another test, she realised with bitterness.

She must have allowed that bitterness to show for he said "You had no need of my help, child. You have been ready to perform the Re-Building, unaided, for some time now. You had only to find the confidence in yourself. It would have been inappropriate for me to intrude."

Te made to move towards him but a giddy aftershock made her stagger. Vo came to her, instead.

"Carefully, Te. The revelation of the first Re-Building is great. For the first time in your existence you have, truly, seen yourself. Every facet of your personality laid before you, the positives and the negatives, even those you would never reveal to yourself. All there for you to control and mould. You have seen what you are and shaped it into what you will become. For most, it is a treasured memory that guides them, fulfilled, into the void."

His words sparked the memory within her and with it came a pang of dread at the nightmare, the chilly ghost of the emotions she had felt. She recoiled from it.

"Not for me," she said with revulsion. "Such terrible pain. A coldness and emptiness I've never felt before. Oh, Prim, it was horrible."

"Yes." Vo's mind projected a comforting wave to accompany the word he spoke. "You have been given instruction in the negative impulses that I could never have given you."

The wave settled on Te's mind, warmed her, soothed her. She felt Vo's understanding of her ordeal in that wave. Though he could not know, he understood the agony her soul had witnessed and saw, with her, that terrible moment, the aftermath, the prelude.

Oh! Could he see her negligence also? How she'd failed his test? Too late, she masked the sudden guilt and it was clear, by his puzzlement, that Vo sensed the emotion.

"I lost my concentration," she admitted, her guilt turning to shame of its own accord, "My mind wandered from the task and I did not sense the wave in time to shield myself from it. I'm sorry, Prim."

The disapproval she had expected never came. If anything, Vo seemed amused at the admission. "There is nothing for you to apologise to me for, Te," he said. "It is you who has come to harm. And, I think, your lack of attention may have saved you from considerably more harm."

"How so?"

Vo said, "I doubt that there's a single Dweller who didn't receive a jolt from this wave, it was so powerful. Certainly, no one I passed on my way to you escaped the effect, even with the rock wall to protect them. You had no such protection but, I think, your wandering mind missed the worst of it. Had your senses been concentrated to receive the wave, it would've taken more than my teachings to heal you."

The comfort came again, though the implication of his words menaced the air. He moved to the brink of the ledge and gazed at the sky as though on a search of his own. "As a matter of interest," he said, at length, "what was it that so distracted your mind from your search?"

Te felt her soul deflate a little. The disapproval was coming after all. She said "I was speculating about the reasons for the search. Wondering what purpose it would serve." Then with a defiance she did not truly feel, "If any."

Vo remained where he was and, for a second, Te glimpsed a faint ripple of satisfaction, something she had hardly expected.

"Indeed. I had hoped that you would, rather than accepting my tenuous reasons with blind trust." He turned to her. "You have proved your mental discipline to me many times, Te. I have no need to test it further. And, valuable though it is, it is nothing without the inspiration and guidance of speculative thought."

His words gave her no congratulation but the satisfaction and pride he radiated was unmistakable. Te let them wash away the guilt and shame. Without realising, she had passed the test he'd set for her.

Vo turned back to his search. "Did you reach any conclusions?"

"No. A supposition only."

"Yes?"

"Presumably, you learned of the existence of another consciousness from the Beyonder."

Vo said "The Beyonder is still comatose. Until the Bio-form can be accommodated, It seems best that it should remain that way. Directly, there is nothing to be learned from it."

"You knew something, nonetheless. I felt it in you."

"Did you, now? It was clumsy of me to let it show."

"What did you know?"

"Nothing. I...suspected," Vo conceded. "The Beyonder's emotional vortices are still highly active despite its deep sleep. The state has randomised them greatly but, among them, I sensed loss. Also a deep bond recently severed, selfless concern, a need to search, many other similar impulses. The accumulation led me to suspect that the Beyonder may not have been alone when it arrived here, by whatever means that was. Tenuous evidence, I admit, but the possibility could scarcely be ignored. And, it appears, that my suspicion was correct."

"You think the wave was caused by a second Beyonder?" asked Te, doubtfully.

"Well, certainly no Dweller, here or on any other world, could've generated a wave of that magnitude," said Vo, "even if they possessed such negative emotions, which is unheard of. The Beyonder, however, may well be capable of them. Even in sleep, its mind vibrates with emotional impulses, some never encountered before. It is more than likely that the wave came from one of its kind."

Te joined him at the brink, her vision straying down across the rugged contours beneath her. To her dismay, she saw only grey, solid rock, barren and unmoving. She had remoulded her mind and taken the step into adulthood. The old magic had gone. But still in the back of her mind, a small voice seemed to be speaking, wondering what thoughts had shaped those contours, what lay at the bottom of those dark cracks. Wondering.

She turned again to the sky and began, tentatively, to reach out with Vo. "But what could make it fear so?" she asked, "What could provoke such anguish in any creature?"

"Envisage it, child. A living mind, trapped in darkness and impotence with no physical body to rescue it. A terrible enough fate for a Dweller's mind."

"I know it," said Te. "It is what the lost ones suffer, cut off from their purposes."

"My process will put an end to their suffering," said Vo. "But it is not Dweller minds we are concerned with, now. These are creatures beyond our experience. What must it be like for them? Consider this, Te. When we allowed the first Beyonder to Bio-Form, it instantly selected a set of dimensions. Almost an automatic reaction. What does that suggest?"

Te considered. "That the Beyonder is used to existing in one fixed natural form. Rather than attempting to adapt to the new environment, it simply replayed the model of that previous form."

"Good," said Vo. "I agree with you. But consider what else that might imply. If these creatures are so attached to that one form, it may mean that they have no conception of transmitting the mind from the body. The confusion in their minds suggests that they may not be capable of it, as we are. If this is so then they are existing outside their natural state and one of them is now awake and aware of that fact. Small wonder that it should panic."

Te felt the horror welling up again. But, this time, she understood it. Named it and knew it. "We must help it. Bring it to us."

"Yes, we must," said Vo. "This time, though, you will guide it here, Te."

"I? But I have no experience."

"No more had I when I brought the first here," said Vo. "These are beings outside our knowledge. There are none with experience. I have, only, a single encounter with a sleeping mind that followed my call without realising. A conscious mind will require subtler coaxing. Its fears will make it suspicious of us and a single mistake could be enough to drive it away, no matter how desperately it needs our help. You, Te, have touched its mind, albeit briefly. Long enough, though, to understand its feelings."

"Yes." Te could sense them clearly, now. She did not allow herself to recall the memory but just glimpsed it, like shading her vision from a bright light to see the source. "I will know what to do."

"You will know what not to do." Vo corrected.

"Do I have the skills necessary?"

"That, child, is for you to decide." Vo broke his search and faced her fully. "Not even I can direct you in this. You will be the first. There is no advice I can give you, there is no preparation you can make. Only you will know and only when the time comes. Ah!" His mind, still gently probing of its own accord, had sensed something and his attention snapped back to the search and locked on. "There!"

Te's mind followed his, a single tendril this time, following the trail out, past the voids, out into the empty mists beyond. And her mind heard, distant but quite clear, a plaintive sob.

3.

"Are you calm, now?" asked the voice from the shadows.

There was no answer. Sobbing only, the sound of a soul in fear and despair.

"Answer me. Pull yourself together and answer me." There was a new drive in the words, now. They shook the being, forced it to listen. "This will not help you either."

"Nothing can. No one can."

"Then you must."

"I cannot."

"There is no one else. Only you can."

"But there is nothing."

"Look again."

The eyeless vision persisted. Still the negative space, contradicting the very basis of the reality gone before, worse than any nightmare. The smothering mist, the terrible voids.

"Yet it has beauty."

There was a scientific symmetry, common to both versions of space and equally wondrous. A miracle working before the vision. There was motion, now, too. Not much. The movement of a breeze, no more, insufficient to disturb the heavy vapour all around. The voids, though, gave it away. They moved, passing slowly beyond the picture's frame, falling behind until the mist closed over them, finally gorged and engulfed. A drama of giants on an infinite stage. The symbols of power and might succumbing, at the last, to the inevitable end of all things. An immense play before an audience of one.

"Beauty."

"Good! Good!" The voice of the hidden mentor, softer this time but close. "You begin to see, now. You begin to understand, at last. That is good." A voice from behind, deep and shrouded. Cajoling words, urging words. From where?

"Who are you?"

"That matters little, surely. You hear me."

"I hear nothing but you are there. You talk to me but hide from me. What are you?"

Laughter, loud, reverberant, terrible. "I am you, you fool. All of you and more than you'll ever be. I am within you and beyond you. I am you."

Then it was gone. Only the mist remained. The last of the voids passed from view, the last mouth shut, snapping off the words. Only empty space was left.

"But not empty."

The luminous haze pervaded the scene, yielding without protest to the motion, silent and still as manifest peace.

"Not still."

The mind saw the mist in motion of its own. Behind, where the hidden voids still fed mercilessly, the mist contracted into a thousand swirling eddies, turning with the orbit wheel in a kaleidoscopic ballet. Ahead the ethereal blanket, unruffled by the voids, drifted on a lazy errand only known to itself, unhurried, and unordered. And yet there were shapes in the shapelessness, brief and hazy as wandering thoughts. For a second the aimless wisps converged and solidified, a patch of radiance intensified while the surrounding mist darkened and a perfect circle shone for a twinkling before vanishing back into the idle stream. Other forms, also. Some perfect geometry, others soft and irregular and all for the briefest of glimpses.

"Not silent."

Listening, beyond hearing, the mind could hear the sound. A whisper so faint and so regular that it could not be heard above the silence. But it was there. Not words, not syllables, not even letters but a gabble of countless incoherent fractions, minute particles of sound that never joined into language. A symphony of possibilities. Wonders beyond dreams.

"Such beauty."

The soul revelled in the tranquillity, the mind marvelled at the spectacle. The horror lapsed into the forgotten shadows. And the low, satisfied laughter from the depths of the consciousness went unheard.

Suddenly, the mist began to thin. The random shapes dwindled and died, the whisper silenced.

"What is this?"

The haze parted to reveal a wall of darkness. The motion abruptly ceased. Then, there was the sound. A hollow clang, an impact on glass. But not glass, vibrating away through the substance without matter, not quite solid but unyielding to the collision.

"Some kind of barrier."

It stretched away above, below, to left and right. Not behind, though. Behind was the mist, now seen from outside, a vast cloud.

The mind tried to move forwards again. Again the movement was arrested, the ringing tone sounded once more. It tried to move along the barrier, testing the surface all the time for a single vulnerable spot that might submit to pressure. But there wasn't one.

"An impervious wall."

A wall alive with lambent blue light. On the left-hand horizon a speck of light appeared, grew with immense speed and flashed passed the vision, a broad ribbon of blue flame that receded to a speck again on the opposite horizon. So the barrier defined itself.

"Transparent. It could almost be glass."

The darkness lay beyond. The barrier itself was crystal clear, thick and distorting, holding back a shadow dark beyond imagining, a midnight without the light of stars to alleviate it.

"No. No darkness."

The mind turned away, back towards the radiance of the mist to soothe away the dread of the ordeal in the dark. A terror, visible once more, repelled by a vast window. As it turned it noticed the window's curve. Slight, almost beyond perception, but a definite curve. And inwards.

"Another prison. And I am inside."

To escape from the dark's unwalled jail into a cell defined by transparency and the darkness waiting outside. No way of escape and nowhere to run to except that infinitely repugnant infinity.

"No escape. I'm stranded here."

Always there had been the hope. Even with the negative cosmos to erode it, always the hope to cling to. The prayer that a way back might be found.

"Back to the life before." Though the memory still shrouded the details, the feeling persisted. "I had so much. All lost."

The treasured possibility began to disintegrate as the facts revealed themselves and blotted out the options, one by one. Once again, hopelessness leadened the soul, clouded the thoughts.

"Must I watch over you every instant?" The voice of the mentor sliced into the sorrow.

"I was wondering when you would show up."

"Do not mock me. Your existence is my purpose."

"I would have both ended if I could."

"You would not. You cannot."

"I would sooner embrace death than face this empty life."

"No, I will not let you."

"Your words could not stop me. There is nothing for me here."

"What of the beauty?" The angered voice tried to soften itself. "Can you ignore the beauty?"

"Beautiful it is. But it is still only a single picture. No comparison to the diversity there was before. So much existing. So much to experience. More than a thousand lifetimes could absorb."

"You don't know that,"

"Don't I? My memory is clouded but I still know. And so do you, if you truly are me. Do you lie to me, now?"

No answer.

"Are you there? Speak!"

Silence.

"You, too, have deserted me, then. Abandoned your purpose."

Nothing. All that remained was the seed of doubt that the voice had sown, a nagging echo germinating.

"Can I know? Do I know what life I have lost? Can I be sure that it ever existed?"

The memory stirred again, struggled against the shadows that clasped it. Their folds were unbreakable, no facts could escape. But the whole combined mass of the memory began to vibrate with a message, born from the knowledge trapped within. The soul grasped it, absorbed it and swelled with new resolve.

"I do know. I have an existence waiting for me to return to it. I came here so there must be a route between the two. I must find it again. I will."

But how? There was no knowledge, no memory of the departure or the journey. Only the arrival that told so little. No way to determine between accident and design as the means.

"Without my memory, I'm useless. Alone, I can never retrieve it. I need help." The mind called out to make the voice hear. "I need your help. Answer me!"

There was no reply.

"Alone, I'm helpless. And there is nobody to help me. There's nobody here. Nobody."

"I'm here." Not the rumble of the erstwhile advisor. A new voice, light and warm, from ahead, not behind.

"Who said that?"

"I!"

"Who are you?"

"I am one who wants to help you. You need help so desperately, don't you." The soft words soothed the pain, the frustration.

"You didn't answer my question."

"My name would mean nothing to you. My purpose, as I said, is to help you, if you will let me."

"Where are you?"

"You are not far from me. I live among the mists, far enough away from the darkness."

What could this be? Another voice, another illusion from within or a friend without? Help freely offered and, it was true, badly needed.

"Where do you call me from?"

"From the Rock. My home. It is not far. Come."

"Can you help me?"

"I believe we can."

"We?"

"There are many of us here. We all want to help you, if we can. If you wish us to, you must come to us here. Then we will know what help we can give you."

"Where will I find you?"

"Follow me." The voice became softer, receding into the mist cloud, "Follow me."

There was no argument. Slowly the motion began again, moving always to hear the voice clearly. The mist enveloped the mind once more, the shapes and whispers going unnoticed. The mind's attention was focused solely on the guiding voice.

"Follow me. Follow me."

4.

Vo gazed out into the bright night, with both vision and mind, and said with satisfaction, "It is coming."

They had moved from the outside down into the Rock, to one of the multitudinous chambers that speckled the interior. To the hive of the Dwellers.

The room lay just below the outer surface and one of the rock walls, carved to smoothness, receded to let in the hazes of space and, more importantly, to let out the mind of Te that, ever so carefully, reached into the lightness and called out with softened words.

She reluctantly allowed part of her self, her own personality, to join her mind in its task. She needed the emotions that lay there to understand and manipulate those of the Beyonder. Only a small part, though. She dared not risk the Beyonder seeing her fear of the emotional forces it possessed, forces that could blast her mind to the mists in an instant if it so chose. Nor could she allow her immature impatience to creep in and corrupt her mind. She had to command the creature without its realising. She could afford no mistakes.

As her mind whispered, the remnant of her Self released gentle, soothing waves. Not too strong. It must not feel the touch. Gently. Softly.

The rest, retained within her body standing next to Vo at the window, concentrated, supervising and controlling the baited hook far out into the mists. It was awake, as Vo had said, and it had answered her call rationally. The panic, the fear, both gone. Had it come to terms with the reality it found itself in?

No, not quite. The remnant had sensed the pounding of frustration in the Beyonder's mind, a hammer hurling itself time and again against the wall of facts that held it in. A wall as solid, in its way, as the Barrier where she had found it. As she'd watched and listened, from a safe distance, the pounding had quickened, stroke after stroke, increasing in force as desperation began to set in once more. She had waited for just the right moment, the moment before the attacks became frenzied out of control and drained the strength away.

Then she had called and it had followed her.

Vo's mind, though powerless to assist hers, reached out and watched. He was careful not to interfere, maintaining a much greater distance from the wandering mind and masking every wave of his presence, blending into the mist itself.

"Excellent!" his body said. "The moment was well chosen, Te. It follows without apprehension."

"Not for much...longer." Enough of Te's mind remained unoccupied to make her body speak, though with some difficulty. "Its...desperation has kept it from distrust...so far. That will fade...with the hope I offer. Soon...it will remember...to be suspicious."

"Can it be countered?"

"Not...directly. Caution and distrust...are integral down to the primary level...of its being. The first... reaction to any new stimulus... will always be suspicion. I could only...dull the reaction at best and only then... with a full mind-touch. It would...never allow that."

"No. You are wise not to attempt it." Vo shifted his vantage point a little to better appreciate her diagnosis. "A mind with such a basis may react instinctively to any perceived interference. It could flinch away or, worse, lash out. And we know the harm it can cause. You must find another way."

"Yes." Te hesitated a moment as her supervising mind considered the options. "Persuasion will...be difficult. While it doubts our sincerity... there are no reassurances we can offer... that will convince it. There is one... factor in our favour, however. The Beyonder is at...a considerable disadvantage... in its present condition. Its desire to...find a way out of... its predicament may be...powerful enough to override...its basic fears. If I can...." She broke off, her mind concentrating harder, straining to catch again the glimpse it had sensed. Then she said, simply, "It begins."

"Come, This way."

The mind was back among the mists again, listening for and following the guiding words. The voids, once again, opened their maws before it but the guide wove a trail easily between them, never too near to the danger.

"Danger!" A low, hoarse whisper floating with the motion, just ahead of the closing mist. "Danger! Danger!"

"Is that you?"

The voice from without had not heard. "Follow. This way."

"Danger!" It could almost be the voice of the mentor, hollowed of conviction, faint and uncertain.

"What danger?"

"Danger!" The same drawn syllables, echoing over and over.

"What danger can there be?" The question lingered, unanswered. "What danger...can there be?" The mind slowed its motion and hovered, listening for the guide again.

"Come. Follow."

"Wait!"

"Yes?"

"How do I know I can trust you? How can I know that you speak the truth when you offer me help?"

"You can't."

"What!"

"Think about it. Is there really anything I could say to you that would dispel your fears? Is there any fact that you would accept from me as proof of my good faith?"

"No, I suppose there isn't."

"Of course, there isn't." The voice's tone just avoided admonishment. "I could stay here into eternity arguing my sincerity with you. It would change nothing. You have no way to tell if I lie or not. At the end you must decide for yourself whether or not to trust me."

"How do I decide?"

"It is not for me to say. You want help. I offer help. If you want it, you must follow me." Again the stranger's voice began to fade, quicker this time, moving again on its homeward journey. "Follow me. Follow me."

Friend or foe? Gaoler or benefactor? Which? Whichever, soon it would be lost. The decision had to be made now. There was no time to debate. There were no facts to consider. The instinct, silently computing with almost no data, had to take the decision, and quickly.

Still there was the warning whisper. "Danger! Danger!" Intangible menace. But weigh that against this existence, the mind thought. Any amount of time, shut in with the darkness and light transposed. Say, then, "Decide!" and the choice is made.

"I will follow."

It began to move again. The ethereal invitation had dwindled to a word among the whispered confusion.

"Which way?" It had lost its bearing. The mist offered no reference points. "Where are you?"

It moved experimentally along the course that had led it this far. But the call waned and was lost completely. The mist closed in once more.

"Have I hesitated too long?" The whisper jabbered no reply. "Where are you?"

"I am still here." Behind, and quite near. "But you must come this way. Follow."

Follow, then, The decision was made and final. Listen only for the directing words. Ignore the whisper on hearing's edge. "Danger!"

"It comes...again." There was satisfaction in Te's hesitant words. "It will...resist no longer."

Vo's mind, which had watched the exchange in silent fascination, withdrew wholly into his body. "An interesting manipulation," he commented aloud. "I must admit, I did not expect that reaction. But, then, I cannot sense its emotions from my standpoint."

"They go...deep." Te's speech became more laboured as she concentrated harder. "Its motivations are...almost, completely dominated by them. I threatened to...abandon it to its predicament...and gave it no time to consider...its decision to follow me. In those...circumstances, with no facts...to guide it, it would...act on the prevalent...emotion."

"Namely, its desperation," said Vo. "Interesting. But take care, child. Remember that it is a Beyonder you are controlling. It may be capable of responses we cannot predict or control. In those seconds it was alone, it could've rushed into the mists and become lost or stumbled into the grip of a void. Do not let it slip from your control."

"I...have not forgotten," Te whispered. "There is...always that risk. For a time...I almost lost it."

"I know," said Vo. "It almost blundered into me and I was watching from a good distance. Fortunately, it didn't detect me otherwise it would've fled for sure."

"I...will be careful." Te's words became more indistinct as her quarry drew nearer. "It follows...without fear, now."

"Will it continue to, though?"

"If it reaches...here at all...we will...have our answer. The...results... will...tell." She said no more, totally absorbed in her labour.

"They will tell, indeed, child," Vo thought to himself. "They will tell of your success, I am sure."

He moved from the window to the rear wall and began to manipulate a large panel of controls set into it. A hum, the sound of a thousand voices trying to sing the same low note, made itself heard, rising in volume to vibrate the very air. Higher, pulsating notes joined the rumble, running along the seamless walls and congregating in an area of the smooth rock floor to Vo's right. Cracks appeared, eight perfectly straight fissures forming two large rectangles, one within the other, in the centre of the chamber. The space between them, no more than two inches, began to rise above the level of the floor, a uniform rectangular box growing out of the rock. The floor area within its walls remained motionless until, as the sides rose to a half metre, the inner cracks sealed themselves as suddenly as they'd appeared and the floor, too, rose with the box for a further half metre and came to a halt.

The soprano song ceased, the bass tone softened into the background. Vo operated one more control, turned and fixed his gaze on the box. Slowly, the four sides began to thin as though an invisible vice were squeezing at the molecules. Their thickness halved, quartered. The greyness in them faded away into a crystal transparency and a casket of glass stood before him on a stone pedestal.

Vo relaxed his stare and simply watched as the casket began to fill. There were no pipes or inlets of any kind connected to it. The heavy mist that began to swirl behind the glass, accumulating with every second, appeared there out of nowhere. And, though the casket had no cover, the mist made no attempt to escape from it.

And Vo thought to himself "it is ready."

A point. A dot of black, one that did not suck hungrily at the substance of the vast cloud. No void. And the softly whispering trail did not move to avoid it. A point at the vision's centre, growing with the passing seconds.

"Come!" The voice clearly radiated from there. "You are almost with us."

"That is your world?"

"It is. The Rock."

The expanding point began to reveal its contours. The circle mutated, elongated. A rough triangle. No sphere.

"Sphere?" Another glimpse from the shrouded memory. "Spherical. Why isn't it a sphere? Worlds should be spherical."

"Should they?"

"Of course. A gravity field will always...." Another certainty showed itself for a tantalising second and then dissolved back into the shadow, "...will always attract matter equally from all directions. Will always form a sphere. I think."

"Does it really matter? I dwell here and it makes no difference to me. Does it to you?"

"I.... No. No, it doesn't."

The form resolved to clarity. The blackness of silhouette gave way to grey, the grey of rock. Perspective extended into the third dimension. A pyramid? No. A cone.

"A mountain?"

Too rough for geometry's work but too uniform to be entirely random. From a base, roughly circular, the rugged slopes tapered to a sharp apex at the exact centre of the initial disc. A mountain suspended alone in space. Uprooted, perhaps, from the surface of a lost home and cast to the winds.

"Where do I find you?" The Rock, looming to fill the vision, revealed no activity, no sign of life. The slopes were too barren to accommodate any; no plants clung to them.

"I am within." The voice, louder and clearer than ever before. "We are within. Look!"

A beam of light, brighter by far than the pearl of the mist, lanced out from the side of the floating mountain.

"What must I do?"

"Come into the light. It will bring you to us. Come!"

There was a moment's hesitation. The senses probed the beam, warily. They received a warmth from it, radiating from the heart. Gold-pure waves of welcome, incapable of menace.

"You see," said the guide. "There is nothing to fear."

"I can feel so." Gingerly the mind rose to meet the light. The first touch, the softest contact at the consciousness' edge and the light washed in, a light too bright to dazzle, too beautiful to turn away from. It filled the vision and penetrated beyond, flooding narcotically into every impulse. The consciousness reeled as warm, contented waves caressed the soul and lulled it into a happy stupor. And the light slowly receded back into the Rock.

Te held the crystal before her and directed her mind energies through it. The facets absorbed them, twisted them within the complex lattice and projected them, as a beam, through the window into the mist.

The casket was full, now, and the mist within had stilled, waiting as Vo was. Having produced the ensnaring crystal and passed it to Te, there was nothing he could do until Te brought in her prize.

Te's body gave a start as her mind and self abruptly returned to it. The crystal she held still glowed, the beam still seared through the mist.

"We have it!" she cried, excitement forcing its way irresistibly into the words. "We have it!" Carefully she backed away from the window towards the vat of mist, holding the beam as steady as she could. Slowly she lowered the luminous gem into the casket and let the mist swallow it up.

Both turned towards the window. Both saw the errant shaft of brilliance receding. At its tip, a sphere of brighter whitened light rode the beam, returning to its origin. The glow of the crystal in the casket, muted by the dense vapour, intensified as it reclaimed its lost energies. The tip entered the chamber, homing in on the crystal that had briefly given it life and plunged into the casket.

Something shattered. Both heard it though their hearing sensed nothing. The light in the coffined mist pulsed and spread, infecting every wisp. It was mist no more. The casket now brimmed with liquid light, thick and oily. A writhing pool of particles searching, linking and breaking. Forming positives, negatives, indefinites. The twists and turns of reasoned thought. A mind.

The second Beyonder had come to the Rock.

TWO: RE-FORMATION

5.

Through the veins of the Rock, invisible trails running through every wall and every floor, Vo sent his message. Simple and to the point, his mind projected it. A mere fraction of a second was all it took. The message runnelled through the Rock, twisting its way through the labyrinthine corridors, seeking out the one Dweller, among the thousands, to whom he had sent it. A fraction of a second was all it took.

A fraction of a second later the reply came, retracing the steps of the first to where Vo's mind waited.

"Oa will come shortly," he said. "We are to begin without her."

Te was not listening. She was staring, vacantly, into the casket as though she expected to see the dreams of the sleeping mind within.

Vo moved to her and followed her gaze. "You see," he said, "you can still wonder. You've been afraid that you would lose that power as you mature, haven't you."

Te's reverie broke and she turned to him. How had he known that?

"I've felt it in you," he said. "You feel the magic beginning to dwindle but it will still be there. It has merely been separated from your logical mind by the Re-Building. Segregated so that it should not interfere with your reasoning processes. That is as it should be. But as long as there are things to wonder at in this existence you will never lose it. And you will always have need of it. It is the most invaluable of the tools you will need to complete your purpose."

"And when all is known, when there are no are mysteries, what then?" asked Te.

Vo said, "That is a question best put to Ra, I think. Whether his answer would satisfy your question or not, I couldn't say. What I will say is the discovery of the Beyonders suggests there are mysteries enough for a while yet."

Pulsing. The light from the casket was fading and brightening in a slow rhythm, colours beginning to infect the whiteness. It caught the attention of both.

"The activity is increasing," said Vo. "The creature is waking. We must delay no longer." At his bidding, two flat panels rose out of the floor besides the casket, their surfaces encrusted with crystalline fragments. From the upper edge of each grew a smooth sheet of smoked transparency and, as Vo and Te took their places before them, these screens sprang to glowing life.

The pulse of the casket quickened, shaking all the colours of the spectrum from the viscous light. Vo touched the crystals of his panel in a rapid sequence, extracting a signal and a rising vibration from hidden machinery. The display in front of him blazed with a flurry of symbols. Beyond, the transparent walls of the casket took on a glow of their own, not one of white light but of deep, drawing purple on the brink of darkness.

Vo said, "The link is complete. Offer the Beyonder control."

Te's console came to life under her touch. "Primary control?" she asked.

Vo hesitated. "Yes. Let it choose a body for itself. Let us see what it wants."

"Will we need to use the Basic Integrity Programs?"

"I expect so. Certainly, if it chooses the same form the first Beyonder chose. That body could never have survived here. It would have disintegrated in moments without the adjustments the program made to it."

"Perhaps we should feed the programs to the Beyonder. Maybe if it knows what is needed to stabilise the body, it will add those elements to the model."

"I think not." replied Vo "Let us not confuse it. All the Beyonder needs to know is that the Imager will translate its thoughts into a model of the body it wants. We can stabilise the model properly when it has finished."

Te's display blanked and a row of dots appeared across its width just above the panel surface. She picked out a deep red gem in the centre of the cluster and, with a light pressure, caused a momentary spark of scarlet flame in its heart. The concealed machine chirped a signal, a brief cluster from the higher octaves that ran from the briefly luminous crystal down to the floor, along and upwards into the body of the casket, intensifying the purple radiance for a moment.

"No response." The display remained empty, save for the flowing dot-line that refused to change.

"It doesn't understand yet," said Vo. "Send the offer again."

Te touched the crystal a second time and, though the casket itself reacted to the repeated twittering, its occupant remained uninterested.

"Again, Te."

The red crystal flamed once more, in vain it seemed for some moments. But, just as Te reached forward to send the message again, an answering signal came. A single ping, no more. On the display the dot at the farthest left of the row became a short vertical line that scuttled along the row, vanishing beyond the opposite edge and leaving dots in its wake. A response, but not much of one.

"A random pulse?" Te asked. As if to answer her, the apparatus emitted a second ping and another isolated line passed across the display.

"I think not," said Vo. "We have its attention, at least." The indicator bleeped another line, affirmatively, at him. "But still it doesn't comprehend the offer. Transmit the secondary message."

Te touched another crystal, again red, and a new melody scuttled across the floor into the casket. A demonstration, this time. See this, it said, see what you can do.

This time the indicator remained silent. The Beyonder pondered.

Vo listened to the silence for half a minute and then said, "Now make the offer again."

The red crystal blazed another barrage of sound towards the casket. It never made it there. A torrent of impulses exploded from the casket and swamped the repeated message as it passed. Te's console leapt to feverish activity as a raucous cacophony of sonic interpretations filled the room. The indicative row of dots on the display began to flicker with lines, a rapid binary code flowing from left to right, too quickly for Te to interpret. But not for the machinery. As the screeching continued, a point appeared on the empty screen above the indicator line. Then another. Then a line was drawn between them. More points appeared and were joined together by more lines.

"It has taken control," said Te. "It's already feeding in measurements."

The points appeared more rapidly, turning the lines back on themselves to form a three-dimensional, wire-frame mass on the display.

"So it was with the first," said Vo. "Little or no hesitation." He looked over at the form materialising on the display, slowly rotating to reveal all three dimensions. Only a basic shell as yet, lacking features and organs. But he recognised enough. "As I suspected."

"The same form?" Te asked.

"There are minor differences, even now. But, basically, yes. It is the same."

The pitch of the signals altered. The Image on the display began to sharpen as fine detail was pumped into it. Te watched it, trying to envisage the completed Bio-form in solid living matter, moving to the command of the resident mind. The vision, when it came, provoked a pang of disgust. Such a form, she thought. How could it exist so?

Vo's console emitted a sharp signal. He adjusted the controlling crystals but the alarm continued to sound.

"What's wrong?" asked Te.

Vo attempted another combination, which again failed to silence the persistent signal. "Our control matrices have cross-connected," he said. "Sever it, quickly."

Te manipulated her own panel but could only elicit a defiant signal from it. "I can't," she said. "Something is overriding my commands."

"The Beyonder's input is contaminating the programs," said Vo. His panel sounded another signal, sharp and pointed. The display came alive with symbols and gauges. The background rumble of the room rose a little. "It has tripped the activation relay," he said, a slight edge of alarm tingeing the statement. "The Bio-Formation has begun."

Te glanced down at her own display. The indicator was still speckled with lines and the contours of the grotesque form above it still flowed in fluid alteration. "The model is not yet complete." she said "You must stop it."

"The Beyonder has control of the activator," said Vo. "If it chooses to proceed with the Bio-Formation, it will not allow me to stop the process."

Across the room, the evil glow of the casket walls changed from deep purple to black. Among the mists a darker shape, a greyness in the centre of the white mass, began to form. The rumble rose further.

Vo left his panel and crossed over to Te who moved aside to let him see. "We need not be too concerned," he said. "The process will take time. Enough to complete the model if the data flow is maintained."

"But not enough for us to adjust the pattern," said Te. "Look at it. It's certain to need Basic Integrity Intervention to exist in this environment, let alone survive."

Vo considered, quickly. "Then we'll have to intervene now," he decided. "Load the Basic Integrity Programs into the auxiliary terminal."

A third panel rose out of the floor and Te went to it.

"Be sure to isolate the terminal from these two," warned Vo. "We can't afford to lose that to the Beyonder's control."

Te did not look up from her rapid manipulations. "But how can I intervene on the model without a link into the Imager?" she asked.

Vo said, "You can't. You'll have to intervene directly on the Bio-Formation."

Te's movements faltered. "What?"

"There's no other alternative. The Beyonder is, obviously, fixed in its intention and will resist any interference with the model it has chosen. Our only option is to force the adjustments into the Bio-form by direct injection."

"But if we inject the wrong adjustments, we might kill it."

"It'll die for sure if we do nothing." Vo positioned himself between the first two panels to get a clear view of both. "Now, align the programs and stand by to insert them, one by one, on my instruction."

Te hesitated, then continued her work. "I am ready," she said, presently.

The pattern on the first display, the model, was nearing completion, the last refinements settling into place. The second display, aside from the fluctuating gauges, showed the same form but in the early stage of its evolution. The Bio-form, slowly growing, as yet nothing more than a soft skeletal shadow in the bath of light.

Vo concentrated his attention on the second screen, casting only brief glances at the other. Te waited, poised over her controls.

The figure in the casket became more defined. Its darkness deepened and it seemed to suck in the liquid light, swelling as it fed.

"Prepare to inject the first program," said Vo. The metronomic movement of his gaze between the displays broke rhythm and flicked upwards to rest briefly on the casket. Then down again, to one display then the other. It fixed there. "Inject!" His mind said it, quicker than his speech would have.

Te caught the thought and stabbed down on a green crystal fragment, releasing a short burst of deep throaty impulses that caused the walls of the casket to throb in protest. The form on the monitoring display flickered then continued its growth, though the course of that growth had changed slightly. Slightly, but significantly.

"The form has taken the program matrix," said Vo. "Good. Prepare to send the second and third together."

The stream of data from the casket suddenly silenced. The indicator went dead. Above it, the completed body, the blueprint of a living form, somersaulted dreamily.

"I'm ready," Te said into the silence.

"So, too, is the Beyonder. Wait." Vo's alternating gaze froze on the panel beneath the floating image. A few seconds passed, seemingly unused. Then, there was an energetic crackle and the panel exploded with sparks, then flames. A few of the smaller crystals popped out of their mountings, flew across the room and shattered against the opposite wall. Vo relaxed his will and the flames instantly went out, leaving a blackened mass of chipped and discoloured crystals where the panel had been. The screen above, however, was untouched, not even smoke-stained, the dancing figure oblivious to the conflagration. The dot line, though, had vanished.

Vo flashed out a thought, "Inject now." An instant later the casket shuddered to a duet of notes in harmony.

The flowing light within was fading, losing its life as the dark shape drew it away. But it felt the interference from without and reacted with what anger it had left. Its failing pulsations gained intensity and pace as it tried to resist. The wreaked panel erupted in a brief shower of sparks.

You are too late my friend, Vo thought to himself. You cannot change your body now. You must accept what we give you. If you wish to live.

The door to the chamber opened and Oa entered. Without a word to either, she crossed the room and stopped, facing Vo. Their minds met, exchanging a simple greeting highlighted with respect for each other's particular skills. Then she turned to Te.

Te's mind sent the same polite welcome, her respect laced with the awe that youth automatically awards to greater experience and wisdom.

Usually, to a Dweller child such as she, the respect in the greeting would be omitted until they earned the purpose that would define their lives. It would be replaced by encouragement and an understanding of the struggle they faced to develop their skills for that purpose. It was this that Te expected, having been greeted in no other way throughout her existence. But it did not come. Instead, she felt, for the first time, the respect returned to her. Oa already knew what she had done, that which no other had nor ever could have done. All would know by now how she had guided the turbulent being to the safety of the Rock. All the Dwellers would greet her thus from now on.

There was a silent second while the salutations lasted, no more, and when it ended Oa turned her attention to the casket. The desperate pulse of the reluctant mind in the light had faded, beaten. There was only a pearly glow that still yet dwindled to grey wisps of dull fog that softened the lines of the dark form within to uncertainty.

"It will be complete soon," said Vo. "Complete and sufficiently stable to survive. For a while at least."

Oa transferred her gaze to the display that monitored the changing shape and studied it carefully. Then she moved over to the damaged panel, waved the lingering smoke out of her way and scrutinised the floating image. Only then did she speak.

"For long enough," she said, "though not, perhaps, in the greatest of comfort. The internal mechanisms appear to be less developed than they were with the first."

"Are they different forms, then?"

"No. The internal structures are identical in arrangement and basic design. But this form seems to lack finer operational details present in that of the first Beyonder."

"Will these mechanisms function adequately?" asked Vo.

"I'm not sure that they'll function at all, though that need not necessarily be of concern to us. Presumably, the minds are sentient so they should be self-sustaining. The mechanisms themselves are not needed to keep the creature alive in our environment. Still, there will have to be some restructuring."

"I suspected as much." said Vo.

Oa transferred her attention to the creature itself, touched its mind.

"Confusion. Too much confusion. It will need to be calmed down before we can get it to consent to the alterations."

"You think that necessary?" Vo asked. "It will be difficult to get any coherent responses from it for some time. Longer than we have before that Bio-form starts to break down."

"I think it wise to do so," said Oa. "A being so particular about its form that it must wreak the equipment to preserve it is not likely to welcome any changes being forced upon it. We have seen how it reacts when in distress."

"Very well," Vo conceded. "How shall we proceed?"

"I think," said Oa, "that we should keep the Beyonder unconscious for a while. Give the mind time to acclimatise itself to the new body and a period of peace in which to calm down. The mind of the first Beyonder is still unconscious and I have noted that its emotional activity is much quieted."

"The mind of this one is already active," said Vo. "You will need to use a suppression wave?"

"Yes. And while it is suppressed I can examine its body and that of the other Beyonder. A close examination may show us what these Bio-forms need to operate properly. If we can alter the environment so that these needs are satisfied then, when they awaken, they will be more comfortable and, so, less distressed."

The hidden machinery chimed, once, twice, once more. All three looked up. The casket walls were transparent once more. The mist within had gone, no longer able to hide the dark, rubbery Bio-form that lay there motionless. Thin, spindly limbs immovably joined to a grotesquely contorted trunk. The place where the mind dwelt, what might once have been a sphere now dented out of shape, crowned the whole from a thick stalk, flexible but as inadequate as the rest.

Vo moved quickly to the panel he had left. "It is finished," he said. "We must suppress the mind quickly, before it wakes."

Oa joined him, producing a small, clear crystal that she touched to the display. It glowed as the terminal accepted it and activated it.

Te remained at her own panel, but she did not look at it. She was staring, instead, at the figure in the casket, the form that, a short time ago, her mind had shuddered to envisage. A nightmare stepping out of her mind into reality, in living Bio-flesh. She found herself moving towards it, her will unable to stop the motion. It silently drew her up to the casket, drew her vision down to look full upon it.

This was the creature she had rescued from the darkness. This was the creature that had no place in the creation she knew. This was the creature that had blasted her mind with a fear that she could never escape from.

It drew her vision to the misshapen face, past the sharp protrusion at its centre to the twin depressions above, hidden beneath shutters of stretched flesh. Its vision, perhaps.

She stared down at them. The lids flicked back, flicked wide, and two glistening pools of darkness stared back at her. Stared into her and held her. She could not look away nor shutter her mind against it. Those eyes, wide and staring, reached in and filled her mind. To her horror, Te felt the pain it had placed there waking again, the anguished cry filling her hearing. She brought all her will to bear against it, to force it back into the shadows where she had buried it but she didn't have the strength after her exertions.

In desperation, her mind cried out to whatever listened, "Leave me! Whatever you are, leave me! What are you?" The last, a question with no place in her appeal, a question that had burned to be asked and had waited for a convenient time to arrive. But not now of all times. It burst impertinently from her mind before she could stop it. She stood, transfixed, now dreading the answer she would get. "What are you? What do you call yourself?"

The cry ceased, suddenly, leaving her mind filled with a noisy silence, worse in its way than the noise before it. Then clearly, simply, the answer came. One word, one she didn't recognise, a name.

"Human."

She got no more from it. Vo came up behind her and physically pulled her away, "Don't, Te! Close your mind. Protect yourself."

Te felt her own thoughts flooding back, washing away the dread silence. "I'm...all right," she said, shakily.

Oa was still at the panel, making rapid manipulations of her own. "The suppression wave isn't working," she said, in agitation. "I do not understand." She looked up at the Bio-form. It was shaking, uncontrollably. One of the pipe limbs reached stiffly upwards and its end unfurled into five flexible manipulators, which clutched at the air. Her mind looked at it also. "I sense a discrepancy. The body is sending some kind of signal to the mind. It is overriding the wave."

"What kind of signal?" Vo asked.

"I am not sure. It feels like a malfunction warning but I've never felt one so intense before." She paused, shifting her position a little as though to see at a different angle. "Panic is setting in. That signal must be neutralised. One of us must touch the Beyonder's mind and block out the warning."

Fear shot Te another glance as she realised Oa meant her. "Must I?" she quavered.

"You have already touched it, child," said Oa, "you have guided it here to safety. It may trust you where it would trust no other. The Beyonder must be persuaded to accept the suppression wave. And quickly. The mind is being told that the body is dying, though it is not true. The mind may decide to shut itself down to stop the pain messages. You must convince it otherwise."

A rebellious impulse in Te said "Let it die, if it so wishes." She pushed it quickly aside, ashamed. An alien mind it may be, but still a living one. Having brought it so far, she could not abandon it now, despite all it had done. Such actions may, after all, be beyond the control of its will. She would not know until it was brought to consciousness. Besides, she could see its pain now. Her mind did not have to look. The shaking had become convulsions, the eyes widened to bulging. An orifice beneath the central protrusion in the face, up to now sealed invisibly, broke open and widened, but emitted nothing and nothing entered. She had led it out of darkness, now she must lead it again, out of ignorance.

She steadied herself, bringing the mind barriers ready to hand should she need them, then moved back to the casket and looked down into the staring eyes. This time they did not attempt to seize her. She read in them, instead, a trace of pleading. She held her vision there and her mind reached out along that line into the other's torment.

"Help me!" it said. "You said you would help me. I...can't...." The rest was drowned out by insistent signals, demands and refusals.

"You have no need," she told it. "All minds can live here. Yours can live. You have no need."

There was no reply but she was sure it had heard her. But still the signals of failure sounded and, with the arrival of each new impulse, the panic increased. Te adjusted the mind barriers to shield herself from it and reached in deeper.

Oa's mind watched from outside, monitoring both. Out loud, she said "You must hurry, Te. The mind is beginning to close off secondary functions." As she spoke, the desperately waving limb with its clutching fingers fell to the casket floor and became still. "The shutdown is beginning."

"I cannot persuade it," said Te. "It is almost as if..." Then she sensed it. Deep down beyond the turmoil, a signal, a regular pulsing rhythm. She reached towards it and the confusion faded around her. She was leaving it behind. Soon there was silence, save for that one inexorable beat. There! Again! Again!

"I've found it," she said, aloud. "The mind is sending autonomic signals to the bio-mechanisms, but they're not operating. It thinks it can't live without them."

"Deactivate the signals, Te," said Oa. "That will stop the failure messages. Quickly."

Again! Again! Te concentrated on it, timed the rhythm. Again! Again! Again!

Then she matched it. "Stop! Stop!" The beat continued but she kept pace with it. "Stop! Stop! Stop!"

Then stop it did. There was silence. Te's mind listened to it for a moment in case the pulse should start again. It did not. She brought her mind out, sensing only peace as it travelled. The suppression was taking effect. But before her mind exited and before the Beyonder went fully into the sleep they had given it, she felt the slightest wave of gratitude from the drowsy mind.

"It is done," said Oa. "The Beyonder is fully dormant. Clearly we have more to compensate for than we believed."

"You had best begin your study of them immediately," said Vo. "Hopefully that will tell us what we must provide them with when they are awakened."

"There is no immediate hurry. The Bio-forms will hold for some time yet, though it may be best to keep them near the Re-Formation machinery in case they become unstable. Their minds will come to no harm while they rest and it will give this one's mind a chance to heal its wounds."

"You sensed wounds?"

"I did," said Te. For some reason, she found that, if she let her gaze wander, it always strayed to the casket, and the peacefully sleeping... what had it called itself?...human. "The memory, for one."

6.

The name came first. The first basis of memory, the identity.

"Kass...Kasstovaal! Malkan Kasstovaal!" That was the trigger. It punched a hole in the shadow curtain and let the light flow through. Under the force of memories, a whole lifetime fighting to get out, the dark wall crumbled and fell away.

Then it came in a torrent; a vast wave of life and sound that would've blinded had it not been what his eyes had once seen, would've deafened had it not been what his ears had once heard, all too fast to comprehend. Memories. They surged past, leaving him only a glimpse, sought out their place and lodged themselves there.

Memories of his childhood, things he couldn't even remember remembering before, each day scrolling past in sequence. They had been joyful days to the bright young man who had lived them, each one different and always full, never long enough. Visions of his home, one he had not visited for so long, of friends he'd left behind. And he'd forgotten all of this. It was like watching a stranger's dreams, better than any he had. For the first time, Kasstovaal realised just how much of his life he'd lost, had abandoned to become....

Then a wash of knowledge, facts and figures, disjointed to begin with but soon linking together, each joined to every other in the pattern of all things, the logic of the universe. His academy days passed before him and it was as though a dark cloud had settled over him. This was where it had begun, the degeneration of his life, his soul. This was where he had begun to empty his life of all that magic, of all those dreams and surround himself with cold, hard reality. He watched those years with a leadening heart, wondering whether the choice he had made had been the right one. His choice to turn the path of his life towards....

Too fast. All too fast, too brief to understand. Not enough to form the picture. Try to find the one factor that governs the rest. Try to focus. Fix on one memory, one that recurs perhaps. There!

A sea of faces. He had seen that before. He concentrated, looking for the same image to appear again. There it is! Focus on that.

A sea of faces, Young faces, looking up. Looking up at him, or where he would be. Yes, he'd been here a few times before, talked to many such groups of expectant faces. Time was when he, himself, had been among them, listening to the words. Now it was him doing the talking. Talking about what? Start at the beginning. Start from...the calling of his name.

"...Pilot-Captain Malkan Kasstovaal."

He rose from his seat and made his way up onto the platform. The man in the Principal-Master's robes stood aside to give him access to the podium. Kasstovaal was there, on his invitation, to give the customary Active Pilot-Captain's address to the new entrants on their first day. He knew the Principal of this Academy of Space Navigation quite well and knew the words "Come and scare as many of the little bastards out of my Academy as you can," to be the nearest be would ever get to an invitation.

The Principal, himself, had been a Pilot-Captain in his heyday but had now turned to teaching others about it, being the only profession that would accept him in his latter years, after the expiry of his license. All that specialised knowledge and experience had turned out to be good for nothing except commanding a space ship. Or this. On the whole, though, he counted himself fortunate to have seen his latter years at all, the life expectancy of Space Pilots being as precarious as it was, and accepted his fate as quietly as could be expected of one of his kind. And he took no offence at the opinion that an Active Pilot-Captain would be better suited to give this talk than he was. The reputation that preceded them tended to drive the message home more forcefully.

Thus it was that Kasstovaal was here; for what, his fifth time? Maybe more. To try and tell the unsuspecting assembly what they were letting themselves in for. As far as he was allowed.

He marched up to the podium, carrying a thick black file under one arm. He had given this speech enough times, now, not to need notes to refer to. What the file actually contained was the result of a year's subscription to a bondage sex magazine, which he had applied for when he was pissed out of his brain one time. Needless to say, it had absolutely no relevance to what he was going to say and he only brought it with him for one purpose, to which he now put it. He slammed it down on the podium, causing a number of gasps from the audience and one or two jumps out of seats. All extraneous muttering ceased and every pair of eyes fixed on Kasstovaal as though they didn't dare look away in case he noticed. A heavy silence formed around the hall to make way for his words.

He cast an eye along the rows of startled faces before he spoke. The hall could hold three hundred and, on this opening day, usually did. Three hundred hopefuls beginning a course of training which spanned seven years and culminated in a single test. He knew well that, of those three hundred, only three, perhaps four, would ever complete the course up to Pilot-Captain level. About a quarter would realise that, despite the academic prowess that got them into the Academy in the first place, they didn't have what it took to be Space Operatives and would drop out. Another fifty per cent, though insufficiently qualified to be Pilot-Captains, would be merited at individual skills, the best of which would be developed and would qualify them for Operative service in those fields. From the remainder came the expulsions, the failures and even one or two suicides. Only half a dozen or so would emerge to take the final test. And only three, perhaps four, would pass.

Kasstovaal surveyed this particular class and made a mental note of those who looked most likely to go the full distance. It was a popular sport among the Supervising Prefects to put money on a student's ability to be among the few pass-marks after the test and, before he left, Kasstovaal was bound to be asked for a first day estimate. Then he spoke.

"The time has come for a few truths" he began, in a voice low but still clearly audible at the back of the hall. "So far, in this hall today, all we've heard is a load of self-congratulatory horseshit about pride and honour and privilege on the part of the Academy, your planets and yourselves. Well, now that that's all done with, I'm here to tell you how it really is. I'm here to give you the grim and grimy reality of being a Space Operative."

One youngster in the front row gulped and Kasstovaal wrote him off there and then.

He continued, "You have been selected from the best of all your worlds to come here. And, no doubt, some of you still harbour poetic visions of being Space Pilots. Romantic dreams of adventure and discovery. What's the popular line at the moment? 'Sailors in Infinity.' 'Wanderers at one with the Cosmos.'" He allowed a dreamy smile to cross his lips as he spoke and, at the same time, watched to see how many of the faces attained the same glazed expression. Then he leaned forward, the grin dissolving into a glare.

"Forget it!" he said, harshly. "Space is at one with nobody. It is a place which neither you nor I nor anybody has any right to be in and it will find a million ways to rid itself of you. It will exploit your every mistake and bring every force it contains against you. My advice to you is to leave such ideas at home on those worlds of yours. Many have tried for such oneness. Many have tried to tame Space. They lost."

He paused and watched the implication sink in. About a hundred faces before him bleached white, a few flushed red and the rest were just too goggle-eyed to worry about changing colour. He noted, this time round, one youth who neither blushed nor blanched but merely frowned and exhaled breath as though he'd had one of his fears confirmed. Kasstovaal marked him as a possible at that time, an estimation that future events were to prove correct.

"Space is the one thing that Man cannot tame," he went on, "no matter how hard he tries. You can't control Infinity. That's the prerogative of gods, if you believe in such things. Is anybody in here stupid enough to think he or she is a god? Or a god in the making? If so, I've got news for you. You're not. And our training isn't going to turn you into one; never think it will. We can't give you divine powers. We can just show you how to stay alive a little longer.

"So that's lesson number one, boys and girls. Space will always work against you. That is the Space Operative's mantra. Repeat it to yourself constantly. Write it on your shaving mirror, include it in your prayers if you're religious. Have it tattooed across the inside of your eyelids, if you want. Just don't forget it. Space will always work against you. Even travel within it is impractical. Physical movement causes time distortions and speeds greater than light cannot be maintained long enough under conventional propulsion. Therefore, we must use something else for our travels."

He placed both elbows on the podium and leaned on them, "What is Space?"

It took a few seconds for the assembly to realise that he was asking them for a response. Then a few tentative hands went up. Kasstovaal didn't straighten up but, simply, uncoiled a finger from the fist of his right hand and pointed it at one of them. The student, looking as though he expected Kasstovaal to shoot him with it, took a deep breath and blurted out his answer before his courage deserted him, "A void!"

That was the answer that Kasstovaal had expected to get. It was the answer he always got. "Wrong!" he said. All the other hands went down instantly. "Space is not a void. It has substance. You can't see it because it does not reflect light and has no illumination of its own. Matter and energy can pass through it. But it is there, nonetheless. Space is a curtain, a dark curtain which holds all the light and matter and energy in its folds. And any curtain can be drawn aside if you can but grasp its edge." He paused to give emphasis to that sentence. Every Pilot-Captain knew it.

"Those are not my words but you will learn about the great scientist who first said them. That is what we have learned to do. To open the curtain and see what lies beyond. The space of this universe will not allow us to pass through it easily so what is needed is a space that will. And that is what lies beyond the curtain. A second universe, a second set of dimensions similar to our own in some ways but significantly different in others. For one thing, though this second mode of existence inhabits the same area as our universe, it is some six hundred thousand times smaller. Furthermore, physical laws that bind us here do not apply there. We can open the curtain and pass a ship into the Second Mode. Once there, it can travel faster than light without difficulty, with no distortion of relative time. It can travel the length of a single sector, reopen the curtain and emerge into this universe six hundred thousand sectors away from where it began. That is the secret of Second Modal Transit. A technique, perfected many centuries ago, that gave mankind the means to spread out into the universe from Origin. In the keeping of the Pilot-Captains, it binds his dominions throughout the galaxy together.

"Perhaps some of you may qualify to be Pilot-Captains and earn the right to have this technique at your command also. But be warned that the Second Mode has its dangers, some more potent than those in our universe. For one thing, the electro-magnetic energies that hold all matter together in our universe begin to decay when you enter the Second Mode. Stay there for too long and your ship will begin to disintegrate around you, as the molecular bonds give out. First your ship then your own flesh and that of your passengers and crew.

"There are other dangers, too; clusters of anti-matter debris; storms made up of time and energy drawn from the First Mode through black holes into the Second Mode; Ghost Planets that fade in and out of existence as the energy of their molecular bonds alters in strength; Energophilic dust clouds that can drain all the energy out of your instruments; a hundred other purely physical dangers.

"And navigating within the Second Mode is a delicate skill. Re-enter the First Mode at the wrong point and you'll find yourself sitting in the heart of a sun or on the event horizon of a black hole or six feet under the surface of your own home planet. There is no room for error, complacency or distraction. That includes poetic ideas about the nature of creation and feelings of mastery over it. If you cannot put these things aside, as I have advised you to do, better that you should leave now rather than waste our time and effort in training you. There are quicker and much less expensive ways of killing yourself."

He paused and looked round at the signs of extreme nervousness that now dominated every face without exception. One at the end of a row near the back looked as though he was, indeed, about to get up and walk out. Kasstovaal remembered, with some amusement, that, one year, a whole group of students from the same planet walked out on hearing this advice, much to the delight of the Principal-Master. It was interesting to note that no Applications for Entry were ever received from that planet again afterwards.

When nobody moved, he continued. "The skills you will be taught here will qualify you for many professions within the Space Service: engineering, navigation, mathematical skills - these and many more besides. Many of you will find a talent in yourselves for one of them. But to be a Pilot-Captain, you need to be proficient at all of them. A Pilot-Captain is an entire spaceship crew in one person's body. He must be able to take on the job of any crew-member who falls incapable. He has to know his spacecraft down to the last microcircuit. To instantly sense and rectify any malfunction. He is the one in control of all the others and takes into his hands, not only his own life, but those of his crew and his passengers as well. He is the one who will take them towards certain death and bring them out alive."

There was a slight snicker under somebody's breath behind him. The Principal-Master knew, as well as Kasstovaal did, that this was the line that did half the job of the address on its own. Ninety-nine per cent of them would now be doubting their capabilities and questioning their self-confidence. That was good. That would make them careful, at least. It would now be the job of the tutors to find among them that one per cent, those three or four individuals who still held true to their convictions, and cultivate them for the test.

Kasstovaal had no qualms about using that line. This was more than an opening address. He was giving them their first and most important lesson. Knowledge that would save their lives one day. Looking round, however, it was clear that none of them were very grateful for his advice. In all probability, the only ones who would ever fully recognise the value of his words were those who left the academy, seven years later, with a Pilot-Captain's license in their hands.

He recalled one occasion when he had been invited to present the licenses to a graduating class to whom he had given the address seven years earlier. Six from that class, all on Kasstovaal's first day estimate list, came through the test that season. And, as each took the precious scroll from Kasstovaal's hand, he saw in their eyes and heard in the "thank you" that each gave, that they recognised the wisdom he had given them and were truly grateful. He remembered wondering if he truly deserved their gratitude. Even to these three hundred faces he was not telling all the truth he knew. He moistened his lips. "Perhaps there are some among you who have what it takes to be such a person." As he spoke, he reached slowly into a pocket and withdrew a neat scroll of embossed plastic, which he unrolled for the assembly to see. "Perhaps there are a few of you worthy to possess one of these. A Pilot-Captain's operative license. Perhaps there are. Perhaps not. It is for you alone to decide. Decide wisely, I warn you. We do not expect perfection among our number. Perfection is not good enough. If you can prove capable of more then, and only then, we will welcome you." He lifted the extraneous file from the surface in front of him and after a few stunned seconds a short ripple of uncertain applause emerged from the assembly. Kasstovaal absorbed it with little relish.

Nothing he had said had been untrue and the wisdom within was invaluable without a doubt. And yet he felt like a traitor to those three hundred faces. Every time he gave an address of this kind he felt that he was betraying them, not by what he'd said but by what he hadn't said. What they wouldn't let him say.

He had warned them of the physical dangers that awaited them in the Second Mode. That much he was allowed to say. But he had knowledge about the Second Mode that few people across the universe had. The Principal-Master, for example, did not know about it. Space Central did know and they also knew that he knew and who it was that had told him. They would not let him warn the students about what happened to Space

Operatives after a few tours of duty. About what the Second Mode did to their minds, their souls. What they would become.

We will welcome you, he had said. Oh yes! Welcome to a life where you cannot help but look behind you all the time to see if death is following you. No matter how good you are or how well you're trained, no matter how confident you may be, the Second Mode will rob you of it and the ultimate realisation of mortality will leaden your soul.

It was almost always that way with Space Operatives. Trained, as they were, to compensate for the unpredictable physical hazards of the Second Mode, few could admit to having no fear of falling victim to them. With every transition through the Second Mode the feeling grew, amplified by the invisible invader that dwelt there and which no training could fight off. The fear would grow to certainty but would not reach mortal terror and with the conviction would come dark depression and resignation.

Welcome to a life where you dare not allow love to grow, to spare others the pain of your death when it came.

It was not unheard of for Space Operatives to break all ties to even their closest family. There may not, after all, be another chance to say goodbye.

Welcome to a dark mood that can repel company at a range of twenty yards.

They all but cast themselves out of society and settled into a solitary existence, only able to seek friendship and understanding from among their own kind. Most sought other solace from alcohol bottles and, in some cases, bottles containing far more dubious substances. Some to escape their predicament, others in an attempt to have as wild a time as possible before the inevitable end caught them up.

Kasstovaal would not wish such an existence on anyone. But Space Central would not let him warn the new students. The required level of excellence meant that potential Space Operatives were hard enough to come by; if they knew of the emotional damage they risked, there would be far, far fewer applicants. Space Central could not allow that no matter what, or who, it cost.

Some said that Space Operatives abandoned their lives.

"They were taken from us long ago."

Some said that Space Operatives placed no value on life.

"Yet we would die to preserve it."

Some said that Space Operatives wished for death.

"We are already condemned."

He didn't remember much about the rest of the assembly. He tended to shut off, after he'd said his piece, and brood on what he'd just done to all those youngsters. He'd used everything he could think of, short of the whole truth, to put them off and make them think twice about their vocation. Hopefully some of them would take the hint. But it was a half done job, the best he could do, and he doubted its efficacy.

Afterwards, the Principal-Master invited him into his study for a drink and chance for things to be said that could not be said in front of the students. While Ex-Pilot-Captain Lauritious Calantina didn't know the whole truth of the matter he was, nonetheless, fully advised of the subjects he was not to mention. As such, he had an inkling of what it cost Kasstovaal's conscience to make this address and had made a habit of making this private time available so that the bile could be let out.

His secretary, a prim old spinster who disapproved of the language he used, had left them a tray of coffee. Calantina picked it up off the desk, turned and dumped it, tray and all, out of the window. The study was on the fourth floor so it was a few seconds before they heard the crash of crockery and someone yelping.

Calantina motioned Kasstovaal into a seat, reached into his desk drawer and produced a bottle of Origin Vintage Brandy.

"Grab a glass," he said, "this is my crash course in forgetfulness. Thirty creds a bottle and worth every one of them." He poured for them both and sat down himself. "Anything you want to get off your chest?"

Kasstovaal shrugged. "Nothing you haven't heard me bleat about before. How did I do?"

Calantina raised his glass. "Your usual thorough job, as far as it goes. I reckon we'll have a few bags packed before the end of the day."

Kasstovaal sighed and sipped his drink. It was liquid fire all the way down his throat and set up a hearty glow in his stomach.

"I know how you feel, Kass," the Principal-Master said. "Why do you think I'm still doing this job, at my age, and not beating the shit out of my garden on Tasma 5, like I should be?"

Kasstovaal chuckled. "Cal, I never worked out why, exactly, you took this job in the first place. You've never gave me a satisfactory explanation, the times I asked you."

Calantina threw back his drink in one gulp and refilled his glass. "I'll tell you why, my boy. The truth, this time. Guilt, plain and simple, just like yours. I know what thirty years in the Service did to me and my own battered and corroded conscience won't let me stand by and watch three hundred fresh-faced kids a year line up to have it happen to them. So when they offered me this job, I took it and since then I've been cultivating a reputation as the most ill-tempered, cantankerous old bastard ever to stalk the corridors. That way, I'll either scare them off completely or I'll make them doubly careful about everything they do for fear of having to explain to me what they did wrong. It's not much but it's the best I can do to make them see sense."

He sat back in his chair and examined his drink for impurities. "But, despite the best efforts of both of us, the Academy remains almost as populous as before. I don't know, Kass. We get nothing but the most intelligent and academically proficient of the children from the planets in this sector; they have to be, to pass the entry exam. And yet, they're all too thick to take a simple hint when it's offered. I despair of kids today."

"Now you're beginning to talk like an old man," said Kasstovaal. "Save it, Cal. I'm not fooled for an instant."

Calantina snorted. "I feel old, that's for sure. I won't be doing this job next year. I'm almost resolved on that point. Time I stopped kidding myself that I can make a difference."

"You will have made a difference" said Kasstovaal, "to a few of them."

"Maybe."

"Who do you think they'll offer the post to next?"

"Buggered if I know." Calantina downed his brandy again and placed his glass on the desk. "Do you want it?"

"Me?"

"Sure. It would suit you. There are worse places to be put out to pasture, when the time comes. I could put my oar in for you, if you want."

Kasstovaal shook his head. "I haven't reached that point yet."

"You're sure of that, are you?"

"Fairly. I'm half your age, for a start."

"Since when did age become a factor?" Calantina sounded very sober, despite two industrial-strength drinks.

Kasstovaal asked, "Is this a private lesson, Principal-Master?"

"You bet it is."

And Kasstovaal found himself considering it, asked himself the question that Space Operatives tried to avoid asking themselves.

Just how far down have I really gone?

So, that was it. Malkan Kasstovaal again knew what he was and, not for the first, it bothered him. The stream of returning memory gave him an objective view of the life he had led. He saw himself as others must have perceived him for so long; closed in a cynical world of his own, shut in and shutting out. And it dawned on him just how much he missed...people. He found himself reliving the simple interactions of his youth, the friends who had grown with him and learned with him. He had forgotten how much he needed that simple symbiosis. To be wanted and not just tolerated.

"If I were to die today," he thought to himself, "who would grieve for me?" A simple, if selfish, way to gauge your worth in the great scheme of things. It horrified him to realise just how little his demise would affect the universe. In a couple of hundred years even his gravestone would have vanished. Always assuming that anyone realised he was dead in the first place.

This revived the question "Where am I? What has happened to me?" When he awoke, would he be back among those people he had left behind? Was he, in fact, truly asleep? Memory. Wait for the last memory to return.

The voyage of his life swept on before him. Piece by piece, one thing leading to another, the path he had chosen for himself, mapped out with all its intricate twists and turns. He found himself looking, sadly, at the alternative routes he could have taken, the other choices he could have made, and wondering, futilely, where they would have taken him. And the sadness grew keener as he watched the life path sink lower and lower towards the depression and emptiness he recognised as his own. But even that life would be preferable to the emptiness he had found here.

The question remained stubbornly unanswered. How much more could there be to run through?

Then a bright, blinding light. Then darkness.

The memory flow ceased. Everything was there, all in place. Yet something still defied knowing. Light, then darkness. Then light again. And a voice. Whose?

"What will I find when I wake?"

7.

Oa thought to herself, "How you must struggle to survive."

An internal scan of a Beyonder's body floated on the display before her, the malformed mechanisms pulsing with convulsive purpose.

But what purpose? Physiology was a simple science on the Rock; it had no need to be complex, and nothing in the considerable experience she had gained in its pursuit bore any resemblance to this creature.

Her only choice, she decided, was to treat this as a problem of logic. Each of these mechanisms must have a specific purpose, she began. A purpose which must, ultimately, contribute to the proper functioning of the mind, which is the centre of all things. And she knew where the mind resided, that much she was certain of. So how does the mind connect with the rest?

It was possible, she reminded herself, that the structure of such an alien creature might not admit of such a logical analysis. Some, if not all, of these mechanisms may have no bearing on the workings of the mind. May have no purpose at all. That, she reasoned, was unlikely. Why waste so much matter and effort on useless bio-systems?

The basic trail had been easy enough to follow. Educated guesswork had to suffice for the rest. She was still employing it when a small section of the smooth wall behind her quietly disappeared to form a perfectly rectangular opening onto the corridor beyond. Through it passed Vo, then Te, - then a third, taller than those ahead of him, his head passing within an inch of the top of the doorway though no reflex compelled him to duck. With all three safely entered, the perfect doorway filled, once more, with rock, the smooth wall healing itself, silently, to uniformity.

Oa did not permit their entry to interrupt her train of thought and her three guests waited for her to acknowledge them, patiently and without offence. To have interrupted the inevitable flow of logic within another's mind would have been the more impolite.

The wait was not a long one. Oa reached her new conclusion and, mentally, fitted it into place with the others. With each addition, she reflected briefly, the complicated mess seemed to make a little more sense. An alien sense, though. It possessed a kind of half-hearted logic that, on the one hand, implied a great evolutionary complexity while, on the other, omitted many of the logical results of such a state.

She ended her speculation, turned and touched the minds of Vo and Te in the brief welcome. Then she turned to the third.

The mind of Ji, Thought-Healer and the master of minds on the Rock, greeted hers first. The greeting was conventional enough but the underlying respect that these two shared held deeper meanings. The doctor of the body and the doctor of the mind, holding between them an uncertain mastery over the elements of existence.

Vo asked, "Have you completed your analysis?"

"There is little that conventional analysis can tell us," Oa replied, indicating the display. "Many of the mechanisms present in this Bio-form do not appear to function. Assuming that each had some function to perform, this would indicate that the original molecular structures were not successfully re-formed."

"I suppose a non-re-forming life form would have no need of so detailed a knowledge of its own form," said Te, "unless it were a healer, perhaps."

"Quite so," Oa replied. "The greater development of the first Beyonder may suggest that it was a healer. Or, at least, one possessing a healer's knowledge. I have been concentrating my study on that one's Bio-form. Even there, most of the mechanisms have reverted to inert masses, I have only conjecture to offer as my analysis."

"Very well."

Oa touched the controls of a panel in front of the display and the picture swelled and focused to closer detail in response to her narrative. "One thing is clear. The conscious mind resides, solely, in this mass of tissue housed in the upper portion of the body. This mass is connected to the rest of the body in two ways. Firstly, by a network of fine fibres. I've never seen anything like them. See here." She pointed. "They start all over the body. Virtually every surface, inside and out, is a mass of them, microscopically small. These fibres lead inward, converging and tangling and connecting together. They all, finally, terminate at the mind tissue, by which time they've become a tightly compacted mass."

"What purpose do they serve," wondered Vo. "Do you know?"

"I have analysed a few of the fibres. They appear to be energy conductive. I have relieved the suppression a little to allow the mind to operate at a low energy level. At this level, the mind is passing rhythmic electrical impulses through the network, which are presumably intended to stimulate the mechanisms into action. Observe." The picture moved and centred on a mass that quivered with each signal it received.

Te asked "Could this be the autonomic signal I suppressed in the second Beyonder?"

"No" said Oa. "Though the signal frequency and characteristics are similar. It appears that the Beyonders use these fibres to carry all their autonomic instructions around the body, rather than using direct stimulation as we do in our bodies. There is clearly enough capacity, within the network, for thousands of such impulses, all for different purposes. The signal you detected, Te, was but one of them. This mechanism here responds to another. It is the only one that is responding to the stimulation at this time."

Vo examined the image. "It appears to be a compression pump of some kind," he said.

"Correct. It is pumping a liquid through a system of channels that extends throughout the body but, primarily, to the mind tissue. This is the second link. The liquid passes into the tissue at this point and then leaves it by this channel here. The channel system forms an unbroken circuit with a fixed volume of liquid circulating within it."

"A cooling system, perhaps?" Vo ventured.

"The liquid, also, has not maintained its original structure," said Oa, "so I cannot be certain. But I think it is more than merely a coolant. During the circuit, the liquid passes through other mechanisms, inoperative ones, which are, clearly, not designed merely for pumping action. These two structures here," she indicated, "are, I believe, the most important ones."

"They look like empty vessels," said Vo.

"Ah, yes. But they are closely connected to the liquid channel. These fine membranes, here and here, are apparently designed to keep the liquid within the channels but, also, to allow something from these vessels to enter and leave the liquid."

"Chemical intake?" said Te, astonished.

"It appears so," Oa said. "Either that or some form of energy which could be conducted through the body by ions present in the liquid. But, in that event, surely there would be no reason for the liquid to move."

"Chemicals, then."

"Most likely. And more than one form of chemical, it seems, as there are two separate vessel structures. The liquid would carry these chemicals to the mind tissue, deposit them and return for more. Perhaps, even, taking unwanted elements away with it."

Vo considered. "There is no way to determine which elements are required?"

"Even if we knew, I doubt that the circulating liquid would carry them, in its incomplete state."

"Then we cannot hope to satisfy the Beyonders' needs in their present form. If we awaken them without providing for those needs, the malfunction signals will shut down their minds. We may have to proceed with the reconstructions without their agreement."

Ji spoke for the first time. "For my part, I will not act before they have been consulted. More than merely halting the autonomic signals that control these mechanisms, I must also give them the illusion that our form is similar to their own."

Te asked "Is that necessary?"

"Your own observations prove it to be so. These are emotionally motivated beings, cautious to the deepest levels. I doubt that they could accept the strangeness of our forms as easily as we can accept it of theirs. And we know how powerful their emotional reactions can be. Even if we could calm them so that their first sight of us would not shock them so much, they could never bring themselves to trust us fully. It would be a hopeless basis for interactive study."

"I agree," said Vo. "Surely, then, it would be better to place this illusion in their minds before they are brought to consciousness. They need never know how different our true form is. It would spare them the initial trauma."

Ji said, "If I were to do so, the illusion would break down in a very short time. We are different in more than just appearance. We move and manipulate in more ways than their rigid forms can and the illusion cannot possibly convert all of these differences into forms they would accept. A single discrepancy will be enough to make them suspect that all is not as it appears and, with that realisation, their minds will struggle against the illusion until they break it, which they will eventually do. Their behaviour, thus far, shows that they have the determination necessary.

"However, if they know how we appear in reality and, as a result, choose to be given the illusion, their minds will accept it and will not struggle against it because they have decided that it should be put there.

"Besides," Ji turned to face the wall, part of which, at the command of his will, faded to transparency to show the two Beyonders lying, unconscious, on raised slabs, "it would be unethical to act otherwise. Let us not forget that these are sentient beings. Even if it transpires that they do not reason as we do, that fact remains. If they can choose, we have no right to alter their bodies or invade their minds before they have made that choice."

"You are correct, of course," said Oa, "and a method may yet exist to allow them to make that choice."

"How?"

"Given that none of the Bio-mechanisms have re-formed in their original state, it follows that they will no longer require the specific chemicals they were originally designed for. Since the minds are naturally sustaining themselves, within the Bio-forms, we need only provide the correct type of chemical." She centred the display on a set of the organs she had indicated. "These vessels correspond to the autonomic signal that Te detected and interrupted after the Bio-Formation. They connect directly to the orifices in the upper body and we can assume that the desired substance is drawn through these orifices into the vessels. If we can satisfy the command to draw in the substance, that should be sufficient for the Beyonders' immediate needs."

"And it will be safe to bring them to consciousness?" Te asked.

"I believe so. I also have reason to believe that satisfying this need will allow the Beyonders to communicate. I have examined the fibre network closely. Its complexity suggests it is capable of much more than just controlling and powering these mechanisms. The vast majority of it seems to be designed to pass information to the mind. Of what remains, the output circuits, I find, the connection with the most potential to pass any complex pattern out of the body terminates in the pipe that connects these vessels to the orifices."

The display moved with her words. "Here. It controls this small, flexible membrane structure across the pipe. Assuming that the substance is passed out of the body by this route, as well as in, this membrane could be made to cause very specific vibrations in the expelled chemical."

"And you believe this to be their method of communicating?" asked Vo.

"I do. The design of these other openings at each side and the similar membranes within would indicate a method for receiving such vibrations for translation into language. It might be the opposite way around, I suppose, but I do not think so. The only question that remains is which form of chemical to provide."

Vo perused the displayed organ. "It is a delicate structure." he said "Too fine to hold a solid."

"Agreed. A liquid form, perhaps."

"Or a gaseous one."

Oa considered, "If we were to try a gaseous form first, it would do the least damage if it proved to be the wrong choice."

"Very well. Fill the observation area with a non-reactive gas and then remove the suppression wave. Be ready to replace it again if the Beyonders fail to function. We must observe them with the greatest care."

8.

"What will I find when I wake?"

The question hung in air, weighted with doubts and fears and hopes. Fortunately, Malkan Kasstovaal had no time for his troubled dreams to speculate too deeply on the answer, to create nightmares or hopeful desires from it in their wanderings. No sooner was it asked than the heavy waters of sleep that had held him in a smothering embrace for what felt like an eternity, began to flow away.

The first sensation he felt was the floating airiness of his mind as the pressure was removed from it. He let it drift awhile, safely detached from both dream and reality, in the no man's land between where neither nightmare could reach. But, no, he could not hide here. He had to know the answer.

He became aware of his body beneath him. The sensations dull almost to numbness, the limbs unmoving. But at least he could feel it was there. Had he, in fact, ever actually lost it? He could remember the fearful sensations, the absence, the lost responses. Had they all been dreams?

No. There had been another. The crushing sensation, the great heaviness across his chest though there was no weight. He hadn't been able to breathe.

Panicked, his body lurched, instinctively, and drew in a mighty breath, filling his lungs to their utmost in a second and holding them full in case the precious atmosphere deserted him again. He held it until his lungs ached, until it forced its escape in a shuddering exhalation. Desperately he drew another. Then another. The air remained. He relaxed, allowing his breathing to settle into a panting rhythm.

The feeling in his limbs began to return. He felt that he was lying on his back, on something hard and smooth. He felt comfortably warm but could feel no movement in the air. The only sound he could hear was his own breathing slowing to normal.

Did he dare to open his eyes? To see where he was, to answer that question. Would he find himself as blind as he had been before? Did he dare to look?

I must, he thought, I must know. He braced himself, like a child ready to enter cold water, and opened his eyes. The light, the old friend he'd missed so much, burned, cruelly, into them. He snapped them shut. Too fast. Take it easy. His eyes had not seen light for so long. They would need to adjust. They felt strangely dry and itchy.

He waited for the pain to subside before he tried again, slowly this time. Gradually the vision opened onto a soft, blurred white. Gradually it brightened as his eyes opened fully and their focus shifted to reveal the world to him.

A plain surface was before his eyes. I'm lying back so it has to be the ceiling, he thought. He flicked his eyes around it. A bare stone ceiling.

Not even a light fitting. Yet there was plenty of light up there. It seemed to hang there in a way that light, by definition, should not be able to do. The ceiling had light also, it seemed. It appeared to him not painted white but, rather, bleached of its natural colour, freeing a gentle glow from within the stone itself.

It was hard to perceive, with the brightness of the two shifting and merging into each other, just how far up the ceiling was. For a moment, the surface stood out clearly then the misty radiance, closer to his face, closed into a brief solidity.

Annoyed, he threw up an arm to wave the mist out of his way. It froze in mid-air as his eyes caught sight of it.

"That's not mine!"

It was not the tanned and well-nourished arm that should have been there. Not the heavy palm and precise fingers. This limb was thin and undeveloped as though the skin alone clung to the bones. The skin was completely jet black, like carbon, darker than any human skin, and completely hairless. His hands had shrivelled to childlike proportions with featureless palms and long, reedy fingers without nails. He brought the other arm and hand up to touch the first. It was the same. He rubbed and pinched at the alien skin. It did not yield, as skin should. It clung to him tightly, slowing his movements. It had a dry, rubbery feeling to it, as though a wet suit had melted into his skin. The arm felt his explorations but the sensation was muted. No matter how hard he pinched himself, the feeling would register, a full second after the event, as nothing more than a brief and dull ache.

He let his arms fall. One impacted dully with the hard surface on which he lay. He felt the other fall onto his stomach, palm down. Curiosity got the better of his horror and moved the fingers across the surface before he could stop them. They felt the same smooth, spongy texture beneath them. For a moment he couldn't bring himself to look though he knew what he would see. Then he lifted his head on a stiff neck and beheld his naked and featureless body lying there, dark as night.

He stared at it, unbelieving, until the ache in his neck forced him to let his head drop to the hard surface. His eyes still stared, sightlessly gazing into the floating light above. His breathing quickened, though he did not notice. Out loud, he said "What's happened to me?" and his voice emerged, dry and broken, from his throat. But, at least, it was his own voice.

As if in answer, the air suddenly vibrated with a loud belch from somewhere to his left. The sound shook him back to life and he sat up, too quickly, his joints somewhere under the sponge-rubber skin clicking in protest. For the first time, he saw the room in its entirety. The walls, like the ceiling, were featureless, without even a door, and were made of the same smooth, blanched stone, as was the floor. There were no visible joins between any of them, as though the room had been carved out of a solid block rather than built. The surface, on which he now sat, was a smooth slab of the same material, raised from the floor by a stone pedestal. These, too, joined invisibly to each other. It looked like something that had grown out of the floor under him.

A few feet away stood another slab on which another dark figure lay, still asleep. It was shorter than he was and bulkier, the limbs more muscular. The shape of the body suggested a man, though the impression was muted by the soft skin. The head was bald, showing no sign of ever having hair in the past. It provoked Kasstovaal to pass a hand, unconsciously, across his own head and feel its baldness. The other man's facial features were blurred and undefined, the spongy flesh muffling them like a mask.

And yet there was something about the figure that struck a cord in Kasstovaal's memory. It seemed to him that he should know that person.

He swung his legs over the side of the slab and, hesitantly, stood upright. He felt weak and off balance. How long had he been asleep? His mouth was bone dry as though all the moisture had been sandblasted out of it. Across his lower body, a soft, heavy ache lingered.

Steadying himself as best he could, he took a slow step towards the second slab, head down, watching and controlling every movement with minute care. In this way, he covered the few feet across the room and, leaning on the slab for support as the room swayed about him, he looked down into the other's face.

He was sure he recognised that face. Completely devoid of its hair, on face and head, it was difficult to place but he knew this man. And, as confirmation of his suspicions, the mouth opened and belched loudly into his face. It could be only one person.

"Jeryant"

It could only be Space Medical Operative Doctor Bryn Jeryant. Unique in the known universe, that one characteristic would always give him away in the end. It was Jeryant's contention that generations of multi-racial inter-breeding by his ancestors had conspired to provide him with an epiglottis which, in the relaxation of sleep, diverted two or three per cent of all the air he breathed into his stomach, which he then had to burp out every few moments. It had condemned him, in recent years, to sleeping in a space helmet, particularly in the cramped confines of survey ships as an alternative to being thrown out of the airlock by his shipmates. By the same virtue, however, it blessed him with far more than his fair share of postings to large and spacious luxury liners.

Now that he recalled his friend to mind, Kasstovaal could appreciate how he had not recognised him more quickly. The Jeryant he remembered was several pounds heavier, a few inches shorter and, generally, sported a thick, filthy beard. The fine, precise hands on this form were, also, out of place on him. The old Jeryant had hands a wrestler would have been proud of; large, meaty and hairy. They were the sort of hands that cleaved meat for a living, the sort of hands you wouldn't let anywhere near you in an operating theatre, and this explained much about Jeryant's failure to make any headway in public medicine. These new hands, though, definitely belonged on a surgeon and were, perhaps, more what Jeryant would have chosen for himself, had the choice been given him.

In fact, the whole body seemed to be nearer Jeryant's ideal self. Kasstovaal had heard him moaning, frequently, about how he'd like to be taller, lighter, fitter. "If I'd kept my body in trim," he used to say "I wouldn't have to hang around you miserable bastards all my working career." It would then be pointed out to him that no medical organisation, other than the Space Service Medical Division, would have him in their employ, and that his body was beyond the point where miracles could reasonably be expected. He would then punch somebody in the teeth. Now, it appeared, someone had given Jeryant his wish. Up to a point.

So why did Kasstovaal's body feel so....imperfect? It was certainly not what he would have regarded as the perfect body. It still felt incapable of holding him upright and, though he felt no direct pain, he was sure that it was not functioning as it should. His mouth was still dry despite all his attempts to salivate.

The figure of Jeryant stirred slightly on the slab. The lips parted to allow the tongue, black as the rest of him, to pass once across them, leaving an enviable layer of moisture on the surface. Jeryant sniffed the air, unconsciously, and shifted his weight, making ready to turn over. Unfortunately, the slab on which he lay was almost exactly as wide as he was and so he rolled straight off the slab and fell, face down, to the floor with an impact which forced out one last burp from his inflated stomach.

Kasstovaal made his way round the slab as quickly as he could manage and found Jeryant lying flat on the floor, still face down and still, apparently, in the process of waking up. His drinking habits being what they were, Jeryant was used to waking up in odd places and in odd positions and waking up face down on a hard floor that he didn't recognise was nothing new to him. Rather than allowing the impact to jolt him awake, he raised himself slowly to consciousness, automatically bracing himself for a raging hangover. He was pleasantly surprised, therefore, to find that his head was clear, in the face of the evidence.

"I should be feeling like dirt," he said to the floor. "Either that or I'm missing something important. Which is it?"

Kasstovaal opened his mouth to speak but the dryness within had stiffened his throat and tongue making them difficult to control. With an effort, he croaked "Jery!"

Jeryant rolled over stiffly and propped himself up with both hands. As he caught sight of Kasstovaal he started and gave a gasp. That was the limit of his surprise, however, since he was an experienced spaceman, a medic moreover, quite used to coming face-to-face with humanoid mutations. That fact stopped him being afraid but it hadn't yet taught him to be diplomatic.

"What in the fifteen bloody suns are you?" he demanded. There was nothing, apparently, wrong with his voice.

Then he frowned as his darkened eyes took in the gaunt creature that had spoken to him. "Kass?" he said, his eyes squinting to recognise his friend. Eyes that were black from edge to edge, Kasstovaal saw. No pupils, no irises, just black. So must his be, he realised.

"Yes, Jery. It's me."

"Good grief, man! What's happened to you?"

"What's happened to US, Jery."

Jeryant looked down and noticed his own blackened body for the first time. He sat upright and brought his arms and hands in front of his eyes. He turned them over and over in horrified fascination. "If this is a joke," he said, "its not very damn funny."

"I don't hear anybody laughing."

"Do you remember how we got here?"

"No."

"Me neither." Jeryant hauled himself onto his feet and stretched the stiffness out of his limbs. "What's more to the point, I suppose, is where here is. Can't say I recognise it. Mind you, a place with no doors or windows I would call a prison. I wonder what's outside."

Outside. Something like a chill washed across Kasstovaal's new body. He realised that he knew what was outside. Somehow he had seen it. He tried to dismiss it as his imagination, but the conviction would not go away. He knew. He had seen it. "Jery. I've...."

"I don't remember doing anything illegal. More than usual, I mean." Jeryant had a surgeon's inability to panic in any situation and an almost infuriating practicality. "Say, do you think one of us is supposed to be getting married, this morning? Must be you, I reckon, sunshine. I don't get caught like that, even when I'm dead drunk."

"Jery!" Kasstovaal started forward towards Jeryant but his balance finally failed and he pitched forward into the doctor's arms. "I've seen it out there."

"Careful, Kass" said Jeryant, lifting his friend and placing him on the slab. "Sit down before you injure yourself. Gods, you're in a state!"

"I've seen outside." Kasstovaal insisted.

"When?"

"Before I woke. I...saw it in my head. Light where the darkness should be. Darkness where light should come from. It's not our universe out there. Not our Mode."

"You were dreaming."

Kasstovaal grasped Jeryant's shoulders and shook them feebly. "It was no dream. It was real. I could feel it. I was there. I was...I had no body. Just my mind floating in it all. But I could see it. I could hear. I could hear her calling to me."

"Her? Who? Who, Kass?"

"I don't know. She didn't say. I can't even be sure it was a she, it was just a voice. It said it could help me. It...she guided me here."

"Where's here, then?"

"I'm not sure. The Rock, she called it."

Jeryant glanced around. "Well, it's certainly rock, no doubt about that. Could it be somewhere in the Second Mode? A stable area?"

"No. That Space is the other side of our curtain. It's dark too. You've seen it. This Space is light. I know it. And the suns shine darkness into it. It's the opposite of what we know." His face, such as it was, froze suddenly. His eyes widened in horror. Then he laughed, a hollow and involuntary noise in his dry throat.

Jeryant knelt down. "What is it?" he asked.

"You don't see it? My dear Doctor, it's so obvious what's happened to us. Everything we knew is gone, even our own bodies. It's finally happened."

Jeryant grabbed Kasstovaal's head and drew the man's eyes to meet his own. "No, Kass! It's not true."

"We're dead, you fool. We must be." The laughter was turning to sobs. "Our souls have been detached from our bodies. What do you call that if not death?"

Jeryant's grip tightened. "Stop this" he ordered, loud enough for the room to echo the command. He glared into the maddened eyes. "You shouldn't have let it go this far" he said, more softly. "Why didn't you tell me how bad it was, you stupid bastard."

"What can it matter now?" stammered Kasstovaal. "We're gone. Nothing matters."

"You're jumping to conclusions, Kass. Shut up jabbering and think. You're an intelligent man. You have to be, in your job. Think!" Jeryant released the shaking head. "We're here aren't we? We have bodies. Well, almost. Wherever we are, we are alive. Everything we are is still here, isn't it. The only thing we've lost is our bearings." He stood up. "Besides, this doesn't look much like my idea of a heaven. Or a hell, come to that." His eyes reached wall level and stopped short. "Kass. Do you feel like receiving visitors?"

"What?" Kasstovaal looked up and saw Jeryant staring at something, behind him. The feeling that he was under scrutiny tingled on his spine.

Jeryant said "Our hosts have arrived."

For a few seconds, Kasstovaal couldn't bring himself to look. The feeling of eyes upon him and the sick sensation of fear in the place where his stomach had been, rooted him to the slab and kept his eyes staring at the opposite wall. He had to concentrate to force his head round, to lift his body from the slab and turn it after the head.

There they were. Part of the stone wall had become transparent and on the other side of this new window four figures watched them. Or, at least, they appeared to be watching them. They did not seem to have eyes in the human sense of the word. In fact, there was nothing even remotely human about them. Four cylindrical masses of some black, oily substance like a thick syrup, clinging to some invisible surface beneath and held in by a thin, filmy skin. The semi-liquid flesh moved constantly, as they watched, making the skin undulate in random patterns. The only parts of them that appeared solid were two thin white bands that stretched, unbroken, around the circumference, one beneath the other, just below the top edge of each. They appeared to have no limbs but, as Kasstovaal watched, the skin of one of them split open, about half way down its body and a stream of the black, viscous liquid shot outwards, solidifying, as it touched the air, into a thick branch of an arm. It stopped growing outwards and a thick bubble of the stuff began to grow on the end of it. It swelled like a balloon and suddenly exploded into six long, reedy fingers that reached down and began to play along the surface of a panel, dotted with gemstones, with incredible dexterity. They paused for a second and the ball-like 'hand' swelled again, split and spewed out a seventh finger that landed, accurately, on another stone. Then, the whole grotesque appendage melted and contracted, was sucked back into the body. The split skin sealed up neatly after it.

"Incredible!" Jeryant watched the manipulations with fascination. "A metaphysiology. They create or discard any limbs at need."

The lower band on one of the beings, the shortest among them, glowed a pearly white and emitted a multi-coloured beam of light towards the nearest of its fellows. The colours struck the upper band of the other which glowed as it absorbed them. The second being sent out a different colour pattern from its own lower band but in separate streams to each of the other three.

"Communicating by light waves," Jeryant said. "We're going to have fun trying to talk to them."

"Talk to them?" Kasstovaal had been watching with far less scientific interest and much more horror and disgust. He felt, if he had the organs for it, that he was going to be sick.

Jeryant clapped an arm across his shoulders. "Yes," he said. "It's the most direct way I can think of to get us out of here before we starve or suffocate or dehydrate. Besides, this is a First Greeting situation. New frontiers of knowledge. Friendly relations. 'We come in peace.' All that horseshit. You've done it before. I've seen you."

"Those were humanoids, at least," hissed Kasstovaal, afraid that the watchers could hear him. "These are.... They're...." He searched for a sufficient word but could find none.

"Yes. Well, I don't suppose they consider you as much of an oil painting, either" said Jeryant. "Let's just hope they don't treat us with the same contempt. We are in their hands, so to speak."

There was a click, a report like a muffled gun shot that bounced around the smooth walls and was lost.

Kasstovaal jumped. "What was that?"

"You don't expect me to know, do you? I'm new here as well, remember."

The air began to vibrate with a soft, almost insect hum. Then a clear, precise, male voice said "Welcome, Beyonders. Can you understand me?"

The two humans exchanged glances. "They seemed to have solved the problem for us," said Jeryant, under his breath. Out loud he said, "Yes. Yes, we can, thank you."

"That is good. I have adjusted our gas emitters to produce vibrations that you can understand. Now we can communicate. You are both welcome here."

Kasstovaal spoke up. "You called us Beyonders. What do you mean by that?"

"Forgive me," said the voice "It is a term only. A description. We know, only, that you are a new species. Beings beyond our experience. We do not know how you prefer to identify yourselves."

"We call our form human," said Jeryant. "Individually, we are identified by names. Mine is Bryn Jeryant and my friend is Malkan Kasstovaal."

"I see. We are Dwellers of the Rock. I am called Vo."

"We're glad to meet you," Jeryant elbowed Kasstovaal in the ribs, "aren't we?" he hissed savagely.

But Kasstovaal's dulled senses didn't feel the jab. "Could you tell us where we are?" he asked. He couldn't determine which of the creatures on the other side of the window was Vo, if indeed he was among them. So he had to cast his question to the air rather than direct it at any of the Dwellers in particular.

"I have told you. This is the Rock."

"And where is that?"

Vo's voice paused. "Without a common reference point, I do not think that I will be able to describe to you where the Rock is in relation to your own point of origin. You are, as I said, outside our experience so it is unlikely that we shall be able to find one easily."

"How did we get here?"

"Again, without knowing where you came from, I cannot answer you fully. But these are matters for another time. What is of greater importance at the moment is your physical and mental well-being."

"Is it?"

"Yes. We first detected you as disembodied minds. We guided you here and gave you the opportunity to Bio-Form suitable bodies for yourselves. The ones you now inhabit. But these are proving unable to survive in this environment for very long. If they are to continue to operate, it will be necessary for us to adjust them into forms which will remain stable."

"Why haven't you done that already?" asked Jeryant.

"We must first obtain your consent to the operations."

"Surely, if our bodies will die without them, it goes without saying that we agree."

"Does it? For all we know, you may not wish to be imprisoned in a body at all. It would be unethical to proceed without your agreement. Not to mention impractical."

"Why impractical?"

"For your own comfort, we, also, propose to re-program the perception centres of your minds to give you the illusion that your modified bodies look and feel more like your original forms. The illusion will also make us appear, to you, as your own kind. It is clear from your reactions that you feel uncomfortable with our forms as you now see them."

"We're sorry if we gave you that impression," said Jeryant, glaring at Kasstovaal. "Your forms were strange to us. We were taken by surprise."

"There is no need to be embarrassed," Vo's voice said. "It was a perfectly natural reaction, under the circumstances, and not unexpected. This is why we offer you the illusion. I'm sure you will agree that it will make our interaction far easier and if you accept the illusion willingly it will operate far more effectively."

"How long do we have to decide?" asked Kasstovaal.

"As much time as you need. We will not force these alterations on you. However, I must point out that your bodies can only be sustained for a short time in their present form. We shall need a decision before they begin to degenerate. After that there is little we can do."

Jeryant said "Give us a few moments."

"Of course."

Kasstovaal turned away from the window and motioned Jeryant to do the same. "Do we risk it?"

"I don't see that we have much choice," said Jeryant. "Either we get comfortable or we get dead. Properly this time."

"If we believe what he says."

"You're a suspicious bastard, aren't you."

"You bet I'm suspicious." Kasstovaal glanced back at the window. The Dwellers were still there. But how could he tell if they were still watching them? What did they actually see with?

He went on, "I mean, if our kind had two of them locked up in a tank, how do you suppose we'd treat them?"

"With considerably less courtesy than we've been shown up to now, I expect."

"Bloody funny idea of courtesy," Kasstovaal gestured at the body he was now wearing. "I've been asked to wear some weird things on a First Greeting but being expected to change my whole body is taking diplomacy too far."

"So you accept, then, that they've given us these bodies? That much is the truth?"

Kasstovaal hesitated. "Well, yes, I suppose. At least I know we couldn't have done it."

"Well then. I don't see any other candidates."

"But what about our own bodies? What happened to them?"

"I don't know. Vo said we arrived without them."

"We only have his word for that. What if they have them, somewhere?"

"You what?" Jeryant chuckled. "You're not suggesting that they've taken our minds out of our original bodies and then gone to the trouble of creating new bodies to put them in?"

"Why not?"

"For what purpose?"

"Well, experimentation maybe. Studying our bodies. Playing with our minds. Or both."

"They could do that just as well by leaving us in our own bodies," said Jeryant. "You're not thinking straight, Kass."

"Well, perhaps they've destroyed our own bodies."

"So what if they have?" asked Jeryant. "This is the point, Kass. Right now it doesn't matter whether the Dwellers destroyed our bodies or whether an accident did it. Maybe we blew ourselves up for the fun of it; I can't remember. The important thing is that the Dwellers have given us new ones. They've given us a second chance. True, they haven't got it right yet, but they're offering to correct the mistakes. Does that suggest malevolence to you?"

Kasstovaal was silent, remembering the white space, remembering the voice. Not Vo's voice. It had offered help. Hadn't he received it? He could see. He could feel again. He had a body, of sorts, where he hadn't had before.

Jeryant continued, "What's more, Vo's given us the opportunity to refuse. If you want to use that opportunity, you go ahead. Stick around and see what happens. Look at you. You're not exactly a picture of health now, are you. You reckon you can afford to turn down the only offer of help we're likely to get?"

And when Kasstovaal hesitated to answer, he went on "Or perhaps it's true what they say about Pilot-Captains. Your life really does mean nothing to you."

"You know that's...not...." Kasstovaal trailed off as an intense wave of dizziness and nausea swept over him. His legs buckled underneath him and he fell into Jeryant's arms, which had instinctively raised to catch him.

Despite his greater bulk, Jeryant's arms could not take even that light a weight. He managed to lower Kasstovaal more gently to the floor but could not hold him up. The effort made the room spin around Jeryant. He sank to his knees, next to his friend.

"Convinced yet?" he asked, his words slurring, "I think we have less time to make up our minds than we thought."

Kasstovaal's head throbbed. His vision dropped in and out of focus. His whole body felt as though it wanted to tear itself apart. Through it all, he fancied he could actually feel himself slipping away, feel his mind struggling to free itself from the thing that had become his body. Could this be what death felt like?

"No!" Something in his mind, that was not entirely his will, made the decision for him. He did not want to go yet.

Whatever it was forced his lips apart and squeezed out of them the words "I....agree." which came out as a dry whisper and, under even that small exertion, Kasstovaal passed out.

Jeryant had heard him, though. To the room in general, he said "You hear that? We both agree." He almost shouted it in his desperation to have it said before his speech failed completely.

Vo's voice filled the room again. "Good. We must begin at once. It seems that the Bio-forms are degenerating more quickly than we had thought."

Jeryant gave a weak chuckle. "I had sort of noticed."

He looked up at the slabs. "I don't think I'll be able to get him back up on there," he said. "In fact, I don't think I'll be able to climb up myself. You'll have to help us."

"There is no need," Vo said, "just lie down where you are and we will begin. Have no fear. We shall make you both unconscious again first. You will feel no discomfort."

"I'm ecstatic...to hear it" said Jeryant, lying back, almost falling back, in fact, onto the hard floor.

Through his own weakness and disorientation, he vaguely felt his body rising. Was the floor lifting up under him? He turned his head to look sidelong at the slabs on which they had woken but they were not there anymore. He caught sight of one of them just as it receded and disappeared into the floor, became part of it. And the floor was falling away from him, slowly and smoothly.

Then he felt a great heaviness settle on his mind, pushing him down the short distance to unconsciousness. He knew, instinctively, that he could not resist it, so he did not. Instead he let go and allowed the darkness to take him into its folds.

This was not the waking darkness that Kasstovaal had feared and fought against. This was a peaceful old friend that they both knew well and trusted to look after them until they woke again. If they woke again.

And while the two humans slept, the Dwellers worked.

Behind the transparent screen, a neat opening appeared in one of the walls and four Dwellers filed silently into the room. They formed up in a line before Oa and Ji, who were making feverish preparations for the task ahead of them.

Oa looked up from her work and acknowledged each of them in turn. "You all know what you must do," she said. "Quickly, now."

The group split into two pairs and stood themselves before the window, two concentrating on Kasstovaal, two on Jeryant.

Oa said "They will apply their wills to the molecular bonds. They will force the Bio-forms to stay together until we are done."

"That is good," said Ji. "The work will take some time to complete. Are you prepared?"

Oa scanned the displays before her and was satisfied with what she saw. "Yes," she said.

"Then we should delay no longer."

Ji turned to face the window. His mind reached out towards it, through it into the room and down into the sleeping mind of the first Beyonder, the one called Jeryant. Deep down.

With the skill only a Master of Minds can achieve, Ji's mind probed down through the myriad pathways of Jeryant's thoughts, seeking out his in-built perceptions, his knowledge of himself and his body. What it looked like and felt like.

"Interesting," he thought to himself. "Most interesting."

… THREE: RECEPTION

9.

"This is going to take some getting used to," Jeryant said.

Despite Kasstovaal's misgivings, they had woken up, more or less at the same time, to find themselves still lying on the raised slabs.

With the time distortion of the deep sleep, they could not tell how long they had been unconscious. From the way Kasstovaal now felt, clear-headed and refreshed, restored, it must have been a good long time.

No sooner had the two of them opened their eyes than the clear voice of Vo came to them out of the air, as before. The operations had been a success, he said, and they should rest easy for a while, to fully recover from the ordeal. After that he, Vo, and his colleagues would come to speak to them properly.

In the meantime, they should awaken themselves fully and, perhaps, take the opportunity to examine themselves. Vo put it in exactly those words, causing Jeryant to laugh out loud before he could stop himself.

But his laughter soon faded when he started to do as Vo suggested and realised that, despite this second attempt to re-form his body, or at least to re-form the way he saw his body, things were still not quite right.

Their bodies were still black and there was no visible change in the sponge-rubbery quality of the skin. It did, however, appear to be more sensitive than before. This time when Kasstovaal pinched himself, he felt it quite distinctly and the slab underneath him seemed to have taken on an extra hardness for his benefit.

Their eyes also appeared to have changed. Instead of the dark glistening globes that had been there before when they looked at each other, each had his own original pair of human eyes; Kasstovaal's green and worried, Jeryant's brown and inquisitive; both in incongruous contrast to the jet-black skin that surrounded them.

Their teeth seemed not to have survived, at least not as individual units. They found that they had a bone-hard ridge around their upper and lower jaws, widening at the sides and thinning to incisor sharpness at the front. It was as though all their individual teeth had been seamlessly welded together. And they were black, disconcertingly so. It put them both off smiling at each other.

They found that they were still completely hairless all over their bodies and this absence quickly led them to discover that other things were missing too.

"What the hell!"

They were, obviously, both naked but the illusion of wearing an all-over wet-suit was complete and their perfectly smooth skin, they suddenly realised, was exactly that; perfectly smooth. Not one item of genitalia seemed to have survived the process. No nipples. No testicles. Nothing but smooth, unbroken black skin.

For the first time he could remember, Kasstovaal saw a look of panic cross Jeryant's face as he watched the medic half-turn to pass a hand under and behind himself.

"Sealed up," he wailed, "who sealed up my asshole?"

He rolled back over, sat bolt upright on the slab and began threatening the blank walls with his fists. "This is intolerable," he roared at the empty air. "Call yourselves scientists? What sort of asshole doesn't know what an asshole's for, eh? And you can stop bloody laughing as well."

This last he said to Kasstovaal who was appreciating, not for the first time, the entertainment value of Bryn Jeryant in a rage. A lot of pent-up tension was being released with the merriment, as well.

"Whoops!" he laughed. "Slight slip of the knife there, Mr Surgeon."

Jeryant simmered down a bit. He could see the good it was doing to have his friend laugh. "That's buggered my Saturday nights for a start," he said. "And most of the rest of the week, come to think of it."

"Show off!"

After that, they resolved to put their new bodies through their paces, as far as was possible within the room's confines. Kasstovaal found that he had regained almost all the build he remembered having, and the sensations beneath the rubber skin as he raised and stretched his arms and legs, felt much like the flexing of his own muscles.

He swung his legs over the side of the slab and stood upright. His balance seemed to be all right. He felt none of the giddiness that had brought him to his knees before.

He walked forwards. At least, that was what he intended to do; what actually happened was that his legs walked out from under him and he toppled backwards, throwing out his arms to catch at the slab and break his fall.

"Pissed again, I see," smiled Jeryant from his own slab, as Kasstovaal picked himself up. "I've warned you about those cheap bars."

When he too fell backwards when he tried to walk, they both agreed that they should take things a little more carefully. They found that if they began by walking alongside the slab, holding onto it with one hand like a banister, by the time they reached the end of it and let go they could continue walking normally, if a little unsteadily. The problem appeared to be in keeping their balance when they started off. That natural shifting of the weight and adjustment to the balance, needed at just the right moment to compensate for the inertia as the legs moved away, was suddenly beyond them. The same problem, only in reverse, occurred when they tried to stop, no matter how many attempts they made to adjust to it.

"I hope nobody's watching," said Kasstovaal as they picked themselves up off the floor for the umpteenth time, "we must look a right pair of clowns, prat-falling all over the place."

In the end they contented themselves with some on-the-spot drill that Kasstovaal dredged up from his academy days. Their bodies responded easily, almost too easily, to the exercises. Even Jeryant, who was chronically unfit at the best of times, kept pace with Kasstovaal throughout the sequence. When they stopped, they found that their bodies had not reacted to the exertion at all. They were not out of breath, they were not sweating, not a single muscle felt as though it had just been in use. And their searches for an accelerated heartbeat revealed to them that they did not, in fact, have a heartbeat at all.

They made their way back to their slabs, on all fours, and sat silently for a few moments, absorbing this latest revelation.

Then Jeryant said "I'm going to try something. Can you give me a mental time-check?"

"Sure."

"Alright. Let me know when you get to ten minutes."

Kasstovaal started to count silently, spacing his numbers to a rough second's length. Jeryant just sat there looking at the walls, occasionally twiddling his thumbs.

At last, Kasstovaal reached six hundred and said aloud, "Okay. Ten minutes. Now what?"

"Now," Jeryant replied "I suppose you'd better bury me."

"Pardon?"

"It's just that I've been holding my breath for the last ten minutes. So, by rights, I ought to be dead. Or, at the very least, unconscious. But I don't feel any ill effects at all."

Kasstovaal suddenly became aware of his own breathing. It seemed regular enough. He tried holding his breath, just stopped breathing because he wanted to. Nothing changed. The expected burning in the lungs and mounting desperation did not come. He drew in a deep breath and the rhythm started up again as though nothing had happened.

"We don't need to breathe, do we?" he said.

"No."

"Then, what are we breathing now?"

"I don't know. Are we actually breathing at all, I ask myself?"

Kasstovaal checked again. Still regular and deep. "Feels like it to me," he said.

"Ah! So it might," said Jeryant, "but it might just be an illusion. Remember what Vo said. Part of the operation was to alter our perceptions and give us the illusion that our bodies are operating normally. To make us feel more comfortable. Now, if we don't actually need to breathe, there may not actually be any gas in this room to breathe. If the illusion wasn't preventing us from knowing that, how do you think we'd react?"

Kasstovaal swallowed. From the haziness of his recent memories, before his first awakening, he remembered exactly what suffocation felt like. "I know what you mean," he said.

"The missing heartbeat is probably a mistake," Jeryant went on, "I shall have to ask Vo about that, when he shows up."

"If you're right, and there is no atmosphere in here, how can we still be speaking?" asked Kasstovaal. "You need an atmosphere for normal speech."

"What we call normal, perhaps," said Jeryant. "The Dwellers use light waves to communicate. We've seen them. That doesn't need an atmosphere to work. Perhaps they've adapted us so that we can communicate by light waves, as well."

"You mean we could be speaking to each other, now, in light waves?"

"Sure. Why not?"

Kasstovaal's hand went up to his face. No, it couldn't be true. He touched his lips. He could feel them there where they should be.

"That won't tell you anything." said Jeryant "If the illusion they've put into our minds is that good, it won't let you realise that they've altered your laughing gear. Or anything else, for that matter, that might disturb you. In reality, we may not even look remotely humanoid anymore, for all we know."

He got up off his slab and started himself off walking, aiming himself directly at the other slab so that when he tried to stop, and inevitably fell forward, his outstretched palms smacked against the stone and held him almost upright.

"Don't worry about it," he said as he righted himself and sat down. "More probably, they've fitted us with some sort of translation device, like a Vocaliser. Something that doesn't necessarily need to fit over the mouth and ears. That's what I'd do. Anyway, it doesn't matter what's real. Only what we see and feel and sense actually matters to us. Like any sensible animal, we react to the universe as we perceive it. And as far as we're concerned, this illusion the Dwellers have given us is what the universe is like. As long as it makes the universe react in the way we expect, what's the problem?" He rolled his shoulders. "Feels all right to me. Of course, if you'd rather, I expect they could take the illusion away for you so you could see things as they really are. Reckon you could handle that, do you?"

Kasstovaal sighed. Or, at least, he felt that he had sighed. That was something you couldn't do if you weren't breathing. "No," he said, resignedly. "You're right, it's better this way."

"Good." Jeryant clapped him on the back. "So stop moping. Things could be a lot worse. Still, when our friend Vo shows up, he and I are going to have a serious talk about quality control. Amongst other things."

To say that a door opened, a short while later, would not be strictly correct. What happened was a section of the wall quietly faded out of existence leaving a perfect, rectangular doorway leading out onto a corridor beyond. Through it walked three humanoids. They had the same black rubbery skin as the two humans; smooth and hairless, and also, like them, wore no clothes. A suggestion of swelling at the chest and hips of one of them, the shortest of the three by a head, seemed to imply that it was a female while the other two, lacking such contours, were presumably meant to be male. They had no facial features to speak of, but as Kasstovaal looked at each in turn a second time, he found that he could see something in each which distinguished them quite markedly from the others, though he could not say what it was.

The one feature of their faces that did stand out was their eyes. These were two perfect circles of a pearly white substance, like ivory or shiny plastic. Kasstovaal recognised it from his first sight of the Dwellers in their true form. The two bands, which they used to communicate with each other, had been made of that same material. Not made, though. It was part of them.

The two humans rose to meet them, using the slabs for support. One of the male humanoids, the shorter of the two, stepped forward, opened a lipless mouth and said, in what seemed to be quite normal English, "Greetings, Beyonders. I am Vo. I trust you are feeling better."

Kasstovaal felt himself blink involuntarily. This was Vo? The same creature he'd seen through the glass. Even as the thought crossed his mind, the humanoid figure in front of him flickered and for an instant that same cylindrical creature was standing before him, shooting a stream of coloured light into his face. Kasstovaal blinked and shook his head. The humanoid was standing there again, looking puzzled. Then, for another instant, the creature reappeared before Kasstovaal's eyes and he staggered back, gasping at air that wasn't there at all. Then everything returned to normal again.

The other Dweller male stepped forward holding out a calming hand.

"Do not fight the illusion, Beyonder," he said. "It will only break down if you try. Accept what you perceive."

"Yes." Kasstovaal took a deep breath, a metaphorical one he presumed, let it out and relaxed a little. "Thank you. I'm sorry about that."

"Not at all," said the Dweller, kindly. "You are strong willed. I sensed that within you. It will take you a little while to get used to the unreality of your situation."

With a mental effort, Kasstovaal willed himself to calm down. The humanoid forms, standing before him, seemed to become more solid, more real, as he relaxed.

"That's better" the tall Dweller said.

Kasstovaal nodded. He could feel that it was better, that all was well. He had taken the Dweller's advice and it had worked and the Dweller was gratified that it had helped. Kasstovaal could feel the gratification and it warmed him. But only for a moment.

Then it dawned on him what the feelings, and the Dweller's words, must mean. "You read my mind, didn't you?" he said, suspiciously. "It wasn't just my body language telling you I'd relaxed."

The Dweller nodded. "Of course. We can, all of us, sense each other's minds and yours. My own talent, in that regard, is developed to a much higher degree. I can reach in and sense the perfect pattern, see the whole landscape that it forms; the peaks and troughs that shape the whole mind. As such, I am, currently, the Master of Minds among my people. I am called Ji."

"But it's more than just sensing minds," said Kasstovaal, "you're projecting something into mine. I can feel it." His tone was edged with new hostility.

Ji seemed a little taken aback. "I was only sharing my gratification with you," he said. "I had thought that it might help you in your effort to calm your mind. I did not mean to cause any offence."

Vo said, "We must remember, Ji, that they are of an alien race. Even something so simple as wave-sharing they may never have experienced."

Jeryant edged towards Kasstovaal and hissed urgently into his ear, "Will you, please, sit on your bloody paranoia for a few seconds. Of course they must be a telepathic race. How else do you suppose they managed to transplant our minds into these bodies, eh?"

"Telepathic?" Vo had heard the whisper as though it had been said out loud. Now he appeared to be considering the word. At least his expression, such as it was, seemed to give that impression. Or was it something else?

"Yes," he said, after a few seconds, "I think that is more or less the correct way to describe us. Empathic would certainly be true for all of us. It is our way to sense and share our emotions, feel the shape of each other's minds."

"Is that how you managed to get a grip on our language so fast?" Jeryant asked. "You can't have heard anything like it before."

"It is a simple skill," said Vo. "The language centres of our minds reach out to touch the language centres of yours and sense the meaning of the..." he stopped and considered "...concept labels you are saying to us."

"Concept labels?" Jeryant thought about it. "You mean words."

"Yes. Words. The words of any language are nothing but arbitrary labels attached to concepts. They could mean anything to anyone. But by tapping into your language centres we can sense what each word means to you. As long as we can comprehend the concepts you use, we shall be able to communicate without difficulty."

He paused. "I take it, from your reaction, that your race does not have such skills."

"That's right," Jeryant said. "Very few of our people have any telepathic ability."

The three Dwellers looked at one another in what appeared to be astonishment. Vo said "I see. Then we must ask your forgiveness. Our mental openness is something we take for granted. It is so much a part of us that we do not even have a ...word to describe it to each other. There is no need for one. It just is."

"For us, it's different," said Kasstovaal. "We've only got our own thoughts and feelings inside our minds. That's enough to contend with. There are a few Telepaths, among our race, who can see into minds like you can. But the rest of us don't trust them. We don't want them intruding on our private thoughts."

"Yes. I can see that," Vo said, "your minds are used to being sealed off from one another. That makes you secretive and private on an instinctive level. It is only natural that you would resent any intrusion from outside. We did not realise this before. Forgive us."

Jeryant gave Kasstovaal an encouraging nudge in the ribs and he felt his First Greeting training kick in and start telling him that he was behaving like a moron. So they were Telepaths. Or Empaths, or whatever. You couldn't trust them but there was no real need to fear them. Was there? Now that the rational part of his mind examined the black fear and suspicion that were flooding his thoughts, it shocked him to realise just how powerful his own fear of them was. He could not remember ever feeling so passionately about Telepaths before. What had come over him? Shock, maybe. Or some side effect of the process that had put him in this body, whatever that was. He had to pull himself together. Never show fear or distrust on a First Greeting, his training told him. To do so could get you killed. Be diplomatic.

"Of course," he managed, moderating his voice with an effort, "in fact I should be apologising to you for my rudeness. It's just that your world is very strange to us. And these bodies," he gestured down at himself, "the word strange doesn't begin to describe them. Apart from that, we can't remember how we got here and we don't know where we are." He chuckled, slightly, "It's a lot to contend with when you've just woken up."

Vo nodded. "We understand. And we shall respect the privacy of your minds until you are ready to let us in. All Dwellers shall be told not to touch your minds unless you allow it. Would you see to that, Ji?"

"I will." Ji turned away and walked out through the doorway into the corridor. The doorway silently sealed itself up behind him, leaving no mark in the smooth wall to show that it had ever been there. Kasstovaal wondered what sort of technology had come up with a door mechanism like that. But it was a question for another time.

Vo said, "Clearly, there is much that needs to be learned. By both you and us. The Dwellers have never encountered so alien a race as you before. We are most curious to find out about you."

"The feeling's mutual,." said Jeryant. "We'll answer anything you ask, if you'll do likewise for us."

"Splendid," said Vo. "Though I think it will be a long process. Before we begin it, however, my people wish to meet you formally. A Ceremony of Welcome has been arranged."

"What? For us?" Jeryant asked.

"Yes. It is customary for visitors to be received in this way, though we have never welcomed visitors the like of you two before."

"I'll bet!" said Jeryant. "When is this ceremony?"

"The ceremony awaits your convenience." said Vo "We can go now, if you feel strong enough."

"I'm fit for it," said Jeryant "let's go."

"Wait a moment," said Kasstovaal, "could I ask a favour of you, first?"

"Of course," said Vo. "What is it?"

Kasstovaal searched for words. It was a request he'd been growing more and more desperate to make. He had hoped to pick a diplomatic moment for it but now he had started to blurt it out and he couldn't contain it anymore. He had to know.

"Could we see what is outside this place?" he asked. "Could you show us?"

The third Dweller, the female, took a step to Vo's side and spoke for the first time. "Are you certain that you wish to see?" she asked Kasstovaal. "I think that the sight will cause you distress."

It appeared to Kasstovaal that she had a light, musical voice, though in reality she probably had no voice at all. But, more than that, she had a voice he recognised.

"You!" he said "I know you. I heard your voice out in the mists. You called me, didn't you."

"That is so," she replied, simply.

"Te is my...offspring," said Vo. "I gave her the task of guiding you here."

Kasstovaal found himself lost for words. What did you say to someone who had, quite literally, brought you back from the dead? And that was what she had done. He had no doubt about it. "Thank you" hardly seemed sufficient, but he said it anyway. "Thank you, Te. I'm very grateful for what you did for me."

Te smiled, or was that just an illusion. More than that, it seemed to Kasstovaal that she swelled, literally, with pride. She seemed to grow a little taller and Kasstovaal realised that, though he had not been able to find the words to sufficiently express his gratitude, she knew exactly how grateful he really was. She must have seen it in his mind and now he was glimpsing into hers. For an instant he felt just how pleased she was to have done such a service for another being and to realise how much it meant.

Vo placed a hand on Te's shoulder. "Now, child, you are bubbling over. Remember your control. And remember that our guests are not used to waves."

"It's all right," Kasstovaal protested. "Really, it is. I'd be glad to feel like that more often myself."

"That is good," Vo said. "But nonetheless, child, remember your lessons. Your mind must control you feelings, not vice versa."

"Yes, Prim." Te gathered her control and the waves of emotion ceased. Kasstovaal felt them stop.

Vo said, "What Te says is true. What you see outside the Rock may well disturb you. Perhaps it would be wiser to wait until you have become more comfortable with your situation."

"No." Kasstovaal bit the word back, stopping himself from shouting it out in his desperation. "Please! I need to see."

"Very well." Vo turned and walked towards the wall, opposite the observation window. "This wall connects to the outside."

Kasstovaal and Jeryant moved to join him, using the slabs and each other for support.

"Can we see through it?" Kasstovaal asked, as they came to a stop against the wall.

Vo turned and regarded them both for a few seconds, as if in speculation. Then he said "Of course" turned away and stared fixedly at the wall. A few seconds later, a large rectangular section of it disappeared in front of the startled humans' eyes. And the whole ghostly panorama was there before them. Kasstovaal felt his throat constrict as his eyes took in the sight for the first time. His mind, though, had seen it before. It had been no dream. The dense white mists were there in front of him, at once both a solid mass and a movement of, almost, intangible wisps. And the Voids, a multitude of black, staring eyes watching him, seeing easily through the mists.

"By Gods!" Jeryant's mouth had dropped open at his first sight of it. This whisper was all he could manage, before it.

Slowly, still hanging on to one another, the two of them stepped up to the new window. Leaning on the sill, they found that it was, as it appeared to be, an actual hole in the wall: there was no glass. The sill's width showed that the wall was over a foot thick here. But, nonetheless, a section had simply ceased to be and had opened the room to the sky.

There was no sign of the ground, though. Cautiously, Jeryant leaned outwards, beyond the sill, and looked down. "Would you look at that!" he breathed.

Beyond the lip of the sill, the stone of the wall became rough and craggy and did not slope straight downwards, as he had thought it might, to be the lower storeys of a building. Instead, it sloped outwards from the window, still at quite a steep angle but by no means sheer. It was, Jeryant imagined, what the downward view must be like from halfway up a pyramid. Except that the base of this one, which he could clearly see like a horizon beneath him, was very roughly circular, not a straight edge. And, more importantly, it did not appear to be standing on anything. Above the horizon of the base, where he expected to see solid ground at a ninety degree angle, he could see only more of the sky. Underneath them, as well as in front of them.

"We're spinning," he said, suddenly. "Those...black stars, or whatever they are. They're moving. And I can see new ones appearing over the rim. It's just fast enough that you can see it." He pushed himself upright. "This place is floating free in space, isn't it."

He turned over to look upwards. He had to hang on to the sill to lean out far enough to make out the rock wall, tapering inwards above him to a summit some distance away, pointing towards more sky above.

"This is our reality." Vo had stayed to one side, watching them. "There are different places, the Rock is but one, and there are different races living on them. People and objects come into being, change and eventually pass away. But this; the sky; the Voids; remains constant. That you do not recognise it confirms to us that you come from outside our reality. Our...universe. I think that is the term you use."

"Gods!" exclaimed Jeryant, pulling himself up. "Even my most psychotic dreams never came up with anything like this. And I've had a few, I can tell you. You were right, Kass. Strange doesn't even begin to describe it."

Kasstovaal didn't answer, hadn't said a word since that negative image had come before his eyes. Nor had he moved. The spaceman in him, the trained and tested Pilot-Captain, saw that sight as a wonder, incredibly strange and beautiful. But his heart sank to see it. A large part of him had been holding on to the hope that he had, after all, imagined all this, dreamed it up in a delirium that would admit of a normal explanation. He had hoped to see something familiar, anything. A star, a planet, anything would do. It didn't matter where. Then there might have been a chance to contact his own people and tell them where they were. Organise a pick up ship.

As it was, he realised as he stared out into the mist, there could be no messages, no rescue. He and Jeryant were about as far away from home as it was possible to be. The length of at least one entire universe away, in fact.

10.

"How do you do that?" Jeryant asked as he walked behind Vo.

The doorway that had simply appeared in the wall to let them out into an arch-shaped corridor had just faded back into an unbroken rock surface, leaving no trace that it had ever been there. The window looking out into space had done the same thing. Not, in itself, a particularly astounding effect. Jeryant was sure that a few of the more technically minded worlds could probably have created a technique for fading a door in and out like that; probably had done already, if truth be told. But not, he felt, in different places along the same wall. The doorway they had just used had appeared several feet away from the one through which the Dwellers had originally entered. And, now he thought about it, the one that Ji had left through had been in a completely different spot, as well.

Moreover, the doorways were, apparently, capable of being different sizes. He and Kasstovaal were still finding walking difficult and were having to hold onto each other for the small, extra support they needed. This required them to walk side-by-side, each with a hand on the other's shoulder, and, in recognition of this, the latest doorway had been twice the width of the others.

"It is a simple technique," Vo said, but not before exchanging a glance with Te, walking beside him, which Jeryant noticed. To him, it seemed that the unspoken message that passed between them went along the lines of "you realise what that question implies about them, don't you?"

Vo continued, "It is merely an exercise in matter-forming and un-forming. The simplest, in fact. It is the first one that our young are taught."

"Sorry!" said Jeryant "I'm afraid I'm not following you here. What do you mean by matter-forming?"

Another glance. "Creating matter," said Vo, "bringing objects into existence."

Jeryant said "I still don't..." and then stopped as his mind began to connect what Vo had said directly to the vanishing door itself. Understanding began to dawn. "Is that how you build things?" he tried. "Is that what you're trying to say?"

"Well, yes," said Vo, "in its simplest form, that is what the term means."

"But how does it work?" asked Jeryant. "There's something I'm missing here. I mean those doors just materialised out of nowhere. How is it done? Do you use machines?"

"No," Vo replied. "We use out minds. We will objects into existence."

"Will them? You mean you just think about an object and it appears out of thin air?" Then Jeryant regretted using the phrase as he saw Vo struggling to make sense of it, in a lengthening pause. "Sorry," he said, "that last part was a colloquialism. It doesn't mean what it literally says."

"I think I understand it," Vo said, hesitantly. "Yes. It does describe the concept quite well, in fact. To ordinary vision, matter-forming would appear to be objects appearing out of nowhere."

"And that's completely normal for your people, is it?"

"Oh, yes. But it is more than just for my people," Vo said. "It is the normality of this reality. This universe. It is the way matter comes into existence and how it continues to exist after it is created. And how it ceases to exist, when it is no longer needed."

"Tell me..." Kasstovaal hadn't shown any interest in the conversation until now. Ever since the window had opened in front of him and confirmed his fears, he had been sunk in silent brooding, hardly responding to Jeryant or the Dwellers as the four of them left the room to go to the reception. He had been barely aware of the rough rock walls passing to either side of him and the smoothed floor beneath his bare feet. Then something of the conversation filtered through to his numbed brain and woke him. Something vital had just been said and Jeryant was going to miss it because he was a Medic, with little knowledge of physics. But Kasstovaal thought he knew what Vo was describing. He reached forward and took hold of Vo's arm to get him to stop and turn to face him. The arm felt real, rubbery like his own but cold under his touch.

"Tell me," he said again. "Tell me exactly how matter is formed. What is it made of?"

Vo nodded. "Of course. Stupid of me. The differences between our realities may extend all the way to the very building blocks of creation. I had overlooked that. I apologise."

"Never mind," said Kasstovaal, looking straight into the Dweller's face. "Just tell me."

Vo took a few seconds to assemble his words, reflecting that those things taken for granted by some are the most difficult to explain to others. "At the most basic level," he began, "matter consists of minute particles, too small to be seen by normal vision. All forms of matter are made up of these particles and the different forms are defined by the pattern in which these particles are joined together."

Kasstovaal listened carefully to the words, interpreting their meaning as Vo did. "You're describing atoms and molecules, aren't you?" he said, excitedly.

Vo's face broke into a smile and relief came off him in waves. "That's right," he said. "You do have words for them. You understand the theory."

"So far," said Kasstovaal. "Keep going. What holds the atoms and molecules of any piece of matter together? What keeps them in that pattern?"

"Mental energy," said Vo, promptly. "The will of the being that formed the pattern in the first place."

"Ah!" That was it. It made sense to him now. "That's the difference," he said. "Matter in our universe is held together by a different force. Electro-magnetic energy. That's the basis of our reality."

"Is that so?" Vo said. "I am familiar with this energy form. Potentially quite versatile, I understand, but it has no force outside special laboratory conditions. Quite useless, for all practical purposes."

"That explains it." said Kasstovaal "That's what happened to us."

Jeryant looked at him, sharply. "You think this explains how we got here?" he asked.

"No, not that. I still can't remember how it happened. But don't you see, Jery. It explains what happened to us when we got here. Every atom and every molecule in our bodies, our clothes, even the ship we were using, assuming we were in one. Everything was held together by atomic and molecular bonds made of electro-magnetic energy. Suddenly we enter an environment where there is no electro-magnetic force holding things together. What do you suppose is going to happen? All those bonds are going to disappear and every single atom is going to break down into its component particles."

Jeryant gaped at him. "You mean we just dissolved away into nothing? Just like that?"

"We atomised, Jery," said Kasstovaal, darkly. "We broke down into a cloud of sub-atomic particles. We couldn't have survived. But, somehow, we have. That I don't understand."

"No mystery there, I'd say," said Jeryant. "It seems to me that if any part of us is going to survive in a universe made up of mental energy, it's our own mental energy. Our thoughts, our minds. Isn't that right, Vo."

"Indeed," Vo agreed. "The process of sentient thought generates mental energy, here. What you describe is consistent with the state in which we first found you. Disembodied minds held together in the mist by the power generated from your own thoughts. It is a condition we are familiar with among our people."

"How come?"

"One of the skills we have learned is to send our minds out of our bodies into the outer mists. It allows us to see other places and communicate with those who live there. It allows us to perceive great expanses of space, all at once, and travel great distances at the speed of a thought. Only one thread needs to be left behind, attached to the body so that the mind can find its way back. If that tendril breaks then the mind becomes lost and cannot find the way again. It becomes as you were. Drifting, helpless and without purpose. A terrible fate for a reasoning mind."

"Yes." Kasstovaal had no need to imagine what that must feel like. He knew now that he had experienced it first hand. It had not been a dream.

Vo turned and began walking again. The others followed. "Since we mastered the skill," he went on, "several of us have been lost in this way. Many of us tried to guide them back to the Rock and show them the way back into their bodies. We came close to success many times but we could not achieve re-fusion. Without the original link, the mind cannot re-enter the body. And, without the mind to sustain it, the body quickly loses cohesion and crumbles into atoms. Once that happened, we could not help them."

"Now, though, we know that we can. I was set to the purpose of finding a method of capturing and focusing a disembodied mind so that it can be re-implanted into a body. And another of us, Oa, was given the task of creating an artificial body, a Bio-form, to replace the old body if it degenerated too far. And we have both achieved success." A hint of triumph entered Vo's voice as he said it.

"You have?"

"Yes. With you two. You are the result of our first field experiments with both processes. Of course, we did not expect to find you, out there. We were searching for one of the lost ones, though they will have drifted far in all this time. Even so, I thought that I had found one of them, when I first detected your mind, Jeryant. You were quite close to the Rock, then. But it quickly became obvious that you were not one of the lost ones. Your mind felt quite different. But we were still able to draw your mind in and fuse it into a Bio-form."

"So you'd never done this, before us?" said Jeryant.

"Only in laboratory simulations. But now we know that it works in practice. You two have done my people a great service by helping us prove the efficiency of these processes."

"They're not one hundred per cent efficient yet, you know," said Jeryant, looking down at his new body. "When I meet Oa, as I soon hope to, there's going to be a very frank exchange of views."

Kasstovaal smiled to himself. He knew what Jeryant thought of as a frank exchange of views. It usually involved a lot of shouting and variously coloured blood spattering the floor and generally ended with someone having to bail the Medic out of a jailhouse. Kasstovaal had done this himself, five times as far as he could remember, and from five different jailhouses. Oa had best watch out.

"Admittedly," said Vo, "the Bio-formation process still needs improvement. Though, I think, you stretched the program far outside the limits Oa was planning for when she built it."

"How do you mean?" Jeryant asked, making a mental note of the "she".

"Oa designed the machine with flexibility in mind. Creating an artificial body is all very well and, in functional terms, one Dweller's body is much like another. But what of the characteristics of the individual? No two Dwellers are ever alike in all respects." Vo paused. "I don't think it would be appropriate for me to list where the differences are to be found on our bodies. It might upset your Illusion programs."

Kasstovaal forced his mind not to remember the sight he'd had of them. The real Dwellers behind the glass window, staring in at him. He could not push the memory far enough away and it kept jumping across his eyes. Keep calm, keep calm, he told himself. He could almost feel himself straining to hang on to the illusion. In his eyes, the figures of the two Dwellers began to soften, losing their definition.

Te, walking a pace or two in front of him, sensed his mind struggling. Vo, next to her, did not seem to have noticed. That she didn't understand. Should she try to soothe the Beyonder? The one who called himself Kasstovaal, whose mind she had touched. She thought that Vo would not approve, if she did. He had told Ji, and through him all Dwellers, that the privacy of the Beyonders' minds should be respected. And yet the poor creature was battling within its own mind. She could almost feel the Illusion faltering as its mind writhed. It would come to distress, even harm, if it broke down completely.

She was no Thought-Healer. How could she be sure how much of a battering one of Ji's mental constructs would stand up to. But then, in an alien mind, would Ji himself know?

She came to a decision and sent a calming wave out behind her into Kasstovaal's mind. Just one brief burst.

As it washed over him, Kasstovaal suddenly found that he had won the battle. His mind stilled and the figures of Te and Vo, in front of him, became solidly humanoid once more.

Vo was still talking and showing no sign of having noticed anything wrong, much to Te's relief.

"We decided that it was not for us to dictate how the Bio-forms should appear," he was saying. "That choice belongs solely with the recipient. After all, it is they who must wear it. So Oa designed the machine to accept input from the mind caught in my focusing device and to change the Bio-form's structure according to that input. The mind inside the crystal can dictate what form it wants and the machine will create it. Within reason, of course. Certain aspects of a body cannot be changed otherwise it won't operate properly and the body will die. The machine is meant to allow for those."

"Sounds reasonable to me," said Jeryant. "What went wrong in our case?"

"I think Oa would be better able to give you a full answer," said Vo. "But I believe that the machine found you altogether too...different to reproduce accurately. Forgive me, I mean no insult by that. But the program was designed to expect only variations on a standard model of a Dweller body. The bodies you told it to create were so far from that model that it could not compensate for the differences."

He took a sharp turn to the left, leading them into a connecting corridor that curved away to the left and the floor began to slope downwards. It was only a gentle slope, hardly noticeable under other circumstances. But Kasstovaal hadn't seen it coming, hadn't been paying attention to where he was putting his feet. He was still slightly zonked from the effect of the wave Te had sent to him, not much above the effect a headache pill would have had on him but enough to relax him just a little too much. When his foot encountered the slope the tenuous hold he had on his balance and co-ordination deserted him completely. His legs tangled, as they sought to regain the rhythm, and he stumbled sideways, pulling Jeryant with him. Instinctively, his hand came up to stop himself falling and the palm smacked against the rough rock surface of the wall.

Then he gasped as thoughts flooded into his mind. Thoughts that were not his own. It was as though a hundred different voices were talking to a hundred other voices, gentle conversations passing back and forth across his brain. At first it was a babble, all jumbled together and indistinct. But he found that, if he concentrated, he could isolate them and hear what they said.

"The first pattern is stable," said one, and it seemed to Kasstovaal to be coming from somewhere to his left. "But the second pattern is still fluctuating."

"Perhaps the fifth sector needs to be modified again, " said an answering voice, to his right this time.

"I am not yet convinced that the problem lies in that sector," said the first. "Perhaps we should begin the second pattern again, from the baseline."

"A radical approach. You think it necessary?"

"Unless a satisfactory explanation for the instability can be found, then I think that is the only alternative."

"A pity. Much time and effort has gone into this construct."

"The effort is not wasted. No effort is ever wasted. If we can discover where we went wrong."

"Of course."

"Shall we begin now?"

"Later, I think. We must attend in the Gathering Place, now."

"Indeed. I am looking forward to meeting these Beyonders."

"So am I. If they truly come from outside reality, think what insights they could give us."

Then there was a pause. "One of the Beyonders is with us, now," said the first, with mild surprise.

"Welcome, Beyonder." said the other, kindly. "I am Na. I hope we may speak at some time. There is much I would like to ask."

Kasstovaal felt the guilt of an eavesdropper discovered in the act. He wrenched his hand away from the wall and the voices ceased. He found himself still standing in the corridor, staring at the wall with his mouth hanging open. He stumbled back a couple of steps and collided with Jeryant, who was still trying to regain his footing.

"Watch out," Jeryant exclaimed, catching him, "you'll have us both over again."

Kasstovaal pointed a shaking finger at the wall. "I heard voices," he gasped, "I touched the wall and then there were voices in my head. Talking to each other. Talking to me, even."

Te walked back to him. She gently closed a hand, or the illusion of a hand, around his outstretched one, closing the pointing finger and tenderly guiding the arm back down to his side. She looked up into his face, her hand not letting go.

"It's all right." she said "You have touched the veins in the Rock. It is how we talk to each other if we are some distance apart. It is nothing to worry about."

"Veins?" Kasstovaal's eyes darted back up to the wall, but could see only plain grey rock. He brought his eyes back to meet Te's. Those two perfect white discs held him. He could not look away because, suddenly, he did not want to look away.

"Veins," said Te. "Impurities in the rock itself, formed into channels along which we can send our thoughts. In this way, all the Dwellers can speak to all the other Dwellers; at the same time, if need be. That is how all Dwellers know to come, now, to the Gathering Place to meet you two."

"All Dwellers?" said Kasstovaal. "They're all coming to meet us? Now? The whole population?"

"Oh, yes. They are all most curious. They all want to meet you."

"Well, how many are there of you?"

"A few tens of thousands. But the Gathering Place is quite big enough. Come with me." She turned and led him by the hand. "I will show you."

The term "big enough" did no justice to the Gathering Place.

The corridor had spiralled gently downwards for almost half a mile, or so it felt to Kasstovaal. And then they had turned off into a straight flat corridor that ended abruptly in an archway, opening onto a large circular area with what looked like a podium set in the exact centre of the floor.

It wasn't until Kasstovaal and Jeryant stepped through the archway, after Vo and Te, that the sheer size of it became apparent. The cavern they had entered was not so very wide. But it was tall. The walls stretched up and up, every inch of four thousand feet, if Kasstovaal was any judge, terminating in a distant roof. At first sight, the walls maintained a straight line upwards, creating a long thin cylinder. But as Kasstovaal looked more closely he saw that the walls tapered ever so slightly inwards, so gradually that he might have missed it, had he not had a Pilot's eye for perspective.

The wall at floor level had half a dozen archways leading off from it, including the one they had just entered through, equidistant around the circumference. Above these stretched a band of smoothed stone, standing proud of the wall by two feet or so to form a ledge, all the way around the cavern. The face of this ledge, about a foot thick, had been intricately carved, a swirling pattern of objects and symbols, more mathematical than artistic. At one point on it, he thought he could make out the standardised shape of a DNA helix.

Six more archways opened out onto the ledge and were, in turn, crowned by another ledge seven feet higher up. It continued like that all the way up, as far as either of them could see. At every tenth level or so, the ledge extended out into a stone bridge, stretching across the expanse of the circle. Not all the bridges reached directly across the centre; some merely cut across a side, and no two seemed to stretch at the same angle. With those, and the inward tapering of the ledges, Kasstovaal could see that anyone standing anywhere in that cavern would have a virtually uninterrupted line of sight directly down to the floor below.

Vo and Te led them both, still goggling upwards, across the floor to the podium. Like everything else here, it seemed to have been carved out of rock.

"This is the Gathering Place," said Vo, and the cavern filled with echoes. Every sound made in here must carry all the way to the ceiling. "Here we meet to ponder only those matters that must involve us all. Every Dweller must have a say. It is quite rare for it to be used."

"How rare?" Jeryant asked.

"It has only happened four times during my existence," said Vo. "Te, here, has never attended a gathering until now. Only matters of great moment will draw all Dwellers from their work to attend. None will stay away."

"Well, that's flattering," said Jeryant, "I've never been called a 'matter of great moment' before."

"And what, exactly, are they going to discuss this time, Vo?" Kasstovaal asked, flat voiced. "What are they all going to have their say about?"

Vo looked at him quizzically. He had caught the edge of hostility in the words. "Why, nothing is to be decided. The Dwellers merely wish to welcome you among us. What could there be to decide?"

"Well, how about whether or not to allow us to keep these new bodies of ours? How about whether or not to let us remain here at all?"

Vo looked shocked. "Neither of those matters are in question, I assure you. We have no desire to cast you out of the Rock. And as for you bodies...well. Haven't I already said that they are the proof that our process works. They are much too valuable to destroy. Never think we would do either of those things."

Kasstovaal relaxed a little. "I just needed to hear you say so," he said, "to know that you had actually thought about it."

Vo nodded. "The point is well made. You need have no fears."

"I never had any to start with," Jeryant hissed in Kasstovaal's ear.

"I had to ask, didn't I?" Kasstovaal whispered back.

"No you, damn well, didn't." Out loud, Jeryant asked, "So when are the others going to start arriving?"

Vo said, "They are already here."

The two humans looked up. Every ledge and every bridge was crowded with Dwellers. They had arrived silently, each had taken their place silently. All were looking down at them, absolutely silent. All the way to the ceiling, a sea of black humanoid forms. Twenty, thirty thousand? Kasstovaal couldn't begin to count them.

At floor level, more Dwellers appeared out of the archways and moved softly to form a circle around the small group by the podium. One Dweller, taller and bulkier than the others and male in shape, stepped out of the crowd and walked towards them.

"I welcome you, Beyonders," he said. His voice was deep and throaty and made the walls boom as the words floated upwards. "My name is Azu. I am the First Voice of the Dwellers. It is my purpose to preside in this place when the time for gathering comes. When the Dwellers speak with one voice, that voice is mine. So it is that the duty of welcoming you among us falls to me also."

He mounted the podium. "Let all know" he boomed, "that these two strange and wonderful beings have come to us out of the mists. Their like has never been encountered before. They are from beyond our reality, from another plane of existence. They bring with them new knowledge and there is much we can learn from them. Already they have assisted us in the purposes we strive to complete. And they too can learn from us."

"These are the Beyonders. Bryn Jeryant" he gestured with a hand, "and Malkan Kasstovaal." He paused to let the echoes die. Then he said, simply "Welcome them."

It sounded almost like a command and Kasstovaal found himself instinctively bracing to receive a blow. After all, he didn't know how Dwellers welcomed people, nor what they understood the term to mean. He'd heard of one primitive race who welcomed ambassadorial parties by roasting the ambassador's first deputy on a spit. Perfectly normal behaviour, as far as they were concerned. That was diplomacy for you; all terms were relative to your understanding of them.

Then somebody behind him said "Welcome, Beyonder."

He turned. There was no one standing behind him. The Dwellers nearest to him were several yards away, still standing quietly. Then he realised that he had not heard the words. They had been sent into his mind, directly, and with them had come a feeling of sincerity. He knew, beyond doubt, that the Dweller who had sent the words meant them, wholeheartedly.

Then it descended on both of them, like a tide. A surge of warm, friendly welcome that could only be felt in the mind and the soul but which was so powerful they felt that they could reach out and take handfuls of it. It warmed them from within and caressed them from without.

Jeryant felt that he glowed with it. He had been made to feel welcome before, but only in the clumsy, fumbling, physical ways open to humans. This was that feeling distilled and focused into pure energy.

Kasstovaal could feel it washing away the fears that haunted him. They welcomed him. They wanted him. They were glad that he had come among them and was going to stay. He turned his eyes upwards to look into their faces. Every time his eyes rested on another Dweller's face, a different voice said inside his head "Welcome, Beyonder called Kasstovaal. Welcome."

Then he felt the discord.

His eyes had been travelling along the length of the lowest bridge, nine or ten storeys up, and had settled on a tall, thin male Dweller who had somehow managed to have empty space around him in the tightly packed crowd. Even without that, he would still have stood out among them for he wore a cape, the same black as his own skin, looking like wings reaching halfway down his back. This distinguished him from the other Dwellers all of whom, like Kasstovaal and Jeryant, wore no clothes. The clip that fastened it, at the centre of his breast, was of a silvery metal and Kasstovaal recognised the sideways figure-of-eight symbol, broken at one end. The mathematical symbol for an infinite value. A symbol from his universe.

Their eyes met and locked. There were no welcoming words. The warming wave faded into the background and, in its place, Kasstovaal felt a surge of the most intense hatred and loathing he had ever encountered in his life. A surge directed straight at him.

11.

The room they were shown into appeared to be quite large until you realised that the reason it looked like that was because it was completely bare. It was a perfectly cubical room, the walls, floor and ceiling all made of the same smoothed rock surface, bleached bone-white. There was not a single feature to define any of the surfaces: no seams; no shades in the colour; not a single imperfection in the smoothness. Kasstovaal found his eyes hurting as they strained to make out the points where the surfaces joined.

"This will be your...private place," said Vo. Then he paused, reconsidering. "No. Those are not the right words. Your...."

"Quarters?" suggested Kasstovaal.

"Yes. That's the word. Quarters. A very rich language, you have. Yes. This room will be yours, Kasstovaal, and there is another room for you, Jeryant, on the opposite side of the corridor. In these rooms you can be alone to quiet your minds and think your own thoughts. No one will disturb you, if you do not wish it."

"Can we get some furniture for them?" asked Kasstovaal "They are a little... well...empty."

Te said, "We will form any objects you need for you. What would you like?"

"How about a bed, for a start."

Te put her head on one side in a manner Kasstovaal was becoming very familiar with. "What is a bed?" she asked.

"Well, it's...it's a thing about so high with a flat surface on top, slightly longer than I am and about twice as wide as I am."

"Four times," Jeryant put in. "I like to stretch out."

Kasstovaal gave him a wry glance. He knew Jeryant's preoccupations all too well. "Stretch out what?" he asked.

"Whoever comes to hand."

"Filthy swine."

Jeryant grinned at him. "Still on form" he said.

"Forgive me," Te said, "I think you are describing a table, are you not. That's what it sounds like."

"No, no," said Kasstovaal. "The surface of a bed is deeply padded. You lie down on it to sleep."

"Amongst other things," said Jeryant, not quite under his breath.

"Sleep?" The incomprehension was back in Te's manner. Not an expression on the face, as such; there were not enough features to communicate anything definite; but her whole body language seemed to transmit her perplexity. This time, she even looked to Vo, who also seemed to be having difficulty with the word.

"I'm afraid I don't understand," she said, at length. "What is to sleep. I can see the word in your mind but the concept eludes me. Please explain to us."

"You don't know what sleep is?" said Kasstovaal, incredulously. "Well, it's the action of...well... losing consciousness."

The Dwellers looked puzzled. "We know what unconsciousness means," said Vo. "We use suppression waves to induce it if one of our kind becomes ill and needs healing without pain. We only use them when absolutely necessary. Is that what this 'sleep' is for?"

"No. It's...well...oh, bugger. Jery, you explain it to them. You're the Medic around here."

A little, sadistic part of Jeryant had been enjoying watching his friend struggle to put into words something that didn't usually need describing. "Damn! Show's over", he thought.

He said "Sleep is part of the process we humans use to re-energise our cells. We slow down all of the processes taking place inside our bodies so that we are using the smallest amount of energy possible. That includes thought processes, of course. Our bodies can, then, store up the energy we're not then using so we can use it while we're awake...that is, not asleep."

The Dwellers took a few silent moments to absorb this.

"So, if I understand you correctly," Vo said, hesitantly, "your bodies don't normally generate enough energy, at any one time, to operate at full capacity."

"That's right."

"So you need to store energy to make up the difference."

"Correct."

"I see." Vo's tone suggested that he wasn't overly impressed. "It does sound somewhat inefficient."

"There's not a lot we can do about it," Jeryant told him. "That's the way evolution works in our universe. It differs from person to person and from race to race but in almost all life forms there's a considerable gap between the rate at which food can be turned into energy and the rate at which that energy is used. It's a pain but everybody has to live with it."

Then he caught Vo's expression. "Where did I lose you, this time?" he asked.

Vo hesitated, as if embarrassed to ask. Then he said "Forgive me. What, exactly, is food? Is it another process, like this 'sleep' you describe?"

Oh boy, said a small voice inside Kasstovaal. Not only do they have no concept of sleep, they don't know what the word 'food' means. We're dead.

"Fuel," Jeryant tried. "A mixture of organic solids and liquids which our bodies use to burn and make energy. That's how we subsist."

"Ah! Interesting," said Vo. "You remember, Te, the vessels Oa detected in the Bio-forms for chemical intake. This explains them."

"So, you would need a constant supply of these solids and liquids to continue operating," said Te.

"Not constant, as such," said Jeryant. "We have to fill up two or three times between sleep periods."

"More in some cases" muttered Kasstovaal, just loud enough for Jeryant to hear.

Jeryant ignored him. "This does raise the question of whether or not we still need to. As I understand it our new bodies are based, at least in part, on the design of our old bodies. Does that mean that they re-energise themselves in the same way? If so then we have a problem. I can tell from your reaction that there is no food to be had around here."

Vo said "I doubt that food will be necessary to you now. Or sleep, for that matter. I assume that these processes are designed to generate the electro-magnetic energy which, you say, is the power in your universe."

"I think so," said Jeryant. "One form of that energy anyway. That right, isn't it Kass?"

"Yes."

"Well then," said Vo, "that energy has no use in this reality. All things here, Dwellers included, are powered by mental energy. Mental energy is generated by the process of thought. Thought is promoted by the condition of sentience. Because we are sentient we can think and, because we think, we subsist. The same, I believe will now apply to you."

"You're sure of that, are you?"

"Do you feel the need to take on fuel or to recharge your storage cells?"

Jeryant patted his stomach. "Now you mention it, no I don't. I don't feel tired or hungry. You, Kass?"

"No."

"And I think we ought to be feeling one or the other by now, given how long it's been since we woke up. Let alone the time we were under."

"Then we have our answer," said Vo. "Oa will be able to confirm it. But if either of you feels any signs of weakening, lose no time in calling for one of us. Indeed, if you feel any ill effects. These Bio-forms are still experimental after all. And they were never designed with you in mind. There may be side effects which laboratory experiments cannot predict."

"All right," said Jeryant. "But I think we'll still have a bed each, if it's all the same to you. I think better lying down."

"Is that what you call it?" murmured Kasstovaal.

"Shut up, Kass. There's a good boy."

Te turned and began staring into the empty room. A perfect seven by three block began to rise out of the floor, coming to a stop at exactly the height Kasstovaal had indicated. As they watched, the smooth upper surface seemed to become soft, like melting chocolate, and then turned to a liquid which, for some reason, failed to run off the sides. Large bubbles started to appear in the liquid, spreading all over the surface and swelling like balloons. At last the swelling stopped and the bubbles solidified into a thick mass of air pockets, an ideal mattress.

"Is that right?" asked Te.

Kasstovaal stepped into the room and walked up to the bed. He gave the padding bubbles an experimental push with his hand. Then he lay down on it, sinking comfortably into the bubbles, which shifted and gave to fit his body but did not break.

"Feels good to me," he said. "Thanks." Then he sat up and asked "Could you teach us to do that?"

"Certainly," said Vo, "I had intended to suggest it in any case. It is a skill you will need, if you are to spend any time with us."

"If only so we can open the doors," said Jeryant.

"Quite so. We should begin as soon as possible. But, first, there are a few matters I must discuss with Oa and Ji which must take priority."

"What matters?" Kasstovaal asked.

"Your progress so far. Everything that has happened must be recorded. No detail must be left out. For instance, I notice that you are both still having difficulty in walking. That requires an explanation and a remedy."

"Not before time either," said Jeryant, "I don't stagger about this much when I'm blind drunk. And it's not as though I've had the pleasure of drinking anything." Then, to stop the puzzled silence, he added, "I'll explain the concept later. Oa will love it, I'm sure."

"Very well," said Vo. "Te. Stay and help the Beyonders settle into their...quarters. Form for them any item they need for the time being. Come and join us when you have finished. We will need your observations, also."

Then to the humans he said "Until later, Beyonders" and walked away down the corridor.

When it came down to it, Kasstovaal had some difficulty knowing what to ask Te to form for him. It wasn't so much a question of selecting the things he felt he wanted or needed in the room as which of those things he could actually describe to Te in terms she would understand.

He tried to base it on the items he remembered keeping, habitually, in the cabins on board the various ships he had commanded. Those, as far he could remember, were the nearest he'd ever got to having a permanent home. Ever since he'd left the academy, with the ink still drying on his Pilot-Captain's licence, he had been either in flight or just waiting in dock to re-board. Those cabins briefly became the storage rooms for him and his life, somewhere where he could shower and crash out for a few hours and a place to leave the few personal belongings he had, stuffed into his kit bag. Image plates of family and old friends he hadn't contacted in years and places he'd never been back to. His music collection, compressed into music tubes, that helped him to sleep when sleep had become more and more difficult. A few book chips, to while away the waiting time. A facsimile of the licence, in a frame. And the symbol of a religion he could no longer remember the name of, a small statuette of three hands clasping each other, plated in gold. That had been a gift from one of the few women he had managed to be intimate with. Right now, he couldn't remember her name and felt guilty about it. She had been a deeply spiritual woman. Perhaps that was why they had come together. She always sought to see the inside of people, rather than just be guided by external appearances like most people did. She had recognised his need for love and took pleasure in fulfilling that need. And she had understood that he would not stay, could not. She had given him that symbol of her religion to remember her by and, perhaps, to give him some of the solace it offered her. Something for him to pray to, if he ever reached the point of praying. He had kept it, treasured it, but he had never prayed to it.

All these things were almost certainly beyond a description accurate enough for Te to recreate them. So he would have to forget them, for now. Maybe he'd be able to do it himself, after a bit of training.

That just left the more practical items of the average cabin. Certain of those, he reflected, didn't apply here. If Vo was right, he didn't need a food dispenser, even assuming he could have got Te to create all the components for him. There didn't seem to be any need for a lamp or other light source. All the rooms and corridors he'd been in so far had been well lit though he had still not been able to work out what they were lit by. Air conditioning didn't seem to be necessary either. The air felt comfortably warm and, just slightly, on the move all the time. It smelt a bit sterile for his liking but not worth making a fuss about.

In the end, both he and Jeryant settled on having a bed, a table and two chairs, one to sit up at the table and one large armchair padded in the same way as the bed. They debated on whether or not to try and describe a shower to Te, but decided to leave it for the time being. For one thing, there were no obvious sources of water.

"I doubt if they wash anyway," Jeryant said. "If they get dirt on their hands, I suppose they'd just will it out of existence. A good deal more efficient than our way, when you think about it."

As for wall adornments, the only thing Kasstovaal could think of was a mirror. "Er... a reflective surface," he explained. "It's usually made out of a sheet of transparent material over a very shiny metal backing surface. Does that make sense?"

Te thought about it. "Something like this?"

A full length rectangular mirror appeared against one wall and Kasstovaal got the first really good look at his own body and the first sight he'd had of the face that he now wore. It was recognisable as his own, the one that mirrors usually threw back at him, but the lines were blurred and softened. The spongy skin gave it a puffy appearance and the surface stretched unnaturally as he moved his jaw. His eyes stood out in stark contrast to the absolute jet black of the flesh. Then he remembered that it was all an illusion. The mirror would not show him what he really looked like. His mind would not let it. Even as he thought that, the image of himself in the mirror softened even more as the illusion faltered. He looked away, quickly. He didn't want to see that. Didn't want to know what the Dwellers had turned him into.

"On second thoughts," he said, trying to keep the quiver out of his voice, "I'll do without it. Take it away, please."

Te noted the reaction and quickly vanished the mirror out of existence.

"Would you like a window to the outside?" she suggested. "Your room does connect with the outer surface. I could make one for you."

"No!" The word snapped out of Kasstovaal before he could slow it down. The memory of that sight still haunted him and it would be some time before he could fully accept the fundamental wrongness of the reality out there. The last thing he wanted at the moment was to catch a sight of it every time he turned his head. "No," he said, more gently. "No, thank you."

"As you wish," said Te.

"I would," said Jeryant. "If it's all the same, I'll swap with you, Kass. Then, I'll have the window. Could you just alter this bed a bit for me, my dear?"

Eventually, though in far less time than it would've taken them in their own universe, the two humans were established in their quarters.

"I must leave you now," said Te, "I must meet with Vo and Oa."

"But you will come back?" Kasstovaal asked.

"Oh, yes. Soon. I shall come back and collect you for your Matter-forming training, once we have finished our discussion."

"All right. See you."

Te's face gave a small smile, though what that signified in reality Kasstovaal couldn't tell, and then she left.

"Well," said Jeryant, making his unsteady way into Kasstovaal's room and sitting down on the bed. "Not so much a case of 'I think therefore I am' as a case of 'I think thereby I continue'. Fascinating situation, isn't it?"

"I'm glad you're enjoying it," said Kasstovaal, dryly.

"Sure I am. It's an exercise in pure anthropology. I love it. Just look at these people, Kass. They don't sleep, so they keep operating 24 hours a day. They don't eat; they get all the energy they need from their minds. Now you think about how much of our time and energy we use up just trying to make sure we can keep ourselves supplied with food and somewhere to sleep."

"Work to eat, eat to work and sleep to do both!" said Kasstovaal.

"That's right. But the Dwellers aren't in that sort of vicious circle. They don't have to expend energy to get more energy. That means they can concentrate one hundred per cent of their faculties on other things. And, on top of that, they can create objects out of thin air, just by thinking about it. That is almost the full set of qualifications for godhood, you know. I wonder how long they live?"

"Personally," said Kasstovaal, "I don't intend to stay long enough to find out. We've got to work out a way to get back to our own universe. We don't belong here."

"What?" exclaimed Jeryant. "We're sitting in a brand new universe with a whole new set of frontiers to explore and you want to leave. What happened to your pioneering spirit?"

"I never had any. I don't run explorer missions. My priority is always to get the ship, its contents and me to the destination safely. Scientific curiosity doesn't usually play a major part in that."

"I think it might have to, in this case." said Jeryant "Still assuming, of course, that we started off in a spaceship..."

"We did," Kasstovaal interrupted. "It came back to me a short while ago. A definite memory of you and me in the cockpit of a spaceship. A two-man job, a Star-runner I think. Then a bright light. That's all."

Jeryant rubbed his forehead, "Still a blank, to me," he said. "If you're right, though, it does tell us something positive."

"What?"

"It means there aren't any more of us floating around out there. What did Vo call it? Disembodied minds. At least we don't have to worry about leaving somebody behind. I don't suppose you've remembered what went wrong."

"No. Not a detail. I can't even remember where we were supposed to be going or why."

Jeryant said, thoughtfully, "I suppose there is a chance that nothing went wrong. On the contrary, everything might have gone exactly right."

"What are you talking about?"

"Well, isn't it possible that the aim of the trip was, in fact, to get us here. Into this...I don't know. Third Mode, I suppose you'd call it. Might it have been an experiment to do just that? To penetrate past the Second Mode and into a Third."

"Are you serious?"

"Well, why not? I know, as well as you do, why the Second Mode is used for space travel. Because it's smaller compared to the space it occupies. Now I may only be a layman in these matters but it seems reasonable to me to think that a Third Mode would be smaller still, probably by the same factor as the Second Mode is to our universe. If you could pass a ship through that, you could cross the span of the universe in a matter of days."

"It's a popular theory," said Kasstovaal. "But the scientists all discount it as a practical possibility. It's only just possible to use the Second Mode within safety limits. The normal laws of physics start not to apply. It's like our problem here, only less so. The effects in the Second Mode can be shielded against with certain alloys and energy fields. And limiting the exposure, of course. The theory goes on to say that, while a Third Mode would be proportionately more compressed, the physical laws that apply there would be even less compatible with ours, by the same proportion. Almost certainly beyond the capabilities of any shielding. It's always been considered far too dangerous."

Jeryant shrugged. "Knowing those bastards at Space Central, sitting on their money bags, that wouldn't deter them from trying for very long. The sort of profits they could pull in if it worked would easily be enough to justify risking a couple of operatives. In their eyes, anyway. They've got a very precise idea about how much a human life is worth."

"The man's a cynic."

Jeryant leaned forward. "I have very good reason to know," he said, firmly. "Believe me."

Kasstovaal didn't press it. "Anyway," he said, sitting down at the table, "I doubt if they'd send us two on a mission like that. We're not the best qualified to go prospecting in a new universe, are we. They'd send a science team, wouldn't they?"

"Not if they weren't sure it would work," said Jeryant. "In that case they wouldn't risk a whole team of valuable scientists. For the first sweep they would send two people to tell them the two things they first need to know. They would send a Pilot-Captain to see how the ship reacts and they would send a Medic to see how human tissue reacts. If they come back with positive data...hells, if they come back at all...then the scientific team could be sent in. And we, sunshine, have one unbeatable qualification for a mission like that."

"What?"

"In the eyes of Space Central, we are eminently dispensable. And we both know why that is, don't we."

Kasstovaal saw the truth in it. "Yes. We do. And they would do that to us, wouldn't they."

"We both know it."

"It could still have been an accident, though," said Kasstovaal. "This is all just speculation. Either way, if we can recreate the effect that got us here we can get back. If they want to send a scientific team in here to research these Dwellers and their Rock, let them. They'd be better at it than we would."

"You're not thinking, Kass. It's not just a question of doing what we did in reverse and you know it. Even assuming we could get hold of a ship and work out how to make it take us back into our universe, you know what will happen when we get there. Exactly the same thing that happened when we arrived here. We'll atomise, as you put it. Molecules held together by mental energy have no more place in our universe than molecules held together by electro-magnetic force have in this one. And that's what we're made of now, Kass."

He paused. "Now, I don't want to speculate about whether or not a disembodied mind could survive for any time in our universe, like it can here. The conditions here are, after all, uniquely suited for that. In our universe, you're entering the realms of the occult and the religious. But, again, assuming that our minds survive the transition and keep going, I can't think of anywhere in the universe where we would find anyone who could make us artificial bodies, like the Dwellers have. Again, I am in the best position to know that is true. And you know it as well, Kass."

Kasstovaal banged a fist on the tabletop. "No. I won't believe there's no way back. There must be one."

"I'm not saying there isn't," said Jeryant, "what I am saying is we don't want to rush things. If we do we'll end up dead. We don't have all the answers yet. But one thing is certain. Whatever the solution is, our best chance of finding it and exploiting it lies with the Dwellers. They're obviously quite advanced scientifically and with their matter-forming powers they can provide us with whatever materials we might need. At the moment they seem to be willing to do that. But I think it would help if you cut them some slack."

Kasstovaal looked shifty. "Don't know what you mean," he muttered.

"Don't give me that. You've been looking over your shoulder from the moment you woke up. And it doesn't take an Empath to sense what your feelings towards the Dwellers are. I think that the only way you could've made the fact that you don't trust them any more obvious would be to have it tattooed across your arse in big, white letters."

"I'm just trying to watch our backs. I don't accept these people on face value like you do, Jery. You said yourself that they're only a couple of steps off godhood. Compared to that, we're on a level with the rodents. How much compunction would they have in disposing of us if our value as an experiment runs out or if we cease to be interesting enough? It wouldn't take much, either. They could just think us away. I don't like the idea of anyone having that sort of power over me."

"You can't judge them by human standards, Kass," Jeryant protested. "So far they've gone out of their way to make us comfortable. That should count for something, surely. And are you going to deny what we felt at that welcome ceremony? Gods, it was powerful enough to pacify an army. I should've thought that would've convinced you that they mean us well. I certainly didn't have any doubts when I walked out of that cavern."

"You didn't pick up what I did," said Kasstovaal and told him about the Dweller on the bridge. "I could feel hatred, real black hatred coming off him. Aimed straight at us. And, before you say it, it wasn't my imagination."

"It's just one Dweller," said Jeryant. " One out of thousands. Much as I hate to think there are people in the universe who hate me, I have to accept the possibility that there are a few scattered around. It does not alter our situation. Soon they are going to start teaching us those useful little matter-forming tricks of theirs. If we can wrap our heads around those, we'll be on an equal footing with them, won't we."

"Will we? Don't forget they've got practice on their side. Not to mention greater numbers."

"Al lright." Jeryant got up, used the bed to start him off and walked around the table to face his friend. He leaned forward, knuckles on the tabletop. "All right. Let's suppose, for the sake of sheer bloody-mindedness, that you're right about them. They can't be trusted. We're shit to them. They're going wipe us away the moment they get bored. What, exactly, can we do to prevent that happening?"

"I don't know," said Kasstovaal, savagely. "I don't know at all."

"Nor do I. Yet, " said Jeryant. "But if we learn about them, observe them, study them like they're studying us. If they have any weaknesses, ones we can use against them if it becomes necessary, then that is, surely, the way to find them."

"You're right, of course." Kasstovaal had to concede.

"Good boy." Jeryant patted the other's bald head. "Don't forget, though. The Dwellers can pick up on emotions. If you want to keep yours from them, you've got to simmer down. Get a hold of yourself and start thinking rationally."

"I'll do my best," said Kasstovaal. "Te, I think, I can trust. But I can't rightly say why."

"Innocence of youth, perhaps."

"Is she young? By our standards, who knows. No, I don't think that's it. I just feel that I...know her mind. It sounds silly but that's what it feels like. I just know that I have nothing to fear from her."

"Well that's a start." said Jeryant.

"But, then, she's just one Dweller, too. The argument cuts both ways. Even after that ceremony...and yes I did feel it too...I can't claim to know the minds of the other thousands of them."

"That's no excuse," said Jeryant. "Not here. If you asked these people what was in their mind, they wouldn't just tell you. They'd let you look for yourself. They'd probably show you how to do it, too. But that wouldn't convince you either, would it?"

"No, it wouldn't. Thoughts can be concealed. Even I could do it, if I tried hard enough. You're probably right in what you say. The majority of them may have no ill intentions towards us whatsoever. But with the sort of power they have, how many of them would it take to dispose of us. Just one, I suspect. One Dweller with a reason to hate us."

"All right," said Jeryant. "Confine yourself to Te, if it makes you any happier. And if they'll let you. You'll probably learn more like that anyway. Find out anything you can about how they live, what they spend their time doing. Remember everything you see. I'll do the same, though I shall be doing it for different reasons to yours. This is one scientific opportunity I am, definitely, not going to waste."

He turned away and headed for the door and his own quarters.

"Jery!"

Jeryant turned back. "What?"

"You don't suppose the Dwellers ARE gods, do you? I mean THE gods?"

Jeryant stared at him. "What are you on about?" he asked. "And don't tell me all this has made you find religion. I know you better than that."

"It's nothing like that," said Kasstovaal. "I mean, you know how many religions there are knocking around back in our universe."

"Don't I just. You can't throw a brick in any city without hitting some sort of priest."

"Well, I was just thinking. There's a theory that says popular legends have some basis in fact."

"Sure. I've heard that one."

"Well," said Kasstovaal, "suppose the same applies to religions and their deities."

"That's what the churches would have us all believe."

"Sure. But suppose the basis for those deities is the Dwellers and their powers."

"Huh?"

"Well, why not?" said Kasstovaal. "They've got most of the qualifications, according to you. Suppose they are, in fact, the gods that the religious saps back home have all been worshipping? It's possible, isn't it?"

Jeryant thought about it. "No," he said, at length, "I don't think so. The Dwellers lack one fundamental qualification, namely knowledge of us. One of the very few things all the religions agree on is that the gods are fully aware of our existence and form, either as our creators or our controllers. The Dwellers have never seen us before; that much is obvious."

"This generation, perhaps," said Kasstovaal. "But earlier generations might have known of us and influenced us."

"And then forgotten about us completely, keeping no records for their successors to find?" said Jeryant. "No, Kass. It won't wash. I grant you that they might be somebody's gods. But I don't think they're ours."

"An interesting problem," Oa was saying, as Te entered the room and took the seat waiting empty for her. The conversation paused, while greetings were exchanged. Then Oa said "We were just discussing the difficulty the Beyonders are having with their motion. I suppose it may, merely, be a flaw in the reconstruction. Their motive limbs are very strangely designed and there may be components I have missed. Have you any thoughts on this, Te?"

Te was still not used to having her opinion sought by her elders. She had just crossed the boundary into adulthood and suddenly her views had enough value to be considered by them. To her mind, the validity of her opinion had not changed from when she had been considered a child. But, now, they were interested and she still felt under pressure to justify that interest. As such, she took time in considering her answer.

"It appears to me," she said, "to be an error in the co-ordination of the limbs. If it is so, it is strange that the Beyonders' minds have not yet adjusted their co-ordination to correct the error."

"As you say," said Ji, "it is strange. From my observations of their mind constructions, I would say they are capable of making an adjustment of that kind. Perhaps the error margin is too large for their minds to adapt to."

"It may be so," said Oa, "I must give the matter some thought. Are there any other problems which need to be considered."

"No physical problems," said Vo. "The Bio-forms seem to be holding well, this time. There are no signs of degradation and the Beyonders have complained of no other malfunctions."

"Good. But we must keep them under observation. The test of time will be the most rigorous for the Bio-forms."

"I have advised the Beyonders to seek assistance the moment any malfunction is detected," said Vo. "I hope it will not be necessary."

"Our experiments say that it should not," said Oa. "But experiments are no substitute for testing in reality."

"What of their mental states?" asked Ji. "How are they responding to the new environment?"

"Te," said Vo, "perhaps you should answer this."

Te thought back, compiling her recent experiences into an answer, all the time feeling, acutely, the gaze of the other three Dwellers on her. "The one called Jeryant seems to have settled into the environment very well. I sense no apprehension or instability from him. The second

Beyonder, the one called Kasstovaal, is very much the opposite. I sense fear in him. Fear of us."

"Fear?" exclaimed Ji. "For what reason?"

"I do not know. It may be the sight of us he had before the illusion was installed. That memory seems to persist in his mind. I have noted how he reacts when he is reminded that the illusion is protecting him. The memory of our true appearance starts to conflict with the image the illusion is giving him and his mind starts to fight against it. I do not think he wants to see us as we really appear but his mind seems unable to accept the illusion, either. I have felt the illusion weakening, during these episodes. Do you think it will be strong enough to withstand the conflict, Ji?"

"I cannot be certain," Ji replied. "It might, perhaps, be wise to strengthen it a little, in view of your observations."

"Te was able to calm him, during one of these attacks," Vo put in. "Kasstovaal does respond to waves, even in those circumstances."

He did notice, Te thought to herself, guiltily.

"Did the Welcome ceremony help him?" Ji asked.

"It started to," Te said. " I was observing him closely during the ceremony and I felt him begin to relax. The fear in him started to break up and I thought it was going to resolve his apprehension for good. Then, suddenly, it all came back again. His fears solidified and all the healing that had taken place was undone. I do not know why?"

The three elder Dwellers looked at one another in puzzlement. Ji said "Such a reaction is hardly reasonable under so much positive wave energy."

"And yet it happened," Te insisted. "I definitely felt it."

"Of course, of course. We do not doubt what you tell us, Te. The question is why."

"Could it be," Oa suggested "that one of us was not projecting positive waves during the ceremony? Could Kasstovaal have detected a negative emotion directed towards him?"

"It would explain the reaction," Ji said. "But which of us would do such a thing? Who would sully the Ceremony of Welcome by sending a negative wave?"

"No one has raised an objection to the Beyonders' presence here," Vo said. "I can think of no one with reason to wish them ill."

The four of them considered in silence for a few moments.

"We cannot resolve this," Vo said, at last. "We have too little information."

"I can make some discreet enquiries," Ji said. "Perhaps someone else sensed a negative wave being generated during the ceremony. That would help us."

"Very well," said Vo. "In the meantime, we shall begin the Beyonders' matter-forming training. It may help Kasstovaal if he has something to occupy his mind."

"They will need amplifiers," said Oa. "It will be as though we were training children."

"Indeed. However, I suspect that they will learn far more quickly than children would. And they have the experience of adults to draw on for patterns. It will be interesting to see what results."

"I look forward to hearing about it," Ji rose to go. "Te, could I speak to you for a moment before I go."

"Of course." Te rose and the two of them went out into the corridor.

When they were alone, Ji said, "You have an affinity with Kasstovaal, do you not?"

"I touched his mind fully, during the Bio-forming process. I do not understand his fears but I can sense them and counter them."

"Very well. Clearly, you are the best qualified among us to keep his fears in check. But beware, Te. I have looked into his mind, also. There is latent power in there. We all felt it when he cried out from the mists. I advise you to tread carefully."

"Thank you, Thought-Healer. I will."

FOUR: CREATION

12.

"So, you're Oa, are you?" Jeryant's face spread into a large, dangerous-looking smile. He let go of Kasstovaal's shoulder and strode, past Te, on into the laboratory, bringing himself to a stop against the workbench where Oa was waiting for them. "Delighted to make your acquaintance, dear lady. I can't tell you how much I have been looking forward to meeting you face-to-face."

Kasstovaal wondered whether he should, or in fact could, intervene on this first encounter and stop it from going the way he could see it going. For Jeryant to, automatically, turn on the charm and start chatting up any creature possessing curves in the right places, as Oa did, was no more than normal for him, regardless of how well defined those curves might be. But Kasstovaal's ears detected the unmistakable rumblings of an imminent explosion in Jeryant's tone and manner. At best, something seriously undiplomatic was about to happen and it was about to happen to Oa.

"I am gratified," Oa said. "I, too, have been anticipating this meeting with some eagerness. I gather that you are a healer of your species, which explains why your first Bio-form was so much more complex than your friend's. You were able to give the machine very precise data to build with. It has given me great insight into the physiology of your species. We shall have much to discuss."

"Oh, indeed we shall," said Jeryant, the menace starting to rise into his voice. "Why don't we begin by discussing these new bodies you given us. There are a few vital components missing, suddenly. Components I, definitely, remember having about me when I woke up the first time."

"Indeed?" Oa showed genuine concern. "I thought I had left in all the essential components. But, then, I only had inference to guide me. It is true that I did remove a few items but only ones which appeared to serve no useful purpose."

Oh Gods, thought Kasstovaal, everybody stand back.

"No useful purpose!" Jeryant suddenly thundered. "The bits I'm thinking about have a very definite purpose. More than one, in some cases. I'm talking about my genitals, Gods dammit. The reproductive organs. The old on-board entertainment system." He pointed at his significantly unoccupied crotch.

"Oh, those," said Oa, surprised. "Yes, I removed those. When I scanned them, they read as completely inert masses."

Jeryant made a small, strangled noise in his throat.

"Er...Jery!" Kasstovaal came up beside his friend. "Perhaps this isn't...."

"Madam!" growled Jeryant, through gritted, black teeth, "I'll have you know that those organs are vital to the continuation of my species, not to mention my personal reputation. And what about my arse?" He twisted and pointed downwards. "That's the terminal point of the whole digestive system, that is; a poetry of chemical interplay it has taken millions of years to perfect. There's meant to be a hole down there."

"Very well," said Oa, calmly. She reached down to the bench and picked up a thick tool with a large blade on the end of it. "Bend over and I'll make one for you."

Jeryant's mouth dropped open. The onrushing tirade gargled in his throat and the words died unspoken. Kasstovaal clapped a hand to his mouth and nose but failed to fully stifle the laughter that spluttered out of him. Oa just stood there in puzzled innocence, still holding the cutting tool ready.

After a long moment, Jeryant turned slowly to towards Kasstovaal, a stunned expression on his face. "I think I'm in love," he whispered, hoarsely.

"Idiot!"

A doorway appeared in the opposite wall and Vo walked in carrying a metal tray. "Is all well?" he asked, taking in the frozen tableau before him and not understanding any of it.

Jeryant snapped out of whatever trance he had slipped into. "Er... fine. Thank you. Oa and I were just discussing some of the finer points of human anatomy. It can wait for another time, I think. If that's all right with you, Oa."

"As you wish." Oa put the cutting tool back down on the bench. Kasstovaal saw Jeryant's eyes follow it all the way down to the bench top and saw him swallow hard when Oa let go of it.

Vo brought the tray across the room and placed it carefully down on the bench. On it were two thick, rectangular strips of a hard, shiny material, like polished black plastic. Set into the centre of each was a green crystal, the size of a large coin.

"You will need these." Vo said.

Jeryant gingerly picked one up and turned it over, carefully, between his fingers. It was heavier than it appeared, feeling more like ceramic than plastic, though it was warm to touch. The blank underside appeared, at first sight, to be smooth and featureless. But as the light caught it at an angle, Jeryant thought he could see a tracery of fine lines and tiny shapes, like circuitry, just below the surface, black on black.

"What are they?" he asked.

"Pattern Amplifiers," said Te. "We give them to our young to help them with their matter-forming until their minds are developed enough to form things without them."

Vo said, "You will also need them, for a time at least. Your own minds are at their full development point now but the amplifiers will help you to focus your minds on the process of forming."

"What do they do?" Kasstovaal asked.

"Their function is twofold. Firstly they help your mind to form a clear picture of the pattern of molecules you wish to form. That is the extent of the task itself; putting together an entire object molecule by molecule. To one who has never formed before, it is a daunting prospect, is it not?"

"I can't see that it's even possible," said Jeryant. "The amount of data needed would be more than one memory could hold, surely."

"But the memory does not have to hold the full pattern of any object," said Vo. "Knowledge of a molecular formula is sufficient. Or, for a pure element, only the structure of a single atom is needed. Since you both have knowledge of the nature of such structures, presumably you must have been shown the structures of some atoms and molecules to demonstrate the theory."

"Sure," said Kasstovaal. "Diagrams for the most part, though. I don't think I've seen that many Nano-scan pictures of real structures."

"Me neither." Jeryant put in.

"No matter," Vo assured them. "Diagrams are sufficient for the purpose and you shall only need knowledge of a few structures to begin with. Enough to practice on. Any others you need, we can teach you from our records."

Jeryant said, "That's all very well for a single molecule. How do you turn that into a full blown object?"

Vo said, "Any object is, after all, just a mass of the same molecules joined together. All you need to have is the beginning of the task, the molecular formula, and the end of the task, the finished object. When you have those, the path between the two becomes a simple logic problem, like putting a puzzle together. It is a task your unconscious intelligence centres are quite capable of working out."

"Unconscious what?" asked Kasstovaal.

"Unconscious intelligence centres."

"We may have a problem, then," said Jeryant. "Human minds don't have those."

"But you are wrong. All intelligent minds have them. Permit me to demonstrate." He searched among the objects littering the workbench and found a small spherical object, which he tossed speculatively in the air. "Now," he said to Jeryant, "catch this."

He tossed the ball across the bench. Jeryant automatically reached out, two-handed, and caught it, neatly.

"Now," said Vo. "Consider what you have just done. You estimated the force with which I threw the ball, you measured the angle of its trajectory, you calculated the point at which the force of mass attraction would begin to take hold of it and bring it down, you adjusted for the effect of air resistance on the surface of the ball and from all this you accurately calculated the point in three-dimensional space where the ball could be most easily intercepted by your hand, taking into account the average response time of your arm and wrist muscles. And you did all that calculation in the split instant just after the ball left my hand. Are you going to tell me that you did all those calculations consciously? I know that you did not."

"Of course not," said Jeryant. "I couldn't begin to work that lot out consciously. With a computer maybe, if I had a few hours to spare."

"And yet all of those calculations were performed. And as a result, the ball was caught. That is your unconscious intelligence at work. It is capable of millions of calculations in that small unit of time. For an intelligence source that can accurately perform calculus of that complexity in so short a time, the construction of a simple molecular matrix is no challenge at all. The difficulty lies in training yourself to use that intelligence source. What the amplifier does, first, is help you establish the link between your memory, where the molecular pattern and the end result are stored, and the unconscious intelligence centre. It sets the task."

"And the unconscious intelligence does all the working out?" Jeryant said.

"Correct. In a matter of a few instants, a complete molecular model of the object in question is available in your mind and can be used in forming it."

"Forming it out of what?" asked Kasstovaal. "Where does the matter come from?"

"It is all around us," said Vo. "Millions upon millions of free-floating particles. Sub-atomic particles, I think you called them. A cloud of them surrounds us, even now. Every cubic unit of free space in this universe is full of them. Too small to be seen, of course, since they are all disconnected from one another. It is only when we start to join them together into atoms and molecules that they become evident.

"For larger or denser structures, the Rock itself can be used as a source of matter. The process, then, involves breaking down the existing molecular bonds, first, so that we are left with a mass of freed particles.

"The amplifier's second task is to help you focus your will to the correct frequency to form atomic and molecular bonds. Once you reach that frequency and start to form the first bonds, all that is then needed is for you to project the complete molecular pattern at that mental frequency. The object exists, for a brief instant, as nothing more than a mass of mentally generated energy bonds. The bonds seize the appropriate particles from the air they come into contact with. More are drawn in from the surrounding air until all the bonds have been occupied. The result is the desired object."

"And it's that simple?" asked Kasstovaal.

"Oh yes," said Vo. "Eventually you won't even need the amplifier to help you. You mind will become used to forming and won't need any assistance."

"What happens when we stop projecting the pattern?" asked Jeryant. "Don't the bonds just fade out and let the object fall to pieces again?"

"No. Consider that any object you create in this way is held together by the power of thought. In a sense it is made of thought. That makes any object just a little bit intelligent. Not much. Just enough for it to know that it exists, nothing more. The capacity for that one thought is just enough to generate the mental energy needed to keep the pattern in place."

Kasstovaal said, "I'm not sure I like the idea of my bed thinking to itself while I'm lying on it. There's no telling what it might decide to do while I'm asleep."

"There is no danger," said Vo, "the objects we create are not sentient in any way. The intelligence level is far too low for that. To all intents and purposes, they are inanimate and should be regarded as such."

Oa took the amplifier Jeryant was still holding in his hand. "We will need to fit these, first," she said. "Then you can begin to practice forming."

"Where do they go?" asked Jeryant.

Oa pointed to her forehead. "Here," she said, "at the optimum point of transmission for the mind."

"Well, we'd best get on with it then," said Jeryant. "Eh, Kass?"

Kasstovaal looked dubiously at the amplifier on the tray. "After you, I think."

"Suit yourself."

Oa said, "If you would lie down on that bench, over there." She pointed towards an area of completely empty floor, which suddenly sprouted a flat, padded couch on a thin, raised pedestal.

Jeryant felt compelled to test it with his hand. It didn't look substantial enough to take his weight, quite apart from the fact that it hadn't even existed a second ago. Did these things need time to set properly? But the couch felt quite stable and appeared to be still fixed to the floor. Or still part of it. He lay back and sank into the padding. The couch didn't even wobble.

Oa carried the amplifier over to him, holding it carefully by the edges. "Do not worry," she said. "This will not give you pain."

"I'm a medic too, don't forget," said Jeryant. "That line doesn't fool me. I've used it too often myself."

Oa held the amplifier over Jeryant's head and delicately laid it on the skin at the exact centre of the broad forehead. For a second or two nothing happened. Then, to Kasstovaal's eyes, it appeared that the black strip began to melt. First the edges then in towards the central crystal, all became a thick black liquid which showed no inclination to run away down Jeryant's nose but maintained the original rectangular shape. Then, one or two bubbles appeared on the surface and the liquid began to sink down into the skin, drawing the crystal down in with it. In a moment, all the liquid had disappeared, leaving only dry skin. The crystal still protruded, sinking a little way further into his forehead before coming to a stop.

Jeryant went a little cross-eyed for a second before blinking and then sitting up. "Is that it?" he asked.

"Yes," said Oa. "All done."

"Didn't feel a thing." Jeryant pushed himself off the couch, "All yours, sunshine," he said to Kasstovaal.

Kasstovaal hesitated and then walked over and lay down before he could change his mind. He saw the amplifier pass briefly in front of his eyes as Oa brought it into position and then felt the hardness of it touch his skin at the centre of his forehead. He winced involuntarily. After a few seconds he felt the strip begin to liquefy and half-wished he hadn't seen it happen the first time. It felt like a small slimy creature had attached itself to his forehead. Then there was a small, sharp pressure, right at the centre of the wetness as though someone were resting the point of a knife against his skin, pressing in just a little as if to draw a dot of blood. Then the pressure stopped, the wetness faded. And, suddenly, all of Kasstovaal's perceptions seemed to leap several feet, straight upwards. For a spilt second, he seemed to be looking down at the room from ceiling level, looking down at himself, lying flat and staring upwards. Then everything snapped back and all he could see was the blank ceiling above him. He blinked, trying to reassemble his thoughts and then sat up.

"I thought you said you didn't feel a thing," he said.

"I've felt a lot worse than that in my time," said Jeryant. "Don't be a baby."

They regarded one another, examining the green crystal that poked out of the other's forehead.

"I wonder how many channels you can pick up on that," Jeryant commented.

Oa picked up another tool from the bench, a flat clear sheet with a handle on it, and held it up to each man's crystal in turn. Small red symbols passed across the transparency as she scanned them both. "Good," she said, "the amplifiers have activated. We can begin the lesson, now."

"Come this way, Beyonders," said Vo, and led them towards the wall where the door he had entered through had been. It had sealed itself up invisibly behind him.

"This will be you first test," he said. "Beyond this wall is the training room we shall be using. You must first learn how to create a doorway into it."

He stared at the wall and a perfect, rectangular doorway appeared in front of him, "Like so." The doorway faded back into a plain wall.

"You make it look easy," said Jeryant.

"It is easy," said Vo. "Virtually no pattern calculation is required in this. All I am doing is willing a section of the Rock out of existence. I am breaking down the bonds that hold that piece of wall together so that the particles are liberated and can be walked through. Putting the wall back is just as simple. I do not need to create a new molecular pattern. I merely have to continue the pattern that already exists in the surrounding rock. Come, both of you. Stand to either side of me."

They obeyed, taking small careful steps to keep from losing their balance unsupported, and stood facing the wall with him. "Now," said Vo, "concentrate on the piece of wall immediately in front of you. Know in your minds that, solid though it is, it is only collection of particles bound together. Push your thoughts forward out of your bodies. Connect with the bonds binding the wall and instruct them to let go. Order it and they will obey."

Kasstovaal stared in front of him at the blank wall, listening to Vo's words. How the hell did you push your thoughts forward? What did that mean? He furrowed his brow and formed the command in his mind. Let go, he thought. Let go. Nothing seemed to be happening. He gritted his teeth and built the words up in his mind, making them louder and louder until his brain seemed to be shouting. Let go, I say, let go.

The wall in front of him faded uncertainly, hovering on a point between being there and not being there. Kasstovaal summoned up one big, final push, almost howling the words out loud in his concentration. The wall faded away and he could see into the room beyond.

"A good effort," said Vo, "for a first try, certainly."

Kasstovaal took a step backwards to get a look at his handiwork. The hole in the wall was about five feet high and just as wide in a couple of places. Its general shape was circular but it was the irregular sort of circular hole he would have got if he'd tackled the problem with explosives. You could use it as a doorway if you bent down and didn't mind that the doorway didn't reach all the way to floor level.

He could see that Jeryant, further along the wall, had done no better. Between the two ragged holes, Vo had opened another perfect rectangle and the comparison was rather deflating.

"Now," said Vo. "We need to seal up these holes. The Rock must be put back as it was. Come. Concentrate with me. This is the easier task."

They took their places again. "This time, reach into the Rock around the holes. Feel the pattern of the molecules, the shape of the atoms.

Picture the wall growing, healing itself. Concentrate on repeating the pattern until all the empty space is filled."

Kasstovaal concentrated. He focused his eyes on a section of the rough doorframe, staring hard as if to memorise every contour and jagged edge. Was it really possible for him to sense the pattern of the molecules, he wondered? Did his mind already contain the pattern? He had seen microscope images of molecules before and, now he came to think of it, one of those had been a sample of a rock formation; granite or something like it. Perhaps this rock formation was similar to that.

An instant after the thought crossed his mind the wall suddenly filled itself in, neatly and completely. Kasstovaal blinked at it. "Did I do that?"

"Yes, you did," said Vo. "Well done."

Jeryant's hole was still in the wall. He was frowning furiously at it. "Damn!" he said, "I can't get it to happen."

"You haven't locked onto the pattern," said Vo. "Here, let me help you see it." He moved and stood behind Jeryant, looking over his shoulder at the wall.

After a few seconds, Jeryant said "Oh, that's it!" and the hole closed up in front of him.

"Good" said Vo. "Now let us try the same thing again. This time you will find it easier."

This time, Kasstovaal gathered his effort into one single burst of power, now that he had an idea of how much force was needed. The wall vanished in front of him. A clean transition between being and not being this time, no hesitation. But it was still as ragged as the first one had been. Jeryant managed a little better, achieving a hole that didn't splay outwards in all directions, but began to approach a rectangular shape.

Filling the holes in hardly took any effort at all. Their minds seemed only to suggest it and the walls obediently sealed up.

"Again," said Vo. "This time, try to focus the energy into a shape. Look at the wall and imagine the shape you want to create. Draw an imaginary rectangle on it. Now, keep that outline fixed in you mind and then push to open the door."

Kasstovaal concentrated, trying to hold the mental stencil still in his mind. Hold it there, don't let go of it while I...push. He sent the command, funnelling it through that shape. The doorway that faded out before him was a rectangle. The edges were a little rough to the touch, compared with the absolute smoothness Vo created in his doorways, but he was nearly there. He felt oddly proud of himself.

They both tried it a few more times, both eventually achieving doorways as near to Vo's in shape and neatness as made no difference.

Jeryant filled in his latest effort, looked speculatively at the wall for a few seconds and then stared at it again. The doorway that appeared this time was rounded and bulbous and had a small extra protrusion cut out at the top. It took a few seconds for Kasstovaal to recognise it as the cut out shape of an apple.

"Good, eh!" said Jeryant, beaming.

"Very...decorative." said Vo, "I think you have both mastered that exercise quite well. As with all things, the more you practice the simpler it will become."

"At least we can get around on our own, now," said Jeryant.

"Quite so," said Vo. "And now," he stepped through the apple-shaped doorway, "we shall proceed to more complex exercises."

The others followed him through into the room beyond. It was larger than the one they had just left, high-ceilinged and wide-floored with a lot of empty space to it. There were two small tables, each with two stools beside them, in one corner but that appeared to be the entire contents. Vo made his way to the tables and motioned for the two humans to sit, one at each. Oa and Te took the other two places; Oa opposite Jeryant, Te opposite Kasstovaal.

"Now" said Vo, "I want you both to form a sphere made out of plain stone. Like this." He held up a hand and a small, grey sphere appeared in his palm. "Oa and Te will help you."

Kasstovaal furrowed his brow. "Where do I get the molecular structure for this from?" he asked.

"Your memory will have it stored," said Te. "It is the same pattern as for the wall. You managed that alright."

"Yes, but I'm not sure exactly how I managed it. As far as I can tell, I just told the wall to copy itself, over and over again. I didn't make any effort to memorise the pattern."

"Nevertheless, your memory will still have retained the pattern. The memory retains every piece of data and every experience you are exposed to during the course of your life."

"That can't be true. There are thousands of things I can think of which I can't recall in any detail."

"That must be very inconvenient," said Te, sympathetically. "But the data will still be there. Even if your conscious mind is unable to access it, your unconscious intelligence will know where to find it. Try."

Kasstovaal concentrated.

"Remember" said Te, "this time you are trying to create a three-dimensional object. Instead of focusing on a flat surface, you need to focus on a three-dimensional area of space. Pick a point just above the tabletop and visualise the sphere in that spot."

Kasstovaal selected a spot just in front of him on the table and brought into his mind a picture, a three dimensional image of the sphere Vo was holding.

"Want it to be there," said Te, encouragingly. "Want it as hard as you can."

I have the picture of it in my head, Kasstovaal thought to himself. All I have to do is take it out of my head and put it there. On the table, in front of me. Move it from my mind and out into reality. Make it real.

A piece of empty air just above the tabletop shimmered with the motion of millions of microscopic particles converging on that one spot. Then a small stone sphere faded into existence and lay there, as solid as the table itself.

"Well done," said Te, "you see how simple it is."

Jeryant was finding it less easy. "Focus," Oa was saying to him. "Do not lose the shape in your mind."

Jeryant blinked. The mass of matter that splatted suddenly onto the table was dark brown, wet and organic-looking.

"Oops," said Jeryant. "Sorry. Lost concentration there for a moment."

"Nice one, Jery," said Kasstovaal. "I've often thought that was what your mind was full of. Now I've got proof positive."

"Never mind," said Oa, vanishing the mass with a thought and leaving the table completely clean again. "Try again."

On the second attempt, Jeryant managed to bring forth a sphere, identical to the other two. He picked it up and tossed it in the air. "Success!" he said, triumphantly.

"Good," said Vo. "For the next phase, I want you to alter the structure of that sphere and turn it into a metal."

"Which metal?" asked Kasstovaal.

"Any one you wish. You have many metals in use in your universe?"

"Yes. Hundreds."

"Very well then. Select one and then turn the sphere into that metal."

Right, thought Kasstovaal. Basic chemistry lessons, the sought of thing you got taught when you were seven years old. Somewhere in the hidden recesses of his memory there must be a copy of the Periodic Table. He could remember what it looked like but couldn't remember all the details. Never mind, though. According to Te, it's all in there. Pick a simple one. Iron will do.

He focused that thought on the sphere. This time, he could almost feel parts of his mind linking together, passing data back and forth, calculating and transmitting the result towards the sphere.

The sphere changed colour, sinking to a darker grey, becoming a ball of iron as he had willed it to be.

"'Ere! Mine's shrunk." Jeryant was holding up his own sphere, now pure gold but considerably smaller than before. He could hold it up between his fingers.

"Of course it has," Kasstovaal said. "Gold is a lot denser than stone. You can bet that it weighs exactly the same as the original sphere. But the particles are more tightly packed so it's bound to take up less space."

"I do not think we have encountered this metal before," said Vo. He took the small gold sphere from Jeryant's hand and examined it closely, rolling it between his fingers as if to feel the quality of it. "Interesting," he said, at length. "A very soft metal, for all its density. Very little durability. I cannot see it having any practical use in construction. What do you use it for?"

"Ornamentation, mainly," said Jeryant. "It's nice to look but that's about all it's good for."

"It's a very efficient energy conductor," Kasstovaal put in, "but it's very rare and there are better materials, which are easier to come by."

"Indeed," Vo said. "We, of course, can form as much of it as is required. Perhaps we should show this metal to Tinu. He is looking for an efficient conductive metal for his experiments. Perhaps this will serve."

He held the gold sphere in one hand and formed an exact replica of it in the other hand. He gave the original back to Jeryant. "Now" he said, "let us continue."

And so the lesson went on, hour after hour. It was hard to tell exactly how long; the Dwellers didn't appear to use chronometers or anything to mark the passage of time. Since they didn't need to regulate their time with eating or sleeping, Kasstovaal reflected, they probably didn't need to mark time, except in measuring an experiment, perhaps. In truth it didn't really matter to Jeryant and himself, either. They still felt no signs of tiring, even with all the mental effort they were putting in. So they kept at it and each new exercise increased the feeling of power that had sprouted inside both of them, that strange and wonderful realisation that they were doing magic, real magic, and could keep it up forever.

They continued with metals, as many as they could think of. First spheres then cubes and pyramids, prisms of all shapes and sizes. Then plates, pipes, any and every formation of metal they could imagine.

Then they moved on to other materials. Crystals, glass, plastics. One by one they ran through every substance they could remember from their early schooling. Then they began to combine them together, creating increasingly intricate structures as control became easier.

Kasstovaal created a perfect replica of the religious statuette he had been given. He showed it to Te.

"What is it for?" she asked.

Kasstovaal didn't fancy his chances at explaining religion to Te. "It's a piece of artwork," he said. "A friend gave it to me. The original, that is. It meant a great deal to me."

"It helps you to remember your friend?"

"Yes, it does. We parted ways a long time ago. I like to remember the time we spent together."

As for the objects Jeryant created, Kasstovaal hoped nobody would ask him to explain what they were, though it would be fascinating to hear what explanation Jeryant would offer.

They moved onto more everyday items. Tools, knives, forks, dinner plates, coffee cups. Jeryant tried his hand with nylon and succeeded in producing a large white handkerchief, which he blew his nose on theatrically.

Then came the question of organic molecules.

"Organic structures are no different to any other," said Vo. "More complex, perhaps, but the basic forming principal is no different."

"I know some organic structures," said Jeryant. "But they're mostly of human body parts. I don't think I want to start producing those. Could be very nasty."

"I don't think I've ever seen any," said Kasstovaal. "There isn't much call for those in my line of work."

"The only way to produce true organic structures is to learn their patterns," said Oa. "We have many on record, those that have been discovered during scientific research. Though, outside the laboratory, we have little use for them. Organic substances do not play much of a part in our existence."

"We, on the other hand, use them all the time," said Jeryant. "That could be tricky. I can't see us getting hold of any samples, any time soon."

"We have found" said Vo "that where it is not necessary to have the genuine article, chemically speaking, a simulation of the substance will suffice."

"How do you mean, simulation?"

"You know what the basic elements are, I presume"

"Well, most of them are carbon and water. So I understand."

"That is enough," said Vo. "If you feed that information to your unconscious intelligence it will be able to calculate a pattern based on that and the end product you want. It will know, from your memory, exactly how you expect the object to appear and feel and how it stimulates your other senses. The pattern that it calculates will be for an object that stimulates your senses in exactly the same way as the original would. The only difference would be that, if you subjected the object to analysis, it would probably not be the true organic structure of the original."

"I think I get you," Jeryant said. "Let me try it." He stared at the tabletop again. After a few seconds, a big red apple appeared in front of him.

"What is this?" Oa asked.

"It's a fruit. It's one of the things we eat for fuel."

"It will not be any use to you now," said Oa. "Even if you needed fuel, which you don't, it is only a simulation. It will not contain the fuel elements present in a real one."

"You're wrong there." said Jeryant "Some of us find eating a great pleasure." He picked up the apple and sniffed at it. "Smells like an apple to me." Then he took a big bite. Underneath the shiny, red skin, soft white flesh dripped with juice.

An expression of bliss came over Jeryant's face as he chewed. "Gorgeous. Just like the ones I used to pinch out of the trees, back home." He tossed it to Kasstovaal. "You try a bit."

Kasstovaal turned it over and took a small bite from the uneaten side. It was good.

"And this is how you take on fuel?" asked Oa.

"That's right," said Jeryant. He swallowed. "I would recommend you try it. Only I don't think you would be able to."

"Interesting," said Oa. "At some time, you must explain to me how you extract the fuel elements?"

Kasstovaal had a try at forming, searching his memory for a picture combined with a smell and a taste. Suddenly the room was filled with the aroma of freshly baked bread. The golden brown loaf was still warm as Kasstovaal took it in his hands and tore a piece off of it. It was soft and moist and tasted exactly as he remembered. In fact, it matched the memory he had used precisely, in every detail.

After that, they took it in turns, trying to outdo each other with their culinary recreations and the training room rapidly began to smell like the kitchen of a very busy restaurant.

Eventually Vo said, "Enough, now, I think. You both have a good grasp of the techniques. All that remains now is that you should practice. Do so in the privacy of your own rooms. Create anything you wish for yourselves. For now, I think we have all worked enough."

"I thought you didn't rest," said Jeryant.

"We do not sleep," Vo corrected. "But we do take time away from out labours. For private thought or recreation. It improves the efficiency of our minds for when we turn back to our labours. For myself, I feel the need to contemplate on some of the things I have encountered during our time together."

"Suits me," said Jeryant. He looked at the walls, one at a time. "This is the one into the corridor, isn't it?"

"That's right."

"How did you know that, Jery?" Kasstovaal asked.

"I don't know. I just looked at each wall in turn and I knew what was behind each one of them. The information just appeared in my mind. Behind that one is a corridor."

"The Rock remembers," said Vo.

"What was that?"

"The use that a room is put to" said Vo, "leaves an imprint in the walls, a mental echo of what has taken place there. If a room is normally used by one Dweller then the room will reflect the mind of that Dweller. A corridor, of course, holds the residue of many people passing by. It is enough to distinguish one from another."

"Well then, Kass!" said Jeryant, opening an arched doorway into the corridor, "Let's see if we can't find our own way back to our quarters. I feel the urge for some redecoration coming on."

13.

By Kasstovaal's reckoning, at least three days had passed since he and Jeryant had woken up in their revised bodies. It must be at least three by now. He had lost track, one way and another. His body was giving him no clues, operating as it was on a constant medium turnover, midway between restlessness and fatigue. All he had to go on was the accumulation of events that had taken place since that time, but he couldn't be sure how long each had taken.

Putting together a simple electronic chronometer had been no challenge for him, once he'd focused his matter-forming skills finely enough to produce micro-circuitry. For a man trained to know every last component of a spaceship, nose-to-tail, it was preschool stuff even down to the chemicals needed for the power battery. Now that the light-emitting diodes were alive on its face, he had been debating what time he should set it to. Hells! For all the difference it made he might as well set it to noon and have done with it.

He flopped down onto the bed and stared at it for several minutes, watching the numerals change. Bloody pointless exercise, he thought. After all, he didn't have anything accurate to calibrate it against, only his own mental time-keeping, so it would only be as good at keeping time as he was.

But it was little projects like this that were keeping his mind occupied. He found that, when he had nothing particular to do, he started to brood about his predicament.

The showers he was quite proud of. Not nearly as complicated as the clock but plumbing wasn't really his field and he'd had certain local problems to overcome, which had called for a certain amount of ingenuity. The simple answer had been to create two closed water-tanks, one mounted on the wall about eight feet off the ground and another on the floor immediately beneath it. Those had been simple enough to create. They had just expanded the pattern of the wall and the floor and the two stone tanks had just grown where they were wanted, immovably fixed in position and, having no joins, perfectly watertight. All that was needed then was a pipe, leading from the base of the upper tank to a shower head, passing through a tap on the way. They indented the top of the lower tank, sloping all the sides inwards and downwards to a hole in the centre where the water would drain into the tank.

All they had to do if they wanted a shower was to stand on top of the lower tank and matter-form a quantity of water in the upper tank, the simplest molecule of the lot. They learned from Vo how to excite the molecules to make the water hot and then they just opened the tap. Jeryant had even cooked up a species of soap from one of his chemistry lessons. Once they had finished, they had to un-form the water again, where it had collected in the lower tank.

That was another taste of home. It refreshed his body, somewhat, but not for very long. It was just one of the small niggling ways in which his body failed to react in the way he expected it to.

It didn't sweat, for one thing. Kasstovaal had put himself through dozens of combat-level training circuits around the room, just to see if he could tire himself out. He hadn't been able to do that, but the activity had increased his body heat and it took him ages to cool down afterwards because the pores of his skin remained resolutely dry.

The two of them had also discovered that being able to simulate food was not the blessing it had first appeared to be. Jeryant had produced a couple of huge, juicy steaks with potatoes for them to celebrate their handiwork. The experience of eating had been as pleasurable as they could have hoped for. The after-effects were not so; their stomachs were still intact but their digestive systems had not fully re-formed and so Oa had shut them down. In consequence, the food just sat as a dead weight in their stomachs, not going anywhere. This might not have been so bad had not the false molecules in the food started to degrade and react with each other, producing some very strange and unpleasant gases. In the end they had sought guidance from Oa about how to un-form the food in their stomachs without un-forming parts of their own innards in the process.

At least the Dwellers had found the answer to the problem of walking. The problem, Oa had said, was that they were too used to giving commands to their legs using their nervous systems. She and Jeryant had begun spending time together, comparing notes on human anatomy, at least as far as it applied to their Bio-forms. When he had confirmed the purpose of the fibrous network that stretched throughout their bodies, the answer had become obvious.

"It is not the most efficient of control systems," she had said. "Inevitably, there is a slight delay between the time at which you decide to begin walking and the time your limbs receive the command to move. It is not a long delay but it is significant. Presumably, you have become used to using that delay as the time you need to adjust your balance and orientation to compensate for the inertial force of the movement. In your new bodies, however, your limbs are receiving commands directly from your mind, by mental impulse transmission. The signals are reaching your muscles much faster than your...nerves could have carried them. That means that you no longer have that delay in which you can adjust your posture. Your legs are moving away before you are ready."

They had referred the problem to Ji who, with the agreement of both humans, had touched their minds long enough to install a slight delay in some of their response times. The result was most satisfying.

But even with that problem out of the way, his body still bothered him. It didn't feel right. The skin still felt tight and constricting and seemed to lack the elasticity of real skin. If he pinched it, the peak of gathered skin between his fingers would stay in that shape for fully three seconds after he let it go and would, then, sink very slowly back down flat.

Lying there now, he raised his left arm up to eye level and stared speculatively at the smooth surface. Then, on an impulse, his lifted his right hand and called up a pattern in his mind. A steel scalpel appeared in the palm and he closed his fingers around it.

Carefully, he positioned the blade against the skin of his left forearm and made a thin, shallow cut down towards the wrist for about two inches. The skin split apart, the tension pulling at the lips of the wound and he felt, keenly enough, the sting of pain as his nerves protested. But no blood came forth, nor anything that might have taken its place. The wound stayed dry. He brought the arm nearer to his eyes and looked more closely. Beneath the surface of the skin, the flesh was revealed as a honeycomb of tiny air pockets, like a fine sponge, formed out of the same black material as the skin.

As he stared at it, the wound began to close up. The lips pulled themselves together and split skin sealed itself invisibly. Within a few seconds, it was as though the cut had never been made.

Damn. Even that simple control over his body and his life had been taken away from him. He felt robbed. This wasn't his body. This wasn't him. The Dwellers could adjust it and fiddle with it and poke around in his mind all they liked, it wouldn't make any difference. His body was gone, lost, taking with it everything that had distinguished him among his people, everything that he could recognise as Malkan Kasstovaal. The face that had stared back from the mirror, the limbs that had carried him through his life and his work. The fundamental realities that defined what he was. All gone, atomised. And now? Hells, could he even be called human anymore. The accident, or whatever it had been, had taken his life away from him, his existence. This...thing the Dwellers had dumped him in wouldn't give that back. Some second chance.

On entering this universe he had ceased to exist, literally. And I still don't, he thought. Malkan Kasstovaal died in that accident. For good.

Just then, a doorway began to appear in the wall from the corridor and Kasstovaal instantly knew that it would be Jeryant coming in. That was something you could always say about Jeryant. Wherever he was, you could always detect him coming a long time before you actually saw him. He always seemed to generate a field of charisma like a wide bubble all around him, a mobile atmosphere of expansive noise, rude jokes and suggestive remarks. You could usually detect the wave front of it by the ripple of incredulous, and slightly embarrassed, laughter that used to precede him into crowded rooms. At other times you could just feel it in the air.

This trait appeared to hold true even in this universe. Here, it manifested itself in the doorways he created for himself, which were never simple rectangles. Not having Kasstovaal's technical abilities, he had practised with his door forming and had got it to a point where he could form any shape he liked with a clarity and definition that Kasstovaal would not have thought possible in a simple outline. But you were never in any doubt about what shape he was trying to create, more was the pity. His natural infantilism had found an outlet in this skill and the shapes he was creating were, at best, comic, at worst, downright lewd. It was, perhaps, fortunate that the Dwellers did not know what any of them were.

As such, this particular doorway was the unmistakable shape of a pair of boobs, pointing upwards. Jeryant had to duck slightly to make his way in through the left breast.

"Top of the morning," he said, heartily.

"How would you know? There aren't any mornings here."

"It just feels like it." Jeryant gave the left nipple of his creation an affectionate pat before vanishing it away. As he turned back, he caught sight of the scalpel in Kasstovaal's hand and could see from the way he held it what it was he had been doing. The smile dropped off his lips and his face hardened. He marched across the room and snatched the blade from Kasstovaal's hand.

"That's a dangerous road to go down, Kass," he said sternly. "It only leads to one place. That one place I told you I wouldn't let you go, like it or not."

"Stop worrying," said Kasstovaal, "I don't think I could end my life here if I wanted to. Certainly, not that way, it seems. We don't bleed."

"That's not the point," said Jeryant, waving the blade in Kasstovaal's face. "The last thing you want to be doing is contemplating ways to die, Kass. Not even in the cause of scientific enquiry, so don't try using that as an excuse. There are other ways of finding those things out."

"All right! All right!" said Kasstovaal "I'm sorry. It's this body. Sometimes it just seems like one big irritation. It's like having an all-over itch I can't scratch."

"You've put up with worse," said Jeryant, dissolving the scalpel into nothing. "And I dare say there'll be more to put up with before we finally get out of here. Don't start slipping away from me now, Kass. I need you. You're the technical brains of this outfit. If we do work out a way of getting home, it's you who's going to have to make it happen. I can't do it, I'm only a Medic. I'm relying on you. Remember that."

"I hear you, Mr Medic." Kasstovaal put up a smile. "You haven't lost me yet. I'm not going to cut my throat before I've found a way out of here."

"What about afterwards?"

"I suppose you'll have to hurry up and find that cure, won't you. I know what you're thinking. You're thinking the De-phase syndrome is pressing my buttons, aren't you."

"It's certainly getting more pronounced. It may just be that the experience of...."

"Almost dying?" Kasstovaal suggested.

"If you must put it like that. The trauma of that experience may still be draining your mental faculties. That leaves you fewer resources to fight off the De-phase symptoms. Hopefully, as time goes on, that trauma will decrease."

"The Dwellers seem to know a lot about how minds work," said Kasstovaal. "Perhaps they can help you find the answer."

"That's what I'm hoping," said Jeryant, "I've been bombarding Oa with every piece of human anatomy I can think of. And there's a fair bit of that, I can tell you. She's soaking it up like a sponge."

"Not your usual chat-up strategy, surely," said Kasstovaal, slyly.

"Don't you believe it, pal. Many a young female medical student has succumbed to my extra tutorials."

"Dirty old man!"

"Still the champion."

At that moment, a doorway opened in the wall. Te stood in the corridor. "May I enter?" she asked, tentatively.

"Of course, my dear, of course," said Jeryant, heartily. "I was just leaving, anyway. The fair Oa awaits her next lesson in the attributes of the human body. I have made it my mission to acquaint her with all of them." He overlaid a doorway of his own, on top of Te's. It was heart shaped. "I shall leave you two kids to get to know each other better. Try not to do anything I would do in your place. And if you can think of anything I wouldn't do, definitely don't do that. Ta Ta!" The doorway sealed up behind him.

"What was he talking about?" Te asked.

"Ignore him, said Kasstovaal. "He's being facetious."

"Ah! I have noticed this about Jeryant. His mind seems preoccupied with non-essentials."

"I think he just has a different set of priorities to everybody else. That was true of him even in our universe." He motioned Te towards the armchair and sat himself up on the bed. "And what can I do for you, Te?"

"I should like to talk with you, if I may," Te said, sitting down "Vo is engaged with his work and has no need of me, at this time. I have time to pursue my own curiosity. I'm curious about you. You are like nothing any

Dweller has ever encountered. There are so many things we must know, it is hard to know where to begin. Nobody has been given the purpose of learning about you. Not yet. So the task falls to anyone who has time to spare and is interested to learn. I am interested."

"I'm happy to answer if I can." said Kasstovaal "And we want to learn more about your people, as well. The problem, I think, is going to be finding common reference points. From what I've seen of your reality so far, I can think of hundreds of things I could try and tell you about that you wouldn't understand, simply because there's no equivalent here. Or anything approaching an equivalent."

"And yet we must try," said Te. "Perhaps if we break everything down to base principles we may make some progress."

"Perhaps. But, then, we're back to the question of where to start."

"We could start anywhere. Your names, for example. The very basis of your individual identity. They are strange to us, in their construction. They are so long."

"That's a well accepted phenomenon in comparative sociology," said Kasstovaal. "It's all to do with the total size of the population. I come from a society that spans thousands of planets and has a population that goes into quintillions. In order for all of us to be sufficiently identifiable from each other we need to have a very large number of name combinations. And the best way to maximise those is to have long names with lots of interchangeable syllables in them. My name is quite short, by comparison with most people I know. Whereas in a small society, like yours, with only thirty or forty thousand people in it at any one time, names of only one or two syllables are quite sufficient to distinguish you all. It's been encountered in my universe, a few times, with small isolated societies."

"I see." But Te looked troubled.

"Is there something you didn't understand?"

"Quintillions of people, you say. And thousands of worlds. It is difficult for me to conceive. Is your reality so large?"

"Those are only the inhabited worlds and they only account for one per cent of the planetary bodies explored so far. The outermost limits of our universe have not yet even been charted, let alone explored. And it is expanding all the time. It is doubted that my race shall exist for long enough to ever have explored it all."

"Incredible! What could not exist in a reality that size?"

"How big is your universe? Do you know?"

"Very small, by comparison. A physical form can cross it in only a few cycles. There are two hundred and five worlds, but only thirty-eight have people living on them, including the Rock. Some of those have greater numbers than we have, but not by much."

"Quite a difference, isn't it."

"Quintillions." The word seemed to fascinate Te. And why not, Kasstovaal thought. If she's ever had cause to use the word at all, she could never dream of applying it to a quantity of people.

Te asked, "How do so many people find enough purposes for themselves?"

"Purposes?" Strange way to put it, he thought. "If you mean 'what do we do with our lives', well, most of the time we have to concentrate on obtaining food and keeping a roof over our heads. That's oversimplifying the situation and, admittedly, it's not as hard as it used to be but that's what it boils down to. And it doesn't leave us much time and energy for other things. But we make time to enjoy ourselves and, on several thousand worlds, there's no shortage of ways to do that."

"Is that all?" asked Te. "How do you find time to learn anything?"

"Some people devote their energies to scientific research. The rest of us give them food and quarters in return for their efforts. Again, that's a simplification. What they learn is made available to everybody else. Those that want to know about it or make use of it."

"And the rest? How do they learn?"

"We pass on a basic education to our children. Over and above that, we learn what we need to know to perform our function in life. Nothing more."

"It seems very inefficient/" said Te. "But then, I suppose, it is the best way to compensate for the way your bodies work."

"What we lack in efficiency we can usually make up for in weight of numbers. And what about your people, Te? You seem to set great store by purposes."

"Our purpose is our reason for living. We devote all our thoughts and actions to the completion of that one task."

"Just one task?"

"Yes. Every Dweller has a different task which occupies them life long."

"They must be quite complicated ones if they take a whole working life to complete."

"Some are extremely labour intensive. Others are less so."

"What's yours?"

"I am not mature enough yet to have a purpose," said Te, a little tone of regret edging into her voice. "But soon, though."

"How will you choose one, when the time comes?"

"We do not choose our purpose. It is given to us."

"By whom?"

"I do not know."

"Pardon?"

"I do not know where the purposes come from."

"Sorry," said Kasstovaal, "I don't understand you."

"I will explain. When the time comes, we go to the Chamber of Purpose and wait. After a short time, we receive a purpose."

"How, exactly?"

"I do not know of my own knowledge. We each only enter the chamber once in our lives. I have been told that the purpose just comes into your mind and lodges there. However it is, everyone who leaves the chamber does so knowing, without any doubt, what their purpose is."

"And these tasks just come out of nowhere."

"Yes."

"Hasn't anyone ever asked where these…thoughts might be coming from?"

"I think everybody speculates about where the purposes come from, before they go into the chamber. Afterwards, the purpose itself becomes all important. Of all of us, the Keeper of the Chamber is the only one who may, actually, know. And he will not say."

"What do you think?"

"I have followed the usual paths of speculation. One thought is that the purposes are born out of the mists of space."

"You mean the mists outside the Rock?"

"Yes. Any volume of it contains an amount of thought energy. A small amount. But some think that the whole volume of mist in the entire universe may combine that small amount of energy into coherent thought. The result would be a very large and very complex mind thinking its own thoughts and, perhaps, deciding the tasks which must be undertaken and the things that must be learned. Perhaps it is that which injects the purpose into our minds so that we will carry them out. Another theory is that the purposes are transmitted from the voids."

"The voids? You mean those black spheres out in the mist."

"That's right. They draw in energy constantly. Nobody has yet determined where the energy goes to. Scientifically, at least. Again, Ra might know but he will not say."

"Who is Ra?"

"For now, he is our Voidseer and Keeper of the Chamber of Purpose. He is the only one of us who may send his mind towards the voids and see what lies there."

"Does he tell you anything about what he sees there?"

"Only to tell us if our purpose is completed satisfactorily. When we feel that we have completed our task to the fullest extent possible, we go to him and ask for his confirmation. The voids guide him as to whether to say yes or no."

"Really?"

"So he says," Te said, guardedly. "The truth of it is something we cannot know. It is a question of belief. But none of us can or will make an ending without the word of the Voidseer."

"A belief system," Kasstovaal tried the word. "A religion?"

"Yes. You could call it that."

"Strange. I couldn't quite picture your people having a religious belief. You seem too...I don't know...in control to need one."

"Even for the most logical minds, there are mysteries that cannot be fathomed. Belief suffices to account for the ineffable."

"So the theory is that the voids dictate the purposes in the first place and then confirm whether or not they've been completed properly."

"That's right."

Why not, Kasstovaal thought to himself. Either explanation might be possible in this place. They both seemed feasible, even to him. But, then, it surely couldn't have been beyond the skills of the Dwellers to prove or disprove either one. With their powers and their obvious thirst and drive for knowledge, it should have been a piece of cake. That was what belief and religion could do, he supposed. There were some questions which you just did not ask and that was all there was to it, logical or not.

He asked "Are there any other theories?"

"There is a popular one among the younger of us," said Te. "It is believed that somewhere in the Rock there is a great book, an enormous ledger in which are written all the purposes that must be completed during the lifetime of the universe. At the beginning of the book are the very simple tasks, those that were completed long ago shortly after the Rock came into being. The tasks become more and more complicated as the book progresses until on the last page is found the most difficult and complex of problems which must be solved. It is believed that the Voidseer keeps this book hidden somewhere. And when a Dweller comes to maturity and enters the Chamber he goes to the book and reads the next purpose down, in sequence. Then he projects the purpose into the chamber himself, telepathically, and crosses out that purpose in the book so that it should not be used again."

Kasstovaal chuckled. "Sounds like a few of the stories I was told when I was young," he said.

"It is fanciful," Te agreed. "But, again, it has never been disproved."

"Has anyone ever asked Ra whether or not it is true?"

"Some may have. If so, he has never answered definitely. It is generally difficult to get definite answers from Ra, so few of us try."

"That's about normal for a religious leader, in my experience."

"Your people have religions too, then."

"Thousands," said Kasstovaal, contemplating briefly on the minefield that was the religious landscape of the inhabited worlds. "Thousands of contradictory belief systems, all falling over each other to prove that they're right and everybody else is wrong. Most people let them get on with it and believe, within themselves, whatever gives them comfort."

"They need religion for comfort?" Te asked, puzzled.

"Yes. There is one universal fear we all have which is the source of all the other little fears we keep within ourselves. All of those break down to a basic fear of the unknown and the unknowable. All the questions which have not been answered or cannot be answered. Religion gives us answers to those questions, which we can convince ourselves are the right ones."

Te filed that away in her mind, but decided to say nothing until she had discussed it with Vo. There may be implications.

Kasstovaal asked,. "So, what do you do while you're waiting for a purpose? I presume you get an education of some sort."

"Learning that which all need to know is not a long process for us," Te said. "When mind can touch mind, knowledge can pass between at the speed of a thought and be known forever. A Dweller child is given into the care of their Primary Parent, after birth."

"Primary Parent? How many do you have?"

"Four are needed to create a new life. One out of the four is chosen to be the Primary Parent and take on the responsibility of training and developing the new Dweller's mind and readying them to receive their purpose."

"So, presumably," Kasstovaal said ,"Vo is your Primary Parent." And then, enlightened, he continued, "And that's why you call him 'Prim', isn't it? It's a diminutive of Primary."

"That's right. Vo has taught me many things. More than just the transfer of the knowledge I will need. He has had to guide me in the control of my emotions and waves."

"I remember him saying something about 'waves' and 'wave-sharing'. What does that mean? What are 'waves' exactly?"

"Waves are emotions that are...projected between beings. We are empathic, remember. If we feel a certain emotion within ourselves and we want another to feel it as well we can send it to them. We turn the feeling into a wave and project it towards that person. When the wave touches them, they feel the emotion also. You, yourself, have felt them. During the Welcome ceremony."

"Of course," said Kasstovaal. "I remember how it felt." All too well, he thought, privately.

"For a young Dweller" Te went on, "it is tempting to project almost every emotion you feel and hope to receive back the waves of all the emotions felt around you as a result. Part of the training you receive from your Primary Parent is how to keep your emotions and waves under the control of your reason, rather than allow the opposite to happen. We are taught that emotions are important; they give us the drive we need to take our task forward to completion and they allow us to see possibilities which logical reasoning alone could not show us. We must learn to keep them under control, store them away until we need them and access them when we want them."

"Sounds like a tall order."

"It is by no means an easy task. One way of achieving it is to actually take your mind to pieces and reassemble it in a new order, an order in which your emotions are enclosed by your reason."

"Have you tried it that way?"

"Yes." Te remembered it. And the cry that had made it happen. The cry from this being, sitting in front of her, talking rationally to her. "Not long ago. It was quite a struggle."

"It sounds it. I don't think I'd like to try it."

"There is a skill in it," said Te, pulling herself away from the memory. "Vo taught me how it should be done. But it is something you have to experience to know what it is really like."

"What else has he taught you."

"Discipline, mainly. The regimes by which research can be done most efficiently."

"I think all parents have to teach their children something of the sort. Trouble is, when you're on the receiving end of the lesson, you never appreciate the worth of it until a long time after."

"That's true enough."

At that moment, Kasstovaal realised that that thought was the first one he had devoted to his parents in some months and he instantly felt guilty. Not so much because he hadn't thought of them as that he had chosen that he would not. The goodbyes he had last said to them, he had tried to make the final ones. He should've known that no goodbye can ever be enough. What would they be thinking now that he had disappeared? Did they even know?

"What are you thinking about?" Te interrupted his thoughts.

"Unfinished business," he said. "Nothing I can do anything about now."

"Unless, perhaps, you find a way back to your own universe."

"Yes." Then he looked up at her sharply. "Are you reading my mind?"

"Not at the moment. Merely observing your reactions. And I know that that thought has been foremost in your mind for some time. I have felt it there. You are eager, even desperate, to leave here, are you not. Do you really find us such unpleasant hosts?"

"Well I...." It was embarrassing. All his instincts warned him constantly to be on his guard. But, suddenly confronted, they weren't providing him with any reasons to give. He tried to sound casual, offhand. "Perhaps I don't know you well enough."

"That is simply remedied." Te rose, walked to the wall and formed a door. Then she looked at him and motioned him to follow. "Allow me to introduce you to the Dwellers."

14.

Finding your way around the corridors of the Rock should have been virtually impossible, to Kasstovaal's mind. They all looked much the same, arched and roughly hewn out of the rock, but with floors smoothed down by wear. The only noticeable difference appeared to be that some corridors ran straight and level while others curved and sloped in a seemingly endless spiral.

Always they were lined with rooms, sometimes open to the corridor so that he could see inside as he and Te passed, sometimes closed behind a blank wall, though he could still sense they were there. There were no signs, no markers and no maps to tell him where he was in relation to anywhere else. No visible ones.

And yet he knew. Whenever he glanced into a room or at a wall where one should be he instantly knew what room it was. The knowledge just inserted itself neatly into his mind as though he were recalling it from his own memory.

Glance to the left. That's the laboratory where Rin conducts his experiments. He is in there now, working, though he is hidden behind a wall.

Glance to the right. Through that doorway is Udi's room, where she contemplates her formulae before putting them into practice.

Up ahead, where this corridor ends in a blank wall. That leads to the outside.

Once, he found that they had come to the Gathering Place, not at the floor level but high up onto one of the ledges. For the first time in a long time, Kasstovaal experienced a giddy wave of vertigo as his eyes strayed over the edge and looked down at the arena far below. It came as a surprise to him. Vertigo was something you got out of your system when you started your space training. You could hardly operate in space if you were susceptible to it. He put a hand to the wall and steadied himself.

Te was walking, unconcernedly, along the ledge towards a bridge that stretched across the diameter of the cavern. She looked back at him. "Are you all right?" she asked.

"Er...yes," said Kasstovaal. "The drop caught me by surprise, that's all."

"You need not fear it," Te said. "You cannot fall if you do not wish to. Observe." And, with that, she sidestepped out onto thin air and stood there, watching him calmly. "You see," she said.

I shouldn't be surprised, Kasstovaal thought. Hells, they can do virtually everything else. Defying gravity shouldn't give them much trouble. Out loud, he asked, "How do you do that?"

"It's easy. Come and try it for yourself."

Kasstovaal swallowed away a lump that seemed to have formed in his throat. Pull yourself together, he thought. It's no different than doing an EVA. And how many of those have you done in your life?

He made his way, cautiously, along the ledge, stopping just short of where Te still hung in mid-air. "What do I do?"

"Just tune your mind to the force that pulls you downwards," said Te. "Focus on the floor below us. That is where the force emanates from. All you have to do is shield yourself from it. Push it away so that it cannot touch you."

With an effort of will, Kasstovaal turned his eyes downward and stared fixedly at the smooth floor, waiting for him down there. He tried to shift the focus of his thoughts this way and that, trying to see the floor in all of its aspects, using the amplifier to sense more than his eyes could. Every frequency of light that came off it, the infinitesimal movement of the molecules that formed it and, if he really focused hard and sharp, the small energies that radiated from it. Then, he found what he was looking for. The impression of a powerful sucking energy, drawing at everything it could get a hold on. Once he could see it, it seemed the simplest thing in the world to push it out of his way, force the energy to flow around him and prevent it from taking hold of him.

He sidestepped. It was an odd feeling, bare feet on thin air. But he wasn't falling. He chuckled to himself as he realised what he was doing. He was telling gravity to get lost and it was doing it. He took a couple of steps backwards, placing his feet on a new carpet of air molecules. He stepped towards Te, a full blown laugh making its way to his lips. Then he lost concentration and started to drop.

Te reached out quickly and closed her hands around his wrists. He stopped falling.

"You must be careful not to lose your focus," she said, reproachfully. "Otherwise you will fall."

"Are you holding me up?" gasped Kasstovaal. He had only dropped a few inches but it seemed to have taken all the breath out of him. Assuming that he had any to begin with, of course.

"I am holding back the attractive force for both of us," said Te. She stepped back onto the ledge leading Kasstovaal with her. "It takes some mental effort to do. We find it easier to use the bridges." She turned and led him onto the bridge, walking coolly across, as before. On the other side, she selected an archway and the corridors took over again.

As time went on, the indistinguishable labyrinth started to make sense to Kasstovaal. It appeared that the Gathering Place was at the very centre of the Rock. Between it and the outer surface were three main spiral corridors, equidistant from each other, reaching almost all the way down from the summit to the base and becoming further apart as the circumference increased. These were connected to each other, at intervals, by the straight corridors, which criss-crossed each other in between the spirals. On many levels, these opened out onto the ledges of the Gathering Place, which would then have to be crossed or circumvented, depending on whether or not that particular level had a bridge. Above and below the Gathering Place, the straight corridors continued until they, once more, intersected with the spirals. All very orderly.

"It was not always that way," Te told him. "In the early times, the Dwellers burrowed into the Rock more or less at random, making spaces for themselves to work in and tunnels to join them together. As more and more Dwellers came into being it quickly became clear that the volume of the Rock would have to be used in a much more orderly fashion. Otherwise the available space would soon run out. And, in some places, the structure of the Rock itself would be weakened, due to too much tunnelling. So the old caves were filled in and the present structure was put in their place."

"Is there still enough room for everybody?" Kasstovaal asked.

"Plenty. Our population reached a peak several thousand cycles ago and has not changed significantly since. As it is, there is room for everyone to do their work and have a place to themselves, for privacy. And we still have something of a surfeit, over and above that."

"Do you know what the population is at the moment?"

Te appeared to think about this for a moment, as though she were working it out in her head. "At this moment, thirty-one thousand, nine hundred and seventy-five," she said, finally, "including yourself and Jeryant."

"And that's the exact figure, is it?"

"Oh yes!"

"How did you get that?"

"I just counted them."

Kasstovaal was about to protest at that, but realised it would be futile and closed his mouth. If she said she'd counted them then, somehow or other, she had done. No point in protesting the impossibility of doing a spot count of all the thinking beings on the Rock. They could all touch minds in an instant. So how long could it take to count all the minds touching yours?

He decided to change the subject. "You keep a record of your history, then."

"Most carefully," said Te. "We take great pains to ensure that everything that is learned or experienced by the Dwellers is recorded and preserved for future Dwellers to call on, if they need to. Ever since a suitable recording medium was found, we have been storing all the information we could."

"Where does it all go to?"

"The data is placed in the Chamber of Knowledge."

"Can I see it?"

"That is where we are going now."

They had turned onto one of the spirals and ascended for a short way before taking another straight tunnel. About halfway along this, Te brought them to a stop.

"This is the Chamber," she said, and opened a doorway into it.

The room they entered was large and square and stretched upwards for five or six levels above them and, as Kasstovaal looked over the edge of the wide balcony they were now standing on, another three below them. Like the Gathering Place, each level was defined by a balcony, though these were much, much wider than the narrow ledges he had just encountered. Again, the gap in the centre of the room was crossed with bridges, though here there was one on every level. In the very centre of the room, a vertical tube of some transparent substance ran from the floor of the lowest level up to the ceiling and connected to each bridge on the way up. There were openings at the bridge levels and, as Kasstovaal watched, he saw a Dweller drifting gently down the tube from one of the upper levels, coming to a stop one level below him and stepping out onto the bridge. Some sort of elevator, he thought. Or, perhaps, they just needed the tube itself to move in.

There were many Dwellers in the Chamber, several dozen, moving among the racks set along the walls of each level. It put Kasstovaal in mind of one of those antique multi-storey libraries, with books stacked up to the ceiling and ladders on wheels to reach them with.

But then, of course, this was a library. Not containing books, though. The racks in this library contained gemstones. Thousands of crystals, perhaps millions, in every colour of the spectrum, arranged in reverentially neat rows. As Kasstovaal watched, he saw a Dweller select a crystal and lift it, carefully, to his forehead. The crystal glowed on contact and the Dweller's face took on an expression of deep concentration.

"All the knowledge of the Dwellers is stored here," said Te. "Those crystals contain everything we have learned in the course of our purposes."

"How much does each crystal hold?"

"There is one crystal for every Dweller. It is enough to hold the sum total of all their work."

"In how much detail?"

"In every detail. Every conclusion they reached in their work and all the calculation and experimentation that was done to reach it. Those crystals are memories in solid form."

She led him among the racks, exchanging a few brief greetings with some of the younger Dwellers as they passed by.

"Would you like to try one?" she asked.

"Try one?"

"I mean would you like to interrogate one of them for information?"

"Yes, please. I would." Privately he was thinking, this is exactly what we need. All their discoveries in one place, waiting to be accessed when we need them. Or, possibly, destroyed if we need a bargaining chip.

Te drew him up to a rack. "They are arranged by subject," she said, "and then by age. This section is for those Dwellers given purposes in connection with movement through open space and propulsion. Your own purpose has to do with those fields, does it not?"

"You could say that." said Kasstovaal "Certainly in their practical application, though we have to be well up on the principles and theories."

"These should be of interest to you, then." She took a crystal carefully down from the rack, a deep blue one. "Try this one."

"What do I do with it?"

"Hold it to your forehead and reach your thoughts into it. It will become an extension of your own memory. You will be able to remember anything that the original Dweller could remember about their work when he or she recorded the data. Try it."

Kasstovaal took the crystal, gingerly, from her fingers, afraid that he might drop it. It was quite heavy for its size. How much does a thought weigh here, he thought dryly. It was also slightly warm to the touch. He supposed that somebody had just been using this one, until he remembered that all the Dwellers had cold skin, compared to himself.

Slowly, he lifted the crystal to his forehead and placed it against the skin, just above the amplifier.

Nothing immediately happened. All right, he thought, tell me what you know. And it did.

At the forefront if his mind, he suddenly found a detailed plan of a machine. He wasn't seeing a projection, he realised, not with his eyes. His mind's eye, though, could pick out every detail and he quickly recognised it as a model of an accelerated hydrogen thrust engine, a propulsion method his people had abandoned a couple of millennia ago. It was one of the historical curiosities he had had to learn about, taking its place in the evolution of the space propulsion system which had begun with the crude burning of hydrocarbons and had culminated in the Anti-ion interaction drive that now kept his universe moving.

This model, though, was not the one he remembered learning about. There were differences, quite significant differences. It appeared to be perfectly functional, all of the basic components were present and assembled correctly. But it lacked certain refinements present in the commercial model he'd taken apart, the sort of adjustments that would be needed for faults that only use would reveal. In short, the model now on display in his mind was a laboratory model, the product of pure theory and experimentation without the benefit of any actual field-testing. It would work but it wouldn't work well. Not by a Pilot-Captain's standards.

Even so, he recognised it for what it was; a remarkable example of parallel development. He found himself wondering if the unnamed Dweller had followed the same path of research taken by his human counterpart.

He staggered slightly as a flurry of figures and formulae flashed across his conscious mind. Then pictures, brief snapshots of experiments being set up and conducted, the results meticulously noted and listed for him to read. Whoa, he thought, slow down. The images slowed. He could control it. It was no different to interrogating his own memory for a fact or a picture that he wanted to recall. The difference was his memory didn't give up information this quickly or clearly, if it ever gave it up at all. The only thing that made the experience uncomfortable was the nagging thought that he was remembering things he knew for a fact he had never witnessed. It was a concept his reason was having severe trouble with.

He summoned up the memory of the final experiment. The flickering images vanished to be replaced by a single clear image. He could see the actual engine, exactly the same as the diagram he had seen first, assembled and in operation. It appeared to be fixed down on a stone pillar, presumably in a blast vault of some kind. It seemed to be a single frame picture; there were no signs of movement. But figures started to appear and then patterns, which he assumed must be some form of graph. The figures must be thrust measurements. He couldn't decipher the figures but some quality in the memory he was being given conveyed the impression that it had been a success.

He drew the crystal away from his forehead and reality came back to him. He was still standing facing the rack of crystals and Te was standing beside him, watching him with interest.

"How long have I been standing here?" he asked.

"Very little time," she said. "A few instants only."

"It felt like ages."

"That is quite normal. The crystals feed information at a very fast rate directly into your mind. It can be confusing to your perception of real time to assimilate that much information that quickly."

Kasstovaal examined his own memory. All the pictures and figures, even the diagram, were still all there. "Impressive!" he said.

"Did the subject matter interest you?" Te asked, hopefully.

"In some ways. The method of propulsion that Dweller found was discovered by my people a long time ago. But it was a good demonstration. Who was that Dweller?"

"His name was Li. He, too, completed his purpose long ago. Many thousands of cycles, in fact."

"Really. I wonder which of us came up with it first." That was the burning question, really. Which race was scientifically ahead of the other, and in what fields? Who would learn more from whom?

He asked "What propulsion method are you people using at the moment?"

Te looked puzzled. "Forgive me. I do not understand."

"I mean what kind of engines do your ships use now. You must have moved on from this type by now."

"We have no ships," said Te. "None have ever been built."

"None at all?"

"No. We have never needed any."

Kasstovaal frowned. "Do you mean to say that this Dweller went through all this work to perfect a space engine and then never built any ships with it."

"That's right."

"Did he ever intend to build any?"

"No, I don't think so. There would have been no use for them."

"That's crazy. Why bother developing an engine that you don't need?"

"It was his purpose," said Te, as though that explained everything.

"Sounds like an enormous waste of time and effort to me."

Te shrugged. "We have few unsatisfied needs. It is rare for us to need to apply the results of our purposes for our own use."

"So why do it, then?"

"We have a...craving," said Te. "A craving for new knowledge. It is part of our being. It is a craving we share, it seems, with the force that gives us our purposes."

"Knowledge for its own sake," said Kasstovaal, dubiously.

"It has always been reason enough for us," said Te. "And some purposes are put to use for us. The work of Vo and Oa, for example, will benefit my people immensely."

Kasstovaal cast his eyes around the huge room. "And this is where all that knowledge ends up," he said. "Useless or otherwise."

"Yes."

"So all your history is in this room. How far back does it go?"

"All the way back to the time when the crystals were invented," said Te. "And a little before that, where more primitive records were preserved. It does not go all the way back to our beginnings; we do not know who the first Dwellers were, for example. But the shortfall is small, by comparison."

"What sort of time period does it cover?"

"In all, our history to date stretches across twenty-two thousand, one hundred and eighty-seven cycles."

Not a lot of help, Kasstovaal thought, since he still didn't know how long a cycle was or what the Dwellers measured it by. Still, if he interrogated enough of these crystals he should be able to find a value to compare against. Elapsed time was a vital measurement in many scientific procedures and if the Dwellers' science ran parallel to humans', here and there, he might come across an experiment for which he knew the human time value. The calculation would be child's play after that.

"Would you like to try another one?" Te asked.

"I think," said Kasstovaal, earnestly, "I could spend an eternity in here, just absorbing new data. Much as I'd like to, I'm sure it would be very boring for you. And you were giving me a tour, remember. Where to next?"

"So far, you have only seen the practical side of us," said Te. "Now I shall show you our aesthetic side. You are, perhaps, beginning to think that we do not have such a thing."

"The thought had crossed my mind," admitted Kasstovaal.

"We do take our purposes very seriously. But we, also, know the value of taking time away from them for recreation and thought. Stimulating the creative centres of our minds helps us to view the path of our purpose in different ways and, sometimes, suggests different solutions. Come! I will show you the Gallery."

She led him onto the bridge that served this level and stopped at the entrance to the elevator tube.

"It will be quickest if we rise to the top level here," she said.

Kasstovaal regarded it dubiously. He was coming to know how the Dwellers approached the purely domestic problems of life and, though the tube looked and acted just like an ordinary anti-grav lift, he doubted that this was anything so mechanical. "How does this thing work?" he asked.

"Quite simply," said Te. "The force of downward attraction...."

"We call it gravity," Kasstovaal interrupted.

"Yes, that's it. The force of gravity is repelled by the material the tube is made from. Inside the tube, it has no power to pull you downwards. All you have to do is focus on the exit, above or below you, which you wish to use."

She stepped into the tube and was, again standing on thin air. Then she rose, smoothly and sedately, to the top level and stepped out again. She looked down from the bridge and waved at him to follow her.

His ascent was rather less dignified. At first he couldn't get himself to move at all. And then he took off with a jerk, surging upwards and shooting past the next level before he knew what was happening. He managed to slow himself down but by now his focus on the destination was in pieces. The rest of his ascent was a series of spasmodic surges of upward speed interspersed with brief periods at a snail's pace or a dead stop. He overshot the top level exit at high speed and only avoided banging his head hard against the ceiling by raising his hands above his head to stop himself. He finally managed to drift himself down far enough to step out of the exit to where Te had been watching the performance. She was maintaining a perfectly blank expression but Kasstovaal could feel the amusement radiating off her in waves.

"You haven't quite got the hang of those, have you." she said, with forced mildness.

"Does it really show?"

She actually giggled at that. He hadn't heard a Dweller laugh before now, or whatever it was they did which his illusion translated into a laugh. Coming hot on the heels of the revelation that the Dwellers enjoyed some sort of art as well, it belied the picture he'd built up in his mind of a race of soulless automata. Mobile computers, performing a function, nothing else. But these were people.

The blank wall at one end of the bridge, a blatant gap in the neat racks of crystals, marked the way out into the corridor and Te opened a doorway through to it. From there they rejoined the spiral corridor and began making their way upward.

"For some Dwellers," Te said, as they walked, "their purpose is to create, or cause to be created, a certain number of artworks. There is always one Dweller with that purpose at any one time. It is one of the few purposes which is repeated and passed on to new Dwellers."

"What are the others?"

"There is the First Voice of the Dwellers. The purpose Azu now holds. That lasts for a given amount of time and then the holder can lay the purpose aside for another to be given. Then there are the Masters of Body and Mind. Those are not purposes, as such, merely additional responsibilities that are given to Dwellers whose purposes give them deeper knowledge of the body and the mind. They are our healers. Oa and Ji have those tasks, now."

"And then, of course, there is the Voidseer. That, I understand, is a purpose that has to be held until another Dweller has been trained by the Voidseer to take his place. After a time, the Chamber gives the purpose of apprentice to a Dweller and then he or she will eventually become the next Voidseer."

They had come to another connecting corridor and she paused, as a thought seemed to occur to her. "If we go this way and ascend the outer spiral," she said, "I could show you the Chamber of Purpose if you wish. It is not far out of our way."

"Yes. I'd like that."

They turned down the connecting corridor and came quickly to the junction with the outermost spiral. They were quite high up now, several levels above the Gathering Place, so the corridors connecting the spirals were quite short.

They ascended another level or so until they reached a point where one wall of the corridor widened out in a deep semicircle, at the centre of which was a door. An actual door, not just a doorway. It was smooth stone, but recessed slightly into the wall, as though to slide sideways or upwards. Further along the semicircle was a glass-filled window.

"This is the Chamber," said Te, lowering her voice. She led him towards the window. "We must be quiet, here. See." She pointed through the window. "There is a Dweller in there, now. We must not disturb her thoughts."

Kasstovaal looked. The room beyond was on a slightly lower level to the corridor. He could just see the end of a ramp leading down from the direction of the door. The chamber was hexagonal, the nearest face taken up by the door and the ramp. To either side of that, the next two sides were formed into small stone alcoves with a seat in each, one of which was now occupied by a small female Dweller who sat quietly waiting for her fate to arrive. The sixth wall was dominated by a large, unglazed window, open to the white mists and the black voids outside the Rock.

"I see there's room for four in there," he said, softly. "Is it often full to capacity?"

"Very rarely," Te replied "There has never been a need for more than four at one time."

"Isn't there a danger of getting their purposes mixed up?" he suggested, playfully.

"It would not matter. Any Dweller is as capable of undertaking a purpose as any other. I do not think the purposes are necessarily directed to a specific Dweller. They are just given to whoever is waiting here to receive one."

Does that mean they are all equally talented in all things, Kasstovaal wondered. He doubted it. Being capable of a task and being good at a task were two entirely different things, in his book. Perhaps if they saw all tasks as a logical progression from base principles right up to the completed article, maybe they regarded talent as something that was acquired as a consequence of the process.

"I am looking forward to the time when I may enter there," said Te. "To finally have a purpose for my life."

Just then, a pair of Dwellers came along the corridor from the opposite direction. They did not immediately notice Kasstovaal and Te hidden as they were by the curve in the wall. Kasstovaal looked round automatically and froze as he, immediately, recognised one of them. The tall, male Dweller with the cloak he had seen in the Gathering Place. The other Dweller, also male and a little shorter and fatter, he did not recognise. This one, too, wore an infinite value symbol but had no cloak.

Te had turned with him and seemed on the point of sending a greeting. The two Dwellers had come to a stop by the wall, just short of the curve, and were in the process of forming a doorway into the room beyond. They seemed to become aware of the two of them simultaneously and gave them a short, chilly glance each before disappearing into the room and sealing the doorway behind them.

"Who were they?" Kasstovaal asked.

"The one who wears the cloak is Ra, the Voidseer. The other is Ko, his apprentice."

"Is that so?" That was not good news. Having an ordinary Dweller wishing you ill was bad enough. Having one of the most influential Dwellers against you, one moreover who was privy to secrets that none of the other Dwellers knew about, represented a formidable threat. He would have to let Jeryant know.

Out loud, he said "Not very friendly, were they."

"It is usual for the Voidseer to be somewhat...aloof," said Te. "I suppose the purpose must make them that way. I knew Ko well, before he received the purpose of apprentice. We trained together. He was quite amiable then. Now, though, he is becoming like his master, cold and withdrawn. It is a long time since we last waved to each other."

That confused Kasstovaal for a moment, until he remembered what a wave was to a Dweller.

"Come," said Te. "We shall go on up to the Gallery."

The Gallery bore more than a passing resemblance to the Chamber of Knowledge. Again, the walls were lined with racks of crystals. However, unlike the Chamber of Knowledge, this was all on one level, though the total area of it could not have been much less. One entire level of the Rock had been devoted to this one room, not far below the summit. The three main spirals terminated here, opening out onto a wide circular space where every wall opened onto the outside.

The centre of the room was occupied by rows of what looked like recliner chairs. A few Dwellers were lounging in them, holding crystals to their heads, over the left ear this time, not the forehead.

Te immediately made a beeline for a particular rack and a particular crystal.

"This is my favourite," she said, eagerly. "Try it. I am sure you'll enjoy it."

"Do these work the same as the knowledge crystals."

"Not exactly. These are designed for active input into your sensory centres. All you need to do is hold the crystal to your head and relax. It will do the rest."

She led him over to a vacant pair of recliners and, herself, lay back next to him.

Oh well, thought Kasstovaal, the other crystal hadn't hurt him. He was about to raise it to his head when he felt Te's fingers touching him, just above the right ear.

"What are you doing?"

"I would like to enjoy it with you," she said, placidly. "If that is all right."

"Sure."

What had she said, now? Hold the crystal to your head and... relax. He closed his eyes. But he could still see light, not the dark inside of his eyelids. There was a pure white light in his eyes, the purest and whitest he had ever seen. A dark blob appeared at the centre of his field of vision, a rough triangle. The focus sharpened and the shape resolved. It was the Rock, the whole of it as he had first seen it with his mind's eye; his true vision had never seen it from the outside, after all.

As he watched, the Rock began to fall gracefully forwards, rotating on an invisible axis halfway down its side until the sharp tip of the summit was pointed directly at him. Then the Rock twisted and the whole universe twisted with it.

His body was gone. It no longer made sense for him to have a body. Not in this place. Not where the colours were so fresh and new, a visible spectrum of light born at the very instant of the first creation. Colours too impossible to exist, to even be conceived in his own universe. Colours that seemed to breathe and think and live. Colours existing in three dimensions and more, all visible to him.

He was in a sea of them, borne along in a soft breeze that sang to him in a discordant murmuring that resonated in his brain and became the sweetest of music. Around him shapes fought to exist, struggled to become real. Incredible shapes, geometry folding back on itself and twisting the universe with them as they changed. Geometry defines a universe. If the laws that govern it can flex and bend, so must the universe bend with it.

This whole maelstrom of creation existed, at this moment, in his mind alone. For this while, it was his. It belonged to him. This, he thought, must be how gods feel. He looked upon it, experienced it with every sense, and saw that his universe was beautiful and was amazed at the feeling of power that one thought gave him.

Lying next to him in the Gallery, Te rode the experience with him, touching his mind only slightly, just enough to link into his sensory centres and experience what he experienced. He had a warm mind underneath all that cold suspicion. She liked the feel of it. If only he would let go of his fears how contented he would be, with a mind like that.

She could feel him enjoying the crystal as they rode it together. She had used this crystal many times before and it still had lost none of its potency for her. She had tried many others but this was the one most in tune with her mind. She bathed in its twists and turns, in the richness and depth of its colours and constructions.

She had become so enwrapped in it that she let her control slip just a fraction and her mind touched Kasstovaal's just a little more deeply. The instant she did that a terrible black cloud descended over the colourful scene created by the crystal, blotting it out. A deep voice seemed to growl inside her mind "Go Away!" Then, boiling out of the darkness, came the cry, the same terrible ululation that had wrenched her mind apart, borne out of the mists on a throbbing wave of fear and despair. This time it only lasted for an instant, for she tore her fingers away from his head and shrank away from him in terror at that sound.

Kasstovaal was still holding the crystal to his head, evidently still enjoying the experience as though nothing had happened.

She tried to calm herself down, forcing away the fear that the cry had reawakened in her so efficiently. It seemed she had touched a sensitive spot in his mind, by accident. Something unconscious that had reacted when she touched it and pushed her away. Whatever it was it had known, or sensed in her, that she feared the cry and had used it on her like a weapon. Just enough to sting her, to warn her, forcefully, that she must not trespass.

Ji had warned her about this. She must be more careful, in future.

Kasstovaal's eyelids flickered and the hand holding the crystal dropped away from his head as he came out of the experience.

By now, Te had managed to reassemble her control and could present a calm and composed countenance to him. "What do you think?" she asked.

"That was incredible," he said, in wonderment. "How is it done?"

"All it really is" she replied, "is a pattern of mathematical theorems which conflict with each other. The result of all of those theorems taken together, as one, is a physical impossibility in the known universe. So the mind is forced to create a simulation of a universe in which the result makes sense. That involves a complete readjustment of all your perceptions of reality and that is what you experience. Creating the right theorem pattern is a careful and subtle art among my people."

"Amazing." His head was still spinning with it. It had seemed more than a perception of reality. It had been a certainty of what was. Real and accepted as real. His hand was shaking slightly as he held out the crystal. "Could you put it back for me?" he asked. "I don't want to drop it. And you know better than I do where it goes."

"Certainly." She took the crystal from him and carried it back to its rack. As she laid it in its place she wondered if she would ever be able to enjoy it as much as she used to. Would it always remind her of that sting to her mind?

They were making their way back towards Kasstovaal's room, each absorbed in their own thoughts and their own discoveries. They passed an open doorway, which Kasstovaal barely registered beyond the impression that it was some sort of laboratory rather than a private room.

From within, a voice called after them, "Te, child! And Beyonder Kasstovaal. How fortuitous that you should come by. May I speak with you?" It was a thin, piping voice, the sort Kasstovaal might have attributed to an old man of his species. As the two of them turned and went in through the doorway the figure that came to greet them seemed to confirm his assessment, save that this thin and old-looking Dweller stood upright and strong, still maintaining the height of his powers.

"Greetings, Yua," said Te. "Can we assist you?"

"I think our friend Kasstovaal may be able to," said Yua, looking Kasstovaal up and down. "Tell me, Beyonder. Are you experienced in the creation of power sources? I know your purpose has to do with open space flight. Have you, perhaps, involved yourself with the power generation aspects of that field?"

"Yes, I have," said Kasstovaal. "A pilot is stuck without power to drive his ship. We are trained to repair any system that might fail on us."

"Excellent," said Yua, his face lighting up with genuine enthusiasm. "And, of course, you will be familiar with the properties of electromagnetic energy, since your reality is composed of it. Come and take a look at this."

He beckoned Kasstovaal over to the workbench on which was mounted a large square box of thick plastic. Inside it, Kasstovaal could see a small, metallic device connected to a number of thin filaments or wires.

"I should explain" said Yua, "that my purpose is to devise a method of generating an electromagnetic power flow to a level of not less than one point four million units from a device no larger than...well, this size." He indicated the small device. "It must be no bigger than that. And portable, of course."

"Have you tried micro anti-particle reaction?" Kasstovaal suggested "That's what we generally use in our..." He stopped himself saying "weapons" and said, instead, "...hand tools."

"Yes," said Yua. "That method was developed here a long time ago. But that can only generate one hundred and twenty thousand units maximum. I need to find something much more powerful than that."

Kasstovaal knew the power capacity of a micro anti-particle reactor in his own terms and knew, from personal experience, what even that amount of energy was capable of. He wondered what sort of weapon or tool would need twelve times that amount of energy in a portable form.

"I did think of incorporating an artificial singularity into an anti-particle reactor to hyper-accelerate the particle flow."

"You mean a micro-Black Hole," said Kasstovaal.

Yua squinted at him and then nodded, "Yes. That's correct. A strange term for it but descriptive."

"We tried that," said Kasstovaal. "It multiplied the output, as was hoped, but the weight of the singularity made it too heavy to lift. No good for a portable unit. Even a micro-singularity weighs several thousand tons."

"So I found," said Yua. "I have abandoned that line of research. It is, now, my opinion that the answer lies in tapping the energy potential present in the interface between spatial modes. You are familiar with the technology for creating inter-spatial continuum rips, I am sure."

"Well, yes. It's our principal method of space travel."

"Good. I have calculated that the interface created between the two congruent modes of space should contain enough energy to reach the required level without any adverse physical effects."

"I don't quite follow you."

"Well, we know that when particles are brought into contact with their corresponding anti-particles, an annihilation reaction takes place, a release of natural energy to destroy both particles."

"Okay."

"In the same way, natural energies are brought into play to repair a rip in the continuum, a portal between realities."

"Surely the repair only involves as much energy as it took to create the portal in the first place," Kasstovaal protested.

"Ah!" Yua exclaimed. "My experiments suggest otherwise. I have found that the energy employed in the repair is much greater than...."

He broke off suddenly and both hands went to his head as though he were in pain.

"What's the matter?" Kasstovaal asked, concerned.

Yua let out a long low moan. "No," he almost sobbed. "Not me. Not now." Then he staggered.

Te came to his side and took his arm to support him. "What is it, Yua?" she asked.

"Help me, child," Yua said, hoarsely. "The Compulsion has come upon me."

"Oh no!" Te whispered.

"What's wrong?" Kasstovaal asked. "What's happening to him?"

"He is compelled to procreate," said Te. "A new Dweller is about to be born and he will be one of the parents."

"What? Just like that?"

"Yes. The Compulsion gives no warning."

"You must help me to the Birthing Chamber, child," Yua croaked, "and send the call for Oa to come."

"I will." Te formed a message in her mind and projected it into the wall for the veins to carry it to Oa. "Help me with him, Kasstovaal," she said.

Kasstovaal took the Dweller's other arm and between them they supported him out into the corridor.

"Which way is it?"

"Down." Te said. "It is two levels directly below the Gathering Place."

They started downwards, Yua staggering between them.

"What happens when we get there?" Kasstovaal asked. "Does he have to wait until three more Dwellers get the Compulsion? You said a new Dweller has four parents."

"All four will have felt the Compulsion at the same time," said Te. "He will only have to wait a short time for the others to arrive, if they are not all there before him."

As it turned out, Yua did not have to wait. His laboratory had been on an upper level and it was the best part of an hour later when they finally reached the Birthing Chamber. The doorway into it was already open or was, perhaps, never actually closed. If all Dwellers suffered as much as Yua was, Kasstovaal reflected, it was perhaps an obstacle they could do without. There were observation windows on either side of the doorway, filled in with glass. Beneath one of these, set at an angle, was a flat panel of white glass or plastic with a pattern of crystals set into it, a pattern that suggested controls to Kasstovaal, especially after the things he'd seen recently.

"Thank you, both," said Yua, gratefully, "I can manage now." He eased himself out of their grip and made for the doorway, holding its edge for support.

Kasstovaal moved to look in through one of the windows. Beyond was a small, square room, a little smaller than his own quarters. It was dimly lit, but he could see the other three Dwellers already in there, one male and two female, each standing on a small square podium. These were positioned equally around a central raised stage, also square, all facing centre. He could see Yua making his way, slowly, to the one vacant podium on the far side, holding onto a rail set in the wall for support.

Te turned to walk away.

"Where are you going?" Kasstovaal asked.

"He no longer needs us," she said, flatly. "We can leave them, now."

"But I must see this," he said. "You've been showing me how your people live their lives. Now I have a chance to see how they begin. I can't miss that. Jery would never forgive me, if nothing else."

"But it's...." Te sought for the right word.

"What?"

"Distasteful," she managed.

"Are we forbidden from watching?"

"No, but...." She trailed off again.

"All right. You go, if it makes you squeamish. I can find my own way back."

"No," she said, reluctantly. "If you are determined to watch, I shall wait for you."

"Good." He turned back to the window. Yua had almost reached his place, the other three Dwellers watching his progress. Each podium had a pair of handrails set into the floor and all three we holding on to them to stay upright.

"Oa isn't here yet," said Kasstovaal. "Do they have to wait for her?"

"No," said Te. She was standing back from the window, trying not to watch but fascinated despite herself. "When all four are in place it will begin, whether she is here or not."

"Does that matter? What does she have to do?"

"She only has to make sure that neither the child nor the parents come to any physical harm. As Master of Bodies, she can set right anything that might go wrong. She will also determine which is to be the Primary Parent."

"How does she decide that?"

Te pointed to the control panel. "Each parent gives of themselves to make the new Dweller. That panel will measure how much is taken from each. The Primary Parent will be the one from which the most is taken."

Inside the chamber, Yua clambered up onto the waiting podium and held fast to the handrails. The moment he grasped them, Kasstovaal heard the grating whine of a motor starting up. A section of the chamber wall opened outwards, not just disappearing as Dweller doors usually did but swinging outwards on hinges. Beyond it, Kasstovaal saw the whiteness of open space, dotted with voids.

The mists seemed to thicken, dulling out the voids' blackness. Then they began to pour in, a wide stream of compressed wisps heaving themselves over the lip of the window, writhing and twisting as though they were being sucked in against their will. They gathered in pools around the feet of the four Dwellers, lapping over the edge of each podium and curling to reach up their bodies.

A spot of bright light appeared on the forehead of each Dweller. As Kasstovaal watched, they brightened and then each lanced forward into an incandescent beam of pure white energy. The four beams met at the centre of the raised stage, forming a ball of light that slowly grew in size. At the same time the mists rose up to wrap the Dwellers' bodies in a white shroud, a shroud that grew paler and fainter as though each Dweller were absorbing the substance of it into their body.

Kasstovaal heard footsteps hurrying down the corridor and looked back. Oa approached at a dignified speed that still managed to cover the ground quickly. Hot on her heels came Jeryant, struggling to keep up.

"Oa said there's a birth going on in here," he said. "Is it true?"

"Yes," said Kasstovaal. "Look for yourself."

They both looked. The ball of light in the centre of the stage was still growing and at its centre a tiny spot of pure black was starting to form. Around the square, the four Dwellers were swaying to and fro, as if trying to pull away, mouths open in silent wailing, but all the time the beams of light from their heads stayed fixed to that one spot, chaining them in place.

Oa had stepped up to the panel, which had come to life as soon as the energy began to flow, and was touching the crystals to make adjustments.

"Is it going all right?" Jeryant asked her.

"So far," she said, shortly. She offered no more than that.

Jeryant didn't notice, however. Both he and Kasstovaal were transfixed by the view through the window. The black spot was growing and lengthening. For a moment it appeared to be taking on a cylindrical shape and then both their Illusions kicked in and the shape started to take on human characteristics; arms, legs, head.

"They seem to be using the energy in the mist," said Jeryant. "And using their own mental energy to focus it into a pattern. It can't be like forming objects, surely."

"They don't do it of their own will," said Kasstovaal. "Some kind of urge takes hold of them and they can't help but obey it. I saw it happen to one of them. The Compulsion, he called it."

By now the shrouds of mist around the Dwellers had all but faded into nothing, all their energy drawn away. The ball of light in the centre of the chamber also began to fade. The black form inside it sharpened, became solid. The beams of energy vanished, the ball of light went out. In the centre of the square stage, a small male Dweller, about the size of a ten-year old human, pushed himself shakily upright on his hands and looked about him. Around the square, his four parents stood upright again, looking not at their new offspring but down at their feet.

"Amazing," said Jeryant, softly.

Oa turned away from her panel and stepped into the room. She pointed at one of the female Dwellers. "Ki." she said "The responsibility of Primary Parent falls to you. Take him, now, to the First Voice and Azu will give him his name."

The female stepped down from her podium, took the young Dweller by the hand and helped him onto his feet. Then she put an arm about his shoulders and guided him towards the door. The other Dwellers followed them, silently, out.

"Well," said Jeryant, brightly. "It's congratulations time. Who's for a cigar?" He held up his hand and formed half a dozen of them, impressively large ones. "Anybody?"

Nobody wanted one. Not one of them said a word. The face of every Dweller was fixed and neutral as they turned from the door and went their separate ways in silence.

But before they had all disappeared completely, Kasstovaal caught the edge of an emotion wave. He couldn't tell which of them had let it slip, it was too faint. But he must have misread it, he thought. It couldn't be what it felt like, could it?

For just a moment, though, he could swear to himself that it was grief that he felt in that wave. Awful grief.

FIVE: BARRIER

15.

"It's not so unusual," said Jeryant. "Humans have been warping their perceptions of reality with various substances for thousands of years. I know. I've tried most of them myself."

Kasstovaal had joined him in his room and they were comparing experiences over a pot of coffee so good that it was well worth the inconvenience of ridding themselves of it afterwards.

"As for direct information download into the brain," Jeryant went on, "that's one of the Holy Grails of medicine, that is. We've been after something like it since the Galactic Age began. It won't be much longer before we have it too, so I gather."

"The Dwellers have both of them down to a fine art, believe me," said Kasstovaal. "You should try one of their art crystals. I guarantee that you won't have ever experienced anything like it. And bear in mind that I say that knowing full well the things you've tried in your degenerate life."

"That good, huh!" said Jeryant, refilling his cup, "I shall have to get Oa to take me up there sometime."

"How are you getting on with her?"

"Like the proverbial burning house. I don't think I've ever encountered a female medic who's been so eager for my solo company before. It's a very refreshing experience."

"What? Not having to wash something organic and corrosive off the crotch of your trousers just after you say the wrong thing, you mean."

"Yes, something like that. After witnessing that birth, I should be able to introduce the subject of comparative reproduction techniques without too much difficulty."

"Jery, you are impossible."

"Persistent, my boy. Persistent."

"You're wasting your time, there. Not only does Oa not have the necessary equipment for sex but neither, I'm afraid to say old friend, do you."

"With what I've learned from her about these Bio-forms and how flexible they are, that won't be a problem for very long, old son. I'm sure I can make a few...additions, here and there. Quite sufficient for a practical demonstration or two."

Kasstovaal put his hand over his eyes. "My Gods," he said, "everything they say about you is true, isn't it."

"Every sentence. All hard earned."

"You just be careful. These people can form any substance they like. There's no telling what she might pour into your lap."

"How about you and young Te?" said Jeryant, wolfishly, "I could soon fix you up with the necessary, you know."

"Leave off, old man. Cradle-snatching isn't my style."

"Suit yourself."

"Have you learned anything useful from Oa? Anything not involving sex, I mean."

"Well, I think I can set your suspicious mind at rest about one thing," said Jeryant. "I don't think it's possible for a Dweller to just think us out of existence. I didn't ask her outright, of course. I don't think the concept of causing harm to another sits too well with her. I had to, sort of, skate around the question. But, from what I gather, it's not possible for one Dweller to affect the body of another Dweller, using matter-forming. The molecules that make up a Dweller's body are held together by the Dweller's own thought energy. And since they're all directly connected to the mind that forms them, the molecular bonds are constantly being renewed, second by second. That's what gives them the power to create and discard limbs, as they need them. For another Dweller to try and un-form even a small part of another's body, he would need to suppress every single impulse from the host brain that might reach the molecules and, instantly, reform the bonds. It's virtually impossible. He might succeed in dispersing a few molecules before they could be renewed, but no more than that.

"Apparently, it makes Oa's job, as Master of Bodies, very difficult. You'd think, with their forming ability, medical operations would be a piece of cake. But it's not so. She can't make physical changes happen inside her patients. She has to feed instructions into their minds so that they can effect the changes themselves."

"That's all very well for Dweller bodies," said Kasstovaal. "What about us? We're not Dwellers."

"To all intents and purposes, that's exactly what we are," said Jeryant. "These bodies might be artificial but they are designed to function in exactly the same way as a real one. Remember what the process was designed for; to replace Dweller bodies. The overall construction has been altered for us but, at a molecular level, the substance is unchanged."

"So how did she make the changes to our bodies?"

"Same way as for everybody else. By feeding instructions into our minds."

"I don't remember getting any instructions."

"Well, you wouldn't do. It's an unconscious process. I mean, you're not consciously renewing all your molecules at the moment, are you."

"No."

"There you are, then. But it's still happening. It's like making your heart beat; it's a job you can leave your autonomic centres to get on with, without you having to think about it."

"Okay. You're the medic. I'll take your word for it. We can rule out a mental attack. What about physical force? How susceptible are we to that?"

"Beyond your little dalliance with that scalpel, the other day," Jeryant said, sternly, "I haven't got anything to go on. And, before you ask, I have even less to go on as far as the Dwellers are concerned. They aren't given to cutting themselves with knives. And, in the main, they're too careful and disciplined to have injurious accidents. Oa says she hasn't had to deal with anything like that in a long time."

"I'll take a best guess."

"My best guess is to play safe and don't take any chances. On the face of it, I would say that we are fundamentally the same as the Dwellers. So, to paraphrase an old saying, don't do anything they wouldn't do. Let Te guide you on that kind of thing. Sounds like she's willing enough to do that."

"I haven't seen her since we saw the birth," said Kasstovaal. "She wandered off with the rest of them, when it was all over. Never said a word. I hope I haven't offended her somehow."

"Best go and find her, old son," said Jeryant. "Doesn't do to let these things fester. Take the word of an expert."

"That would be you, would it?"

"You'd better believe it."

Kasstovaal got up. "I will. I wanted to see her, anyway. There's something else I want to see."

"You dog, you!"

"Give it a rest, Jery."

"Don't forget to get rid of that coffee," Jeryant called, as Kasstovaal formed a doorway and went out. "Otherwise, you'll slosh when you move. It doesn't half put a woman off."

Finding Te was easy enough. She had shown him how. He just had to ask the Rock to guide him to her and it would. He felt a bit of a fool talking to a wall, even only mentally. The fact that it talked back to him helped.

"This way," it whispered to him as he came to each intersection, "this way."

It led him, like this, down a few levels and across the Gathering Place until he came to a wall that whispered to him, "Here! She's in here."

Inbred politeness made him wonder if he should knock and, then, his common sense asked how he was supposed to do that on a solid stone wall. The hells with it. Probably the wall would have told him if Te did not want to be disturbed. He formed a doorway and looked in.

Te was lying back on a recliner, clearly lost in her own thoughts. But she came out of them when she saw him. "Hello," she said, brightly.

"Mind if I come in? I'm not disturbing you?"

"Not at all," she said, sitting up. "Please come in."

He entered, forming himself a stool so that he could sit opposite her. "I thought I might have offended you by insisting on staying to watch the birth," he said. "If I have, I'm sorry for it."

"There is no need for apologies. You did not compel me to remain with you. Quite the contrary, in fact. I chose to do so."

"Still, it wasn't my intention to make you uncomfortable. I was curious, that's all."

"Of course. And curiosity knows no bounds, good or bad. I know that, perhaps better than most. It is just that the birth of a new Dweller is..." she paused, in search of words and then went on "...something we find unpleasant."

"Having seen it," said Kasstovaal "I can't see why."

Te looked uncomfortable. "We do not like to speak of it," she said.

Kasstovaal decided not to push it. You had to tread carefully when you came up against social taboos. They could be as immovable as a stone wall to the people who believed in them but could rarely be accounted for rationally.

He changed the subject. "We didn't get to finish our tour," he said. "And there is something I'd particularly like to see, if you would show me."

"Of course," said Te, "what is it?"

"Nothing inside the Rock. Something outside."

She frowned at him. "I thought the sight of the outside disturbed you," she said.

"I'll have to get used to it sometime. It's not going to go away, after all."

"Quite so. What is it you want to see out there?"

"You said to me earlier that your universe could be crossed in a very short time."

"That's right."

"So it follows that you know what is to be found at the outermost limits of your universe. At least one of your people must have seen it."

"A great many of us have seen the edge of the universe," said Te. "We are quite close to it, here."

"Tell me," Kasstovaal said, eagerly. "What do you find there?"

"The Barrier," said Te, simply.

"That's all, is it? Just a barrier."

"Yes," said Te. "You, yourself, have already seen it, I think. You were very near it when my mind found yours out in the mists."

Kasstovaal had wondered about it. He was, now, prepared to accept that what he had seen out in the mists, with a vision that was no vision, had been what was really there. On the other hand, what his eyes were seeing right at this moment was, quite purposely, not what was actually there. How far could he trust his perceptions?

"I'd like to go and see the Barrier properly," he said. "With my eyes, I mean. Is that possible?"

"Of course. We can go now, if you like."

"I'm not taking you away from your work or anything?"

"No. I am taking a period for recreation, at this time. And I do enjoy mist-riding."

"Mist-riding?"

"It's the best way to travel out to the Barrier. Come. I will show you."

From a distance, the Rock appears jagged and irregular, bare grey stone without a trace of plant life hanging on to its surface. Just as a mountain should be, even if it is floating free in space. A closer inspection, however, would reveal the ledges neatly carved into the rough slopes all the way from base to summit. They do not lead into one another to form a continuous spiral all the way up. Instead, each one is a perfectly flat path encircling the Rock, isolated from its neighbours. Climbing the Rock, if one was so minded, would be a simple matter as little more than ten feet of sloping stone separated one ledge from the next and there were plenty of handholds.

About two-thirds of the way up the face, a doorway appeared in the rough rock wall and Te and Kasstovaal stepped out onto the ledge. It was the first time Kasstovaal had done this, actually stepped out onto the surface. It was giving his spaceman's instincts some trouble. The nearest comparison he could make, from his experience, to this situation was walking on an asteroid. In that context, he was quite used to standing on a piece of solid land floating in open space, even being able to step off it and float away. Except, his instincts screamed at him, he should be wearing a space suit instead of which he was bare-arse naked. It was the sort of thing nightmares were made of. Many people dream about turning up for work naked. When you work in open space, at absolute zero and with no free atmosphere, that particular nightmare involves a completely different set of responses.

He took a deep breath and repeated Jeryant's words over and over to himself. Let Te be your guide.

"Okay," he said. "How do we get out there?"

For answer, Te turned back the rock wall behind them. At her command, a stone slab about two feet square and an inch thick slid out of the wall and into her hands. "Hold this," she said, handing it to Kasstovaal and turned back to form a second, identical slab for herself.

"I'm going to give you a molecule pattern," she said. "I shall place it directly into your mind. Is that all right?"

"Sure."

A few seconds later, the pattern arrived in his mind. It was not a substance he recognised, though part of it suggested some sort of polymer chain.

"Now form the slab into that substance," said Te. "You have to do it yourself. It has to be attuned to your mind."

"Why? What is it?"

"It's a psycho-reactive plastic. It will respond to your thoughts, if it is composed of your thought energy."

They focused together, the slabs shrinking in their hands and becoming transparent. When Kasstovaal finished the pattern he was holding a thick plate of clear plastic, shaped like a shield.

Te bent down and placed hers flat on the thin air over the edge, just below knee height, with the point facing outwards into the mists. It sat there, unsupported, and didn't move so much as an inch as Te stepped up onto it. She turned and looked at him, expectantly.

He did as she had done, though with less confidence. He had surfed before, in his youth, but that was some time ago and he was sure that the similarities this had to that sport had already come to an end.

"All right," he said, wobbling a little on his slab, "how do we move?"

"We use the mist," said Te. "Do you know what it is made of?"

"No."

"The mist is all thoughts. Short, randomised thoughts, congealing into a physical form for a few instants of time. Take some, like this." She reached out a hand and waved it, once, before her, cupping it to catch some of the wisps. When she brought her hand back, there was a ball of thicker mist sitting in her palm, not drifting away. She lifted the hand to her face and stroked it up and over her head. The mist spread out from where her hand passed and seemed to sink into her skin. She sighed, in evident pleasure.

He tried it. The mist came easily into his hand and as he rubbed it into his face, he felt his mind surge with extra power for a few seconds. Then the sensation faded.

"Now," said Te, "do the same again, only with your mind. Reach out to take a distant piece of the mist and you will pull yourself towards it. The plate will move with your thought. When you reach the piece of mist you aimed for, reach out further for another piece and another. And so on, until you reach your destination. Try it."

Long unused instincts took over and Kasstovaal turned himself sideways on the plate, bent his knees and raised his arms up to keep his balance. Then he looked out, along the line of his left arm, trying to find a target to aim for.

That was easier said than done. For much of the time, the mist was a blank white wall with no features to lock on to. Then he caught sight of a distant texture in the whiteness, a momentary wisp that, in a few seconds, would fade away again. But it was enough. He locked onto it, reached out for it with his mind.

The plate moved sharply under his feet, almost throwing him off balance as it gained speed, making directly for the point where the wisp had been but was now no more. It continued to accelerate alarmingly and he had to fight to keep his nerve and let his instincts do the work for him, adjusting to every surge of speed under his feet.

Te came up beside him, herself in a sort of surfer's crouch but easier and more relaxed than he was. "That's it," she called. "Well done."

"I thought you said I'd be controlling this thing," he yelled back. "Doesn't bloody feel like it to me."

"But you are," she called. "Now, find another target and follow me." She pulled out ahead of him.

There seemed to be a stiff breeze blowing in his face, created by his own movement, he thought. He risked a look behind him and saw the whole magnificence of the Rock falling away behind him at speed. How fast was he going? It must be every bit of four hundred miles an hour, if the shrinking Rock was anything to go by, and he was still accelerating. It was difficult to tell. He hadn't felt anything like the sort of G-force he would have expected, otherwise he would never have been able to stay upright on this thing. Reaching that sort of speed in so short a time should have knocked him flat. The force of the breeze in his face didn't feel like four hundred miles an hour's worth either, though it did seem to increase slightly in time to his acceleration. All the sensations were muted and out of proportion. It didn't seem to matter. He could feel the old exhilaration starting up inside him again.

He turned his head back and sought out Te. She was pulling away from him, weaving away into the mist. He felt his speed slowing. He must be reaching the point of his first target. He focused on a point a little to the left of the disappearing form of Te and his plate speeded up again. He found that the harder he concentrated on his target the faster he seemed to go and he quickly pulled back some of the lead Te had on him. Another glimpse behind him showed the Rock as nothing more than a small triangle of grey, before the mist closed over it and hid it from his view.

Now the only indicators he had of his true speed were the black specks of the voids around him. He was moving fast enough now that they appeared to move, slipping silently away behind him. This didn't help him much, since he didn't know how big they were, or whether they were moving of their own volition. The weaving course that Te was leading him on headed always for the centre of the gaps between them, always keeping them as far away as possible. They were something he would have to research, he thought to himself. The Dwellers must have stacks of data about them in their library.

Through the rushing of the mist in his ears Kasstovaal heard the sound of distant laughter, carried back to him. A young, joyous, excited sound as Te let go of her adult control and became a child again, enjoying every scintilla of the thrill. A few seconds later, he ran into the wave front she had left behind her, pure joy and excitement bubbling out of her, and he felt them too as the waves impinged upon his body.

Then he lost it. Maybe the waves made him complacent or caused him to lose his concentration. Whichever it was, he overbalanced and fell backwards, arms flailing out desperately to catch a hold of the plate. Somehow or other, his fingers found a grip on its edge and he clung on for dear life. It was still moving at considerable speed, pulling him along behind it like a banner.

With an effort, he managed to pull himself back so that his chest rested on the plate. He hung on as it continued to chase after Te, regardless of the state of its passenger. He debated the wisdom of trying to pull himself up onto his feet again but this was no surfboard he was riding and no surfboard had ever reached this sort of speed. Not, perhaps, the most dignified way to travel but it was secure, at least, and this was no time to be taking chances.

He could still keep his eyes on Te and keep up with her but he would lose her for sure if he stopped to sort himself out. He didn't think she would hear him if he shouted, not at this speed and range.

By now, the voids had thinned out. As each one passed from view, no new ones appeared out of the mist to replace them. Gradually, the mist took over completely, the last of the voids falling away behind him. We must be close, he thought.

Sure enough, Te was slowing down, in front of him, and he was rapidly catching her up. The breeze died away as his own speed diminished and he pulled up beside her.

She turned her head to look at where he would have been if he'd been standing up, looked puzzled for a moment and then looked down at his prostrate form with interest. "Are you all right?" she asked.

They had slowed right down to what felt like a walking pace now, and he felt secure enough to pull his knees under him, then his feet and, then, to stand. "I just thought I'd take the scenic route," he said. He had found that he could, quite safely, use sarcasm with Te. She seemed to be right alongside the concept of it, which had surprised him and she always seemed to know when he was using it, even if the references he used escaped her. It was, perhaps, something she picked up from his language centre, along with the actual meaning of the words. As such, she didn't bother to ask him what he was talking about.

"We are almost there," she said. "Stay close or you might collide with it."

They drifted slowly through an uninterrupted sea of mist. It seemed to be thicker here, with no voids to draw it away. There were more visible wisps, some even gathering together into clouds at the heart of which Kasstovaal could see shapes forming. Cubes, cones and cylinders, the mist solidifying into perfect geometrical prisms as the randomised thoughts gathered together and, just for a few fleeting moments, became coherent.

Then, quite suddenly, the mist parted in front of them and there it was. A solid wall of blackness. Not merely darkness; no amount of light would ever make an impression on it. Complete and total black.

"There it is," said Te, and something about that sight made her drop her voice to an awed whisper. "The Barrier. This is the end of our universe."

Kasstovaal gazed at it in wonder. To his human eyes, it was a completely flat wall, straight up and down. And, of course, it would be. How could you possibly see the inward curve of a sphere that encased a whole universe, even a small one, when you were standing right next to it? And yet he had perceived it before. Some sense that his drifting mind had found to replace his eyes had been able to see it. It could simply be a matter of scale, he reasoned. Unconfined by a physical brain, his mind could have spread itself out, how far there was no telling. He could have occupied a vast area of space, for all he knew, without his mind losing its cohesion. He would have had the perspective of a giant, able to see giant objects as normal size, able to see enough of this barrier to dimly perceive the curve.

The corner of his eye caught a spot of light in the darkness to his left and turned his head to look at it. A tiny spot of pale blue light had appeared in the distance, growing larger as he watched. It extended into a line, lengthened as it drew nearer, a line of light skimming across the surface of the Barrier itself towards them, reaching higher and lower than his eyes could see. Then it flashed past, a band of energy several yards across, tearing open the silence with the rushing scream that followed in its wake. And just for a moment the substance of the Barrier was plainly visible. The blue light reflected on a transparent surface like glass, so smooth and clear as to be invisible against the blackness behind it. The remnants of the blue light were warped and bent through it, giving an impression of lens-like thickness.

The streak of blue light screamed away towards the opposite horizon and the Barrier was once again a featureless black wall.

Kasstovaal made to move closer to it and then realised that that might prove difficult. He hadn't taken much notice of the space immediately around him, his whole attention taken up by the Barrier. Now that he looked about him for some mist to grab hold of and pull him forward, he realised that there wasn't any. There was a significant gap between the Barrier and the mists and he and Te were standing in it. Looking back, the mist was a swirling cloud, seen from the outside. It was as though the Barrier were exerting some force on the mist to hold it away. Or, perhaps, something instinctive in the thoughts of the mist made it keep its distance from that invisible surface.

Then, he had an idea. He drifted back, slowly, to the edge of the boundary where the mist began, reached out a hand and scooped up a handful. He cupped his other hand around it, as though to make a snowball, and then realised that was silly. The mist was already a ball in his hand and had no intention of going anywhere. He drew his arm back and pitched the ball of mist forward as hard as he could. There was a lot of force behind the pitch but a lot of it was wasted. It was like trying to throw a handful of feathers. Nonetheless, the ball of mist drifted gently forwards, shedding some of its substance as it went but, on the whole, maintaining its shape.

Kasstovaal reached out with his mind and grabbed it and he and his plate moved after it at the same leisurely pace, about a yard behind. The ball splashed when it hit the barrier, bursting outwards, in slow motion, into a small circular cloud that spread across the surface of the Barrier in a widening circle, eventually thinning to nothing. Kasstovaal let himself drift and put his hands out in front of him. They came up flat against the Barrier and he stopped. The slight impact caused the substance to ring very softly, a single low note.

It felt solid, cool but not overly cold to the touch, much like glass would be on a winter's day. It was completely dry and so smooth he could barely feel it as he drew his fingers along it.

He tapped it, gently, with his finger. The low chime sounded again, a little louder. He knocked on it with a knuckle. Louder still. On an impulse, he brought his fist back and banged it as hard as he could against the unyielding surface. Then he had to cover his ears as the tone vibrated the empty space between him and the mist, higher than a gong, lower than a bell, louder than any alarm signal he'd ever heard and big enough to fill the space from horizon to horizon. The Barrier rippled very slightly, resonating to the sound and becoming briefly visible. The sound faded slowly, sinking down to bearable and eventually down to a background hum that lingered persistently in his ears.

A little way to his right, another ball of mist floated across the gap and exploded softly against the Barrier's surface. A few seconds later Te drifted up beside him. "I must admit," she said, "I hadn't thought of this method for crossing the gap to the Barrier."

"How is it usually done?"

"You build up enough excess speed inside the mist to carry you across. Not too much, though. The Barrier hurts if you run into it too hard."

"I'll bet." Kasstovaal ran his hand over the surface again. "What's it made of?"

"Some form of energy, I believe, though it doesn't conform to any of the known types of force field."

"Haven't any of your people ever studied it?"

"No one has ever been given the purpose of studying the Barrier and finding out its composition. It has never been properly studied. Some of us carry out rudimentary experiments on it as part of our pre-purpose training or just as a personal project while we wait for maturity. But no more than that has ever been done."

"Strange, that," said Kasstovaal. "Seems like an obvious subject for a purpose, especially as it's so close to the Rock."

"I agree. But, as I said, our purposes are chosen for us. We cannot account for their relevance or reason."

"Are there any notes? Has any data been kept, at all?"

"Some, I suppose. It'll be in the Chamber of Knowledge, somewhere. We never discard any data we obtain, in case it becomes useful later. Is it important?"

"I'm not sure." Kasstovaal leaned forward on his plate and placed his ear flat against the Barrier. He could hear the last fading echo of the tone he had caused but nothing else. He didn't know what else he'd expected to hear. From this angle, if he moved his eyes in just the right way, he could catch brief glimpses of the surface, a momentary shine, the hint of a reflection. There were no imperfections, no cracks. A perfect solid barrier, holding back infinity. And yet.

"Something's not right about this Barrier." He voiced the thought that was niggling in his mind but would not go away. No, he could hardly dignify it by calling it a thought. It was a feeling, a gut feeling, something he could not pin down in his mind.

"How do you mean?" Te asked. "Does it not compare to the barrier around your own universe?"

"I don't even know if there is a barrier around my universe. Nobody has ever been out far enough to find out. No, it's nothing I can account for by a comparison. I can't think of anything to compare it to that would come close. But there is something about it that bothers me and I don't know what it is. It's frustrating."

"Perhaps the stored data will tell you," Te suggested. "If not, perhaps you should conduct your own experiments on it. You could make it a purpose for yourself."

"Perhaps I will, at that." He stood back upright and looked again at the unbroken blackness that lay outside the universe, straining his eyes to catch sight of something, anything that might be out there. Off the top of his head, he could think of a dozen religious leaders who would volunteer opinions on what was to be found outside creation, in the boundary between universes. How they would have envied him, the first human ever to see it with his own eyes.

But there was nothing to see. There were no great creators watching, benevolently or malevolently, over the doings of their creation. There was no great forge in which the universes had been constructed, standing cold and forgotten now that the work was done. There were no great explosions of thunder and lightning as the Gods warred amongst themselves to win the prize of rule over humanity. There was not even the cowled figure of Death patrolling the boundary, ready to reach in with a hand and pluck away a life between his finger and thumb. Even face to face with this most ultimate of mysteries, that one last truth was still hidden from human eyes. The darkness would show him nothing.

He felt a pang of the wanderer's spirit, that pure and irresistible drive that had once made him reach out for the distant stars he saw from his home planet. The desire to go there. It had been strong enough, then, to carry him through the academy and up to his rank. But these days it burned low. Once he had reached those stars they became commonplace, nothing new to him.

Now, he was looking over a whole new frontier and something of that old spirit flared up in him making him want to go there, want to make the unknown known. Later, perhaps. It would have to be later. There was something not right here.

"I think I've seen all that I can here. Let's go back."

"Did you find what you sought?" Te asked.

"No. I was hoping for answers. I just got more questions. I shall have to answer them some other way."

As he and Te turned their plates around and made ready to catch hold of the mist again, Kasstovaal took one last look behind him at the Barrier hoping perhaps to convince himself that he was mistaken, that nothing was amiss and that his paranoia was doing the thinking for him.

But the feeling persisted. Something was not right.

16.

The crystal glowed only briefly when Kasstovaal raised it to his head. It was, visibly, smaller than most of the crystals in the Chamber of Knowledge, almost too small to hold between finger and thumb, and came from among a collection of similarly sized fragments which did not warrant the prestige of being put among the racks. They were set out, instead, on a series of trays tucked away in a corner and didn't seem to attract much interest.

Kasstovaal could see why. There was precious little data to be had from them. Te had helped him sort out the ones that pertained to the Barrier and there were quite a few of them, about fifty or sixty he counted, spanning a date range that reached back almost to the earliest recorded times of the Dwellers and came right up to the present. He had taken them back to his room and had methodically worked his way through every one of them. But they all said virtually the same things.

They said that the Barrier was almost certainly not composed of solid material, given that it maintained its perfectly smooth surface at all times, which no solid material could seriously be expected to do. It must, therefore, be composed of some form of energy, renewing its surface constantly from microsecond to microsecond. However, none of the instruments or scanning techniques that had ever been tried had actually managed to identify the type of energy that was being used.

Nor could they determine where that energy, whatever it might be, was coming from. There was certainly no single source. One enterprising young Dweller had tried analysing the surrounding matter to see if that was giving up any sort of energy which might be fuelling the Barrier. She found nothing.

The only information he could find that was of any real use to him were the basic measurements that all the interested Dwellers started their research with. The Barrier, they all told him, was 10,320.1 units away from the Rock, at its closest point. This appeared to be a more or less constant distance, as the figure did not change significantly from one record to another across the whole date range. That gave him at least a vague idea of the length of a Dweller's distance unit. It had taken him about fifteen minutes to cross that distance on the plate; not much but it was something he could work with.

That was the most annoying thing about these crystals. The Dwellers didn't have individual names for their units of measurement of anything. Any measurement they took was merely expressed as a number of units and you could only tell what they were units of by the context. This might have been confusing to an outside observer had it not been that the Dweller's style of experimentation was, possibly, the most laborious he'd ever encountered. They only ever tested for one measurement at a time, sometimes repeating the same experiment a dozen times to obtain all the data they wanted from it. It never seemed to occur to them that they could, and in some cases should, combine the measurements into one experiment.

Having measured the distance between the Rock and the Barrier, the next logical step that every crystal took was measuring the curve of the Barrier. The only difference in this step was that the older records approached it as an experiment to determine whether or not the Barrier was actually curved at all, while later researchers tended to take that fact as read. They all, inevitably, came up with the roughly same result from which it could be determined that the Barrier did indeed form a sphere with a maximum circumference of 169.8 billion units.

Kasstovaal formed himself a piece of paper and a writing stylus and made a few calculations. If he rode on a plate straight outwards from the Barrier and kept going, he would cross the entire universe in just over one hundred and thirty thousand years, by his timescale, encountering the Barrier again on the far side. By his reckoning, a fairly standard space drive ship would probably do it in less than five years, at a constant thrust. Not big for a universe. Not more than a light year across, he estimated, probably somewhat less.

Aside from that, he would learn nothing else from these crystals. In every one, the research petered out, uncompleted, as each young Dweller had gone away to concentrate on his or her purpose. And he was still no closer to working our what it was that bothered him about the Barrier.

Screw it, he thought to himself. He didn't even know why he felt it so important to find out. If the Dwellers weren't bothered enough about it to research it properly, they obviously didn't consider it as a source of danger. So why the hells should he? The argument failed to convince him.

He gathered the crystals back into the tray and went in search of Te. He found her in Vo's laboratory, working on a panel of control crystals. Above the panel a thin, flat screen was displaying a tightly packed wire diagram that swivelled to show itself in three dimensions. It looked to Kasstovaal like the lattice structure of a crystal. Indeed there was a crystal, the size of a football standing on a pedestal just in front of Te. It glowed brightly and she kept glancing up at it as she worked.

He didn't interrupt her but just watched quietly for a few moments until the sight became uncomfortable. She was working fast and he was starting to get blurred impressions that she had three, and sometimes four, arms and hands. In truth she probably did have, at this moment, and his Illusion was having trouble coping with it.

Vo was seated at the main workbench, across the room, talking to Jeryant. Kasstovaal put his tray down on the bench and sat down with them.

"Oa kicked you out, has she?" he asked. "I knew it couldn't last."

"Apparently she's compiling her notes," said Jeryant. "Going to be some time about it as well, so she says. She's going to call me when she's finished."

Kasstovaal's lips widened into a grin. "She's fed you a line, hasn't she. You must be losing your touch."

"We'll see about that. I don't brush off so easily. I'm biding my time at the moment. I thought I'd chew the fat with Vo while I'm waiting."

"Mind if join in?" Kasstovaal asked.

"Sure," said Jeryant. "But unless you know anything about encephalographic scanning techniques, you're going to be bored out of your mind. And, around here, that phrase could have an entirely different meaning."

"Te is conducting an experiment for me," said Vo. "She will not be long. You have finished reviewing the data on the Barrier?"

"Yes, what there is of it."

"Te told me of your interest. It is a rather obvious gap in our knowledge. But we must be guided by the purposes. We can do no other. You, though, are free to choose a purpose of your own. Perhaps you can help us fill that gap."

"I might," said Kasstovaal.

The glow from the crystal on the pedestal went out abruptly. Te's uncountable fingers continued working.

"Is that the device you used to catch our minds in?" Kasstovaal asked.

"It is of the same design," said Vo. "The devices can only be used once. This one has a few modifications built into it, which Te is now testing. We have learned from the experience of retrieving you two to good effect."

Te finished her manipulations, plucked a small red crystal out of the panel and brought it over to Vo. "These are the results, Prim."

Vo took the crystal from her and held it to his forehead, where it glowed. After a few moments he took it away again and said "Yes. Most satisfactory."

Just then a doorway opened out onto the corridor and a male Dweller stepped in. The infinite value insignia, together with the absence of a cloak over his shoulders, made him instantly recognisable as Ko, the Voidseer's apprentice. He sealed the doorway behind him and stood for a moment looking around the laboratory with the air of an inspector getting ready to disapprove of whatever he finds there, regardless.

Vo rose and they exchanged mental greetings, Vo with ready openness, Ko with reservation.

"What brings you to my laboratory, Ko?" asked Vo. "Does my work interest you or your master?"

"We have no time to involve ourselves in such things," said Ko, coldly. "My business is with Te, directly, and with yourself, indirectly."

Te came up to him, forming a friendly greeting that carried with it overtones of her pleasure to see him. She was disappointed when the greeting she got back from him was coldly formal and, to the two humans, it was clearly visible on her face.

"It is good to see you again, Ko," she said. "What can I do for you?"

"I am here to tell you that the time for your Ceremony of Maturity approaches," said Ko, flatly. "You must prepare yourself. As must you, Vo, being the Primary Parent of Te."

Parent and offspring looked at one another, uncomfortably. Vo spoke up first. "When is it to be?"

"You must come to the Gathering Place in seventy units time. The Voidseer has instructed me to preside over the Ceremony as part of my training."

"This will be your first, then," said Te.

"The Voidseer has trained me well," said Ko, sharply. "You need not fear that I will desecrate the ceremony by making an error."

"Of course not," said Te, defensively, "I never thought it. I would only wish you well in a new experience."

Ko subsided visibly. "I must go to inform your other parents," he said.

"A ceremony." Jeryant jumped off his seat and came over to them. "Excellent. I love a good ceremony. I always say you can learn more about a culture by seeing its ceremonies than any other way. That and attending the parties afterwards. Mind if we join in?"

Te asked, "Is it permitted, Ko?"

Ko turned his head and looked at Jeryant for the first time. It was the sort of look you might give to the slug that had found its way into your salad or the heap of fresh manure that had turned up on your doorstep.

Then he turned back to Te and said, "It may attend if it wishes. So may the other one. There is nothing in the ritual to prevent it."

Jeryant's forehead wrinkled upwards and would have taken his eyebrows with it if he'd had any. "It!" he said, dangerously.

But Ko had already dismissed him from his notice. "Now I must leave," he said to Vo and Te. "I, too, have preparations to make." And with that he turned and headed for the wall leading to the corridor.

Jeryant intercepted him halfway there. "Oh, do allow me," he said, with mock politeness, and formed a doorway for Ko. Ko looked at it and then at Jeryant with an expression consisting of one part puzzlement and one part generalised contempt. Then he stepped into the corridor through a perfect representation of a clenched human fist with an upward pointing middle finger.

"Arrogant little shite," said Jeryant, sealing up his creation. "I'll give him 'It may attend if it wishes' if I ever get him on his own."

"His manners do leave something to be desired," Vo said, unhappily.

"Yes. A good smack in the mouth would be favourite," said Jeryant. "He's a nasty piece of work, that one."

"What's this ceremony all about?" asked Kasstovaal. "It sounds important."

"It is a ritual that dates back to our earliest beginnings," said Te. "All young Dwellers must go through it when they reach adulthood. Until they have, they will not be permitted to have a purpose."

"So it's a sort of rite of passage," said Jeryant. "What's involved?"

The two Dwellers looked uncomfortable.

Vo said, "The ritual is supposed to represent the severance of the last ties that connect an offspring to its parents and marks the time when that child becomes an independent adult."

"It's a familiar pattern." said Jeryant "There are several cultures in our universe that celebrate the coming of adulthood that way."

"For us, it is not a celebration," said Vo. "It is a duty. An unpleasant one."

"Why's that?"

Vo seemed to be struggling to keep something from showing in his voice. "It is a very emotional time. For Te and for the four of us who were her parents. It tries our control sorely."

Jeryant had enough tact in him not to pursue it any further, right now. There would be other times to ask.

"We'll leave you two to get on with your preparations, or whatever," he said, motioning Kasstovaal to follow. "When should we go to the Gathering Place? I don't know how long seventy units is."

"We shall call you when the time comes," said Vo. "The Rock will carry the message."

"Fine." Jeryant created two doorways, a perfectly matched pair of exclamation marks, and he and Kasstovaal stepped out through them.

"They do not understand fully, do they," Te commented.

"They do not see reality in the same way we do," Vo told her. "It is as expected. The best they can do for their understanding is to search for comparisons in their own universe. We do not know their universe so we cannot help them in that. Perhaps they will understand better once they have seen the ceremony."

The message came in absolute silence. It inserted itself directly into both men's minds and neither one of them experienced any doubt that they had actually received it and that they weren't just imagining it.

They came out of their rooms almost simultaneously. Jeryant had to duck slightly to get through his doorway, which exactly matched the shape of the large red-spotted bow tie he was wearing.

"What are you wearing that for?" Kasstovaal asked.

"Formal occasion, sunshine. Got to look your best, you know. It's expected."

"Jery. You only ever wear that tie when you want to take the piss. You told me that yourself."

"What's wrong with it?"

"It looks like a mad butterfly has gone for your throat."

"I'm just trying to lighten the atmosphere a bit. You know me. I'm the one everybody looks to, to break the ice at funerals."

"This isn't a funeral."

"Might as well be, the way Vo and Te were acting."

"All right. But if you make that thing spin, I swear I'll make you eat it."

"Spoilsport! It took me ages to get a working motor together."

They turned and walked together down the corridor, making their way to the nearest spiral and then downward.

"Do we want to be on the floor level?" Kasstovaal asked.

"Probably not a good idea. We are only spectators, after all. And not very welcome ones, either, if young Ko's reaction is anything to go by."

"We don't seem to have ingratiated ourselves with the religious powers-that-be around here. Damned if I can work out why."

"Me neither. I mean, it's not as though we represent a threat to what they're advocating."

"Assuming we've been told the whole of what that is. I don't know. Maybe we should collar Ko on the way out and ask him."

"We could do more than ask him, rude little bugger. But I don't think it would get us anywhere. It's virtually impossible to get an answer out of a priest if he's minded not to give it to you. They devote their entire lives to the practice of not giving people direct answers so they become really good at it. Besides, I reckon I can live without the local priesthood liking me."

"It is just possible that you can't," said Kasstovaal. "You're liable to find that the last words you ever say are something like 'I didn't mean it really, your reverence!'"

"Not me, sunshine. I'd curse the buggers with my last breath, I would. I fully intend to be cursing someone with it. It might as well be a priest as anybody else. How far down are we?"

"Don't know. Let's have a look."

They turned down the connecting corridor and emerged onto the ledge. Jeryant looked down. They were about fifteen levels up.

"Far too high," he said. "Wouldn't recognise my own mother from up here."

They went back and continued downwards. After a couple more attempts, neither to Jeryant's liking, they arrived on the ledge one level above the arena.

"This'll do," said Jeryant. "Close enough for a good view and far enough away from the action so that we don't get roped into anything."

"I shouldn't think they'll be looking for volunteers. It was touch and go whether they would let us come at all. They won't want to get us involved."

"Don't you believe it, mate. Listen to the voice of experience. Never park yourself near the front of a religious ceremony or a comedy performance. It's asking for trouble. Want some popcorn?"

"No. And neither do you. I've seen what you do with it."

They both fell silent as a female Dweller entered the arena below them. She came in slowly, pausing briefly between each step, her head lowered and her eyes turned down to the floor.

She was not a Dweller either of them recognised, but then Te had never introduced them to all four of her parents. She crossed the floor to the central podium and climbed up. She turned to face the archway through which she had entered, but did not raise her eyes from the floor. In a low voice she said, "I am Iya, parent of Te. I am called by that which is due. And I am here." Then she just stood there, waiting, eyes still downcast.

Kasstovaal looked around him and up. The Gathering Place was completely empty, except for the two of them and Iya herself. It occurred to him that she would have said exactly the same thing in exactly the same tone of voice had there been nobody there to hear her. There didn't appear to be anyone waiting outside the archways for her to enter alone and say her piece, for it was fully ten minutes before the next Dweller arrived. A male, who did exactly as Iya had done, standing next to her on the podium and declaring himself to be Or.

Vo came next, close behind him, eyes down like his fellows. He mounted the podium, standing at one end of it, next to Iya.

"I am Vo," he said, "Primary parent of Te. I am called by that which is due. And I am here."

The fourth parent, Ty, arrived a few moments later, taking her place at the other end, next to Or.

The four of them stood there and waited, a still and silent tableau of humility and submission. Or was it something else, Kasstovaal wondered.

Another five minutes went by and the silence in that enormous space became oppressive. Then Ko walked in, maintaining the same slow march that the others had used. Te followed close on his heels, carrying a tray with four small crystals on it.

They came to a halt in front of the podium and stood facing the four Dwellers.

Ko spoke. "The time is now, for the settlement of that which is due. The time is now, when a child must throw off the fetters of youth and take on the power of adulthood."

Then Te spoke up. "I am the one that the First Voice named Te. I come to claim that power, as is my right."

"Child Te," said Ko, "that right is yours. But before you can claim it, all that remains unresolved from your childhood must be laid to rest. All that is due must be settled."

"I am prepared," said Te. "All are here that must be involved. The last of what is due can now be exacted."

"Are all that are called here so prepared?" Ko asked.

The four Dwellers on the podium murmured "I am," in perfect unison, but still did not look up.

"Let it be done then," said Ko, and took a step backwards, leaving the field to Te.

Te said, "When the Compulsion comes, none may resist its power. This I know to be true." Holding the tray in one hand, she stepped forward to stand at the foot of the podium, directly in front of Ty. She selected a crystal from the tray and held it out so that Ty's downcast eyes could see it. Ty raised her head slightly and the eyes of mother and daughter met.

Then Te whispered three words, which Kasstovaal could not make out. His vantage point was at an angle to the podium and Ty was furthest away from him. He saw Ty reach out and take the crystal from Te's fingers. Her hand shook a little as it took the crystal. Her mouth appeared to tremble as Kasstovaal's illusion tried to show him the emotions that were trying to escape.

Ty lifted the crystal, reverently, and smashed it against her breast. It broke easily and crumbled down into a fine cloud of coloured vapour, which hung about Ty for a few seconds before sinking into her body. She tensed and her mouth opened in a gasp; not of pain, it seemed to Kasstovaal, but of pleasure, though it was difficult to be sure, so muted were the Dwellers' facial expressions. The hand still held to her breast shook as whatever force it was contained in that crystal coursed briefly through her body. Then Ty's face relaxed and even took on the suggestion of a smile as her eyes briefly met Te's again. Her arm fell back to her side and she bowed her head once more.

Or accepted his crystal, maintaining an iron countenance throughout. There was just a second though, after his body absorbed the coloured vapour, when his mouth opened and he seemed on the verge of saying something, of blurting something out for his own part. He got control of himself in time, closed his mouth and lowered his eyes back down to the floor.

Iya, evidently the youngest of the four by some way, looked for all the world as though she was about to cry, if you could imagine those two featureless white circles producing tears. She almost dropped her crystal. Te took the shaking hand in her own and helped Iya to raise the crystal to her breast and break it there.

Iya's eyes lingered the longest on Te after the vapour had vanished. It was only with a visible effort that she pulled them away and down again.

At last, Te came to Vo. The crystal she offered him was larger than the rest and it was she who smiled this time as he took it from her. He managed to return the smile in spite of the pain of his own complex emotions. There was a special bond between these two.

All the same, Te whispered the words she had given to the other three and, this time, she was close enough that Kasstovaal thought he could make out what they were.

Vo burst his crystal and there was no mistaking the pleasure on his face as he absorbed the vapour into himself. Then he, too, lowered his head.

Te turned to face Ko. "It is done," she said. "No more is due between us."

Ko stepped forward and Te fell in by his side. "You have heard her," he said. "The last of the ties that bind you to her have been severed. Your part in her is at an end."

The four Dwellers on the podium raised their heads, at last, and looked squarely at Ko and Te. Every face along that line was, now, composed and solemn.

Ko said, "The child that was Te is no more. Only Te, Dweller of the Rock, now exists. All else is gone. All else is at rest."

Then he turned and walked out through the archway, at a normal pace. Te followed him and, one by one, the others stepped down from the podium and filed out after them.

"Well," said Jeryant, breaking the silence for both of them, "what do you think of that?"

They left the ledge and made their way back to the spiral. At the junction they encountered Vo, Te and Or making their way up, towards their rooms.

Kasstovaal wanted to speak to Te about what he'd seen but then he saw her face and thought better of it. She wore on her the signs of an emotional control under heavy strain, a control that would need all the concentration she might otherwise have used for answering questions. He let her pass by and she did not look at him.

"Later, I think," said Jeryant, voicing Kasstovaal's own thought.

They turned in the direction of their own quarters.

"Call me a heartless bastard, if you like," said Jeryant, "but I can't quite see what they were getting so worked up about. I mean, I've seen a few rites of passage in my time and seen a few tears of pride shed in the process. But that was seriously emotion-charged, especially for a group of Dwellers who, we know, don't usually get worked up about anything."

"I suppose that must be part of the purpose of it," said Kasstovaal. "An emotional purge or something. The parents certainly looked better for it afterwards."

"So what do they do the rest of the time? Store it up or something?"

"They might. I can see it working as a method of emotion control."

"Maybe," Jeryant said. "Did you catch what it was Te said when she handed out the crystals?"

"I think I did. I could just hear her when she said it to Vo."

"What was it?"

"Well I might be wrong," said Kasstovaal, "but it sounded to me like she said 'I forgive you.'"

"Forgive?"

"That's what it sounded like. What do you think she meant?"

"Damned if I know. I suppose there is a sort of sense to it. I mean parents can be a real bitch when you're a kid, for one reason or another. I suppose it's worse for Dweller kids because they've got two sets to worry about instead of one."

"But they only have dealings with the Primary parent," said Kasstovaal. "The other three stay out of the way. That doesn't explain it."

"No, you're right." Jeryant stroked his bare chin, missing his beard. "I think we'll have to give them a little time to get over it and then see if they'll talk to us about it."

"They might not want to. If it effects them that much."

"That's why we'll have to pick our time," said Jeryant. "That's the key in psychology. Timing. It's why comedy works on people. The right time will come, you watch."

SIX: VOIDRISE

17.

As it turned out, the right time to ask did not come. Initially Kasstovaal and Jeryant decided to give the Dwellers a full twenty-four hours, by Kasstovaal's clock. After that time, there was too much else to concern them.

They had spent the waiting day just killing time, something that men on deep space flights learned to do very quickly. Being able to matter-form increased their options considerably. A little further down the corridor from their own rooms, they found a room that, the Rock told them, was currently unused. They commandeered it and, within a few minutes, had themselves a very serviceable squash court.

Jeryant found that, as his new body was a lot nimbler than his old one had been, his game had improved considerably. As such, the two of them were now quite evenly matched. They played for hours, neither of them getting the slightest bit tired. It meant that each of them could keep on stepping up the pace to try and defeat the other and soon the game took on an unreal quality as the speed and ferocity reached ever higher. In the end it was only boredom that made them stop and go back to their rooms to shower, for the sake of continuity rather than necessity.

The rest of the time they spent in idle speculation, all of it fruitless, or practising their forming. In all that time, none of the Dwellers came looking for them or sent them messages. Even Oa, who had not been involved in the ceremony, sent no word that she had finished her notes and was able to see Jeryant.

They went to look for her first, when the twenty-four hours was up, and found her in her laboratory, bustling around in what seemed to be a state of some agitation.

"What's up?" Jeryant asked, striding in briskly. "Someone stolen your notes?"

Oa looked around sharply and almost jumped when she saw them. "Ah, good," she said, "I was about to call for you. It has occurred to me that I have forgotten to test your bodies for one particular thing. A most stupid error." This last she spat out at herself with some venom.

"Calm down," Jeryant said. "Whatever it is, it can't be that vital otherwise we'd have felt something wrong by now, surely."

"You don't understand," said Oa, exasperation sounding in her words. "We need to know, one way or the other, before Voidrise."

"What? What's Voidrise?" Jeryant asked, confused. "You're not making sense, Oa."

"Please. Just sit down," she said, waving them towards a bench, "I'll explain shortly."

They sat, exchanging a worried glance. Oa was actually hurrying around the laboratory, gathering tools and crystals on to workbench.

Kasstovaal had never seen a Dweller hurry to do anything before. They could work swiftly, sure enough, when they needed to but still with that calm efficiency that made them seem emotionless. Oa was actually flustered. It was obvious even to him. The way she looked round and about her for the things she wanted, as though she'd forgotten where she kept them, neatly stored. The way her fingers fumbled at a crystal she needed. The way she clenched the trembling fingers into a fist and banged it down hard onto the workbench to try and steady them.

"For the love of the Gods, woman!" cried Jeryant, getting up and going over. "Sit down yourself, before you bloody break something. If it's that important, I'll do it."

"I can manage," Oa snapped.

"No you can't. Just look at you. By the time you've fumbled this thing together, I'll bet I could have done it three times over. Now, just tell me what needs doing. What are we testing for here?"

Oa sagged a little. "I'm trying to measure the amount of mental energy you have in your bodies," she said. "For that, I need to configure a scanning device to measure the rate at which your minds are generating energy and then reconfigure it to measure the rate at which you are expending it."

She pointed to a rectangular metal block, with a moulded handgrip, lying on the workbench. One side of it had a deep groove, running along almost its full length. "That is the device. It's almost ready. Do exactly as I tell you."

"Right," said Jeryant. "What's first?"

"On the shelf behind Kasstovaal, there is a blue crystal pyramid."

Kasstovaal jumped up and looked over the shelf's contents. "Got it," he said, bringing it over.

"That is the sensor plate," said Oa. "Fit it, apex first, into the socket on the tip of the scanner."

Jeryant took the pyramid and pressed it into place. It clicked home and stayed fast.

"Now," said Oa, "slot these crystals into the groove in the following order. Blue, red, black, yellow."

Jeryant searched among the scattering of crystals on the bench, found the ones he needed and set them out in order. At first he tried pushing them straight into the groove, but it was quickly clear that they wouldn't go in that way.

"Slide them in," Oa snapped, in frustration.

It took him a few seconds to see what she meant. Then he realised that the crystals were cut to slot into the groove from its open end and slide along its length. He fitted the crystals into place. "What else?" he asked.

"That grey sphere in front of you is the power cell," Oa said. "Fit it onto the end of the handgrip."

He did as he was told and the device came to life in his hand. The crystals started to glow in their respective colours and a small screen on the top surface lit up with a line of four dashes, ready to display figures.

"Good," said Oa. "Now hold the sensor plate against Kasstovaal's head and press the contact point under your thumb."

Kasstovaal pulled instinctively away from the device as Jeryant pointed it at him. It looked uncomfortably like a gun.

"There is nothing to fear," said Oa, but without any of the kindness and placation that usually went with those words.

Kasstovaal submitted and Jeryant touched the square base of the pyramid against his temple, pressing down on the small crystal chip set into the handgrip. The device made no sound but the crystals on its side glowed more brightly for a few seconds. Then four figures appeared on the small screen, numerals that Jeryant couldn't read.

"Show it to me." Oa demanded.

Jeryant held it out so that she could read the numbers.

"Four Seven Three point Two," she said. "All right. Now you, Jeryant. Scan yourself."

He did so and showed her the result.

"Four Six Two point Eight. Good. Now you must reconfigure the scanner."

"How do I do that?"

"By changing the crystals in the slot. Slide them all out first."

He emptied them out onto the workbench.

"Now, take the red and the blue crystals in your hand and squeeze them together. Re-form them into one combined crystal."

Jeryant did as he was instructed, reaching his mind down and into the crystal structures, welding them together with his will. When he opened his hand again, a single purple crystal nestled in the palm.

"Excellent," said Oa. "Now, the sequence you need is yellow, purple, green, black. There is a green one here on the bench." She reached for it herself but her clumsy fingers knocked it away.

"I've got it." Jeryant reached over for it and slotted it into place.

"All right. Now repeat the scans."

This time Kasstovaal's scan produced the same figure, Four Seven Three point Two. Jeryant's came out slightly different.

"Four Six Three point Zero," Oa read. "An insignificant difference. Not enough to matter." She sounded relieved, though her body remained tense.

"And the result of that is what, exactly?" Kasstovaal asked.

"It is as I had suspected and hoped," said Oa. "You are both operating at stasis level. That is to say that your minds are generating exactly the right amount of energy to satisfy the operational requirements of your bodies and minds. No more and no less. The balance is almost perfect. Quite fascinating."

A doorway opened in the wall and Vo and Te walked in stiffly. They, too, were showing signs of agitation, fingers clasping and unclasping, the rigidity of their limbs, the hard lines on their faces.

"Well?" demanded Vo. He almost shouted it.

"It is confirmed," said Oa. "They have achieved stasis. It's obvious, just by looking at them."

"Too obvious for you to have thought to check them before now," Vo snapped.

"They showed no signs of fatigue or distress," said Oa, forcefully. "I was in time to correct any imbalance, had there been any. But there is not."

"Hey hey! Calm down, kids," said Jeryant, inserting himself between them. "No need for an argument. We've established that there's no problem. There's nothing to get steamed up over."

"Forgive us," said Vo, and the effort in his voice was painful to hear.

Jeryant said, "So, if I understand this correctly, our energy is balanced up. Supply meets demand. And that comes as a surprise to you."

He put his head on one side and looked at the three of them. Vo's body was twitching, Te was rocking restlessly back and forth on her heels and Oa was beginning to shake. Each one of the three looked like they wanted to thump the other two.

"That says to me," Jeryant went on, "that your energy levels aren't balanced like ours are. You're either producing too much energy for your own needs or too little. If it were too little, you'd have to take on extra energy from another source to make up the difference or build up a store of it, like humans do, by sleeping. We haven't seen you do either of those things.

"So, if you're generating an excess of energy within yourselves, energy you don't use, where does it all go? Surely your bodies can't keep storing it indefinitely. Is that why you are all so agitated, at the moment? Is that build-up of spare energy becoming too much to hold? Is that why it suddenly occurred to you to check whether or not we might be building up a surplus, as well?"

Vo said, "You are correct. It is a temporary inconvenience. It will not last much longer. Voidrise is nearly here."

"What is Voidrise?" asked Kasstovaal. "Oa mentioned it earlier. What does it mean?"

"The orbit of one of the voids, out in the mist, brings it close to the Rock," said Vo. "We are approaching the point of perihelion."

At that moment the room filled with a soft ringing tone, as though a bell had been struck. The three Dwellers looked up towards the ceiling, as if looking for the source. Relief showed on their faces.

"At last," said Te. "It is overdue, this time."

The three of them made for the corridor, almost bumping into each other as Vo paused to form a doorway. They hurried out, leaving the doorway open behind them.

"After them," said Jeryant, "let's see where they go."

"I'm with you," said Kasstovaal. "If we're reaching perihelion with a void, I'm not missing that."

They hurried after the Dwellers. More of them were emerging from rooms and adjoining corridors, all apparently heading for the corridors that led to the outer surface of the Rock. The soft ringing continued in the air about them.

"What is perihelion, anyway?" asked Jeryant.

"It's the point at which the two spatial bodies come closest together in their orbits," said Kasstovaal. "It's the best time to get a really good look at one of these voids. I wonder how close it actually comes."

"I don't think it's the spirit of scientific enquiry driving this lot, at the moment," said Jeryant, as a couple of Dwellers came out of a room beside them and actually pushed to get past them.

Up ahead, a doorway had already been opened to the outside and Dwellers were pouring through it out on to the ledge. Kasstovaal and Jeryant followed them out, stepping quickly to one side of the doorway so as not to block the way. As the Dwellers came out, they split off to left and right, filing along the ledge until they reached the vacant space next to the Dweller that had gone before them. They all turned and stood at the very edge, facing outwards.

The flow of Dwellers through the door ceased. Immediately opposite the doorway there was a space still left vacant. The two humans moved cautiously forward and looked over the edge. The lower slope of the Rock stretched outwards into space beneath them. And every ledge was packed with Dwellers. They stood only one deep but close together so that all of them had an unimpeded view of the sky.

Kasstovaal turned his head to look upwards. It was the same all the way to the summit. Row upon row of Dwellers staring out into space. All still, all totally silent.

"The whole population must be out here," he whispered to Jeryant. "Every last one of them."

"Must be important to them, this Voidrise," Jeryant whispered back. "But I don't see...."

Then they heard it. In fact, it was almost too low a sound to hear, a rumble that could be physically felt on the skin if the ears had failed to detect it. It drew their eyes back down the slope to the rim where the grey of the Rock met the white of the mist. The edge of something black began to appear over it, at first no more than a dark line highlighting the rim. Above that line, the smooth sheet of the mist was breaking up, thinning out into visible wisps that waved and coiled in a vain struggle to escape the pull of that darkness.

The line grew to a crescent. On every ledge the Dwellers raised their arms up above their heads and outwards in an attitude of supplication.

Then it dawned on Kasstovaal what it all meant. His mind made the connection it should have made earlier.

"Get back from the edge," he hissed in Jeryant's ear.

"Eh!" Jeryant was still transfixed by the sight of the black shadow heaving itself above the horizon, which was in truth no horizon.

Kasstovaal took him by the shoulder and pulled him back, breaking the spell.

"What're you doing?" Jeryant asked.

"I think I've worked out what they're all doing out here," said Kasstovaal. "I don't think we want to be standing among them it starts."

"When what starts?"

"You said that the Dwellers have a stockpile of energy built up in their bodies. Energy they need to get rid of."

"Yes. Pretty urgently, I should say, by the look of them."

"Well Te told me that the chief characteristic of these voids is that they attract energy. I suppose they must be like black holes in our universe, only not anywhere as strong otherwise we wouldn't be standing here now. Don't you see? What easier way is there of getting rid of a load of energy you don't want?"

Jeryant slapped a palm against his forehead, "Of course."

"And since we're not producing a surplus, I don't think we want to be caught up in it. It might drain us down to nothing."

"Should we go back inside? Just to be safe?"

"I want to see this, if I can," said Kasstovaal, "I might not have any instruments to measure that thing with but at least I'll know what to expect next time perihelion comes round. Just be ready to duck back inside and seal the door if you feel anything happening."

The vibration in their ears grew louder. They both looked out towards space. The void had risen clear of the base and was pulling its bulk up the face of the sky, just coming into view over the lip of the ledge on which the two humans stood with their backs against the rock wall.

An aura started to form around each of the Dwellers ranged along the ledge, a glow engulfing their bodies that grew steadily brighter as the void rose higher in the sky.

The humans looked down at themselves. There was no such aura forming around them.

"I think we'll be all right." Jeryant shouted over the noise. "They must be willing it to happen. I suppose they would need to control the flow of energy somehow, otherwise the void would take the lot. I doubt if it's discerning enough to know when to stop."

The rumbling rose still further and they had to cover their ears with their hands. The Rock under their feet felt as though it were vibrating as well now.

The void dominated the sky, a perfect black disc, larger than any of the suns or moons Kasstovaal had seen from the surface of planets before. It occupied more than half of his field of vision. No, not occupied. It took away half his field of vision, stealing the light he would have seen like it stole away everything else. Anything it could get hold of.

He couldn't make out a single feature on its surface. He couldn't even tell if it was a sphere or just a flat circular hole into...wherever it led. The mist around its edges became ragged as it was sucked in but it disappeared the instant it touched the edge, never seeming to pass across its surface. He wondered if it looked the same from behind or to one side of it.

In front of him, the glow around the Dwellers seemed to reach a peak of brightness and then extended forwards from their bodies, each creating a beam of pure energy lancing out towards the void. The beams maintained a straight line for some distance. Then, as the grip of the void took hold of them, they distorted, bent into random curves and crazy wave patterns by the force that eventually swallowed them up.

The Dwellers kept pouring out the unwanted energy as though trying to glut the void, something their meagre efforts could never do. Every ledge was afire with glowing bodies radiating energy.

Then Kasstovaal felt the first wave escape from the Dwellers nearest to him. That is, he felt a brief surge of elation electrify his body for no reason he knew of and he deduced that one of the Dwellers had let it slip.

Elation? It didn't fit. If he was right, all they were actually doing was performing a natural bodily function, much like a human would eat or excrete. The experience might well induce relief, possibly even pleasure. Elation, though, he would not have expected.

He tried shouting at Jeryant, "Did you feel that?" But it was clear that nothing could be heard over the noise. The protection of their hands was no longer enough to keep it out of their ears.

Stupid, he thought to himself. Why the hells am I using my hands anyway. His visualised in his mind the texture and density of the material he wanted and formed four earplugs of dense sponge rubber on the ledge. He bent down quickly, grabbed two of them in his fingers and shoved them into his ears as fast as he could, wincing in pain at the brief exposure to the racket. The plugs fitted in snugly and cut the rumble down to a dull hum in his ears.

He scooped up the other two plugs and held them in front of Jeryant's face. The medic nodded understanding. Kasstovaal held one of the plugs close to Jeryant's left ear, pushing it home as Jeryant whipped his hand away.

When both plugs were in place, the medic gave an expansive sigh of relief. That was about as complicated as their conversation could be. The only form of sign language both of them knew was the standard hand signals they taught you in Hostile Atmosphere training for when the communicator in your HA suit broke down. Kasstovaal hadn't a hope of communicating what he'd just felt that way. It would have to wait until afterwards.

Instead, he moved away from the wall a little so that he could look along the row of Dwellers. He spotted Te a short distance away to his right and as he watched her, he felt one of her waves flow through him. He recognised the feel of it, the bubbling, childlike freshness that was uniquely Te's. He had felt that same wave from her before, during his wild ride out to the Barrier. The sheer exhilaration of speed and freedom.

He saw her sway on the brink of the ledge, energy still streaming out of her. Was something wrong? Had she given up too much to the hunger of the void?

Before he could think fully what he was doing, he had started easing his way along the ledge behind the rank of Dwellers towards her. He could see her face through the glowing aura placid and unconcerned. She swayed again and stumbled a little as she adjusted her footing to bring her back upright.

Kasstovaal arrived behind her. This close he could feel wave after wave of emotion bursting out of her; exhilaration, joy, fulfilment, relief. And then a hint of sorrow, regret, frustration. It became uncomfortable as his body reacted to each fresh wave wrenching his gut first one way then the other. He had to fight it, to persuade his mind to block them out and concentrate.

She swayed again, forwards this time, and he was sure she was about to topple off the ledge and away down the slope or even out into space. Pure instinct made him reach out to grab her arm and steady her.

The moment his fingers touched the cold skin the full, undissipated force of the waves radiating from her roared up his arm and through his body. Every nerve in his body screamed with the contradictory cocktail of her feelings, many times more powerful than any he had ever felt within himself. Overloaded, they could not pass on the instruction he sent to his hand to let go of her. Then the universe whitened in front of his eyes, became too bright to see.

Jeryant saw him go towards Te but hesitated to follow him. He saw Kasstovaal catch hold of her as she pitched forward and then the aura that surrounded her reached out for him too, wrapping him in light.

Jeryant started forward. Kasstovaal was frozen to the spot and Jeryant knew that if he didn't break that connection soon, his friend would be sucked dry.

To Kasstovaal it was irrelevant. Everything was irrelevant. All the fears and petty worries that his body imposed on his life were gone. He was free, his mind totally unencumbered by the tyranny of the physical universe. Only his thoughts mattered. His thoughts could go anywhere. He could do anything but had no need. There were no obligations, no requirements, no priorities, nothing to get in the way. Only pure thought. He was free, freer than he had ever dreamed possible.

But not yet, something told him suddenly. You cannot have this freedom yet. You have not earned it yet. And the sorrow and regret that swept over him with that thought was more than he could bear. To have such a paradise so near you could reach out and grasp it and yet not be allowed to extend your hand for it.

But these were not his thoughts, he realised. They felt wrong inside his head. He was touching the mind of Te, laid wide open and naked with the purging of her energies so that even he could see the pattern of her thoughts.

Kasstovaal saw them and understood them. At last, he understood them. All the little inconsistencies he'd noticed, things he hadn't noticed but remembered still. They suddenly made sense to him and the new-found knowledge chilled him to the very core of his soul.

But he had no time to react to it. He felt an incredible tiredness fall over him like a solid weight. The impossible brightness before his eyes went out and left him in blackness. The blackness of the Voidrise swallowing him up.

Jeryant reached Kasstovaal and then hesitated about what he should do. There was no way he was touching either of them. Common sense and the little he knew about energy conduction told him that would be an extremely bad idea. Right, he thought, what I need here is insulation. He didn't have Kasstovaal's technical repertoire but hit upon rubber as being a pretty safe bet as a non-conductor. He had to act fast; had to think fast. All he needed was something to push Kasstovaal away from Te and break the connection. Something fairly large and solid and made of rubber.

There was one object that would, inevitably, spring to Jeryant's mind given those three specifications. It was probably just as well that Kasstovaal wasn't conscious of what happened next. Being thumped in the midsection by an inflatable rubber woman is, to say the least, undignified though knowing Jeryant as he did Kasstovaal would not have been surprised if he had known.

But it did the trick. Kasstovaal fell sideways and sprawled onto the ledge. Jeryant un-formed his temporary helper and resolved never to tell Kasstovaal about it. He knelt down and did his best to examine the unconscious man but the bio-form gave him none of the signs he would usually have looked for.

He put his arms under the other man's shoulders and began to haul him back towards the door.

Above them, the bloated void heaved itself past the summit and finally began to shrink as it climbed away from the Rock. One by one the aura around each Dweller went out. As it did so they dropped their arms, turned and began to make their way back inside. There was no hurry anymore, not one of them showed the slightest sign of their earlier agitation. They were back to normal, impassive, in control.

Jeryant got Kasstovaal inside the doorway and propped him up against the wall. The only thing he could think of doing was slapping the man's face but it didn't achieve anything.

He felt somebody crouch down beside him and looked round. It was Oa, looking calm and collected again.

Jeryant took the plugs out of his ears. "I think he got a bit too close for comfort," he said. "You might have warned us about that out there."

"There should not have been any danger," said Oa. "The excess energy must be projected by will. We did not foresee this. It has never happened before."

"I suppose it wouldn't have, if you all let off steam together every time."

"Let us take him to my laboratory," said Oa. "I do not think his energy has been depleted too far but we will make certain."

Outside, the mists took over again, blurring and then hiding the void from view.

Voidrise was over. But it would return. It always did. It always must.

18.

For the first time since he had woken up in his new body, Kasstovaal found sleep. It had evaded him up to now, despite his attempts to find it. Jeryant had advised him to try and keep to a normal human cycle of eating and sleeping, despite the fact that his body didn't need him to do either of those things.

"Our minds are locked into that cycle," he had said. "It's become ingrained into our instincts. It doesn't matter that our bodies don't need them anymore. Our instincts still expect us to go through the motions. If we don't, those instincts will get thrown out of phase and then you're looking at serious psychological imbalance. Much as I hate to remind you, old son, you're already working with a deficit in that area. At least try."

He had tried. Eating was no problem, just an inconvenience, but the nearest he'd managed to get to sleep was a light snooze. Now, though, his drained body plunged him down to a deep sleep frequency, a level that regenerated and healed. And his dreams were full of voids, bloated black eyes watching him, calling to him, offering him a way out. The last way out.

All it takes is our word, they whispered to him. All you have to do to earn our word is to give us something we want. One item only. Then you can be free.

"One item of what?" he asked.

The answer was a word, shouted in a whisper from all around him. "Knowledge!"

He felt himself beginning to wake up, began to be aware of the padding of his bed underneath him, felt his thoughts begin to reassert themselves.

No, not yet. He needed to sleep a little longer. It had given his mind a chance to process and file away the information it had taken on board over the last week, throwing up dreams as it sifted the data. He might not manage so deep a sleep again so he had to make the most of it. There was one thing still missing.

He did not try to will himself to sleep; that was the surest way of waking himself fully. Instead he let himself relax back into the darkness, thinking about nothing, letting his mind do the work on its own.

He felt himself dip back into sleep and then out again. He had reached the borderline, the transitional point where the consciousness switches on and off from moment to moment as the mind walks the line, stepping first on one side then the other. That was the level he wanted.

There was one question that he still wanted answered. The Barrier; what was wrong with the Barrier? He was no longer prepared to mark it down as fanciful thinking on his part. He was thinking like a Pilot-Captain again and a Pilot-Captain never ignored his gut feelings. They were trained to feel the rhythms of the ships they commanded, to feel through the seat of their pants any slightest change in the vibrations. It became instinctive and microscopically honed. Changes too slight for anyone else to notice, or even for the instruments to detect, would ring alarm bells in the mind of the Pilot-Captain, who wouldn't hesitate to have the crew stripping down the circuits on the strength of it. You couldn't take any chances with a spacecraft, especially if you were carrying passengers.

That was how it was now with Kasstovaal. Something in his instincts had detected an anomaly in connection with the Barrier and was trying to draw his attention to it. He had to work out what that anomaly was.

He didn't try to force the question into his mind, just let it slide in of its own accord so that his mind could carry it into his unconscious the next time it dipped in. That was where his instincts lay, his unconscious. Perhaps they would answer.

There was a brief moment of non-time as he slipped back over the boundary. When his mind returned again, it did not come back with an answer as he'd hoped. It came back with the question twisted into another form. Lateral thinking. It was no longer "What is the anomaly?" it was now "How would I have detected an anomaly?"

It was a good question. Detecting an anomaly in the operation of a spaceship was one thing, since he knew spaceships down to the last component. The Barrier was something else entirely, since he knew little more about it now than when he'd first encountered it.

Logically, the anomaly had to be something he had been trained to recognise, otherwise he would never have detected it on any level. He only had the most rudimentary knowledge of the Barrier so it had to be something quite fundamental.

He let that reasoning laze across his mind and waited for it to dip back down into the well of sleep. It did so a couple of times more without coming back with an answer. It was becoming more difficult to keep himself at that level. Staying relaxed was becoming a strain and the moment that happened, one would negate the other and he would be awake and that would be that.

He managed to sink down, one last time, into the darkness and when his mind emerged it had the answer. It was so obvious.

Kasstovaal was suddenly wide awake and sitting up on his bed. Of course! Why hadn't he seen it before? There was no one else in the room with him. They had apparently determined that he had suffered no damage from the draining of the Voidrise and had left him to sleep it off.

He sat there for a few seconds, wondering what he should do. Think like a Pilot-Captain, he told himself. Now that you've got a handle on the problem, the first thing to do is to confirm your suspicions. You can worry about what to do about it afterwards.

He swung himself off the bed and went to sit at the table. Despite all the computers and stylus pads human technology had come up with, he still found that he worked better with paper and pencil. It helped him think a problem through, allowed him to break it down into small components he could work with.

He formed himself a sheet and a graphite pencil and started to work. It wasn't a very complicated device he wanted, not compared to some of the machines he'd built over the years. The actual science behind it was ancient stuff, dating back to the dark times of the pre-Galactic age. As crude as the hells, but effective.

He approached the actual design of his device in reverse, starting with the emitter which would produce the actual effect he wanted and working backwards from that to build up the circuitry that would make the emitter do what he wanted it to. Circuit diagrams came as easily to him as handwriting and creating the circuit design was a simple logic puzzle.

After an hour, by his clock, he had a design he was happy with. He checked it through several times, running his eyes along the circuit and visualising in his mind the twists and turns each component inflicted on the energies from the power pack.

Once again he had to consider the problem of calibration. He'd managed without anything too accurate for the clock, since it wasn't important. With this device accuracy was going to be vital, and moreover, it had to be accurate in Dweller units of measurement. He could no longer put off the task of working out just how much of anything one unit was.

He could just ask one of the Dwellers to demonstrate a unit of everything to him but he didn't want to involve the Dwellers in this experiment. If he found what he expected to find, he wasn't sure that he wanted to let Dwellers know about it.

There was only one alternative. He would have to consult the Chamber of Knowledge. There had to be references everywhere in there, measurements he could compare to the real thing. He just had to find a few of them; three or four would be sufficient to calibrate the device.

He got up and was about to form himself a doorway when it occurred to him that the best way to keep the Dwellers from finding out the results of his tests was to not let them know he was conducting any. That could be easier said than done, since the Rock knew where everyone was and what everyone was doing and wouldn't hesitate to pass that information on to anyone who asked.

On the other hand, who other than Vo, Te and Oa were likely to ask? Those three, and Jeryant as well come to that, might make the reasonable assumption that the first thing Kasstovaal would do when he woke up would be to go and find one of them, if only to ask what had happened. Up to a point, therefore, they would assume that he was still asleep if he didn't show his face. Jeryant might look in on his way past, though, just to check.

Kasstovaal thought about it for a moment and then concentrated his will on the bed. Hells, he looked like a badly made foam-rubber dummy anyway. As such the foam rubber dummy that appeared on the bed a few seconds later was a perfect likeness and Kasstovaal reflected that he probably wouldn't have managed it if he'd still been wearing his old body.

With any luck, Jeryant would just look in through one of his novelty doorways and see the figure on the bed, apparently still asleep, and leave it at that. If he didn't, it wouldn't take him long to work out the deception, in which case Kasstovaal would have to hope that he had the sense to keep his mouth shut.

Kasstovaal folded the circuit diagram and took it with him. He didn't seriously believe that he could deceive them all long enough for him to get finished, not with a dummy. But it would give him some breathing space, after which he would have to bluff it out.

He took a circuitous route to the Chamber of Knowledge, avoiding the corridors that the three Dwellers or Jeryant might have used to reach his room.

It brought him to the top level of the Chamber and he had to descend a few levels in the tube. He managed to make his descent fairly smoothly, this time, and didn't draw any additional attention from the Dwellers moving among the racks.

What he needed were references to measurements of distance, preferably ones that could be measured again now with the same result. The height of the Rock itself would be a good one, for a start. That value probably hadn't changed in millennia, despite the apparently fluid nature of its interior design.

Since, he decided, measuring the Rock was not likely to form part of any Dweller's life purpose he searched for it among the pre-purpose crystal fragments in the side tray. Surprisingly, there were very few references to the dimensions of the Rock. Perhaps it was an exercise so basic for a Dweller child that they didn't bother to record it. Or perhaps it was just another one of those things the Dwellers took for granted, the same way that he took it for granted that planets were spherical.

He found one crystal, however, that contained exactly what he needed. Apparently one young Dweller, in the recent past, had been set the task of building and testing a distance-measuring device, by her Primary Parent, as an exercise. She had settled on the method of firing a radium pulse between two points and then measuring how much the radiation decayed during its journey. It was a very accurate method, producing reliable measurements to ten decimal places. The young Dweller had been very enthusiastic about testing her device and had measured virtually every room and fixture that remained unaltered by successive users.

That one crystal contained not only the height of the Rock but, also the dimensions of the Chamber of Knowledge and the Gathering Place, including the distances of all the bridges from the floor level, and the Chamber of Purpose and the distances to the nearest three planets and the Barrier, as well. She had noted all of these statistics down carefully in the record, along with footnotes to the effect that her measurements more or less matched those made previously, according to her research, though her figures were more accurate. More than enough benchmarks for Kasstovaal's purpose.

He took the crystal away with him; it did not appear to be in demand. The next thing he needed was a workshop, preferably a long way from his room. He made his way down the innermost spiral, taking the shortest route to the base level of the Rock where the spirals ended. This level was, of course, the one with the largest area and, consequently, the greatest number of rooms. Kasstovaal had come down here with the empty idea that Dwellers might prefer to occupy the higher levels, filling those up first, and therefore leaving a lot of the rooms on this level empty. Oddly enough, this appeared to be quite true. He found a corridor, joining two others, in which all the rooms were empty. He opened up the one in the centre, to be as far away from others as he could, and sealed the doorway behind him. The room was bare, waiting for someone to fill it and give it a purpose, a name.

He formed a large workbench in the centre of the floor and laid out his circuit diagram.

He closed his eyes and began to form components in his mind.

The work went quickly, with an almost dreamlike ease, all the more so when Kasstovaal realised he didn't actually need to form individual components, one by one, and then fit them together by hand. If he disciplined his mind and focused clearly on the whole pattern, he could form complete, functional circuit boards that only needed to be slotted into place. Also, for a single-handed engineering job, the power to shrink or expand the dimensions of any component, so that they fitted exactly, was a godsend that many of Kasstovaal's colleagues would have killed to possess.

Programming the processor chips took a little time. While he could form the structure of the chip itself, he couldn't manage to form it with the program locked into the structure. He tried it several times but the moment his mind let go of the new chip, it would reset itself and become blank. He couldn't seem to focus enough power to hold the program in the chip until it was fully formed. In the end he had to give up and wasted a couple of hours lashing together a basic hexadecimal hand programmer and splitting the program down into hi-Basic language.

Eventually, though, he sealed up the last edge on the pair of black rectangular boxes that were the finished machine, a master unit and a smaller slave unit. He had managed to compact them enough to be hand held, which was an un-looked-for bonus.

Now the calibration came in. He started with simple tests, just to make sure the system worked properly. He formed six pieces of wood about an inch thick and of an equal but indeterminate length. He put the boxes down on the workbench, face to face, and placed one of the pieces tight between them to define a distance. He triggered the master box to scan and measure the distance and then, using the programmer, he instructed it to recognise that distance as one unit. Then he used a second length of wood to double the distance and triggered the scan again. As he'd hoped the box registered exactly two units.

He repeated the experiment progressively with all six wood pieces, putting the boxes on the floor to get enough clear space between them. Each time they came out exactly correct.

That was good. Now he had to adjust it to measure in real Dweller units.

He consulted the crystal and jotted down on a scrap of paper the measurements the young Dweller had taken in the Gathering Place. Then he took hold of a box in each hand, lodged the scrap of paper between two fingers, clamped the programmer under one arm and headed out into the corridor.

He passed a couple of Dwellers on his way up the spiral. Both gave him a polite greeting, which he did his best to return, but neither showed any special interest in the equipment he was carrying.

Just as well, he thought. If one of those two Dwellers had asked him what it was he was carrying he would either have had to lie, which they would probably have sensed, or he would have had to explain why he had built it, which he didn't want to do.

The Gathering Place was deserted when he got there. Just how he wanted it. He consulted his list. The first measurement was from the floor level to the first bridge, about fifteen levels up. The crystal had recorded a distance of 0.2105033721 of a unit

He positioned the slave box on the floor right up against the wall to get his best chance of a straight line shot and then carried the master box up to the bridge level.

He had equipped the master box with a telescopic cross hair sight to aim more accurately at the target point marked on the slave. Obviously it would be useless for measuring the Barrier but at the calibration stage he needed all the accuracy he could get.

He crouched down on the ledge, near where it met the bridge, and sighted on the slave box. He was directly above it. He took aim and fired the scan. He could ignore the figure that came up on the display, this time, since it had no meaning outside the workshop. Instead he used the programmer to recalibrate the master box so that it recognised that distance as 0.21050 of a unit.

Now, in theory, the system should measure, pretty accurately, in Dweller distance units. He needed to test just how accurate it was. He moved up to the next bridge, and measured the distance down to the slave box. 0.45109 units. He consulted his notes.

The young Dweller had come up with a figure of 0.4510795569 units, but then she had been using a much more efficient system. Still, the difference couldn't be more than a couple of millimetres and since he was doing this by hand that sort of error margin was more than acceptable.

He repeated the experiment on the next four bridge levels and got the same sort of results.

A Dweller came across the third bridge, while he was lining up the cross hairs on the shrinking target below, and gave him a greeting. He jumped and almost dropped the box. He clung to it desperately and managed to hold on to it.

"My apologies," said the Dweller, obviously contrite, "I did not mean to startle you."

"It's fine," he said, easing back onto the ledge until his nerves stopped jangling, "I was concentrating too hard. I didn't hear you coming."

"You are conducting an experiment?" the Dweller asked.

Damn, thought Kasstovaal, an inquisitive one. "I'm doing some forming practice," he said. "I wanted to see if I could put together some micro-circuitry that actually worked." It wasn't actually a lie. He had wanted to hone his forming skills. He was just being economical with the truth and hoping like the hells that the Dweller hadn't noticed.

"Are you having success?"

"So far. I need to do a few more tests yet."

"Then I shall not keep you from them." The Dweller turned and disappeared through one of the archways. Kasstovaal held on to his relief as long as he could before letting it go in a deep sigh.

He pondered weather or not to run a few more tests in here but decided against it. It would be accurate enough for what he wanted. He might as well stop procrastinating and get on with it.

He circled back down to the arena, picked up the slave box and then headed back down towards the base level. It seemed to be the best place to conduct the test from, being the closest point on the Rock to the Barrier.

First, though, he had to work out in which direction the Barrier was. There was no point in returning to the same ledge they had used before. The Rock was spinning on its axis so that point on the Rock's face wouldn't necessarily be facing in the right direction.

Nor would it have helped if Kasstovaal had managed to take note of the void constellations visible in front of him. The voids themselves were on the move; the Voidrise had proved that.

Te had known instantly in which direction to lead him. How had she done that? Perhaps she could sense it in some way. Or perhaps it was simpler than that.

There was one other thing he needed. He made his way, circumspectly, back to his room, made a non-functional replica of his clock and took the original away with him. The dummy him still lay undisturbed.

He opened a doorway and stepped out onto the lowest ledge of the Rock. Beneath his feet were, perhaps, eighteen inches of rock and then nothing. He could just step off into space, but couldn't be sure of falling.

He needed a bearing. He turned and faced the rock wall and formed a question in his mind, "Which way do I go to reach the Barrier?"

It might know, after all. The thing was at least halfway intelligent and if it could keep track of thirty thousand small Dwellers, then it should be able to keep an eye on something millions of times bigger than it was.

The answer he got back was not the one he wanted, though that was better than no answer at all.

Go any way you like, it said. You will reach the Barrier.

"Damn!" He should've expected that. Of course, you could head off in any direction in three-dimensional space and, if you kept going long enough, you would eventually reach the Barrier. It was his own fault, he supposed, for not phrasing his question carefully enough. Either that or the floating mountain was intelligent enough to be pedantic, and that thought worried him.

He tried again. "Which direction would take me to the Barrier in the shortest possible time?"

That worked. This way, the Rock said to him and urged him to his right. This way.

He made his way along the ledge, carrying the boxes with him and watching where he trod. The Rock led him around about a quarter of the circumference and suddenly told him to stop.

Here, it said.

He turned and looked outwards. The mists, sparsely dotted with voids, revealed nothing.

He formed a piece of red chalk and marked the spot with a cross. Then he waited, watching the clock. All the time, he knew, the Rock was spinning that cross away from the Barrier. He would give himself thirty minutes to reach it, so he had to work out how far the Rock would spin in that time.

When the clock reached thirty minutes he asked the Rock to show him again where the nearest point was. It led him away from the cross about forty paces and then told him to stop. Kasstovaal marked the new spot with a cross and then went back for the slave box. He paced out the distance between the two crosses and then continued on around the curve for the same distance again. In a little under half an hour's time this spot would be nearest to the Barrier and it was here that he set down the slave unit, up against the rock wall.

He hurried back to his equipment. The next thing he needed was transport. The pattern for the plates came easily to his mind and he was able to form one twice the length of the previous one. He fused the master unit and the clock onto the rear and floated it. Then he set out.

There were a number of problems Kasstovaal had had to address when he designed his measuring device. He had realised that the time-honoured and tested method of bouncing laser beams or tachion streams or even primitive radio waves probably wouldn't work on the Barrier. It certainly felt solid but since he didn't know what the hells it was made of he couldn't count on any of those things to bounce off it reliably enough to measure.

So he had to design a terminal at both ends of the measurement, a master terminal to send out the initial pulse and a slave terminal to return the pulse back to the master terminal. The amount of time that took was the determining factor.

He had thought about using the same system as the Dweller whose crystal he had borrowed. The problem was that he didn't think there was any way of reliably sticking one of the terminals to the Barrier's surface, especially with those pulses of light or energy, or whatever it was, passing across it all the time. He would have to actually hold one of the terminals up against the surface in order to make his measurement.

There was also the fact that he wouldn't be able to visually sight on the Rock from the Barrier, because of the mist. That meant that the pulses had to be wide-beamed, otherwise he didn't have a hope of hitting the other terminal, even with the wide reception arc he had built into them. That ruled out dangerous radium pulses, not least because he would be standing in the path of them.

He had settled on old-fashioned radio waves, not so accurate but harmless and invisible.

His ride out to the Barrier, this time, was considerably less hair-raising. He could go at his own pace and built up his speed in time with the growth in his confidence. His course was untroubled by voids and any other obstacles and he was able to maintain a straight line all the way out to the Barrier. He reached it with five minutes to spare on the clock. Somewhere back there in the mist the Rock was slowly turning, bringing the slave unit onto a direct line with him.

He unstuck the master unit from the plate and held it flat against the Barrier's solidity. The surface rang slightly at the contact. He switched on and started scanning. He would have to repeat it several times to catch the moment when the slave box was directly facing him and he could get the reading he wanted. At first he got no readings which meant that the slave unit wasn't receiving the pulses. He shifted his position slightly a few times and finally got a response. That first reading was enough to convince him that he had been right. Even with his perceptions being stretched and squeezed by different physical forms, some part of his instincts, the part that drew on his navigation skills, had sensed that the distance from the Rock to the Barrier had decreased in the time between his first and second visits to it.

The past measurements of that distance, had all been virtually the same, differing only in the accuracy of the methods successive Dwellers had used. The consensus of all of them was that the Barrier should be 10,320.1 units away from the Rock at it nearest point.

Kasstovaal's device said that it was only 10,010 units and that figure slowly decreased as the slave terminal came further into line. It bottomed out at 10,005.7575 and then began rising again as the spin of the Rock took the slave terminal away from him again. That was the figure he wanted and it was not good.

He started back towards the Rock, using the master unit as a kind of tracker, stopping every so often to scan for the slave unit and using that as his guide.

He would have to conduct other tests. See if the nearest planets were the same distance from the Rock they had always been. That would tell him weather it was the Rock or the Barrier that was moving. But they could wait until later. The important thing was that the gap between the two, fixed for countless millennia, was now closing. And there could be only one explanation.

19.

The gun was finished. Kasstovaal, perched on a stool in front of his workbench, checked it over for the umpteenth time and wondered whether he should risk test firing it. It was another fairly crude job, the sort of focused beamer first year cadets lashed up in their spare time to make sure their energetics lessons had sunk in. Weapons were not really his speciality but, in his own universe, it would be quite capable of injuring or killing. Could it hurt a Dweller, though?

It fitted comfortably into his hand, the weight of it reassured him. In his heart he hoped he wouldn't have to use it but its presence took away some of that feeling that plagued him. The feeling of being at a disadvantage, a fatal disadvantage. That small insistent voice in the back of his mind that whispered "Danger! Danger!" all the time. "Beware of them. Do not trust. Keep an eye always looking over your shoulder in case death is coming up behind you. Never let your guard down. Never let go."

It liked the weapon, that little voice. That was the real power that all weapons had. A radiation that effected the emotions of anyone near them. The power to cause fear, even when they were not fired, and to neutralise the fear in the one holding it. They could convince you that you had power you didn't have.

He felt the doorway beginning to form before he saw it. Fear of being discovered had heightened his perceptions, which were already feeling the benefit of his recent mental exercises.

It suddenly dawned on him that he didn't have anywhere to hide the gun. He hadn't felt the need to form any drawers in the workbench or cupboards for the few tools he had put together. Nor did he have a convenient pocket he could slip it into, since he was still completely naked. That fact had slipped his mind completely, now that he had got used to not needing clothes and, since he wasn't feeling self-conscious, part of his mind assumed that that meant he was fully dressed. Pockets and all.

He had a split second of guilty panic and then his eyes registered that the new doorway was arse-shaped. He relaxed, but only a little.

Jeryant strode in from the corridor and looked about him. "So this is where you're hiding, is it sunshine?" he said. "Not very diplomatic of you. Still, you needn't worry. I've covered for you, though I'm buggered if I know why I...."

He trailed off as he saw the gun in Kasstovaal's hand. He gaped at it. "What in the hells are you doing?" he cried.

"We're going to need this, Jery," said Kasstovaal, as calmly as he could.

"Like hells we will." Jeryant marched forward, menacingly.

Kasstovaal instinctively raised the gun and pointed it at him before he realised what he was doing.

Jeryant came on, unafraid. "What're you going to do with it, Kass?" he growled. "Shoot me? I'd like to see you bloody well try."

He fixed his eyes on the gun. Kasstovaal felt it turn to stone in his hand. He dropped it and it shattered on the floor.

"And that's just what I can do," said Jeryant. "A Dweller could do the same thing in a fraction of the time, long before you could pull the trigger. Or worse, they could make it blow up in your face if they had a mind to. Personally, I doubt that they would, no matter how much you provoke them."

"Do you?" Kasstovaal asked, dully.

"Yes, I do. Why don't you, Kass? Tell me!"

"Because I've seen how their minds work. I don't just know from watching them, I've seen it first hand. When I touched Te I saw into her mind. They don't value life, Jery."

"What are you on about?" Jeryant demanded. "They went to pains to save our lives, not long ago, or had you forgotten. Why would they do that if they didn't value life?"

"You don't understand," said Kasstovaal. "You didn't feel what I felt in her mind. For a while during the Voidrise she knew what it was to be really free. Not to be held down by a physical body, just existing as free thought floating among the mists. Becoming part of them. I felt what it was like."

"Well?"

"She knew that feeling, not just from previous Voidrises. She knew what it was like to exist in that form. She remembered it and longed for it. I felt her regretting that she'd lost that freedom and couldn't have it back yet. Don't you see what that means, Jery?"

Jeryant said nothing, struggling to wrap his mind around what he'd just heard.

"Think about how they're born," Kasstovaal went on. "They are formed out of thought energy drawn from the mists outside. We both saw it. Living thoughts being caught and trapped inside a body. Having their freedom taken away from them. No wonder the Dwellers feel grief when the Compulsion forces them to create a new Dweller. They know that they are condemning that life force to a lifetime imprisonment inside a lump of flesh. The same as they themselves were condemned once. That's what the child has to forgive them for, in their maturity ceremony. Imagine what it must feel like. It would be like burying someone alive."

Jeryant asked, slowly, "Are you saying that the Dwellers don't want to live?"

"More than that," said Kasstovaal, "they actively want to die at the earliest opportunity. But they aren't allowed to."

"Why not? What's stopping them?"

"It must be their purposes. Te told me that a purpose lasts a Dweller his whole life. I assumed she meant a whole working life after which they retire like humans do. But she meant it literally. A Dweller is brought into existence for the completion of one specific purpose. Nothing else. Once they have completed that task they can let go and, somehow, free themselves from their bodies."

"Incredible," said Jeryant.

"We should've seen it before now," said Kasstovaal. "We've been spending all our time trying to work out how these people live their lives and we never thought to ask them how they die."

"Well you don't," said Jeryant, "not in the early stages of an investigation. It's morbid at best. At worst, it could be a social taboo."

"Not here, though," said Kasstovaal. "Here the death of the body is the crowning achievement, the goal that they are all striving for. You go and ask Vo or Te or Oa or any of them what they think about death. I'll bet they're not shy talking about it. Quite the reverse, I expect. There's a lot about this universe that's the reverse of what you might expect."

"All right," said Jeryant. "Let's assume you're right. Gods know, it explains a lot of things. But there's still no call for you to start waving guns around. They know we're the aliens around here. They're not going to expect us to automatically follow their customs. Nor do I think they will try and impose their customs on us."

"Would you care to bet your life on that? I wouldn't. In truth, I don't believe Te or Vo or Oa would. I don't know about the rest of them. I wouldn't put it past Ra or Ko, for a start. Priests can get highly voluble about the letter of the law when it suits them."

"Nobody's voiced any reservations about us yet," said Jeryant, reasonably. "We're a scientific curiosity. I would say that's a purpose with a lot of mileage on it. And we certainly don't pose a threat to them, not if that pop-gun on the floor is the best you can come up with."

"Oh don't we?" said Kasstovaal ominously. "Do you know what I've been doing in here all this time?"

"What, apart from tooling up for a war you mean?" said Jeryant, perching himself on he edge of the work bench. "I was wondering, now you mention it. Incidentally, I'm insulted that you'd think I wouldn't know the difference between a sleeping body and a dummy. Even at a distance. I'm not that bad a medic."

Kasstovaal had the decency to look guilty. "How long ago did you find out?"

"About seven hours or so, I would say."

"Seven hours? And you've only now come looking for me?"

"I didn't think there was any trouble you could be getting yourself into. Besides which it didn't take me long to work out that you wanted to do whatever it was you were doing in private. I'm not totally thick, you know. So I went back to the Dwellers and made an excuse for you."

"You told them I was still unconscious?"

"No, actually. That wouldn't have worked. There's only so long you can stay unconscious without arousing concern and I'm sure your dummy wouldn't have stood up to a medical scan, if Oa had suggested one to make sure. What I told them was that you'd just woken up, when I came in, and said you were still feeling tired. And I'd told you to rest up for a few hours more. They accepted that. After that I had to stick around for a few hours. After weaving that story, I could hardly run off to go looking for you, could I."

"Jery, I've been underestimating you all these years. Underneath that dirty-old-man exterior is a really devious son-of-a-bitch trying to get out."

"Don't be sarcastic," said Jeryant. "I'll amaze you yet. Anyway, when I did finally prise myself away from them, I asked the Rock where you were and it said that you'd left. I nearly had kittens. Where the hells did you get to?"

"I went out to the Barrier. I wanted to measure how far away it was."

"Why?"

"I got the feeling that the distance had shortened. I've been out to the Barrier twice before, once when I first got here and was floating around in the mists with no body and then again when Te took me. As a Pilot, you get a feeling for distances, even in space flight."

"I'll take your word for that. Has the distance changed?"

"Yes. By my reckoning the Barrier is now something like fifty-nine kilometres nearer the Rock than it was when the Dwellers last measured it."

"So what? Planetary bodies usually move around a lot, I gather. A damn sight more than fifty-nine kilometres."

"In our universe, yes," said Kasstovaal. "But not here. The Dwellers have been measuring that distance, on and off, for centuries and it hasn't changed significantly once in all that time. I haven't quite got my head around their time units but as far as I can tell the most recent measurement was made not more than a month before we arrived. And that said the same as the rest."

"And now we're here and it's started to change," said Jeryant, "that's what you're getting at, isn't it? You think we're causing it to happen."

"I can't see any other candidates," said Kasstovaal. "It would take something pretty major to cause a change like that."

"Doesn't that rule us out? Alien we might be but I can't see us upsetting the flow of a whole universe all on our own."

"But that's exactly what we are doing. It's all to do with the conservation of matter."

Jeryant held up a finger. "Don't start talking physics to me," he warned. "Physics makes my brain ache. Keep it simple."

"Look," said Kasstovaal, "it's generally accepted that when our universe exploded into being, it contained a fixed amount of matter. During the course of eternity that matter is going to be changed and rechanged into millions of different forms; different elements, different compounds, different reactions. But the overall mass isn't going to change because the existing matter cannot be destroyed and no new matter can be created. When the universe finally ends, however it happens, there should still be exactly the same amount of matter present as when it started. Presumably the same applies in this universe and the Second Mode as well."

"I'm with you so far," said Jeryant. "What's your point?"

"The point is, that's not true anymore. Our universe is now light by the combined mass of two men plus a space ship. And this universe is suddenly heavy by the same amount. We've upset the balance of both universes."

"Not that much, surely!" protested Jeryant. "Our weight and the ship's can't be enough to have an effect on a whole universe."

"You think not? I grant you that, in a big universe like ours, the effect would be hardly noticeable. If it were, we wouldn't be able to pop in and out of the Second Mode as much as we do. But this universe is trillions of times smaller than ours. So the effect on it is going to be trillions of times greater."

"But what effect?"

"I'm not sure. It might be something as simple as gravity. That small amount of extra mass might be generating enough gravity to pull the Barrier inwards, like a microscopic Black Hole. Whatever it is, I'm convinced that we're causing it. And if it continues the Rock and the Barrier will eventually smash into each other."

"How long before it happens?" asked Jeryant. "And don't tell me you haven't worked it out yet because I know you will have."

Kasstovaal sighed. He'd gone to some pains to work it out the moment he got back to the Rock, though a big part if him loathed to number his days.

"Just over five months." he said "One hundred and fifty-nine days, give or take a few. And that's assuming that the rate of movement remains constant."

"Will the impact destroy the Rock?"

"Almost certainly, I would say. It won't be moving fast but, then, it doesn't need to. There's a lot of inertia in a lump of rock this size. If it were solid rock I suppose part of it might survive. But it isn't. It's a big honeycomb of rooms and corridors. There's no way it'll stand up to that much force."

Jeryant got up and started towards the corridor, "Come on," he said, decisively, "we've got to warn the Dwellers. Bring your figures with you. We'll need them".

Kasstovaal went after him and caught his arm. "Hang on," he said. "You want to go and tell them that, because of us, their world is likely to get smashed? What're you going to say? 'Sorry, guys. It's not our fault.'"

"We can't just do nothing," said Jeryant. "The more warning they get the more time they'll have to act. They could evacuate to another planetoid or something. Hells, with their powers they could probably move the Rock away from it. We owe it to them."

He paused, looking Kasstovaal in the eye. "That's why you wanted that gun, wasn't it. You think when they find out they'll turn on us as the cause."

"Wouldn't our people do exactly that in their place?" asked Kasstovaal, and Jeryant detected the slightest tremble in the words. Kasstovaal was genuinely scared.

"They're not our people, you idiot," he said, sternly. "Hasn't that sunk in yet? They are a rational, logical people. They're going to realise that killing us isn't going to solve the problem because the matter we brought in with us is still going to be here. Whether it's in living bodies or dead ones or just a couple of piles of dust. All that extra poundage is going to be hanging around somewhere. That's right, isn't it?"

"Yes. But evacuation or moving the Rock isn't going to solve the problem either, Jery. The effect won't stop with the Rock, it'll keep going on and on until there are no worlds left to run to. There's only one solution that will stop it."

"Which is?"

"We've got to get out of here. We've got to find a way to leave this universe and take all our excess matter with us. It's the only logical answer. If we can put both universes back into balance the damage will stop."

"And how are you going to work out exactly how much matter that is? Down to the last molecule, I mean. You can't even remember what ship we were travelling in."

"We'll have to guess. We know there was only the two of us and I can't see us being a freighter crew between us. The most likely type would be a two-man Star-runner. Small and Second Mode capable. You don't waste passenger space if you can avoid it."

"And if you're wrong?"

"I don't know. We'll have to hope to reduce the excess mass enough so that it won't have an effect. We can, at least, reduce the effect, that way."

"Then there's all the more reason to tell the Dwellers about the problem now," Jeryant insisted. "We still haven't worked out a way to keep our bodies, or the ship, in one piece through the transit. We're still as stuck as we were before and we need the Dwellers to help us find the answer more than ever now."

"But we don't need to tell them why," said Kasstovaal. "Anyway, at the rate that thing's moving it won't be long before they notice it themselves."

"Only if they look," said Jeryant. "They're all engrossed in their own purposes. Unless one of them gets given a purpose to do with the Barrier, why would they bother to check? It'll be months before it becomes visible through the mist and then it will be too late. We've got to let them know what you've found. We don't have to say we think we're causing it. It's only conjecture, after all."

"It won't take them long to come to the same conclusion," said Kasstovaal. "They're intelligent enough. And at least two of them we know don't like us enough to believe it. The two Dwellers best placed to influence the others, as it happens."

"Well what are you suggesting we do? Just leave them to get crushed? No way, Kass! There is absolutely no way that I'm going to sacrifice an entire world full of people to your paranoia."

That brought Kasstovaal up short. It had never occurred to him that his reasoning might be seen like that. It seemed only sensible to him. He said, "I'm not suggesting that we should abandon them. I'm just saying we need to be careful how we break the news to them. At least let me confirm the findings before we start pushing the panic button. There are other measurements I need to make first. Plus I want to measure the distance to the Barrier again, say in a week's time, just to see if the rate is constant. A week won't make that much difference."

"You hope," said Jeryant, sourly. "All right, you win. There's sense in being sure first. I'll give you a week but no more. After that we both go to Vo and tell him the situation. We can debate about how much to tell him when we know more ourselves. Agreed?"

"Agreed."

"In the meantime," said Jeryant, sitting back down on the bench, "the best thing we can do is to apply ourselves to the problem of getting out of here. If we're already working on that when we tell Vo about the Barrier it won't look like we're trying to leave to flee the danger. That might not go down too well. Besides which, it'll do you good to keep busy. It'll keep your mind off your fears."

"'Okay," said Kasstovaal. "So where do we start?"

"Well, for one thing, we'll need a ship, won't we," said Jeryant, "if only to make up the poundage we take with us. You're the engineer here. Do you reckon you know enough about space ship construction to build one yourself? From the ground upwards and single handed?"

"Oh I know I can," said Kasstovaal, grimly, "I've done it once before."

"You're kidding."

"You've never heard about the criteria for the Pilot-Captain's exam, have you?" said Kasstovaal. "The final aptitude test that earns you your licence."

"No."

"I'm not surprised. It's not talked about outside the academy and you only hear about it inside when you become a serious prospect for the rank."

"Difficult is it, this exam?"

"The principle of it is quite simple. The set task is always the same and every entrant knows what it is before they enter. Each one is locked in a hangar on his own and has three months to build a serviceable one-person space ship. They are given access to all the materials they want with the exception of their text manuals and notes."

"Three months doesn't sound long."

"It's long enough if you know what you're doing. After the three months is up, they then have to fly their ship along a test course, determined by the examiners. A tough one, usually involving at least half a dozen Second Mode transits and taking in every space hazard the examiners can come up with - asteroid fields, atmosphere penetration, black holes, the whole lot. It's a course a commercially built ship would struggle to survive."

"What's the pass mark?" Jeryant asked.

"Oh, the pass mark is even simpler still. If you make it to the end of the course alive, you've passed."

"What?"

"Honestly. If you don't get to the finish alive, you obviously don't know your stuff as well as you should. Of course, any candidate can pull out at any time before running the course or even during the course. But if you're the type to be complacent and are liable to make mistakes, it's better to find out about it while it's just your arse on the line rather than wait until you're carrying five thousand passengers."

"That sounds like the administration's way of thinking," growled Jeryant. "It has that distinctive sub-zero blood temperature about it. Obviously you passed."

"It was a close thing, but yes I did."

"How close a thing?"

"Let's just say I know where I went wrong. So yes, I could build a spaceship for us. With matter-forming to provide the materials it should be a piece of piss."

"Excellent!" said Jeryant.

"The only problem might be the Continuum Interface Destabiliser."

"What does that do?"

"It's the crucial component for Second Modal travel. It's the device which creates the portal between the First and Second modes."

"What's the problem? Can't you build one of those?"

"Sure I can. A normal one for First to Second Mode transits. I don't know if it'll work here though. We've been assuming that this is the Third Mode, as in one along from the Second, but we don't know if that's true. Neither of us can remember how we got here. I don't know that if I create a portal polarised for a return transit it'll take us back into the Second Mode. I don't know if I can create a portal at all, come to that. The continuum fabric might not react in the same way."

"You'll have to experiment, won't you," said Jeryant. "But aside from that, how long do you think the job will take?"

Kasstovaal thought about it. "The matter-forming should save me a month on the exam time," he said. "Less with you helping me."

"Oh no! You're on you own with this one, sunshine," said Jeryant. "I've got my own fish to fry."

"Such as?"

"Well, these bodies aren't suitable for survival in our universe, are they. Somehow or other, I'm going to have to build us two completely new Bio-forms, ones which work in exactly the same way as our old bodies did. I'll have to duplicate every function of the human body down to the last enzyme."

"Is that possible?"

"I think so. Though I say it myself, my knowledge of the human body is extremely comprehensive. Oa and I have been compiling it all on a database. Together, I'm sure we can adapt her Bio-Forming process to create operational tissues. Might not be the real thing but it should work the same."

"It's all academic," said Kasstovaal, "until we find a way to hold the patterns together on the other side of the transit."

"Yes," said Jeryant, getting up a beginning to pace around the floor. "That's the problem. I need to get drunk over this one."

"You what?"

"I said I need to get drunk. I get all my best ideas when I'm drunk."

"That's debatable. The sort of ideas I've seen you get when you're drunk are the sort that get you arrested. Almost every time."

"I know what I'm talking about," said Jeryant, firmly. "It's all about randomising your thoughts so that you think about problems in a different way."

"That's certainly true."

"Don't mock. It never fails."

Kasstovaal sighed. "Well, if you insist, why don't you just form yourself some alcohol. I'm sure it's a pattern your brain is quite familiar with."

"Tried it," said Jeryant. "Doesn't work! This body won't absorb it. I've even tried direct injection and that didn't work either."

"Silly of me," Kasstovaal muttered, "I might have known you'd have tried it already."

Jeryant gave him a dirty look. "I'll have to find something else. The Dweller equivalent or something."

"I can't see the Dwellers having an equivalent to alcohol," said Kasstovaal. "It would get in the way of their purpose."

"Nevertheless, it'll be top of my list to speak to Oa about," said Jeryant.

Just then, a doorway appeared and Te stepped in. "May I enter?" she asked, timidly.

"Of course," said Kasstovaal.

Te sealed the door and looked about her. "You have made yourself a workshop," she said.

"I wanted to try a few things," said Kasstovaal "No one will mind me using this room for a while, will they?"

"Not at all. There are plenty of spares."

"That's good," said Jeryant. "Because we are going to need one or two other rooms to work in. You see, Te, we need to work on a method to get us back to our own universe."

Te looked disappointed. "You wish to leave us?" she asked.

"Not immediately," said Kasstovaal. " But we will have to eventually. We don't belong here, Te. You've made us welcome and we're grateful. But our people will be waiting for us back there."

Te nodded. "Of course. You must return, if a way can be found. There are still many things I wish to learn about you. I hope you will stay long enough for me to do so."

"Our preparations are going to take a while," said Jeryant. "I'm sure we can satisfy your curiosity in that time."

"Good," said Te. "We must speak to Vo and arrange the facilities you need. Any help we can offer, we shall."

"I wonder," said Jeryant, walking over and putting a fatherly arm around Te's shoulders, "if you could answer a simple question for me first, my dear."

Te looked up into his face. "Of course."

"Tell me," said Jeryant, "what your people think about death. The ending of your physical bodies, I mean."

And the happy smile that lit up Te's face, together with the excited waves that escaped from her, said it all.

"It is the moment of highest fulfilment for us," she said. "The reward we all work to earn for ourselves."

Jeryant glanced up at Kasstovaal, who gave him an 'I told you so' look in return.

"What form does it take?" he asked, gently.

Childlike excitement began to creep into Te's voice, as though she were describing what it would be like at the fairground, when she got there. "When we have the word from the Voidseer, we wait until the next Voidrise and then we release ourselves fully from the body. Not just an ejection of spare energy but the release of our entire minds and selves. Our minds, with the knowledge from our purpose, are released into the void, where the knowledge is wanted. Our selves are released into the mists to become one with the enormity of space. We shall be free as we once were. Free."

She trailed off, intoxicated by the thought of it. Kasstovaal could appreciate the potency of that image. She had shown it to him, let him feel it. He knew the longing she had in her, the longing they must all have. Small wonder that they should crave for the death that would satisfy it. They were sure of their destiny.

But he had no such certainty. Humans did not have that luxury, no matter what they believed or how hard they tried to believe it. He feared the death the Dwellers welcomed. That one incompatibility, so basic, would forever keep their two species apart. The length of an entire universe apart, in fact.

SEVEN: ATTACK

20.

The *Gateway to Infinity* was one of a long line of one-person spaceships that were destined for a very short career. The shortest conceivable career, in fact.

It was the ship that Malkan Kasstovaal had built with his own hands and its maiden flight was to carry him into the most select of official lists, the Pilot-Captain's register. It had managed it by the skin of its teeth, not to mention his, and like every one of its predecessors and successors its maiden voyage was its last.

Not surprisingly, Kasstovaal harboured fond memories of that ship and had managed to scrape together enough credit to buy the wreck of it from the academy. Traditionally, successful exam ships, or what was left of them, were subjected to a component-level assessment by one of the academy masters, together with the successful candidate, once they got out of hospital. This had nothing to do with the exam itself but was merely to find out how much of the ship was salvageable for parts. It was an expensive exam to run, after all, and the academy were keen to recoup as much credit as they could by reusing any parts that could be safely reused in future exams. However, when the assessment had been done, the candidate was offered the chance to purchase the whole wreck for the replacement cost of the useable components.

About fifty per cent of them did this; feeling, like Kasstovaal, a sentimental attachment to the lump of twisted metal that had saved their lives once and, perhaps, hoping to restore it to working order when they retired. The other fifty per cent couldn't wait to see the back of their creation, remembering the experience with horror, and could often not be persuaded to take part in the assessment.

The *Gateway to Infinity* had been assessed by Kasstovaal's engineering tutor, a large cantankerous old fart by the name of Torroldmann for whom Kasstovaal, nevertheless, had a great respect and fondness, all the more so after his exam. After a meticulous examination of the wreckage, Torroldmann had declared that the only things still holding the ship in one piece were spit and positive thinking.

In his new hangar in the side of the Rock, Kasstovaal remembered those words and reflected on their irony. To say that the *Gateway 2* was going to be constructed entirely out of positive thought was nothing more than the literal truth. What was more, he would have to do without whatever adhesive qualities saliva might have added to the structure, since he didn't know the formula for it.

What he did have at his disposal was fifteen years of practical experience that he hadn't had when he built the first *Gateway* and all the extra precision that matter-forming could offer.

There was not much the Dwellers could immediately contribute in the way of practical assistance, but they had arranged this hangar for him. One or two polite relocations had made available two sets of six empty rooms on adjacent levels, in three by two blocks, with two rooms on each level opening to the outside. Removing the internal walls and ceilings had created a single room twice the height of a normal one, double the width and three times the length with wide access to open space at one end. Quite sufficient for the small, two-seater craft he planned to build. He partitioned off a small section of it, up against the wall into the corridor, placing a thick, blast-proof wall from floor to ceiling and inserting an observation window at eye level. This gave him an antechamber, sealed off from the main hangar, from which he could conduct blast tests. Anyone entering from the corridor would have to pass through this area first and would not be in any danger if they came upon him running an experiment. It also gave him somewhere to retreat to if something went dangerously wrong.

He had, also, acquired a helper, much to his surprise.

He had been poring over the first draft plans for the *Gateway 2* when a shorter than average doorway appeared and a small Dweller peered in, timidly, from the corridor. A young male, very young in Kasstovaal's perception.

"May I enter, Beyonder Kasstovaal?" he faltered.

"If you like."

The little Dweller came in, leaving the doorway open as though for a fast getaway.

"My name is Zu," he said, hesitantly. He seemed to be hoping that that would explain something.

"And what can I do for you, Zu?"

Zu hesitated to answer and Kasstovaal thought he recognised the symptoms. A fine example of youthful curiosity doing its usual bad job of overriding awe. It was a sensation he knew from his own childhood, that time when his uncle had been fixing up that old sub-atmosphere speeder.

"I have heard," said Zu, "that you are constructing a space vessel."

"That's right."

"My Prim has taught me a lot about space propulsion. It is most interesting. I wondered...." He faltered again, hesitating on the last step.

"Yes?" said Kasstovaal, encouragingly.

"I wondered if I could watch you, while you work," Zu blurted it out quickly, before his resolve could desert him. "I've never seen a real spacecraft before." Then, as if in his own defence, he added "My Prim said you might let me watch if I asked you."

"You can do more than watch, if you like," said Kasstovaal, taking pity on him. "You can help me build it."

Zu's face lit up and he grinned hugely. "May I really?" he asked, excitedly.

"Sure," said Kasstovaal. "It'll be a lot easier with an extra pair of hands." Then he remembered that he was talking to a Dweller and corrected himself. "An extra set of hands, I mean. Who knows, you might teach me a few things about space propulsion before we're done."

He had to lean away from the barrage of gratitude the little Dweller was letting off.

"Thank you, Beyonder Kasstovaal," said Zu, enthusiastically. "What shall I do first? Tell me."

"Well first you can simmer down a bit," said Kasstovaal. "I'm sure your Prim won't thank me for encouraging you to wave out all over the place."

Zu deflated a little. "Sorry, Beyonder Kasstovaal."

"Secondly, you can stop calling me Beyonder Kasstovaal. Just call me Kass. That's what my friends call me. It sounds more like a Dweller name, anyway."

Zu nodded. "All right, Kass."

"Good. Now come and have a look at these plans."

And that was it. Whenever Zu could get away from his lessons and his Primary Parent had no need of him he would come down to the hangar and assist Kasstovaal with the construction. He was a good former, better than Kasstovaal, and it was only ever necessary to show him a process once, after which he would perform it reliably one hundred per cent of the time.

Also, Kasstovaal found the exercise of teaching Zu beneficial to himself. It compelled him to organise the facts more clearly in his mind so that they could be explained and he found himself understanding them better for having done so. What was more, Zu's knowledge of propulsion was sufficient that Kasstovaal could bounce new ideas off him and the young Dweller was more than capable of keeping step with him in technical conversation.

Kasstovaal soon found himself looking forward to Zu's company. The little Dweller was the nearest to human Kasstovaal had encountered among the Rock's inhabitants.

His other frequent visitor was Te with her mind full of questions about his universe and his race and his life. His old life. He suspected that life would never be as it had been, even if he did succeed in returning to his own universe.

She did not want to disturb his work, she said, and she seemed quite happy to sit there listening to him chatting about anything and everything while he worked. Now and again she would ask him a question or ask him to describe some aspect of his old life, just to start him off and he would try to give her as full an answer as he could, reeling off every fact or experience that came to his mind.

He had learned that this was the best approach with Te, or any Dweller, come to that. There wasn't, really, any point in being selective in what he said for fear of not being understood. He found that, unless he lapsed into really obscure or colloquial concepts, the Dwellers still seemed to get the message okay. It appeared that the language touch was quite capable of bridging the gaps, somehow or other.

This saved a lot of mental legwork on his part, allowing him to waffle on, disjointedly, about any particular subject and be safe in the knowledge that Te would take from it what she wanted. Whether or not he was providing all the insights she needed, he couldn't be sure. His gut told him that when she left him, she did so without full satisfaction.

He regretted that. He had felt her hunger for knowledge first hand, a gnawing ache in the mind. How did she stand it? He wanted to give her what she needed to slake that craving but always felt himself falling short. But perhaps it was more than he could do to satisfy so ravenous a hunger. Still, he kept trying.

Jeryant, absorbed in his own affairs, visited only to complain that Kasstovaal wasn't resting enough and that he should take a break and eat something to keep his human cycle running smoothly.

But Kasstovaal didn't want to rest. He didn't need to rest. At last, he had a positive task to get on with, something that would start him on the road home.

He worked around the clock, never tiring, never stopping if he could avoid it. The old knowledge came easily back to him as he worked, bringing back memories of the last time he had done this.

Then the knowledge had not come so easily, needing to be sweated out of his memory. Then there had been no willing hands to help him. There had been no one at all, for three long months. Just him, the hangar and the ship.

It was one of three hangars sunk deep beneath the academy's vast landing fields, lined with thick, alloy-reinforced concrete just in case he managed to do something stupid with the reaction core. They had searched him for cheat notes, a search worthy of a penal colony and then had locked him in. He could send and receive vid-calls, all monitored by the examiners, and that was the only contact he had with his friends and family. He was alone and as the access door slammed shut the realisation of what he was doing hit him fully for the first time.

He had spent the first sleepless night, in the small but comfortable living cabin attached to the hanger, racked by mortal dread. He felt as though he had just chosen suicide and was going to surprise himself with the exact details of the execution in about three month's time.

He spent the second sleepless night listening to the silence fifty feet underground and feeling more terribly alone than he ever had before.

After that he slept well. The silence, the solitude and no small measure of the fear focused his mind incredibly and he settled into the task. The hangar contained all the tools and anti-G lifting gear he might need and he only had to enter his requirements into the Order Terminal and whatever equipment he ordered would be sent down the supply tube to him, usually within the hour unless it was particularly specialised and had to be obtained from outside the academy.

He became totally absorbed in the task, pouring into it every bit of mental and physical energy he had, putting his soul into the ship in the hope that it might save his life in return.

He had picked a fairly standard design. There was no point in being flashy and getting yourself killed by the flourishes; you didn't get extra marks for it, after all. Best to stick to the tried and tested slower models that were known to forgive small mistakes. Even so, he added his own touches; extra safety measures and back-up systems, anything he could fit into the systems without compromising the ship's operation or making it too heavy.

One touch he was quite proud of was the Centridium alloy coating he applied to the hull. It was a new substance he'd read about in a magazine article, a metallic solution which, if sprayed onto a ship's outer hull, could increase its durability, resistance to heat and, most importantly of all, its resistance to molecule erosion in the Second Mode by several times. Some of the larger shipbuilding conglomerates were planning to use it on their new models. Kasstovaal had made a number of strategic vid-calls in the run up to his exam so that, when he requested an amount of the coating solution and an applicator on the Order Terminal the academy's quartermaster was able to obtain them for him with the minimum amount of hassle. It was quite expensive stuff but it was only a small ship and only a micro-thin coat was needed.

He completed the work with nine days to spare but resisted the temptation to signal the examiners that he was ready. If he had he could have been out of here and getting ready to fly the course. But he resolved to sit out the remaining time and spend it racking his brains for any small detail that he might have missed. Anything that might still act to destroy him.

He virtually took the ship to pieces again and reassembled it during that time and when he'd done that he just sat staring at it, tracing through the circuits in his mind. It was a talent he had discovered in himself early on in his tuition and it was, perhaps, the thing that had got him to this point, the last hurdle.

The ship just sat before him, innocently, an arrowhead, about fifteen feet long and eight feet high, made blunt to pass more easily through gasses and made seamless by the coating he had sprayed on. It looked invitingly clean and new, if you ignored the test-fire marks on the engine housings. Some stir-crazy impulse in his mind wanted him to jump into the cockpit and blast his way out to freedom. He hadn't put any weapons on the thing so that was out of the question anyway. But the speed-hungry teenager that had not quite died off inside him wanted to get going. Pilot-Captain or bust. All of space or oblivion, it didn't matter. One signal into the Order Terminal and he could be away for better or worse.

But he sat it out, facing his would-be executioner or friend eye-to-eye. Once he even said out loud, "You're not going to let me die, are you?" The only answer he got was his own echoes.

When they came for him, he had fallen into a doze across one of the planning desks. The sound of the locks disengaging started him awake.

Torroldmann came in followed by a couple of porters. "Well, young man," he said, kindly. "Time's up. I must now officially ask you if you want to fly the stipulated exam course in the ship you have built here."

Kasstovaal gave the *Gateway to Infinity* one more lingering look before he answered. "Yes," he said, simply.

He was allowed six hours free time to prepare himself before flying the course. The ship remained locked in the hangar and he was not allowed to go near it during that time. He met up with some of his friends who told him in great detail how pale and wasted he looked before taking him out for the heartiest meal they could find in the city's restaurants, an unofficial tradition of the exam.

There were six of them and Kasstovaal crowded around a table while waiters, having had the urgency of the situation impressed upon them in no uncertain terms, hurried to pile food in front of him. The others took turns to pick morsels off of his plates to nibble at but ordered no food for themselves. It was an odd time of day for serious eating and they were content to watch him do it while the ale jugs passed liberally between them.

"No alcohol for you, my son," said Geomaarcolov, covering Kasstovaal's glass. "Got to keep a clear head. Otherwise you might find your head clear of any brains."

"You're all heart, Geo. You know that, don't you."

The two of them had come up through the academy together and Geomaarcolov was the one in the group everybody looked to to keep the party going, something he was eminently good at. He was scheduled to take his exam a couple of months later.

"My friends!" he said, loudly. "Raise your glasses to the condemned man."

"Rub it in, why don't you, you bastards."

"Seriously, Kass, we have every confidence that you'll get through the course okay, haven't we guys?"

There were grunts of assent.

"Now, we're going to be back here tomorrow night" Geo continued, "and we expect you to be here too. And we'll help you get royally hammered in celebration."

A ragged cheer went up around the table.

Geo reached into a pocket and drew out a small note-file pad. "I'm taking three-to-one odds against," he announced. "Five creds minimum bet." Credit chips started to change hands.

Kasstovaal had to smile. "Keep looking upwards, guys," he said. "Or I might crash land on top of you. I'll be looking out especially for anyone who bets against me."

After that he went back to his own quarters and slept, soundly, for three hours with the help of a time pill. When it clicked him awake again, he showered, dressed in his flight suit and had half an hour left to go over the details of the course one more time before he had to present himself.

The suns were beginning to set when he walked out onto the landing field, heading towards the small group of examiners who were waiting for him. About fifty yards beyond them a set of the huge silo doors were grinding ponderously open. As Kasstovaal approached, the *Gateway to Infinity* rose into view, supported by the Grav-plate that locked into the hole left by the doors.

Torroldmann stepped forward to meet him. "Are you ready, Kasstovaal?" he asked. "You know you can still pull out, if you wish."

Kasstovaal forced himself not to answer immediately, to make himself think about it one more time before answering. But this was not the same Kasstovaal who had stepped into the hangar, three months ago, fearing for his life. He had made his decision.

"No, thank you, sir," he said, "I think if I don't do it now, I never shall."

Torroldmann nodded. "Very well, then." He thumped Kasstovaal on the shoulder. "Best of luck, my boy."

The other examiners stepped aside, forming an impromptu human corridor towards his ship. Kasstovaal set his jaw and walked towards it.

He wondered if Torroldmann had taken the opportunity to look the ship over during the six-hour break. He could have. As an examiner he was permitted into the hangar and six hours would be enough for him to form an opinion about the chances of the ship surviving the course. Of course, if he had he would not be allowed to pass that opinion on to Kasstovaal. Perhaps Kasstovaal should have read more in his parting words and that pat on the shoulder.

No. He couldn't start thinking like that otherwise he might as well turn around now and walk back to his quarters.

He opened the small airlock, not much bigger than he was, and squeezed inside. The inner door admitted him into the pilot's compartment, tall enough for him to stand up in but not quite long enough for him to lie down. At one end was the pilot's seat in the midst of the flight controls, at the other the thickly shielded hatch that opened into the rear section to give him access to the core and the engines if he needed it.

He took his time over the run-up sequences, first firing-up the reaction core to give him instrument power and then activating and test running each system in turn. There was one piece of equipment he had not installed himself, a black cube with the academy insignia stamped on it. That would be the monitor link, a passive scanning and transmitting device that would allow the examiners to monitor his actions and make sure he stuck to the course laid out. It was self-powered and independent from the ship's systems, so there was no danger of it interfering with anything, and was sealed tight so that he couldn't tamper with it.

Finally, he ran the core up to flight power level and swivelled the pilot's seat into position. He took a second to calm his mind, to be sure within himself that everything had been done and done right. This was the moment to be sure. Then he reached for the controls.

The *Gateway to Infinity* lifted itself from the ground on a cushion of nil-gravity and angled its nose skyward. The main engines fired, blasting out short jets of steam as they burned off the internal condensation, and the ship accelerated away from the ground and the watching examiners.

He felt the acceleration. He had tuned down the power on the inertia shield so that he could feel the ship operating under him, feel the vibrations. They weren't quite right.

The instruments didn't detect anything wrong but the throb of the engines felt wrong to him. Could he trust his instruments? He should be able to but he trusted his instincts more. He was sure, now, that the starboard engine was running out of phase with the port engine, not by much but enough to play merry hells with his manoeuvring once he hit open space. He adjusted the power flow to the starboard engine manually and the discordant vibration stopped. That was better. It had increased his speed slightly, as well, which was no bad thing when you were fighting your way out of a planet's gravity.

He cleared the atmosphere and prepared for the first transit through the Second Mode. He referred to the copy of the course specifications he'd been given and fed the details into the transit computer. This was where precise calculation became essential. A few extra kilometres in the Second Mode could span the distance between planets in the First Mode or could drop you too near to a star. In addition to the computer he provided himself with a Dual Mode Parallel star chart from which he could determine his relative position in either mode. If he lost the transit computer, the star chart should allow him to navigate manually or, at least, stop him from emerging too close to anything hazardous. As long as it was charted, of course.

He powered up the Destabiliser and cut a neat slit in the fabric of the universe a few kilometres in front of the ship. The slit widened and spread outwards forming a ragged hole big enough for his ship to pass through. He increased the thrust and plunged through into another set of dimensions. Behind him, the forces of nature that governed both universes set about sealing up the hole he had made, squeezing it shut and healing the tear within seconds.

So far, so good. He looked out on a field of multicoloured stars. You could navigate by some of them, but not all stayed constantly bright. Some would just wink out for hours at a time and then reappear as suddenly.

He kept his eyes riveted on his scanners and the view plate ahead, looking for the telltale signs that might suggest a ghost planet about to appear nearby. There was no way to plot them on a star chart; they could appear virtually anywhere if there was enough matter floating around and it was something other than simple gravity that pulled them together. Nobody had been able to work out what it was or even how to detect it. So there was no way to predict when it would cause an enormous volume of dust to suddenly congeal into a planet, nor when it would let go and allow the planet to vaporise again. More than one ship in its transit through the Second Mode had suddenly found itself buried in the centre of a temporary planet. It was survivable, depending on how deep you were and how densely the matter was packed and how sturdy your ship's hull was. If you were really lucky you wouldn't even need to blast your way out; the planet around you might fade out of existence in a matter of hours leaving you drifting free in space.

The best thing you could do to avoid them was to keep measuring the volume of free matter around you and to steer clear of any areas where it was building up too much. There were a few visual signs; floating clouds of dust colliding with one another, static discharges and, most recognisable of all, the Blotmark, as it had come to be called. About fifteen seconds before a planet phased into existence a circular area of space would suddenly go black, a perfect circle of stars blotted out by a sheet of bonding particles. That would be the position in which the new planet formed and if you were in the middle of it the best thing you could do was to push up to full thrust and hope that fifteen seconds was enough for you to pull clear. A more dangerous alternative was to make a fast transit back into the First Mode and hope not to find worse waiting for you on the other side of the portal. Fifteen seconds was certainly not enough time to check and then decide afterwards.

The exterior scanners showed a low volume of matter outside but Kasstovaal kept checking until the transit computer auto-fired the

Destabiliser again and plunged him back into his own universe. He checked his position. The transit computer had inserted him on an approach to a planet. Rindella 12 the course-specs called it, a barren planet with no atmosphere and no inhabitants. The course-specs called for one low pass over the equator before pulling out to deep space again for the next transit. He gripped the controls and eased the *Gateway* down to ten thousand feet. There were no mountain ranges to speak of along the equator, in fact no real obstacles at all. Just low hills and rocky plains rushing past underneath him.

This is supposed to be difficult, he thought as he pulled up and headed for space.

An instant after he remembered about not getting complacent, the proximity alarm went off and he was suddenly surrounded by junk: Tons of twisted and burned metal in a million shapes and sizes rushed at him and he found himself flying for his life, reacting, not thinking.

There must have been the debris of at least two hundred starships up here and he had fallen beautifully into the trap that the examiners had set for him.

Small pieces rattled against his hull as he weaved and swerved to avoid the bigger chunks of metalwork spinning around him. The proximity alarm rang a continuous note in his ears and he shut it out of his mind.

He dipped under the huge bulk of a troop carrier, broken in two by who knew what, and failed to see in time the slowly spinning tail of a gunship rotating into his path. He hauled the ship hard to port but couldn't avoid the collision. The jagged edge of the tailplane raked across the underbelly of his ship tearing through coating and plating alike and gouging into the equipment beneath.

Several systems, minor ones thank gods, sparked and went offline as the power shorted through them. Kasstovaal wrestled with the ship for control over their course, which might otherwise end abruptly in one more lump of metal.

And then he was clear. The proximity alarm went quiet and the viewport showed clean and empty space in front of him.

He reversed thrust and brought the ship to a stop to assess the damage and let his heart stop racing. The blown systems were replaceable and it took him five minutes to switch over to the back-up modules. Then he put on his HA helmet, depressurised and de-grav'd the compartment and opened up the hatch into the rear section. He had to lie on the floor and pull himself into the crawl-way headfirst.

The narrow metal gantry took him first past the cavity in which the reaction core nestled, surrounded by alloy shielding. The collision had not punctured this section, at least, and as far as he could see everything was operating normally. He pulled himself further aft and was soon lying on the gantry in the space between the two engines. This compartment had a gaping hole in the floor, and part of the starboard engine had been ripped away. He opened the engine up and inspected to damage. Two of the power regulators were completely gone and there was a hairline crack in one of the focusing cylinders but otherwise the engine was all right. He couldn't do anything about the crack in the cylinder but it shouldn't retard the thrust too badly and one of the port engine's regulators could take on the work of the two that were missing. He made the cross-connection and finished up by filling the gash in the hull with sealing gel. All in all, he felt that he'd been bloody lucky this time. But this was only the start.

His guard was up now, one hundred per cent of the time and he needed it. The next transit dropped him into the gravity well of a gas giant planet and he was forced to dip deep into the thick atmosphere before he could attain an escape attitude. The hull began to glow as the dense gases abraded the surface. But the coating held and he thanked the providence that had let him read about it, that one time. The gel patch he had put in the rear section would probably have gone but that wouldn't matter too much.

As he pulled away from the gas giant he sensed the off-rhythm in the starboard engine again, the same as on take-off. He upped the power flow again and the engine came back into balance. He would have to watch that. The starboard engine was pulling ten per cent more power than the other one to produce the same thrust. Maybe that crack in the cylinder had been there to start with.

At the end of his third transit, the specs told him to cross 2.5 AUs of a sector of space in the First Mode before re-entering the Second Mode. This time, though, he was able to spot the danger before he dropped himself in it. The star chart showed nothing in that sector but he noticed, through the viewport, the brilliant column of light rushing in and spreading out into a bubbling nebula of energy that stretched and wobbled as time distorted around it. A telltale sign that a Black Hole was waiting for him in the First Mode, sucking in any matter or energy it could take hold of. It had split the fabric of the universe by its sheer weight and some of that matter and energy was leaking through into the Second Mode. He had noticed it and was warned accordingly. That observation was, presumably, what the examiners were testing him for.

Now he had to decide how to act and quickly. He couldn't stay in the Second Mode for too long at a time, otherwise the molecular bonds holding his ship together would become too weak and begin to break up. Entry into the First Mode would renew them to full strength. And there was still the exam task to complete and they would know if he didn't.

He adjusted his position in the Second Mode to correspond with the sector's outermost limits. He couldn't be anywhere within the sector without the Black Hole taking hold of him but the more distance he could put between him and it the more control he would have over the approach. After all, the specs didn't say which 2.5 AUs he had to cross, as long as they were in that sector. He cranked up the power on the Destabiliser and focused the beam for maximum range. He would be moving fast when he fired it the second time and he would need all the time he could get to allow the portal to open enough to let the ship through.

He opened the portal and started towards it. About two hundred kilometres from the threshold the gravity force grabbed hold of the ship and sucked it through into the First Mode. Kasstovaal was thrown back into his seat as the ship accelerated towards the black spot in the distance where the light could no longer escape for him to see. Using the manoeuvring thrusters, he turned the ship through one hundred and eighty degrees to bring the main engines to bear against the pull and pushed them up to full thrust. The acceleration slowed but he was caught now and nothing he could do would bring him to a stop or pull him away.

He swivelled the Destabiliser to fire aft and waited until the instruments showed that he had travelled 2.5 AUs towards the Black Hole. The instant that was confirmed he fired the Destabiliser and watched the rear-view screen as the newly forming portal rushed up to meet him. It was going to be a tight squeeze. He rolled the ship a few degrees to catch the portal at its widest point and cut the engine power. There was a moment of intense G-force as the Black Hole yanked at him and then he was drifting inside the Second Mode, the portal closing in front of him. Task completed. He realised that he'd been holding his breath and let it out in a sigh as he adjusted his course for the next transit.

It was as he was throttling up, to pull away on the new course, that the starboard engine suddenly misfired and went out. The port engine continued to operate, sending the ship into a fast spin. Kasstovaal cut the thrust, rolled the ship over and used the now inverted port engine to correct the spin. He shut the port engine down to idle at zero thrust and began working to restart the starboard engine. He couldn't afford to be adrift inside the Second Mode with no engines and re-entering the First mode was out of the question: even if he could've manoeuvred the ship through a portal without main thrust, it would've dropped him back into the grip of the Black Hole and that would've been suicide with no engines. But the engine would not start, no matter what he tried with the controls.

Frustrated, he rammed on his helmet and started down the crawl-way again as fast as he could go. The cracked cylinder he had found before had now broken cleanly in two, in the fight against the Black Hole, and was quite useless. He would have to divert the power through the other three cylinders and hope they wouldn't overheat with the extra load. His gloved hands fumbled clumsily with the connections but eventually he managed it, slammed the casing shut and scrambled back to the pilot's compartment.

He tore off his helmet and ran his hands over the controls. There were a couple of false ignitions and then the starboard engine fired. Thank gods! He glanced up at the viewport.

All around him the stars were going out.

With barely a conscious thought he rammed the throttles hard forwards while his eyes searched desperately for the nearest edge. He found it beneath him and to his left and steered for it, racing the edge of the Blotmark to reach the stars first. He almost made it.

The ship jolted as a vice of solid rock closed over the starboard wing tip, crushing it and tearing it off. He managed to regain control but the loss of that wing section was going to make his final atmosphere landing a nightmare.

Don't worry about that now, he told himself, worry about it when you come to it. At this rate you'll be lucky to get that far.

The next couple of transits passed without much trouble. They were minor navigational tests, which he completed numbly with hardly a conscious thought behind his actions. First year cadet stuff. But he didn't let his guard down. He didn't dare.

Overall, the thing that came nearest to cooking his goose was the nebula crossing. It wasn't a huge expanse, just a blot of leftover gases discarded from a completed star system. He could cross it in an hour but he had to take it slowly. The dust cloud was alive with electromagnetic pulses and if he cranked up the power too much he might attract one and blow most of his systems. He shut down as many as he could, to protect them from the worst effects if one hit, but that was all he could do.

The portal had dropped him outside the nebula's outer boundary and he was able to take a run at it. He throttled up to maximum, gaining as much speed as he could, and, as the ship's nose plunged into the thicker layers he throttled back to zero thrust and let the built-up momentum carry him. It was a choice between clearing the nebula and its danger quickly, while increasing the risk of the engine activity attracting a pulse, or crossing it slowly without actively attracting a pulse but with more time for one to strike him at random. This momentum should take him across the expanse in about three hours as long as nothing got in the way. The abrasion of the dust shouldn't slow him down too much. He just had to sit and wait.

Around him the dusts were on fire with the energies pent up inside them. There would never be any suns shining in here but the split spectrum glow lit up space with the colours of a hundred suns. Here and there, the flash of a discharge as the energy broke free and the dust dimmed.

The sensors, probing ahead into the dust for obstacles, spotted the field of asteroids dead ahead of him and sounded the proximity alarm. Damn! He examined the echoes. It was a big field but the asteroids were widely spaced and very large. Planetoids more like, this nebula's feeble attempts to create planets as a testament to its existence.

He could manoeuvre around them but he would need to put on some thrust and that was too risky. Besides, he thought, if I go through them and use their mini-gravity to slingshot me past I should gain a fair bit more momentum. He would only need to use the manoeuvring thrusters and if he judged the course just right he could almost double his speed without using the main engines once. He'd done it dozens of time before in cadet trials, though he'd never tried it inside a nebula before.

He pointed the ship's nose towards the first planetoid, heading straight for the centre of it. It loomed out of the dust cloud ahead of him, a misshapen lump of dark rock. His speed increased as its pathetic gravity took hold of him and pulled him down. He judged his moment and turned the ship aside, putting it into an orbit around the planetoid. The *Gateway to Infinity* skimmed around the equator, the gravity still pulling at it, and at the precise moment Kasstovaal flipped the ship away and the gravity threw it out towards the next mini-world. World by world, he weaved his way through the field picking up a little extra speed every time.

The edge of the field was coming up. One more planetoid filled the forward viewport. He would need to judge this one to throw him back onto his original course otherwise he'd have to correct with engine power. No problem, he thought.

And there wouldn't have been except that an enormous discharge of static exploded out of nowhere and smashed the planetoid into a million fragments. Kasstovaal suddenly found himself in the midst of a full-blown meteor shower, several million tons of rock coming straight at him at speed.

He had no choice now. He throttled up the engines and steered for the edge of the storm where the rocks were smallest, dodging and weaving between them under the guidance of his instincts.

A small shard, moving fast, came straight at him; not at the ship, at him; aiming straight between his eyes. It struck the viewport and bounced away, leaving an ominous crack in the clear steel-plastic. That distracted him for just a second.

The much bigger meteor, tumbling towards him from above, he did not see until it was too late. His attempt to swerve away from it saved his life but caused it, instead, to smash down on the port engine pod, ripping most of it away and exposing the charged cylinders to open space and letting their energy crackle out uselessly. The impact threw the ship into a wild tumble and Kasstovaal fought to correct it but he just didn't have enough time.

In the end, it was the energy escaping from the ruined port engine cylinders that sparked off the pulse in his vicinity. All he knew about it was that the controls he was wrestling with suddenly sparked and then blew up in his face. He had a brief sensation of burning pain and then darkness, a darkness he never expected to wake from again.

But he did wake up. He wasn't sure how long he'd been out but that hardly mattered. He was still alive. The life support system must still be working.

His face raged from the pain of the burns and he fumbled for the medical spray and doused his face in it. He cried out for the sheer pleasure as the cold liquid sealed and cooled the burn and numbed the pain.

Right, time to take stock. The first priority was to place a sealing patch over that crack in the viewport. If that blew out his problems could be over real quick. As he did so he saw that the nebula had given way to open space. That last collision seemed to have knocked him clear of the meteor shower and onto a course out of the dust. The ship was still tumbling but there was nothing he could do to correct that yet.

The emergency lighting, created from phosphorescent chemicals and needing no energy, was already operating and by its light he assessed the damage to the controls. They were in bad shape. The EMP had fried most of the operating circuit boards into uselessness but the systems he had switched off seemed to have survived as he had hoped. With any luck he could cannibalise enough components from those to rig up a replacement flight control system.

That assumed that he had any engines left to control. He helmeted up and crawled back into the rear section. The shielding around the reaction core seemed to have done its job and the core was mercifully undamaged. Back in the engine compartment it was a different story. A full quarter of the section was missing on the port side and there wasn't enough of the port engine left to even consider repairing it. That just left the already overburdened starboard engine. What the hells was he going to do?

For a long time he just lay there on the crawl-way gantry, staring at the stars visible through the rent in the hull. He could just give up and send a distress signal. The examiners' black box would relay it back to the academy and they would send a rescue ship for him. That would be the end of his attempt to become a Pilot-Captain and all the trials of the last few hours and the last three months, all that work, would be for nothing.

No. Suddenly he was damned if he would give up before he was sure there was no way out. That's what you needed to be a Pilot-Captain, the ability to find a way home no matter the odds. That was the test. The nebula had been the last course specification. All he needed to do now was to get back to the academy and land. Right!

If he shifted the fixings on the remaining engine and changed the firing angle of the pod he should be able to get a straight line of thrust out of it. He had all the tools he needed stored in a compartment next to the reaction core. The engine weighed about four tons but he was in zero gravity and as long as he was careful about it he shouldn't have any difficulty moving it on his own. He was able to salvage a working regulator from the port engine to replace one of the missing ones on the starboard engine, but all four of the port cylinders were smashed so he couldn't replace the cracked one.

The job of shifting the engine took him eight hours. There were over fifty fixing points holding the engine in place and he needed to re-drill at least thirty of them to get the engine pointing in the right direction. Moreover, the engine compartment was only seven feet long and there wasn't much room to move in. He was forced to cut away the crawl-way gantry in order to make enough space for the new angle. He didn't want to jettison the remains of the port engine, just in case he needed it for parts. But at last he had one operational engine that would get him home.

He crawled back to the pilot's compartment, heaved off his helmet and slumped into the seat. His wrist chronometer told him that nineteen hours had passed since he'd taken off from the academy. The exam had no time limit on it, only his endurance and that of his ship would determine how long this went on.

He munched on a ration bar and allowed himself to rest for an hour before tackling the circuitry problem. That was going to be another long job. He would have to strip down virtually the entire compartment and sort out which components could still be used. One small blessing he now had was that he only had one engine to control and not two. He also had his talent for mental circuit tracing which now allowed him to design a new control system in his head.

The resulting lash-up did not fill him with confidence. All that could be said for it was that it would work for a while but exactly how long was an open question. But it was his only chance at success.

The cost to the other systems had been great. He no longer had a transit computer, a communications bank, an inertia shield, ninety per cent of the scanning equipment, any fault locators and, most important, no life support regulator. That had had to go too, he'd decided. He needed the components. He would have to rely on his flight suit and helmet. The helmet contained all the life support machinery, including its own oxygen reclaimer and if he wired it up to the ship's main power it would keep going indefinitely.

He was now down to the bare essentials. Apart from his makeshift flight controls, the only systems he had left working were the Destabiliser and the star chart, which had somehow managed to survive the pulse virtually unscathed. It was enough to limp home with.

What he didn't have enough of were anti-grav pods. There was a bank of fifty of them mounted on the ship's underbelly to slow its descent into an atmosphere and bring it down to a landing. Now only eighteen of them were working; a few had been lost in his first collision, some had been burnt out completely by the pulse and he didn't have enough components left for the rest. Still, once he got into an orbit above the academy he wouldn't need the Destabiliser or the star chart. He could strip those down and get a few more pods working before attempting re-entry. Even so, the best he could hope for was a bumpy landing, especially with one wing damaged.

He activated the new flight controls and used the manoeuvring thrusters to stop the ship tumbling. The start chart automatically locked on to the nearest navigation buoy and told him that he wasn't far off his original course. He would have to take the journey home slowly, making several small transits rather than one long one. He didn't want to strain the engine and the exam specs specified only that he should make it back after the nebula; how he did it was up to him.

The engine fired and pushed the ship through the portal he created. In the Second Mode, he would have to be doubly watchful now. He only had a long-range proximity scanner working now and that wouldn't warn him about a matter build-up. With only one engine, he couldn't outrun a Blotmark any more and, the state the ship was in, a ghost planet would crush it like an egg. Fortunately he was not troubled by any. He saw one form way off to his left but not near enough to worry him.

He took seven transits on the way back, the last dropping him into an approach that would insert him neatly into a parking orbit above the academy's base planet, where he could do his repairs. With no communications, he couldn't inform Space Traffic Control of what he was doing so he would have to rely on the examiners to pass the word on for him. They would still be monitoring his actions. The black box was built to withstand an EMP.

For now he was safe. Should he rest awhile before attempting the final hurdle? He was exhausted and a few hours sleep inside his flight suit would clear his mind ready for the approach. No. He doubted if he could sleep, not with his goal near enough to touch. Once he got down he could sleep all he liked. One way or another.

He set to work and got six more anti-grav pods working with the reclaimed parts. There was one more thing had to do. He moved to the rear of the compartment and yanked on the lever that ejected the reaction core into space. He would be coming down hot and if he crashed with an active core on board he was liable to make a crater five miles wide. Procedure dictated that if there was any risk of crash landing the core should be jettisoned into orbit before approach, where it could be picked up and made safe. He would have to come down on the storage cells; enough power to land on but not to get him back into orbit if he aborted.

At least the ejection of the core would signal them down below that he was ready to land. Here I come folks, he thought. I hope you're ready for me.

He fired the thrusters to slow the ship and allowed it to drop out of orbit. As he felt the first jolt of the atmosphere against the hull he activated the anti-gravs to resist the pull of the planet. They helped but even at full power they couldn't slow him enough. The howling of the air rubbing past the hull grew to a roar and vibrations rattled the ship until the controls blurred in front of him. Outside the ship's extremities began to glow sullenly red as the heat intensified. A few droplets of molten metal spattered onto the viewport. The glow spread further and further up the hull towards him and he thought he was sure to burn up if he didn't break through to the lower levels soon.

But the alloy coating held. The roaring faded, the vibrations eased. Suddenly Kasstovaal was trying to fly a brick. With a good part of the starboard wing missing the ship was no longer as aerodynamic as it had been and he had to use the anti-gravs to buoy up that side of the ship and keep him level. And he was still going too fast, something he couldn't do much about with the anti-gravs otherwise occupied.

There was no way he was going to be able to slow the ship to a stop and make a vertical landing on the anti-gravs. He would have to land on the rollers and hope they could take the speed. The landing field was ten miles square so he should have enough braking room if he could make a level touch down. A big "If" since it was all he could do to keep the wings level now.

The landing field came into view ahead of him, a wide expanse of dark green impact sponge, hard enough to land on and soft enough to take some of the force out of an impact. He was going to need it.

The *Gateway to Infinity* screamed out of the sky, trailing smoke and flames from the hole in the rear section where the flammable materials around the engines had ignited with the heat and the oxygen. It was a hundred feet off the ground as it crossed the boundary of the landing field, wobbling unsteadily from side to side as the anti-gravs fought to keep it from flipping over. Its emergency landing rollers were down and it was clear to everybody watching that it was not going to be a smooth landing. Four emergency air-skimmers started out from the academy buildings and raced to meet it.

The *Gateway to Infinity* eased its way shakily towards the ground. It had about thirty feet to go when the power ran out and the anti-gravs died. The starboard wing dropped sharply. The port wing tried to drop with it but not fast enough. The ragged tip of the starboard wing caught the ground and sent the ship into an uncontrollable spin. It bounced twenty feet back into the air and then dropped, still spinning, full onto its belly, the rollers screaming in protest at the excessive speed and constant change of direction. The ship careered out of control for two miles along the ground before the bearings on two of the rollers melted and fused together. The nose dropped and ploughed into the impact sponge tearing a long thin furrow through it. The aft section came up and over and the whole ship somersaulted through the air. It completed almost a full turn before it hit the ground, bounced and turned again, coming down on its roof and sliding with a screech of tearing metal that could be heard in the city five miles distant. It slid like that for another half mile before the friction finally brought it to rest, a tangled heap of metal and smoke.

They found Kasstovaal still strapped into his pilot's seat among the wreckage, unconscious and bleeding into his scorched flight suit.

He spent the next three days in a coma and several weeks thereafter in traction. But he was alive. That was all that mattered. That was all he needed. He had passed. He had done it.

In deference to his injuries, the official presentation of his licence was put off until he was able to walk again, as was the celebratory drinking session with Geomaarcolov and his cronies. And, despite all the pomp and ceremony and congratulations of the former, it was the latter that Kasstovaal remembered the more keenly because a few days afterwards Geo began his exam. And his ship never returned.

Thoughts of the *Gateway to Infinity* always ended for Kasstovaal in memories of his lost friend and endless speculation about where it was, exactly, that his luck had run out.

Somewhere in his universe, the *Gateway to Infinity* lay in its storage shed, a twisted and smoke-stained tangle of metal gathering rust and dust and time. A testament to Kasstovaal's luck and skill and the mistakes he had made.

Mistakes he would not make with this new ship. Whatever else happened, he had resolved that the maiden voyage of the *Gateway 2* would end with a much softer landing.

21.

Jeryant was a happy man. The idiot smile plastered across his face testified to that. The wobble in his gait, as he made his way along the corridors, testified to why.

More than one Dweller along the way, on seeing him weave from side to side and occasionally stagger, had been moved to ask him if he was feeling unwell. Being Jeryant, he had automatically responded with things like "Yes, thank you both for asking," or "I was walking straight earlier on but I'm alright now," or even "Yes but stop making the bloody floor move, will you," and enjoying the looks of puzzlement on their faces. Then he would show them the amber crystal in his hand and that explained it all.

Despite losing touch with the concept of straight lines, Jeryant's sense of direction remained true. A large portion of his life had been spent under one influence or another and his brain had developed its own autopilot system, possibly in self-defence, to get him home, or at least to the next bar, when the time came for him to be thrown out. He boasted that it had never let him down, no matter how far gone he was.

So he found his way down to the hangar with no trouble, which was just as well since the Rock had not responded when he'd tapped it with a knuckle and shouted "Anybody in there?" at the top of his voice.

He formed a doorway, shaped like a beer glass, into the antechamber and another one into the hangar proper, the same shape topped off with a stylised stream of liquid pouring from an inverted bottle. He leaned against the second door frame and beamed his induced smile into the room. "I've done it," he said, the words slurring, "I'm officially in my cups." He gestured to the doorway. He deflated a little when this failed to draw the attention of either Kasstovaal or Zu, who were bent over the workbench in an attitude of deep absorption.

"Bugger!" he muttered to himself, glared at the doorway until it disappeared then aimed himself at the workbench and started towards it.

In the centre of the floor a sat a skeletal framework of metal that was beginning to take on a shape that Jeryant recognised, the familiar outline of a space ship. He wandered up to it, breathed hard on a part of it and rubbed away an imaginary stain with his forearm.

He misjudged the distance to the workbench and came up against it hard. It was solid rock, grown out of and still attached to the floor, and the impact made him curse.

The bench was dominated by a large transparent cube, sealed down onto the surface. At first glance it appeared to be quite empty but as he peered closer he could see one very small metal object, no more than half an inch on any side, attached to the exact centre of one of the transparent walls. A cable trailed out from it through the glass and into the panel of controls that Kasstovaal and Zu were working at. The rest of the bench was a mess of human tools, some of which Jeryant recognised, and a small collection of knowledge crystals scattered at random among the detritus.

Jeryant reached out and clamped an arm hard across Kasstovaal's shoulders. "Gods bless all here," he bellowed, heartily.

Kasstovaal sighed but did not look up. "I didn't think it would take you long." he said, a little sourly. "You could sniff out an inebriant in a dry desert."

"Yes, indeed," said Jeryant, loudly, "Other gods bring forth water. I bring forth booze for the betterment of all mankind."

"And then you bring forth water," said Kasstovaal, wryly. "Usually in a corner somewhere. Not just water, come to think of it."

"Not this time, sunshine." Jeryant held out the amber crystal, rolling it around in his palm under Kasstovaal's nose. "Oa gave me this. Scrambles the brain waves, see. Slows them down. Clean, chemical-free intoxication. No hangovers. No liver damage. No bugger all. It's a dream come true."

Kasstovaal pushed the palm gently out of his line of vision. "I'm sure you'll be very happy together," he said. "Now, would you mind?"

Jeryant rolled the crystal from palm to fingers with remarkable dexterity, given his current state. He held it to his forehead and it glowed dully. His eyes seemed to take on an extra glaze. "Ahh!" he breathed. "I love it when the world moves like that."

"This is not news," said Kasstovaal.

"News you want, is it? Well, sunshine, how about if I tell you that, thanks to this little sucker, I've worked out how to keep us from going to pieces when we get home? How would you like them apples?"

Kasstovaal stopped his manipulations and looked sharply up at Jeryant.

"Maybe you ain't interested," said Jeryant gloomily. He turned his back and began tossing the crystal up and down in his hand. "Never mind. Me and my little friend here can go away and have a good time, if you're too busy. I think I'll go and find Oa. There's a woman who needs a good time. And I'm the man to give it to her."

Kasstovaal reached out and plucked the flying crystal out of the air. "I reckon you've had enough of this," he said.

"'Ere! Give that back," Jeryant protested. "Nobody tells Bryn Jeryant he's had enough except Bryn Jeryant. Not if they want to keep eating solids, that is. Get your own, you bastard."

"Suppose you tell me what you're talking about first," said Kasstovaal, patiently. "I don't suppose I'll get any peace until you have told me, so I might as well ask. What is this marvellous piss-head scheme you've got?"

"Piss-head scheme?" cried Jeryant, affronted. "I'll have you know that my solution was arrived at by the most merticoils...meticules...." He took a deep breath and tried again, "...meticulous application of logic. So meticulous, I can't even say it. And it's so simple, too. So obvious, in fact, even a space-arsed throttle jockey like you could have worked it out if you'd stopped looking for murderers under your bed and thought about it for a while."

"All right, Smartarse. What did I miss?"

Jeryant pointed to the crystal that still protruded through the skin at the centre of his forehead. "Amplifiers, my boy," he said. "Thought amplifiers. We've seen what one of these little babies can do with our minds behind them. What if we put lots of them together, eh? How much extra forming power would that give us?"

"Well, if they work like normal amplifiers of anything, it would be an exponential increase depending on how many you use. So what? What's forming power go to do with it?"

"Everything," cried Jeryant, excitedly, "the power of thought isn't totally impotent in our universe, you know. There are examples of its effects all over the place. Psychokinesis, psycometry, ESP. Thousands of cases on record, there are. Probably take a lot more mental umph to affect matter in our universe than it does here but it is still possible. In theory."

"So?"

"So, genius, if we take enough amplifiers with us maybe we'll have enough thought energy between us to hold our bodies and the ship together for a few seconds after we pop through the portal. After we've been in our own universe for a few seconds natural EM bonds would form between the sub...sub-thingies. Whatever they're called."

"Sub-atomic particles, you mean."

"Yeah, them. All we have to do is hold the particles in the right pattern for those first few seconds so that the natural bonds form between the particles to keep them in that pattern. Might take only a split second but once the mental bonds fade away the EM bonds will take over. And we'll be solid, honest-to-goodness matter again, won't we?"

Kasstovaal thought about it. He was sure there must be a flaw in the reasoning. But he couldn't think of one.

"Well, won't we?" Jeryant insisted.

"Yes, I suppose." said Kasstovaal, slowly. "How many amplifiers do you think we would need?"

"How the hells should I know? I guess the best thing to do is to take along as many as we can and hope it's enough. Too much is better than too little, I reckon. And who knows. If we take enough of them, maybe we'll still be able to matter-form when we get there. Think of that."

"Maybe so," said Kasstovaal, thoughtfully. "It's something we'd need to talk to the Dwellers about. I don't know how these things work." He turned to Zu, who had been listening quietly to their conversation. "How about it, Zu?" he asked. "Who's the best Dweller to talk to about these amplifiers?"

Zu said, "The Master of Minds, Ji, has the task of forming the amplifiers for new Dwellers. He would know the design. I am sure he could help."

Jeryant reached and snatched the amber crystal back from Kasstovaal. "Score one for the drunkard," he said, "never fails."

"Hold your horses, old soak," said Kasstovaal. "If I can't get this thing to work it won't matter two farts how many amplifiers we can take with us." He pointed towards the transparent cube.

"What's that then?" asked Jeryant, peering over Kasstovaal's shoulder and squinting to bring the object into focus.

"The Destabiliser. A miniature model of one, anyway. Zu's been helping me put it together so we can make a few test portals. If it works, of course."

"It will," said Zu, confidently. "The knowledge of Tre and Lu proves that this method is efficient. We have followed their designs exactly."

"It's not their efficiency we're testing for, exactly," said Kasstovaal, "though it is a relief to know that the technology does work in this universe."

"The Dwellers have already tried it, have they?" Jeryant asked.

"They came up with virtually the same system we did,." said Kasstovaal. "Though they took a lot longer to get there than we did. Zu and I have been reviewing their notes. They were set the purpose of finding a space travel method that could span intervoidal distances without any time dilation taking place. They seem to have started from the base principles of objects in motion and worked up to it step by step in completely empirical stages, logically calculating and then eliminating all the possible solutions one by one. It must have taken them three hundred years at least."

"How did we do it, then? Isn't that how scientific research usually goes?"

"We usually build on existing knowledge," said Kasstovaal. "We don't go through all the motions over again, just to prove that they all still apply. I learned about the development of Continuum Interface Disruption at the academy, of course. It's required learning. A guy called Franssart came up with the idea; the Curtain theory he called it, and he spent ten years building a device around the theory. That was the first Destabiliser and even the most modern ones work on the same principals as that first one, though the technology has been refined a lot. That was something like three thousand years ago."

"Ah!" said Jeryant, knowingly. "That's inspiration for you. That wonderful, wonderful gift we have that lets us cheat and cut corners."

"He probably worked it out unconsciously," said Kasstovaal. "That thing Vo was telling us about. The Unconscious Intelligence Centres. That's probably where he got the answer from."

"Rubbish!" exclaimed Jeryant. "The Unconscious Intelligence can only do logical calculation. Inspiration is a jump beyond just logic. It's intuitive. Born of something deeper than mere numbers, my boy. You'll be telling me next that he was doing unconscious viability experiments in his sleep. That doesn't account for it. I don't pretend to know how it happens but I thank providence that it does. Where would the human race be without it?"

"Still in caves on one planet, I should think," said Kasstovaal, "not to mention falling behind the Dwellers. Their design for a Destabiliser came out very similar to Franssart's prototype. The records of their tests are all here and they definitely achieved a continuum rip. So I'm not so worried about it not working.

"What interests me more is where their portal opened onto. Their records don't go into that. They were only interested in creating the method of travel, not in the conditions that existed outside their own universe. They sent a vessel in through one portal and got it back through another, end of story as far as they were concerned. The whole thing was carried out using laboratory models so none of them ever saw what was on the other side."

"Nothing too drastic, I imagine," said Jeryant, "otherwise they'd have lost a lot of models, wouldn't they?"

"That's not the point, Jery. I need to know that if I open a reverse-polarised portal it'll open onto the Second Mode. That's why we've set up this test."

Jeryant peered closer. "I hate to tell you this," he said, "but you're never going to fit on that, you know."

"Try to stop being facetious for five minutes, can't you. I'm not proposing to ride through the portal. Not yet."

"How are you going to know if you've reached the Second Mode, then?"

"There are ways of detecting it without seeing it, fortunately. For one thing, if you open a portal into the Second Mode, a certain amount of the background radioactivity leaks back through it. That radioactivity has a very specific pattern to it and it's very easy to detect if you know how."

"And you do, I trust."

"Certainly. We should know quite quickly if we have a way back or not."

"Anything I can do to help?"

"Yes. Stand back and let us work."

"Sorry, I'm sure."

Kasstovaal turned back to his panel. He had made it with normal human press-buttons rather than the touch-crystal contacts the Dwellers used, which he couldn't get the hang of. As such the panel looked exactly like the Destabiliser controls of a normal ship and was as familiar to him as the contours of his own face. The miniature Destabiliser responded to him just like a full size one would, ready to split open the fabric of space.

He knew the Curtain theory by heart; it was engraved on the inside of his skull in big letters. The matter in the universe is made up of sub-atomic particles, so small as to be almost out of the reach of the most powerful microscopes. But even smaller than those are the particles that make up the fabric of space itself, as small again as the sub-particles of atoms are to a fully grown man.

The whole universe is a tightly packed sea of them, nanoscopically small dots of energy woven together. They are too small for friction so any piece of matter can pass among them without effect or even registering their presence. They do not reflect light so nothing will show them up to the naked eye. They form the curtain, the very fabric of creation, the frail but unbreakable barrier between the universes. Not just one barrier, either, but several, interwoven and intermingling, each one holding out a different universe.

Once you accepted the reality of the curtain, the matter of splitting it open became relatively simple. Like so many other scientific processes, it reduced down to the application of brute force. All Kasstovaal had to do was to insert a thin enough lever in the gap between two adjacent columns of these particles and twist.

The trick here was going to be tearing the right curtain. The energy frequency of the barrier dividing the First and Second Modes was well known so the direction of travel merely depended on the polarity of the energy used; twist one way in, twist the other way out. The Dwellers appeared to have used a similar frequency but polarised for a reverse transit, as he would use for a portal to return to the First Mode. That suggested that the universes were all stacked up on each other and that if you just kept on opening portals in one direction you might eventually emerge into a universe too small for a man to fit into. What Kasstovaal was hoping for was evidence that the reverse of that suggestion would be true as well.

He couldn't have prepared this experiment without Zu's help. The little Dweller knew all about laboratory procedures, Dweller-style, having just learnt them all from his Prim. He had formed the Null-cube for Kasstovaal, a kind of small-scale blast-chamber that, for all its apparent fragility, was reputed to be able to hold in the force of a fissioning star or even a black hole created inside it. The area of space it confined was isolated in every way from the rest of the universe. Only the data cables, built into the structure of the transparent walls could get in or out. For all practical purposes, it was a small, self-contained, artificial universe created specially for Kasstovaal to impose his divine will upon.

It was just what was needed for this experiment. Kasstovaal didn't know what happened to an unprotected human body in close proximity to an open portal, even one made up of artificial Bio-flesh, but he knew that the manuals all strongly advised against trying it. Matter could push through one way, radio activity could leak out the other way, but what else might get drawn through? All your breathable air might go for a start, sucked out into the vacuum on the other side. Not that that was a consideration for him at the moment. Even on the small scale he was working to, creating a rip perhaps six inches long but not more, it was best not to take chances. A flippant part of his mind speculated that, if nothing else, the closing portal might take his finger off if he got it caught in there.

Zu looked up at him expectantly. "The sensor is now ready to detect radio activity patterns," he said.

"Well done, Zu. I think we're about ready for the test now."

"All right." Zu was clearly trying to hold in his excitement but wasn't doing a good job of it. The whole project fascinated him and now he was about to help tear a hole in reality for a ship to pass through. At a corresponding age, Kasstovaal thought, there were things that had made him feel the same way. And he was excited, as well. Why not? He might be about to open the way home. One step closer. He increased the power from the micro-cell and rechecked the settings. "All right," he said to Zu, "start recording now."

Zu pressed down on a crystal at his panel. One half of the screen above it began to scroll off figures while the other half displayed a solid horizontal line across its centre.

Kasstovaal reached down to his own controls and started the sequence. After a second or two, in which both humans held the breath that they weren't actually breathing, a thin vertical line of bluish light appeared at the centre of the space inside the cube. The line widened, stretching outwards from the centre so that the widest points pulled the rest into a diamond shape.

The figures on Zu's display changed, became more urgent, and the solid line started to jump with complicated but rhythmic peaks and troughs.

The diamond hole in the mini-universe pulled itself square. Then the two vertical apices began to contract, pulling towards each other and closing the hole. The diamond pulled itself flat, becoming a single horizontal line of the same bluish light that had marked the birth of this brief doorway. It thinned still further and then vanished beyond the range of vision, leaving the cube empty once more.

All three of them stayed staring at the cube for several seconds afterwards as though they feared to miss something wonderful if they turned away or blinked. Then Kasstovaal broke the spell and leaned over towards Zu's panel display. He pressed one of the crystals to replay the results and traced a finger along the pulsing line.

"A perfect heartbeat!" he breathed, breaking into a smile. "That's exactly what I want to see. Look at that, Jery."

Jeryant looked. "If that belonged to a patient," he said, "I'd start taking his coffin measurements."

"That's the heartbeat of a whole universe," said Kasstovaal. "That pattern is absolutely characteristic of the background radio activity within the Second Mode. In three thousand years nobody has been able to work out what causes the radiation to pulse like that or why. But it's quite distinctive."

Jeryant looked into his face. "That's it then," he said, "you've broken through into the Second Mode."

"This time, we have," said Kasstovaal. "It might be a fluke for all we know. Or if the frequency changes from time to time we might not hit the same mode twice. We'll need to repeat the experiment a few times more to make sure that we get the same results. But it certainly looks good."

"Optimistic, as usual I see."

"Realistic. We're only going to get one shot at this trip. I want to be as sure as I can be that it'll take us where we want to go."

"Still, it's something to celebrate isn't it? Have a crystal."

"No, thanks. One of us has to keep a clear head."

"And you reckon that's you, do you? It'll be the first time in a fortnight, if you manage it."

Zu spoke up. "I cannot assist with further trials now, Kass. My Prim is calling me to a lesson. I have to go."

"That's all right," said Kasstovaal. "I wasn't planning to run them straight away, anyway. If we allow some time to pass before we try again, that will give the conditions a chance to change, if they're going to. I won't start them without you, don't worry."

Zu beamed. "I shall come back as soon as I can," he said.

Once he was out of the hangar and the doorway had sealed behind him, Jeryant said "While we're on the subject of further tests and time delays, isn't it time you got on with those Barrier measurements we talked about. I gave you a week, remember? Hells, I can remember it, even like this. I make it nine days, right about now."

Kasstovaal had pushed the matter of the Barrier to the back of his mind and had all but forgotten about their agreement. "I've been concentrating on the ship," he said, defensively.

"I know that," said Jeryant, patiently. "That's why I haven't come to kick your arse about it earlier. Now that your little helper has wandered off and you have some time on your hands, it might be a good time to get on with them, don't you think? I'll help you."

"In your state? I'd be better off working on my own."

"It wears off fast, this thing," said Jeryant, regretfully. "If you don't keep on topping it up the normal brain rhythms start to reassert themselves and, before you know it, stone-cold sobriety hits you in the face. That's the only drawback. I'll be back to normal in a few minutes."

"Will I notice the difference, I ask myself?"

"Don't knock it, sunshine. I'm the only help you've got. Unless, of course, you want to ask one of the Dwellers to give you a hand."

"You know I don't want to do that."

"Well, then. I'm going to be watching you in any case, just to make sure you actually do those tests."

"Oh yeah?" Kasstovaal chuckled. "Reckon you can ride one of those Thought Plates, do you old man? They go at upwards of five thousand kph, you know."

"I was riding waves when you were nothing more than an itch in your father's underwear. I can keep up with you, whippersnapper, pissed or otherwise. Question is can you keep up with me?"

"You've got a bet, old man."

Just then a black form passed in front of the observation window as a Dweller crossed the antechamber.

"Another of your admiring public," said Jeryant. "It's true what they say about how much extra pulling power you can get from a fast motor. Never had the need for one, myself."

A doorway formed and the Dweller stepped through. The response Kasstovaal was forming to counter the tease faded away unsaid. Even at a distance the metal infinite value symbol on the Dweller's chest was distinguishable.

"What the hells does he want?" Kasstovaal hissed.

Jeryant lifted his nose into the air and sniffed at it, theatrically. "My word," he said, loudly, "there's an unpleasant smell in here, suddenly. I wonder what it could be."

Ko stopped about a dozen paces away from them. "This would be your Beyonder humour, I suppose," he said, coldly. "I have heard some of the others speak of it. It pleases you to make fun of us, on top of all else."

"Not a bit of it," said Jeryant, breaking into his dangerous smile. "If I really wanted to make fun of you, friend, I can assure you that you wouldn't see it coming. You would just know that it had arrived."

Kasstovaal cut in. "What do you mean 'on top of all else'?"

"You feign ignorance," Ko's face contorted, the brow screwing up in anger. "You feign ignorance to my face," he almost snarled. "Is this also how you laugh at us? Is what you have done to us not enough that you should mock those you have afflicted."

"Ignorance of what? What the hells are you babbling about?" roared Jeryant, taking a step towards him. Ko took a defensive step back.

Kasstovaal caught hold of Jeryant's arm as a thought struck him. Did Ko know about the Barrier?

"Hold on, Jery," he said.

"I will not hold on," bellowed Jeryant. "I don't have to stand here being bitched at by some arrogant little scripture-basher without enough manners to fill a teaspoon. You, my lad," he pointed at Ko, "need a tutorial on how to be polite to guests. And it'll be my pleasure to give it to you."

Ko took another step back away from the tirade, raising his right hand out in front of him. A large red crystal nestled in the palm.

"You make my action simpler," he said, icily. "Though it is simple enough as it stands. It is a small enough price to exact for so much suffering but it will have to suffice."

Then Kasstovaal knew what Ko was holding. Some sense told him, not specifically but in general terms, told him just too late.

Two beams of brilliant red light lanced out from the crystal and struck the two humans, pinning them where they stood.

Kasstovaal's world was suddenly awash with a red haze and pain. It was not a violent pain, not yet, but it clawed at the centre of his brain, clutching at it and squeezing away his thoughts like water from a sponge. He knew, with absolute certainty that the weapon Ko was holding was meant to kill. Meant to kill them both.

He made a desperate effort to move forward, to rush at Ko and knock the thing out of his hand. He managed a couple of steps, even managed to raise his arm towards his attacker. But his limbs had no strength in them, his mind had no force to command them. Ko took another step away from him and was out of reach.

Kasstovaal sank to his knees, raised his hands to his head. There was a terrible noise in his ears. Was it the screaming of his thoughts as they were torn out of him and crushed?

Through the sound he thought he could hear Ko's voice.

"Perhaps I can't undo the evil of your people, but I can at least repay a small amount of the wrong that has been done to mine."

"It has been a difficult task," said Te. "Kass does try to give me as much of an answer as he can. But his thoughts are unordered. He has not learned to discipline them the way we do."

"That much has been clear from the start," said Vo.

The two of them were making their way towards the hangar. There was news and it was only fair that the Beyonders should be made aware of its import, since it affected them so closely. But there was no rush about it. They had fallen into conversation about Te's pet project, the creation of a profile of the Beyonders and their reality.

"The information he gives comes out in a random order," Te complained. "It takes me as long again to unravel it all into a logical order. Even when I have done that, I still do not have enough of the whole picture to see it clearly."

"It is an enormous task you have taken for yourself," said Vo. "The fathoming of an entire reality is the work of many cycles. I doubt if you will have enough time to encompass it all before your purpose compels you to set it aside."

"Perhaps my purpose will be to complete the study," said Te, hopefully. "I hope so."

"Perhaps it will, at that," said Vo. "The study of the Beyonders is surely a task worthy to be counted as a purpose. And, I think, there is no Dweller better qualified than you to take it on."

They had come to the hangar area now and Te formed a doorway for them both into the antechamber. It was the red light spilling out through the observation window that, first, made them pause but did not cause immediate alarm. After all, this was a laboratory where any number of energies might be set free. As such they hesitated to enter but moved to the window to see what they might be disturbing.

What they saw was Jeryant and Kasstovaal on their knees, faces contorted in silent screams of pain, and Ko standing across the room from them holding a red crystal that transfixed the two humans.

"What is he doing?" cried Te.

In truth Vo didn't know. It had never been known for a Dweller to attack another Dweller, or any other visiting being come to that. The concept was totally alien to him so he couldn't recognise it, now it was before his eyes. But he could sense the wrongness of it.

He sent his mind in towards the Beyonders, reached in to sense the surface of their minds. He felt the pain in them, ripping away at their minds, their beings. He could feel the power of Ko's thoughts feeding the beams that struck the forehead and reached into the brain to draw away the life. He felt Te's mind in there with him, touching as he touched, consternation building in her thoughts.

"He is harming them," she cried. "Prim, I can feel him hurting them."

"It is more than that," Vo told her, hardly believing what he was saying, "he is trying to end their lives."

Kasstovaal could feel his life slipping away. He had not believed, before now, that you could feel it happening so definitely. To actually sense your last seconds running out. To feel the last of your energy ebbing out of your body and know that it would keep draining away until there was none left to bring light in through your eyes. Then there would be only darkness.

He could not fight the force that was rending his mind. He had tried but he could not push the pain back. There was not enough of his mind left to struggle, now, barely enough to support him, the living entity that was Malkan Kasstovaal. Soon there would not be enough even for that and he would slip away.

Is this how it ends, he thought, through the pain.

"No!"

He was becoming incoherent. It did not register with him that the deep rumbling voice that had said that one word belonged to nobody in that room, nobody he knew on the whole Rock. It didn't even occur to him to wonder how he had managed to hear the word through the screaming of his thoughts.

He was going, fading out. All that was left to him was one last, childlike plea. Did he speak those last words? Did his voice cry them out in a last attempt for mercy? Or were they just in his head?

"I don't want it to end. Not now. Not when I am so close to a way home. I don't want to die. I don't want to diiiie..."

And the voice said, "I will not let you." Then it roared.

All three Dwellers heard it. Vo and Te pulled their minds back out of the way as the roar thundered past, aimed straight at Ko.

Vo sensed the edge of it as it passed him, sensed it not only as a sound but also as a rushing wave of force, a force he had never encountered before.

Whatever it was it closed around the startled Ko like a giant, cold hand and hurled him into the air, the crystal dropping from his fingers and rolling on the floor. It lifted him fifteen feet in the air, threw him across the room and smashed him, hard, against the wall.

There was a loud, sickening crunch and cracks appeared all over Ko's body. He stayed pinned there, fifteen feet up the wall, for several seconds before whatever it was let him go. Then he slid down the wall a short way, leaving a black, slimy stain behind him before his body finally unstuck itself from the wall and fell the rest of the way to the floor.

It all happened in a few seconds. Vo and Te, stunned into horrified stillness could only watch it unfold before them.

Vo pulled himself together first. Action was required. No time for disbelief. No time for neatness, either. He blasted a ragged hole in the wall with his mind and hurried in through it with Te on his heels.

It was the Beyonders they looked to, first. They could both feel Ko's mind still operating, though sluggishly. He could wait, even though his body lay in a broken heap on the floor amidst a widening pool of a thick black liquid, like waste oil, that oozed out through the cracks in his body.

The two humans were unconscious. They could feel a thread of intelligent thought from each, but no more. They didn't know if that was enough.

"Quickly!" Vo said to Te, urgently. "Send for Oa and Ji to come here. This needs their skills. It is beyond ours."

"What about Ko?" Te asked.

They both looked at the crumpled body. The black puddle had stopped growing and, as they watched, it actually shrank in size a little before stopping again.

"I think he will recover," said Vo. "I will call Azu to give word on this. I know of no precedent that will guide us. We cannot act."

They sent their messages, urgent words rushing through the Rock's veins, and waited. That was all they could do.

Oa arrived first, radiating concern, both compassionate and professional.

"Have they given any sign of returning to consciousness?" she asked, briskly.

"None," said Vo. "We can sense their minds only weakly."

Oa bent to examine Jeryant first. "What has done this?"

Vo pointed to the crystal lying innocently on the floor. "Ko was directing his mind energies through that crystal," he said. "I am not familiar with a construction capable of such an effect."

"We must study it closely," Oa said. "Clearly it has caused much damage within them. We must know how it works and what it was designed to attack."

"An attack, you say, this is?" said a voice from the doorway. They all turned.

Azu strode in flanked by two bulky Dweller males. "You, Oa, concur with Vo that this was an attack on the Beyonders? There is not an innocent explanation you can suggest?"

"I have only my preliminary observations to make a judgement on," said Oa, carefully. "I can better report when I have examined the Beyonders more closely in my laboratory. Certainly great harm has come of this. Whether or not it is harm caused of intent is not for me to determine."

"Indeed," said Azu, levelly. "This is a grave matter and it must be looked into closely. Do what you can for the Beyonders. Their testimony may be needed."

"Testimony?" asked Vo.

"Never before has a Dweller attacked another living being, let alone an acknowledged and welcomed guest. There is no precedent for this situation. Whatever is decided and done must be decided and done in the sight of all Dwellers. When all the data has been gathered, it will be brought to the Gathering Place where all may see and decide."

He walked across to Ko and stood over him. The pool around him had been contracting in surges, the black liquid being sucked back into him through the cracks in his skin, pausing only for him to gather strength. Azu watched impassively until the last of the liquid had been reabsorbed and the last crack in the skin sealed itself neatly. Ko groaned and made a feeble attempt to lift himself.

Azu motioned to the two Dwellers with him. "Help him to rise," he said, "and take him to his private room. Hold him there until all have gathered to hear him."

The two Dwellers lifted Ko bodily and led him away. Azu lingered awhile, contemplating the black stain high up on the wall. He was the First Voice of all the Dwellers, the one who must speak for all, the one who must condense the will of thirty-two thousand individuals down to a single word and speak it. He could hold no opinion unique only to himself. His purpose did not allow that luxury.

And yet even he could not help but speculate at the power that it would have taken to do that to Ko. To negate all his control over his position in space and fling him like a toy across a room. A force too powerful for even the Voidseer's apprentice to resist.

Such power, he thought, in the hands of so random a mind. We must, all of us, beware.

22.

When thought returned and Kasstovaal felt himself coming awake, he hardly dared believe it. The last thing he could remember, the last certain knowledge he'd had was that death was closing over him. He had known it as surely as he had known his name, the last two words he expected to retain before the end.

And yet. He thought, therefore, he still was. He tested his cognisance gingerly, afraid that it might wink out again if he probed it too deeply. But it stayed. And he stayed. The wave of relief that washed over him nearly made him pass out again. But he held on, pulled himself upward towards wakefulness.

He became aware of the hard slab under his back and legs, the perception of lying horizontal with his head slightly raised. Then he became aware of the most thunderous headache he had ever experienced in his life. He groaned and brought a hand up to his forehead, rubbing against the temples to try and ease the pain.

Someone said, "Kasstovaal is waking up." It was Te's voice.

Kasstovaal opened his eyes only a fraction to see where he was. The light hurt. He got a blurred picture of a laboratory before he had to shut them again.

Oa's voice, directly over him, asked, "How are you feeling?"

"Terrible," he said, hoarsely. "My head is killing me."

"That was very nearly true," said Oa.

Kasstovaal felt something cold and hard press against the side of his head and the pain faded away to nothing with merciful speed. He opened his eyes. Oa was bending over him, in the act of lifting a crystal away from his head.

"Is that better?" she asked.

"Much. Thanks." He tried to push himself up on his elbows but the room spun around him and he had to let himself back down.

"You must rest awhile yet," said Oa. "It will take time for all the functions of your mind to reactivate."

"What happened to me?" he asked. "What did you do?"

"It appears," said Vo's voice from across the room, "that Ko was attempting to shut down all of your mind functions with this crystal."

Kasstovaal turned his head. Ko's red crystal was hovering, spinning slowly in thin air, about a centimetre above the tip of a transparent pyramid. There were crystal controls around the pyramid's base and Vo was working at them, circling around it to reach the controls he wanted.

"I have never seen a lattice like this," he said, not looking up, "it appears to have been designed with no other purpose but to neutralise mental energies. And yet, it is itself powered by those same mental energies. Most fascinating."

"But horrifying, also," said Te, coming into view beside him. "No such device has ever been conceived among the Dwellers, not even in the course of research. The Beyonders have a word for such a device but we do not."

Kasstovaal said, "You mean a weapon."

"Yes," said Vo. "It is a concept wholly alien to us."

"Not to all of your people, it seems."

"So it appears," Vo conceded.

The air nearby suddenly rumbled with a king-sized belch followed in the same breath by a loud groan and a curse. Kasstovaal turned his head.

Jeryant was lying on an adjacent slab and just coming to. "Will whoever is kicking me in the head kindly stop this instant," he moaned. "Otherwise there will, most definitely, be trouble."

Kasstovaal propped himself up. "What's the matter, Jery?" he asked. "Been overdoing the crystals, have we? I thought you weren't supposed to get a hangover after one of those."

Jeryant opened his eyes wide enough to glower at him briefly. "The amber ones I can handle," he muttered, "the red ones are a bit beyond my palette. Gods, will somebody do something about my head? Amputation would be favourite, right about now."

Oa went to him and held the crystal against the side of his head. The furrows in his forehead relaxed and he sighed with the relief.

"That should feel more comfortable," said Oa.

Jeryant looked up at her. "Woman, you are a godsend," he said. "I'd marry you, if I thought you knew what I was talking about."

Oa gave him a quizzical look before turning away.

Jeryant looked over at Kasstovaal. "You all right?" he asked.

"Getting there," said Kasstovaal. "Scared shitless, more than anything. I got a very clear feeling of how close I just came to dying."

"Tell me about it." Jeryant lifted himself into a sitting position, rubbed his palms hard against his cheeks and then slapped himself in the face a couple of times. Then he swung his legs off the slab and stood up.

Kasstovaal marvelled at him. "How do you get up from something like that so quick?" he asked, wonderingly.

"Friend, I've woken up with more hangovers than you've had hot women. It gets easier the more you do it. Leastwise, it doesn't hurt so much. You'll find that out when you grow up"

"I'm not sure I'd want to." Kasstovaal got to his own feet, still a little unsteady, and the two of them joined Vo at his pyramid.

"So how does this thing work, exactly?" Jeryant asked, pointing.

Vo stopped in front of a screen, displaying a complex lattice pattern. He raised a finger to the screen's surface and traced along the pattern in an action Kasstovaal recognised from his own methods. Vo was tracing a circuit, working out how it bent and twisted the energies that flowed through it. "Accepting that this is indeed a...weapon," he said, stumbling over the unfamiliar word, "the principle of its function is really quite straightforward. It depolarises the mind cells and makes them incapable of conducting energy. They become useless and inert, capable of storing the patterns of information already in them but incapable of releasing or processing that information. It is not a quick process by any means but if Ko had continued for long enough, there would not have been enough operating cells left to maintain your personalities."

"In other words, we would be dead," said Jeryant.

"Your selves would, certainly, have been irretrievable," said Oa. "We could have re-polarised the affected cells to retrieve the stored data from them. But the self is a complex entity. It needs constant renewal and activity and there is always a given portion of the mind's resources devoted to that single task."

"Why didn't he attack that portion first?" asked Jeryant. "If he wanted to make an end of us, that would have been the most sensible way to go about it."

"The mind is a flexible thing," said Oa. "The preservation of the self is its first priority. As the cells cease to function, it will sacrifice the peripheral systems first - movement, speech and so forth - and devote its remaining resources to keep the self operating. As more cells become inoperable, more functions, higher ones, would be shut down in favour of the self until all functions bar that one have ceased."

"And then what?"

"If the damage continues and the mind's resources drop below a threshold level, the self will begin to lose its integrity. It will quickly break down beyond the point where it can be retrieved. You two came very close to that point."

"We know," said Kasstovaal.

"Fortunately," said Oa, "the process was interrupted before that threshold was reached. Enough of your minds remained to keep your selves operating at survival level until we could repolarise the damaged cells and allow energy to flow through them again. Once that was done, we had only to wait until you had recouped your mental energies."

"Lucky for us you stopped him in time," said Jeryant. "If there's a next time I hope you won't leave it so late."

The Dwellers exchanged glances. Vo said, "We did not act to stop him. We assumed that one of you had."

"Not me," said Jeryant. "I couldn't move my little finger, let alone clobber the little bastard. And, Gods know, I wanted to badly enough."

"Same with me," said Kasstovaal. "I couldn't do a thing."

"That is most strange," said Vo. "Both Te and myself experienced what happened. Ko was overcome by an enormous blast of psyonic energy, more than he could have countered or resisted. Neither of us could create such a force unaided. It must have come from one or both of you."

"I wouldn't know how to do that with all my wits about me," said Jeryant, "let alone once that crystal got to work."

"Could one of us have done it unconsciously?" Kasstovaal suggested.

"It is possible," said Oa, hesitantly, "but it is a frightening thought that so much power might not be under conscious control."

"Indeed," said Vo, "there is much about your minds we have still to learn."

"So have we, it would seem," said Jeryant. He smiled to himself. "Perhaps we've picked up a guardian angel somewhere along the way, Kass. Have you been praying behind my back again? I've warned you, it stunts your growth."

"I do not understand that reference," said Te.

"Join the club, my dear."

Kasstovaal asked, "What will happen to Ko now?"

"That has yet to be decided," said Vo. "Clearly there must be some price exacted from him for his action, some...penance."

"You mean a punishment."

"That's the right word. Thank you. Yes, a punishment. That concept, also, is unfamiliar to us. It has never been necessary to demand a punishment of a Dweller. No one before Ko has ever acted so grossly to the detriment of another."

"To the detriment!" exclaimed Jeryant. "The little toad was trying to wipe us out."

"Indeed, it is a grave offence," said Vo, "to assist a being to its death before its purpose has been fulfilled. What worse can any Dweller conceive of doing."

Jeryant opened his mouth to say more and then shut it again. The Dwellers would never see death in the way he did, he realised, no matter how much he ranted at them.

"Who's going to do the deciding?" Kasstovaal asked. "If there is no precedent for punishing a Dweller, who's going to set it?"

"The decision will be put to all at the Gathering," said Te.

"That is so," said Vo. "There is precedent for where there is no precedent. All must have a say."

"You're going to put Ko on trial," said Kasstovaal.

Vo considered the word. "No," he said, "that is not wholly correct. There is no need to establish Ko's guilt or the lack of it in this matter. That much is already proven to the satisfaction of all. Both Te and myself saw it and felt it happen and all may look into our minds to see and feel the truth of it. But even had we not been there, the Rock sees all and remembers all. No one, by now, has any doubts about the action he took."

"So what's going to happen?"

"The question of his motives must be looked into," said Vo. "Only Ko knows why he has attempted this folly. When all have come to the Gathering Place he will be brought to account for himself before all."

"That will be an excuse worth hearing," said Oa. "It is difficult to see what reasons he might have had. He and his master keep to themselves. He cannot have had much contact with the Beyonders."

"Perhaps he has heard about the Barrier," said Te.

The two humans exchanged a glance. Jeryant saw Kasstovaal's body stiffen slightly.

"What about the Barrier?" he asked, keeping his voice neutral.

"It is the news we were bringing to you when we found you under attack. We have had word from Cy, whose purpose it is to develop a navigation technique suitable for ultra-velocity mass transfer. During one of her experiments, she determined that the Barrier is drawing nearer to the Rock with every unit that passes."

"Which is moving?" Kasstovaal asked, quietly, "The Rock or the Barrier?"

"It is the Barrier which moves." said Te "Cy has determined that all the spatial bodies in this area are still in their usual positions, relative to the Rock. The Rock has not moved from its place. The Barrier is contracting towards us."

"It has been theorised," said Vo, "that the cause of this contraction may be the arrival of you two and your craft inside this reality. The additional mass may be upsetting the balance of the forces that hold the Barrier in place."

Kasstovaal looked Jeryant in the eye, daring him to say a word. "That's terrible," he said, slowly.

Vo said, "Of course we do not hold you responsible for this. There is no way you could have known of it and we appreciate that your continued presence here may well be accidental and is certainly unplanned. It would be irrational to lay blame upon you."

Jeryant was still held by Kasstovaal's eyes. Soundless words passed between them. "I'm pleased to hear it," was all he said aloud.

"And even if we thought otherwise," Vo went on, "to dispose of you would not have solved the problem. Indeed, you are already working to solve the problem for us by the construction of your space vessel. You are to be thanked for that."

Kasstovaal turned away from Jeryant and the taut strings of his body relaxed a little. "We are only working towards our own desire," he said.

"If it does your people a service along the way then I am glad. We owe you our lives at least once over."

"But I wonder if Ko thought otherwise," said Te. "It might begin to explain what he did."

"Barely," said Vo, "the hypothesis concerning the Beyonders is as well known as the measurement that determined the Barrier's movement. Surely he must have realised that destroying the Beyonders' minds would not have stopped the contraction. Indeed, it would have exacerbated the problem by making it more difficult for the excess matter to be collected and removed. With the Beyonders alive and working, that will soon be done for us."

"Perhaps he didn't have all the details," Jeryant suggested. "Before he fired that thing he was bleating on about some harm he thought we had done to the Dwellers. Something he wanted payback for."

"It may be so," said Vo. "We shall have to see how Ko accounts for himself and his actions."

"Can we be present?" Kasstovaal asked.

"Of course," said Oa. "As the wronged, you two have a greater right than we to hear Ko's reasons and see him punished. We have only been awaiting your recovery and the results of Vo's tests on the crystal before calling the Gathering."

"What about Ra?" asked Kasstovaal. "Has he said anything about this? The boy is his apprentice, after all. Ra might have ordered him to attack us."

The Dwellers looked shocked. Te said, "To suspect the Voidseer of having a part in this is unthinkable."

"But I'm asking you to think about it," persisted Kasstovaal. "Voidseer or not, he is still a Dweller just like the rest of you. It is no more unthinkable to suspect him of plotting our deaths than to believe it of Ko, or any of you. In fact I would say he's more likely to have found reasons to want us destroyed than anyone else, since he professes to have knowledge denied to all other Dwellers. And if he ordered Ko to do the deed for him, and thereby keep himself safe from accusation, wouldn't the boy do it for him? His master?"

"No!" said Vo, shaking his head vigorously and walking away from Kasstovaal as if to put himself out of the range of such thoughts. "I cannot conceive what you suggest."

"But you can't deny the possibility," said Kasstovaal. "I, for one, will be very interested to hear what your venerated Voidseer has to say at this gathering. Have you finished analysing that crystal?"

Vo stopped in front of the pyramid and composed himself. "Yes," he said, shortly.

"Then perhaps you should call the gathering," said Kasstovaal, gently, "the sooner this is cleared up the better."

"You didn't have to push so hard," Jeryant murmured, as the group headed for the arena.

"I had to, at least, get them to consider it," Kasstovaal hissed back, "I can't believe Ra doesn't know something about this. Are you going to tell me that Ko formed his plan and put that crystal together without his master sensing something from him? If he can send his mind where no other Dweller can, he can't be far behind Ji in mental techniques. He may even be superior to Ji in mental skill."

"That is if you believe that he can send his mind into the voids and see what's lurking in there," said Jeryant. "Religious leaders in our universe all claim to be able to do something that mere mortals can't do. I've not met one yet who could live up to everything he claimed."

"I've felt hate from him," said Kasstovaal, grimly. "Real hate. So strong he couldn't hold the waves in."

"Balls!" said Jeryant. "If his control is as good as you say, he never would have let those feelings slip out. The only reason he let you feel those waves was because he wanted you to. He wanted to intimidate you and he succeeded."

"Doesn't that prove my point?"

"All that proves," said Jeryant, "is that he can push your buttons any time he likes and he knows it. He's picked up on your fear and your paranoia and he knows he can use both of them to bring you to heel, if he needs to. He doesn't have to resort to anything as primitive as violence to get rid of you. Or me, for that matter. I know the Religious fraternity; they like to be subtle rather than take direct action. They'd be proud of out friend Ra, I reckon."

"Nevertheless. I'm going to keep my eye on him. See how he reacts."

"Why not. Save him the trouble of watching your reactions. In fact, I'll tell you what, why don't you go the whole hog and accuse him to his face in front of the entire Dweller population. He'll love that."

"I'm not that much of a fool," Kasstovaal protested. "I know I don't have any proof against him and even if I did we've both just seen how difficult it would to convince the others. He'd tear me up for arse paper if I challenged him face-to-face."

"You'd better believe it," said Jeryant, earnestly. "If you'll take my advice, you'll keep your eyes down and your mouth shut like a good boy. That might make him wonder how tight a hold he has of your strings."

"Perhaps," said Kasstovaal. "But there is a chance something will slip. Who knows, Ko might accuse him or, at least, embarrass him. I don't want to miss it if it happens. Maybe Ra has a string or two of his own I can pull back."

The five of them passed through the archway into the arena and Vo led them, once again, across the floor towards the central podium where all might see them. Dwellers were already filling the ledges as far as the eye could see but there was not the silence that there had been before. A low murmur could be heard, a soft sound but made up of thousands of much smaller sounds, each the tiny thread of disquiet escaping from a Dweller. The murmur carried all the accumulated weight of that disquiet and the whole vast volume of air within the cavern vibrated with it and felt oppressive.

Azu stood waiting for them on the podium. He, at least, remained silent and impassive and only he knew the effort it cost him to keep his mind closed, for now, to all that anxiety. When the time came, it was his purpose to open his mind to all the minds gathered about him, to be the funnel into which thirty-two thousand Dwellers would pour their thoughts and opinions. But not now, not until some measure of calm had been restored and the salient facts were made known.

Vo led the party around the podium to stand behind the First Voice in a single line. They waited, in silence, while the remaining Dwellers came in and found their places.

Kasstovaal swivelled his eyes about, searching the levels above him and soon found what he was looking for. Ra was standing in the same spot he had occupied during the Welcome ceremony, at the approximate centre of the first bridge up from the arena floor. It was, perhaps, the spot he had reserved for himself and always occupied and Kasstovaal considered what an ideal place it was for him. The podium was designed to be the centre of activity in this place, the focus of all the eyes that watched. But whoever stood there to be the centre of attention would know that the Voidseer was standing over them, watching their every action.

Again the crowd had edged away from him to leave a space around him. He stood silent and still, apparently staring down at an empty spot on the arena floor just in front of Azu. As Kasstovaal watched him, Ra very slowly turned his head and stared Kasstovaal straight in the eye. He knows, Kasstovaal thought. He felt me looking at him and he's letting me know that he knows. The two held each other's gaze for several seconds, or was it hours; Kasstovaal had lost the power to know. Then Ra turned his head away again, as slowly and deliberately as before, and resumed his stare at the empty space beneath him.

Damn, Kasstovaal thought. First he lets me know that he can feel what I'm thinking and then he shows me that I am beneath his notice, an insignificance he can just brush away and ignore. He's still calling the tune and I'm letting him do it. Damn, sod and bugger it to hells! He lowered his eyes from the bridge and waited, fuming at himself and trying not to.

In front of him on the podium, Azu raised his arms to enjoin silence. The heavy murmuring ceased.

"Let Ko be brought into the sight of all," he commanded.

On cue, the two burly Dwellers entered through the archway opposite, holding Ko by the arms between them. Ko's eyes were turned down to the floor. He did not look up as he was marched across the floor, nor as he was brought to stand on the exact spot that Ra had been staring at so intently. All eyes looked upon him but he would meet none of them, not even those of Azu who stood before him.

"Ko," said Azu, "you have been called before this gathering to answer for your actions. All here know the events that are in question. We have the testimony of Vo and Te who witnessed them. We have the analysis of the crystal which you were seen to use. We have the word of Oa as to the damage done to the minds of the Beyonders, our guests. And the Rock sees all, knows all, and tells all.

"All these facts are known. What concerns us is how they should be read. The facts suggest that you intended to end the Beyonders' lives and that this action, this assault, was designed to bring that about. But one thing more is as yet unknown and must be known before we can rightly decide on what is to be done. You have closed your mind to us and to the Rock so we cannot see for ourselves the motive that drove you. Will you now tell us, that we might understand your action?"

Ko said nothing and made no movement.

"I ask you again," said Azu. "Explain to us why you have done this. Only with this knowledge can a true and correct decision be made."

No answer, not even a raising of the head to acknowledge that the question had been heard.

Azu said, "All have heard, as the Rock heard, the words you said to the Beyonders before you attacked them. You claimed some grievance against them, claimed a right to take recompense on behalf of our people. We know of no wrong done to us by these two. What do you know differently?"

No answer.

"Silence will do you no service in this," said Azu, more sternly. "If you offer us nothing which could mitigate the action you took, even by a little, what can we do but put upon it the worst complexion, based solely on the bare facts. Is that how you would have us judge you?"

Nothing.

Azu said, "You know that we cannot and will not take the reason from you by force. But the combined will of all may yet be brought to bear to persuade you of the rightness of revealing it. Is that what you want?"

This did bring a reaction. Ko raised his head shakily and looked up into Azu's stern gaze. Then he looked quickly to left and right, to glimpse the sheer numbers that looked down upon him, perhaps weighing in his mind the amount of force that many Dwellers could rain down upon him. The thought seemed to scare him but still he said nothing, lowering his eyes back to the floor. He did not look at Ra, though he must know where his master was standing. Ra, though, still continued to stare directly at him.

"Very well, then," said Azu, "if you will have it so; so it shall be." He raised his arms again. "Let all make known to this Dweller their desire to know the truth. Show him that his silence can only bring harm."

The echoes of his words faded. The cavern became silent. But Kasstovaal felt the wave that descended from the highest ledge, nearest the ceiling, gathering energy and force as it passed circle after circle of minds on its way down, building up and up until its full weight focused down on Ko.

The young Dweller convulsed when it hit him. His head jerked upward and his body became stiff. Slowly, shakily, he brought his hands up to press against the sides of his head, as though he were trying to block the ears he didn't have from a sound too loud for him to bear. His face contorted in pain.

Kasstovaal probed outwards, gingerly, with his mind, trying to catch the edge of that wave. Even so gentle a touch roared like thunder in his head. It was a torrent of words intermingled with the frustration of not knowing: Tell us why, they said; We must know; Only you can tell us; You must tell us; The truth; Only the truth will help you; Only if we can understand; Make us understand; Tell us why; We must know.

The words went around and around, thirty thousand soundless voices speaking them all at once, urging him to give up the secret. All the relentless, driving thirst for knowledge that powered them to pursue their purposes to the end, distilled and focussed on Ko. Kasstovaal pulled his mind away.

Ko was quivering under the onslaught, bending double with the pain. For a moment Kasstovaal felt pity for him. He had had a glimpse of what the young Dweller was experiencing. For all their benevolence the Dwellers knew well how to torture one of their own and did so most efficiently, not from any malice but because it was logical to do so. The truth had to be known.

But Ko would not give in, even under so much pressure. His head shook slowly from side to side and still he uttered not one sound.

Kasstovaal felt the wave fade and die. Ko slowly took his hands away from his head and, with an effort, straightened to face Azu.

"Even now, you continue to resist," said Azu, softly. "Not all the persuasion we can bring to bear will convince you to reveal your mind to us. So be it then."

He turned his face upwards to address the tiers of Dwellers reaching up to the ceiling. "Is there any among us who can give word on the reason for Ko's action? Any word said, any action observed, any wave felt. Any small thing that might have relevance. Speak out now so that all may hear."

Kasstovaal's eyes snapped back to rest on Ra. This was the time. He noticed a few of the other Dwellers also turning their heads to look that way. After all, who should know better than the Voidseer what his apprentice was doing? But Ra said nothing, did nothing, just continued staring down at his pupil, face blank and unreadable.

"So," said Azu. "Still there is silence. Still the truth hides from us. All that is left to us are the facts. Never before has a Dweller attacked another being. There is no precedent for how we should deal. But, still, this matter demands a remedy. We must decide with such as we have."

He paused for a moment and it seemed to Kasstovaal that the whole cavern was holding its breath, waiting for the words that would come next.

Azu said, "Let all make their will known to the First Voice. Let the decision be made."

The cavern fell silent again. This time Kasstovaal did not try to reach out for the descending wave. He had no need to. The power of it was no less than the wave that had struck Ko but it was much nearer, aimed at Azu standing just in front of him. What was different was the complexity. He caught brief snatches of it without trying, not a litany of repeated words but a jumble of arguments and opinions, thirty-two thousand points of view all being expressed at the same time. Azu showed no sign of pain as his mind received them, though his hands trembled just a little.

Kasstovaal looked along the line at Vo, Te and Oa. All three were staring fixedly at Azu, all three having their say, adding their silent voices to the rest. It carried on for maybe ten minutes or more and, with no part of their own to play, the two humans could only stand and wait, uncomfortably. Neither spoke for fear of what they might interrupt.

The wave ceased abruptly. Azu's body sagged a little. When he spoke his voice seemed to have taken on extra harmonics as though two or three others we speaking in time with him. "The Dwellers of the Rock speak with one voice. One will forms the words. This is the will of the Dwellers."

He turned and faced Jeryant and Kasstovaal. "Beyonders," he said, "this concerns you most strongly. It is known that you have a concept, a word, called justice which covers contingencies such as this. But you must understand that it is a concept new to us as it has never been needed before. It may not be possible for us to exact from Ko a justice you would think fitting. As the victims, you may wish to claim your own price from him. We are, however, mindful of your continued safety among us. As the reason for his attack remains unknown, we must assume that it still exists and must, therefore, take steps to prevent him from acting upon it a second time, perhaps with different results."

Jeryant glanced at Kasstovaal, who nodded. Then he said, "With that understood, Azu, we are willing to leave his punishment in your hands. He is one of your people so he should be judged by the will of your people. We shall be satisfied with that."

Azu nodded. "It is well," he said. He turned back to face Ko, his face becoming stern again. "The Beyonders wish no price from you. We, however, are honour bound to protect them during their stay with us. Soon they will be gone from this place, with our assistance and good wishes. It is our decision that, until that time at least, you will be placed in confinement where you can cause them no more harm. Once they have left, we shall consider whether or not you should be set free."

Ko faced the First Voice, the nearest his people would ever have to a leader, and he was calm. He had weathered the storm and had held true to his own secret resolve.

Azu went on, "This may also exact a little of the justice owing to the Beyonders as it will delay you in the completion of your purpose and prolong your existence."

This made Ko stiffen a little. This was a consequence he had not foreseen.

"A pity, it is," said Azu, mildly, "that you are the Voidseer's apprentice. It means that his purpose, also, will be delayed, for he cannot complete your training until you come forth from your confinement. You may wish to think on this while you wait out your time."

Now the distress was clear on Ko's face. He turned and sought out Ra for the first time, gazing up into that stony glare with entreaty in his own eyes. Ra never moved, never made sign. Ko turned back to Azu.

"Is there anything you wish to say before this gathering is dissolved?" Azu asked.

And Ko did speak, spitting out the words as though they cost him great effort. "What I wish to say, I cannot say," was all he said.

Azu waited for more but none came. He nodded to the Dwellers standing guard over Ko. "Take him out," he said. "Keep him fast held until the confinement cell can be made ready."

Ko was marched out. As Azu stepped down from the podium, the low murmur of disquiet started up again, only dying away as the Dwellers filed out taking their agitation with them.

The cell appeared to be a room much like any other. It had been picked for its solitude, situated on one of the emptier lower levels and on the opposite side of the Rock to the hangar where Kasstovaal worked. The main features which set it apart from other rooms were the mechanical door into it, operated by ordinary electric motors and held by mechanical locks, and the similarly motorised window which could be opened to the outside but was barred and too small to escape through. Both could be operated only by the control panel set into the wall outside the door.

"The coating of the walls is the key to this room," Vo explained. He was giving the two humans a tour of the facility, perhaps in reassurance. Ko would soon be brought here and Azu had suggested that they, as the injured parties, should see the sentence carried out. Perhaps he hoped to provoke Ko into revealing more than he yet had.

Jeryant walked up to one of the walls and examined it more closely. The wall appeared to lined by a thin sheet of glass, stuck firmly and invisibly to the Rock beneath.

"What is it?" he asked.

"It is similar to the Psychoactive polymer that our travel plates are made of," said Vo, "except that this variation acts in the opposite fashion. This coating is designed to be resistant to both physical force and matter-forming. It would be difficult for any Dweller to penetrate through it, though for them it would eventually be possible. It will not be so for Ko. The polymer chains have been coded to recognise his mind energy pattern, in particular. Any matter-forming power he tries to use on the molecules of the walls will be absorbed by the polymer shielding. The observation window onto the corridor is also coated, as are the door and the bars of the outside window. Only the opening of the door itself will release him."

"Won't he be able to form something to cut through the material?" asked Kasstovaal. "Presumably he'll still be able to do forming using the free-floating matter."

"That has been taken care of," said Vo. "All free-floating matter has been removed from the cell and a field of force will prevent any more from entering. Even through the window."

"That's another thing," said Kasstovaal. "Is the outside window entirely necessary? Our people have found that the best way to make a secure cell is to keep the openings into it to an absolute minimum."

"The window is vital," said Vo. "We cannot deny him the basics of living, no matter what he has done. He will need the window to vent his energies when Voidrise comes."

"Sorry," Kasstovaal said, sheepishly, "I was forgetting."

"The window will open itself automatically when it is time for Voidrise," said Vo. "And close again when it is over. That way there is no danger of him being forgotten and missing the Voidrise."

"Sensible," said Jeryant. "You're not usually thinking very clearly around that time, after all."

"Quite," said Vo. "We must exit here now. Ko is coming."

The three of them stepped out into the corridor and stood back against the wall. Ko was still between his two guards, held by the arms and marched forcefully. Azu came behind him to see that all was done.

Only when he drew level with the humans did Ko resist his guards and bring himself to a stop. He glared at them with open hatred.

"They think you merciful for wanting no price of me," he hissed, "but I know better. You mock me still with your mercy."

The guards thrust him into the cell and one of them operated the control that closed the door on him. They could see him glaring at them through the observation window.

He shouted so that they could hear him. "They mock me and they mock you too, my people. If nothing else is allowed to me, I shall put a stop to that. One way or another that insult shall end." Then he sat himself on the floor, staring into space and saying no more.

"What does he mean?" Jeryant wondered.

"I wish I knew," said Kasstovaal. "That, above all else, I wish I knew."

EIGHT: MINDSHARE

23.

Time must pass. No power over matter and energy can change that. Time must pass and take with it the ephemeral substance of all the universes, whatever the form it takes.

Much time had passed for Te since she had last stood upon this ledge near the summit, contemplating the crags and fissures in between the ledges of the Rock below her, and the depredations that time had imposed were all too clear. The cracks, once dark with mystery, no longer spoke to her. She could no longer look into the grey and see the treasure of images and inspirations she had once been able to see. The Atlas has fallen into a final sleep and would no longer stir for her.

She had come fully to adulthood. Her mind was hers to control and no longer wandered off by itself in search of dreams. And the Rock was only the Rock, seeing all and knowing all and, in its turn, seen and known for what it was and nothing else.

How many times had she come up here with a problem she couldn't unravel by herself? How many times had she let the Rock carry her mind away into a new dream, a new set of possibilities, a whole new perspective? How many of those new perspectives had given her the key to solving the problem that vexed her? A new problem vexed her now and she had come up here again in the vain hope of recapturing that old magic. But it was not to be.

Way down there somewhere, in the deepest depths of the Rock, the Beyonders' ship was nearing completion. She had watched it grow. It was at once sharp with scientific precision and smoothed with aesthetic line, a combination that could impose its own will on the universe, any universe, and twist it to its own needs and liking as easily as any art crystal could. To all parts of her Dweller mind it was a pleasure to see, even a thing of beauty, and yet at the same time something wholly unnatural.

That was the problem. Not just the ship; everything about the Beyonders was still strange to her. It didn't matter how much Kasstovaal or Jeryant talked to her. It didn't matter how much time and care she put into piecing together the jumble of their ramblings in order to form a logical and understandable summary of the salient points. It didn't matter how much raw data she gathered. They still remained alien.

She had set out to compile a definitive work on the Beyonders and their universe. It was not her formal purpose, at least not yet, and no one had actually said anything to her about it. But she knew that she had to do the most complete and thorough job of it possible. The Beyonders would soon be leaving and there was every chance that their like would never be seen again on the Rock. There may never be another opportunity to gather the information for a complete profile and if it wasn't done now, knowledge of the Beyonders and their wonderful universe, too big to conceive, would be lost to the Dwellers for ever.

She knew that the duty had fallen, unspoken, to her. She was the best placed to glean the data and had the leisure to compile it. She felt the responsibility heavy upon her but she embraced it, nonetheless. She was eager to learn about them. Ever since she had first seen that strange pipe-limbed Bio-form lying in the casket, her curiosity had seized it like a gift and would not let go.

But there was so little time. Soon the Beyonders would be gone and her work was still such a long way from completion. She had accumulated more facts than she cared to count, all carefully stripped out of the Beyonders' descriptions and anecdotes and ordered into a form she could use. But they were all just pieces of an enormous puzzle for which she did not have the pattern. The nearest she could compare it to was the experience of rebuilding her mind after hearing the Beyonder's cry, fitting the fractured pieces together in logical order. But this was a puzzle the size of a universe, not just one mind. A universe, moreover, many trillions of times bigger than her own.

Given enough time, many thousands of cycles it would have to be, she might eventually form an accurate representation of that universe. But she didn't have that much time, even assuming that either Beyonder would be willing to stay and describe their universe to her for that amount of time. But they could not stay. They wanted to leave and, it seemed, that the forces that held reality together also thought they should leave and with the utmost expedition.

They could generalise, of course, she and they, in the time that was left. But, then, she would never be able to do justice to that other universe where the Beyonders lived and worked and built and destroyed and loved and hated. She had been given the briefest glimpses into its wonders and, more than that, had felt the depth and richness of it printed deep in Kasstovaal's mind, something he himself was probably not fully aware of. No amount of spoken words would ever be able to convey that richness to an outsider like her.

There was only one alternative that would do the work and show her what she could not see. As she had, once, been able to see the Rock change through her child's eyes so now she must see the Beyonders' universe through their eyes. Her people could do that. She could do it. The problem was did she dare?

There was such power lurking in those alien minds. Ji had felt it and warned her about it. Twice, no, three times now she had felt its force for herself. Enough power to blast her body and mind out of existence. She was sure the Beyonders meant no harm to any on the Rock, herself perhaps least of all, but it was clear that this force was not under their direct control. Their goodwill would not stop it acting if it chose to. Acting against her.

And yet she wanted to know, wanted to see, had to see. Her raging curiosity, the in-built drive that powered her people inside the prisons of their bodies, demanded that she must know. It was irrational but she could not bare the thought of spending her entire existence, in body and beyond, not knowing where the Beyonders really dwelt, without ever seeing it just once for herself. She could never go there, of course. But a part of it lived in the minds of Kasstovaal and Jeryant, a picture seen through their perceptions, enough to show her what she would see if she could go there.

Did her curiosity outweigh her fear? That was the question. Did the curiosity of all her people and all the Dwellers who would follow after them outweigh the risk of unleashing a random force that might even be powerful enough to destroy the Rock and all of them with it? Did she believe that was possible? Yes, she decided, she did. They had all felt the power of that first cry from the mists, an undirected cry of despair with no intended target. How much more potent would a directed blast be, a blast directed at them?

She could not decide and the Rock would give her no help today, nor ever would again. She knew she could no longer see the Rock with her child's vision, see the other worlds she once had, and she felt the loss of it sorely. But now she had another chance to see other worlds through other eyes, worlds even her imagination would never have been able to conjure up out of the Rock's craggy surface. Had the risk been only to her, that would have tipped the argument and decided her. But she was not the only one at risk.

She would have to talk with Vo about it, the way she had always done with her unresolved theories and incomplete plans. He had always been the one she turned to and invariably he picked out the enormous holes she had left and reformulated and rebuilt her work to something workable which was, suddenly, not hers. He seemed, in all innocence, to make it his own and unconsciously stripped out any value her own efforts might have had. She had hated him for that but she had still always gone back to him, perhaps in search of his approval though she had never found it. That was how the child, Te, had seen it. And perhaps it was so.

But the adult, Te, accepted that Vo had the practical experience that she lacked and might, yet, devise a way by which the risks might be minimised. All she had to do was something the child, Te, had never managed to do; to convince him that it was necessary to take the risk.

Something inside her said that shifting the Rock would be simpler. But she had to try.

She turned her vision once out to the sky, to the mists that called to her soul and the voids that demanded her life. And was there something else out there now? For an instant, a flicker of blue light flashing by? A momentary patch of darkness in the mist that was the wrong shape to be a void?

The Barrier was bearing down on them. Was it really close enough to be visible or did she just imagine that she glimpsed it? Perhaps she could still see, past reality, into her dreams.

She turned away and went in search of Vo.

She found him in the Chamber of Knowledge, saving data. He was reclined on a couch, staring blankly at the distant ceiling. On a small table, beside him, a small yellow crystal was growing in size, facets stretching and new prominences sprouting up all over the surface.

Te waited quietly, watching as the crystal rounded itself out, neatening its random shape into a multifaceted sphere.

Vo raised himself and picked up the crystal, looking into its depths as though he hoped to see the information he had stored in it scrolling before his eyes.

"That is the last of it," he said, as though relieving himself, at last, of a great weight.

Te leaned forward to see the crystal herself. "Is that the report on Igu?" she asked.

"It is. He is doing very well. He has already begun work on his purpose again."

"That is good." Te smiled.

Igu was the first Dweller to be brought back from the mists, using Vo's retrieval system. Newly installed inside one of Oa's Bio-forms and given healing by Ji for the torment in his mind the lost Dweller had found himself back among his people and released from a purgatory that had all but torn his mind in two. He had been trapped between states, a tantalising step away from the freedom his mind sought, another step outside the body he needed to attain it and able to take neither. He was the first to be given a way back, a way out. It was a step back from paradise but it was the only way to reach it and to be relieved of the frustration at his accidental limbo was a deliverance he never tired of being grateful for.

To begin with, he had found it disorientating. Lost out in the mists, devoid of physical activity, he had no way to mark the passage of time in his helplessness, though the experience spared him not one second of the time he spent there. He returned to the Rock to find that all the Dwellers he had known had completed their purposes and had released themselves into the Void. An entirely new generation of Dwellers greeted him on his return.

But they had welcomed him no less vehemently and for a while he had been made a great fuss of, by Dweller standards, even to the extent of his own Welcome Ceremony in the Gathering Place. They had all wanted to know what it felt like; was it as terrible as they thought it could be to be stranded out there? And he had told them, yes it was, and had even let them feel the emptiness and frustration that had been his companions for so long. At last, though, the spectacle ran its course and he was able to start picking up the threads of his research and carrying on with his purpose.

He was but the first. Now a team of young Dwellers was constantly on duty scanning the mists and reeling in the lost with Vo's crystals. The records had been searched thoroughly and a list of one hundred and eighty-three lost Dwellers had been compiled, stretching back to the earliest times. Forty-five had already been reclaimed.

"My work is a success," said Vo. "This report is the last proof. I shall soon be ready to enter the Void."

Te's smile widened. "Really?"

"All that is needed now is the approval of the Voidseer. If he gives it, and I have no doubt that he will, then I shall release myself at the next Voidrise."

Te laughed out loud, a joyous sound that was still a child's, and actually reached out and hugged him. "Oh, Prim, that's wonderful," she cried. "I'm so pleased for you. None can have earned release more than you."

"Ah, child," said Vo, indulgently. "My training of you is also complete. That will not bar my release. I can only hope that I have done that task as well as my purpose."

"You have, Prim," said Te. "I shall not forget what you have taught me."

"Then that is something more you must learn," said Vo. "My knowledge is old knowledge and even that is not immune to the depredations of time. Knowledge must evolve if it is to stay alive. Soon my knowledge will have no use left in it and must, then, be forgotten to make room in your mind for new knowledge. Only new knowledge, the knowledge the young make, will have value in cycles to come. Even the knowledge you make will pass away eventually to become no more than data stored in crystals. Knowledge is a living thing and we must feed it and build it so that it may survive."

Te nodded. "I understand."

"It is well, then," said Vo, "I can go into the Void with a clear conscience. And, I own, I am looking forward to it most keenly. And yet, I feel, there is still one thing that might still hold me here a while longer. I find my curiosity about the Beyonders and their universe still to be very strong. I would know more of them if I could before I go. Tell me, Te. What progress have you made with your profile."

"No more than expected," said Te. "It is that which I came to see you about, Prim."

"Indeed?"

Te marshalled her arguments. "Time is short and grows shorter. There will never be enough time to draw all the information from the Beyonders in words. Not enough even to make an approximation of their universe. There are too many facts and too few common frames of reference. They spend many units explaining something that I can hardly begin to conceive because there is nothing like it here. It would take an eternity to build a true profile of them and their universe in this way. And we do not have an eternity."

Vo nodded. "I feared as much. I suppose it was optimistic to think that we might be able to fathom them in so short a time. But they are truly alien, are they not. They follow none of the rules which dictate our lives."

"And yet," said Te "there is still one way left open to us."

Vo looked at her sharply. Te managed not to flinch in front of it, like she had often done before. "You are suggesting a Mindshare with one of the Beyonders, I think," said Vo, gravely. "Need I remind you of the risk that would be involved? Not only to yourself."

"You need not," said Te, trying to keep her voice firm, "I have considered the risks most carefully and, also, the benefits that could be derived from it. It is even more optimistic to think that there might be another opportunity to study and learn from a Beyonder after Jeryant and Kasstovaal leave. They will tell their people of the conditions here and the damage they will cause if they return. If their people are wise they will not try to come here again. There is so much that must be learned and you and I are not the only ones curious about them. The whole Rock knows and is curious. We cannot afford to let this one chance slip out of our grasp."

"But the dangers, child, the dangers," Vo insisted. "The Rock itself is at risk from the power the Beyonders have and don't know they have. Are we to risk losing all the knowledge that has been learned and will ever be learned in the future for the chance to possess this knowledge. It is no trade, Te."

"But is there no way to limit the risk?" Te urged. "Can we not find some way to isolate myself and one of the Beyonders from the Rock and the rest of the Dwellers, like we have done with Ko?"

Vo paused and considered it. "I suppose it could be done," he mused. "The Rock can recall for us the frequency of the energies that were discharged on the last two occasions. That should be enough to code a suitable polymer shielding. But that will not protect you, Te. You must realise that."

"I do," said Te. "And I accept the risk to myself because my own curiosity demands it. I cannot disobey."

"You would risk throwing away all chance of completing your purpose?"

"For the knowledge that can be gained in its place, yes I would," said Te, firmly. "Who knows but that I may merely be anticipating my purpose by doing so. Besides which, I have touched a Beyonder's mind more than once. I will know what not to do. You yourself said so. I am prepared."

Vo looked her silently in the face for some time, then he smiled. "Far be it from me to try and override your curiosity," he said. "I doubt that I would be equal to that battle. Very well, then. It is perhaps fitting that the master should become assistant to his student once before he dies. It will pay many debts between us."

"But, Prim. All debts have been paid already. The Ceremony of Maturity saw to that."

"Child," said Vo, "that only absolves me from the crime of bringing you into being. There are many other things that could only be between us two, Primary Parent and offspring. Things that, under analysis, might not seem well done. In my teachings I have tried to steer you on the right path and I have had to use harsh tools. For that, I owe you and ask, once again, your forgiveness."

To Te's mind came all the little tests he had set for her, all the traps he had left for her to fall into, all the admonishments, all the guilt he had caused within her when she knew she had fallen short. She remembered the silences, cold with disapproval and more eloquent in their way than words could have been. She remembered how belittled he could make her feel if he chose. And yet, she could see just as clearly how all of those little barbs had prodded her and shaped her into the being she now was, a Dweller, a form eminently suited to the pursuit of knowledge. A being ready for a purpose and capable of carrying it out.

"There is nothing to forgive, Prim," she said, softly. "You gave me what I needed. At the end, I wanted nothing else."

24.

"A what?" Jeryant exclaimed.

"A Mindshare," said Te. "It is, I believe, the only way."

They were gathered together in the hangar; the two humans, Vo, Te and Ji. They would need Ji's skill and Te had taken it upon herself to persuade him. Strangely, he had not taken much convincing and had not opposed her conviction to be the one to perform the Mindshare.

"If it were a question of skill alone" he had said, "the task would have been mine to do, not yours. But there is more than mere technique to performing a Mindshare. You must know the landscape of the mind you enter, know its contours, know the way it moves and shifts. You have touched the waking mind of a Beyonder. I have only touched them while they slept. Your mind will know the landscape better than mine. But I warn you again, Te, to take the utmost care. It is a treacherous landscape. Dangers hide in its shadows. Do not disturb them."

He had, however, insisted on being present during the Mindshare, to monitor and be on hand should anything go wrong, and Te had been glad of the reassurance his presence gave her.

The three of them had come together to the hangar, like a deputation begging indulgence. Both humans were there, Kasstovaal working with his head inside the solidifying hull of the *Gateway 2* and Jeryant leaning nonchalantly against the port wing and passing him tools while he chatted to fill the silence. The ship drew the eye of all who entered, a shining crossbow bolt only waiting for the way before it to be open so that it could pierce the sky.

Kasstovaal had thrown himself back into the work with a vengeance following the attempt on his life, a vengeance driven by renewed fear. Zu had continued to help him but even the little Dweller could feel the black shadow that was driving Kasstovaal to greater speed, even to unwise haste, in his work. As time went on, Zu came less and less frequently, repelled by that shadow, though the lure of the ship itself was enough to bring him back once in a while to marvel at it.

Jeryant remained Jeryant, at ease wherever he was and whatever he was doing. In his time he had been bullied and intimidated by experts. After that nothing phased him if he chose to ignore it. He continued his work with Oa, when she was not bound up with the task of Bio-forming bodies for the reclaimed Dwellers.

Te had seen the new bodies he was making for the two of them, with Oa's help. These, he said, were how human bodies ought to be. They were the images of Kasstovaal and Jeryant as they had been though, in truth, Jeryant had not missed the opportunity to be kind to himself. He had built up the muscles and reduced the flab, had even added a surreptitious inch or two to the height of his new body.

He had offered Kasstovaal the same chance. "Just say the word, sunshine," he'd said. "One carefully judged blast from the amplifier and I could up your sex appeal a hundredfold. You'll thank me for it when we get home."

But Kasstovaal had declined. As long as it looked like him, he didn't care. The ship was the sole focus of his mind, the way out. He still melted a little for Te and found he could soothe the ache in him for the reality he missed by describing it to her, digging up details for her that he would not have found the motivation to search for otherwise.

He stopped his work to listen when Te ventured the idea of a Mindshare. He eased himself out of the service hatch and straightened, wiping his hands absently on a cloth already covered in grease. He had no need of such a thing, since he could just form the grime away if he wanted to, but to a human engineer an oily rag is an essential comfort.

"Explain it to us," he said, mildly. "What do you want to do?"

"In simple terms," said Te, "I would like to join my mind to one of yours."

"Haven't you done that already?" Kasstovaal asked. "When you called me in form the mist. Or that time in the Gallery when you shared the art crystal with me?"

"Those were only light and brief touches," said Te. "Aside from those, we have only exchanged waves, as Empaths can. What I propose is a full sharing. I shall send all my perceptions into your mind, link to all your perceptions, your memories, share your thoughts. I shall not interfere or interrupt the flow of your minds, merely ride passively with you. You will barely feel that I am there. It is the most intimate touch a Dweller can make on another."

"Intimate, huh?" Jeryant said. "I was wondering how you Dwellers got intimate with each other. Especially since reproduction has nothing to do with it."

"When our minds are so entwined," Te went on, "I can see reality through your eyes. It will explain so much to me that words cannot."

"I don't follow you," said Kasstovaal. "Wouldn't everything I see look the same as it would to you if you used your own eyes?"

"Not at all," said Te. "And it's not merely a case of our different anatomies. No two people see the universe in exactly the same way."

"That's a matter of opinion, surely. When it comes down to the practicalities of it, isn't sight just the reception of light frequencies, the same light frequencies as everybody else?"

"No, Kass, it isn't," said Jeryant. "Most of what you see is due to the way your brain processes the information of your eyes. I mean did you know, for example, that your eyes can only bring about 10 per cent of your field of vision into focus at any one time?"

"Rubbish."

"It's true. You can only focus on what you are looking directly at. The rest of it is compensated for by your brain. It's like the illusion the Dwellers have given us, only somewhat simpler."

"That being so," said Te, "does it not follow that, since no two minds are alike, no two minds will process the information in exactly the same way."

"But it must all be similar, at least," protested Kasstovaal. "Otherwise how would any two people recognise the same thing?"

"It's merely a matter of comparative terminology," said Te. "For example." She held out her hand and a small red sphere formed in the palm.

"Tell me what colour this sphere is," she said.

"It's red, of course," said Kasstovaal, promptly.

"Indeed," said Te. "But now for a more important question. How do you know that it is red?"

"Well I can see it is, can't I."

"Perhaps I should rephrase the question," said Te. "How do you know that that colour you can see is red?"

"What?"

"It's a simple question. You see the colour of the sphere and you recognise that colour as red. But how do you know it is?"

"Well...." It seemed such a simple question and yet Kasstovaal couldn't think of an answer.

"Is it not because somebody once sat down with you and showed you a colour and said to you 'This colour is called red'?"

"I suppose that's how it happened, roughly speaking."

"Well, then," said Te. "Consider what you have. You have somebody else's word that a colour that appears to you in a certain way is called red. And from then on, whenever you see that colour you will call it red. It is also true that whoever it was that told you to call it red also recognises that colour, as it appears to them, to be the one called red. The question is, though you both recognise that colour as red, how do either of you know that you are actually seeing the same thing?"

"Well, of course we're...," Kasstovaal began, and then trailed off. How did he know? The names of colours were no more than labels that someone else attached to them for your benefit. As long as the labels were in the right place, it didn't matter what your eyes and mind actually saw, in comparison to others. Now he began to think about it wasn't the truth of it there to be seen. Different people preferred different colours and styles. Some had an eye for the visual arts while others did not. Perhaps it could even explain how one man's temperament could be black and forbidding, if the colours of his world appeared dull, while another man could bubble with a sunny disposition, seeing all colours bright and shining.

He said, "And this Mindshare will give you access to the information you want from us, will it?"

"It will," said Te, "in far more detail and far greater depth than you could express to us in words. I shall maintain a link to my own mind along which the information can pass. It will be like using a knowledge crystal, except that it is more than just knowledge I shall be absorbing. I shall receive understanding, your understanding, of your universe. The raw data will make sense to me, as it already makes sense to you. I shall know your universe as you do, far more thoroughly than I ever could otherwise. At the same time, you will be able to understand my reality, my people, my world."

"Sounds like the ideal learning tool," said Jeryant, "so why didn't you suggest it earlier? We've been talking away for weeks, trying to put you in the picture. You could've saved yourself a lot of work and us a couple of dry throats."

"When you first came to us" said Te, "you were suspicious of us and our ability to feel your minds. We pledged to leave your minds undisturbed until you were ready to admit us of your own will. Even now, I am not certain that you have come to trust us enough to allow us in."

"I didn't have any reservations" said Jeryant, glaring at Kasstovaal. "I certainly haven't now."

"But you, Kasstovaal, still do, I think," said Te.

Kasstovaal felt compelled to turn away in embarrassment. The blank, featureless eyes seemed, nonetheless, able to transmit accusation towards him. He threw down the rag he had been wiping his hands on distractedly.

"It's nothing personal," he said, defensively, "I'm just keeping my guard about me. There has already been one attempt on my life, on both our lives. That time, I'd let my guard down. I don't intend to let it happen a second time."

"It is understandable," said Te. "After Ko's action it must be hard for you to trust us. And yet, do you not feel you can trust me? You and I have already shared much."

It was true. Despite all his misgivings and fears, he did trust her. More than that he felt affection for her, not the prebonding of lovers but more the linking of an elder brother to a younger sister, kindly and protective. Her last words had carried a hint of sadness, almost of pleading in them, and he felt it sting him to the heart.

"I do trust you, Te," he said, gently, "but I cannot be as sure of the rest of your people."

"As you will," said Te. "We shall not intrude if you do not wish us to. Nor shall I force the Mindshare upon you. That would be unthinkable, the most gross of violations."

Jeryant cleared his throat, as if in discomfort, and when he'd got Kasstovaal's attention mouthed the word "intimate" at him. Just for once, Kasstovaal realised, it wasn't just down to the medic's one-track mind. This was the nearest Te would ever come to the human concept of sex, at the same time falling short of its extremes and exceeding by a long way the depth of its entwining.

And yet, to them, the meaning was different. That he could tell. Te was standing there calmly proposing the act with either one of them while two of her elders, one of them her Primary Parent for Gods' sake, watched her do it. She showed not the slightest bashfulness or hesitation, considerably less than Kasstovaal was beginning to feel. It meant no intimacy to her, not in the way he knew it. It was nothing more than a scientific procedure, a means to an end. An intrusive one, it was true, and one for which consultation and consent were vitally necessary but it was no more to her than that. Strangely, that thought seemed to comfort him.

"I don't object to taking part," he said. "I know the power of your scientific curiosity. And you'll never be able to satisfy it if my mind is damaged by the touch and the information is lost. I can trust in that if I could not in your goodwill. And I think I do, in any case."

"Good." Te favoured him with a small smile. "Which of you, then, will be the one to share his mind with me. I think it unwise to share with both of you, even one at a time. There are..." she hesitated over the right word, "...complications in the sharing of an alien mind. It is, perhaps, best that we limit the risks by limiting the exposure."

"What complications?" asked Jeryant, his voice hardening into professional seriousness. "What risks?"

The tone in his voice made Te falter. How much should she say?

Ji spoke up instead, coming to her rescue.

"No dangers to you, as such," he said, "more to us. We have all witnessed the powers that lie latent inside your minds. We have seen what they can do."

"You know already that we have no control over those," said Jeryant. "Accepting, of course, that they exist at all. I'm not convinced of it yet."

"We accept what you say." said Ji "All the more reason for us to be cautious. Te will be inserting her mind into every part of the mind she shares, conscious and subconscious alike. If the trigger for this force is hidden in the subconscious there is a chance that she may disturb it accidentally. If that happens then you, by your own admission, will be powerless to stop it or control it. It will not harm you; indeed it appears to act in your defence. But we have seen how this force acts on others and know the harm it may do to us if the Mindshare unleashes it. Thus we have taken steps to shield the Rock and its Dwellers from the effects of this experiment."

"Will these steps protect Te as well?" asked Kasstovaal.

"No," said Te. "They will not. There can be no shielding between us, otherwise I cannot make the link."

"But then it's too dangerous for you," protested Kasstovaal, "you can't consider doing it."

"That is my decision," said Te and there was a trace of steel in her voice which Kasstovaal had never heard before, daring anybody to try and take that decision away from her. He subsided.

"The question remains," said Te, her voice mellowing back to normal, "which of you will share your mind with me?"

The humans were silent for a few moments, each lost in his own calculations.

"Personally," said Jeryant, breaking the silence, "I'm more interested in the process, rather than the results. It's the scientist in me, you know. I think I'd rather watch."

Kasstovaal said "As excuses go that has to be the tamest I've ever heard."

"It's the one I'm sticking to," said Jeryant. "Besides Kass, young upstart that you are, I dare say you've seen more of the universe than I have, being a Pilot-Captain and all." He thought about it some more and then added, "More of what these people want to know about, at any rate. How about it?"

Kasstovaal was already drawn to say yes. The idea had an odd appeal, the chance to really see how the Dwellers lived with the burden of their bodies holding them down. And yet something was holding him back, something stopping him from opening his mouth and saying "Yes, I will." He didn't know what.

Jeryant drew up close beside him. "Go on, Kass," he leered, conspiratorially, "you know you want to. You and Te." He nudged Kasstovaal in the ribs. "Intimate." He waggled non-existent eyebrows.

"Leave it out, you filthy old fart."

Te said, "There is nothing to fear. Will you do it?"

Don't say it, something persisted inside Kasstovaal's head, don't say yes. Don't you dare.

"Yes" he said, firmly, "I will."

They had adapted Vo's laboratory for the experiment, now that his own work was complete, and the Rock seemed to have latched on to the fact that it was now Te's domain, at least temporarily.

This is the room where Te works to unlock the mysteries of the Beyonders, it said in their minds as they approached. Te could not help but feel proud of that.

Vo had helped her with the modifications, sealing off one half of the room to create a blast chamber in which the experiment could take place. It was not up to resisting a blast of physical force, being compromised by the necessary mechanical door into it. But the thin polymer shielding on the walls and ceiling was made to hold back the kind of mental blast that had shaken the Rock before and whipped Ko across a room with a violence that would have killed a human easily.

Ji had contributed some of his own equipment to monitor the proceedings and he made straight for it, when they entered, and began activating crystals.

There was a wide observation window set into the blast chamber wall, made of the same transparent shielding. Beyond it the chamber was bare save for two straight-backed stone chairs standing about a foot apart in the centre, turned inwards to face each other.

Kasstovaal stared at them, picturing himself in one of them and Te reaching out towards him from the other. What would he feel when she touched him? Would she even have to make physical contact with his skin to establish a link? He had no fear of it but he could not stop his mind speculating about it. Some part of him still insisted that it did not want him to go through with it but he pushed the protest to the back of his mind. He wanted this.

Te was standing quietly beside him. "Take your time," she said, gently, "we can begin any time you are ready."

"I'm ready right now," he said. "Better get on with it before I change my mind."

"Very well, then." Te nodded to Ji and Vo, waiting by the measuring equipment. "We shall begin now. Please be ready to monitor."

"All is in readiness," Ji confirmed. "Begin at any time."

Te reached out and took Kasstovaal by the hand. It was a gesture he would not have expected. For a moment the scientific austerity was gone and, this time, Te was the teenager leading him away for a first hidden kiss.

The door swung smoothly open and she drew him inside.

"Seal the chamber" Vo ordered. Ji twisted a blue crystal close to his hand and the door closed again. There was a faint hiss, as of seals pressing tightly into place.

Jeryant stood back and watched, silently, through the window. He saw Te guide Kasstovaal to one of the chairs and motion him to sit. She sat down opposite him and there was an uneasy moment of stillness as the two of them regarded each other diffidently across a few empty inches. Then Te slowly raised a hand, two fingers outstretched and parted as wide as they would go. She reached towards Kasstovaal's forehead. There was a moment when it looked as though he would pull away, leaning back involuntarily to evade the contact. Her hand froze, waited patiently in midair for him to master the reflex and let himself lean forward towards her again. He did so and her hand began to move again, reaching up to place the tips of the two extended fingers either side of the projecting amplifier crystal in the centre of his forehead.

There was nothing that Jeryant could sense behind the glass. Except, though it might have been his imagination, a slight change in the texture of the air.

Kasstovaal waited for the sensation to come, waited to feel the other mind burrowing its way into his like a hungry parasite. Or perhaps it would settle over him like a cloak, smothering him and making his brain heavy with the weight of two minds instead of just one.

He felt neither of these. All there was was that slight pricking about the neck you get when you sense someone standing right behind you and leaning close over your shoulder ready to whisper in your ear.

That was all, at first, so little that he wasn't sure that the Mindshare had even started. For all he knew Te might be having difficulty linking with his mind. She hadn't said how long she thought it would take.

Then he felt his perceptions change. He felt his body become heavier in his seat. Around his peripheral vision the plain Rock walls seemed to come alive, undulating as though it breathed, rippling as though in motion about errands within itself. Around his ears the air began to talk to him or, at least, seemed to be trying to say something but never achieving the words.

In front of him, the form of Te began to change, blurring and altering in a way he recognised all too well. He knew what her new appearance would be before she reached it. Sure enough, within seconds, the cylindrical body and semiliquid flesh of a true Dweller replaced the illusion of the small female humanoid he had known as Te.

In true reality, she was not sitting down; there was no second chair. The thing was standing over him, touching his forehead with two reedy fingers, the only ones it had just now. He got the impression that they were newly formed and not quite set dry yet.

The pearly white bands that encircled it like a coronet looked down on him impassively.

And yet the vision, this vision, that had so filled him with fear and loathing before seemed perfectly natural to him now. It fitted perfectly into the surroundings he could now see with his new eyes. It belonged in the whispering air among the living walls. It was he that did not, his was the body that did not fit into the picture.

And he didn't mind. It didn't seem to matter that he was different. He was a welcome guest. But, more than that, he was a curiosity, a golden source of new knowledge, one to be treasured as infinitely precious. And even that harsh regard for his worth did not bother him, for he could feel how much knowledge meant to the Dwellers. He felt again that ravenous drive. He knew curiosity; it was a force that had been ripe within him once upon a time. But his conception of what that word meant paled into insignificance next to the torrential need of the Dwellers to know that which they did not know. And he could feel the reason for it, also, the seed from which that blazing curiosity grew. This, too, he had felt before, not from his own life but from the outpourings of a Dweller, this very Dweller standing over him and giving him this sight. It was the promise of freedom, a greater and more complete freedom than a human mind could dream of; the freedom of thought from the bonds of rationality, the liberation of the mind from the fetters of the body. There would be no rules, no obligations, no considerations, nothing to hold you back if you could only grasp that freedom. To Kasstovaal it was all, and more, than heaven promised in a thousand languages.

But alongside the bliss of the promise rode the agony of knowing that this paradise of existence was out of reach, a single step away but a step impossible to take. There was a barrier between, a doorway that would only open to the deserving. He knew, as an instinct, that he could earn his way through with knowledge. It demanded an answer to one problem only and if he could provide it the doorway would open and let him through.

And he knew what he would see beyond the doorway. The blackness of the voids where no light can go, only the knowledge. The answers.

That's what they really feed on, he thought. Answers.

Small wonder that Te should choose the danger of the Mindshare over the safety of knowledge lost and lamented. With such a prize to win. He felt his own body weigh heavy upon him, weigh him down. There was a golden moment, maybe no more than an instant, when he knew the whole of her. And, by inference, he knew the whole of them.

No, not all of them. Not every last one.

Te inserted her mind, moving as gently as she could along the physical link and laying herself softly over the mental landscape like a silent fall of snow. She did not interfere, just laid her mind over the contours of the alien mind, letting her own mind take on its shape and texture.

Then she relaxed, mentally closing her eyes to her own perceptions. She opened them again and looked into a new universe.

Every conception she had of size expanded around her; a thousand, a million-fold. Numbers became incapable of holding the universe in. It just kept growing and growing, further than her mind could begin to reach.

The voids were gone. Or were they? It seemed to her that the whole universe was one enormous black void, a darkness from which there was no escaping.

She thought she might find the bliss of the voids all around her and searched for a sea of freed minds revelling in the vastness. She did not find it.

She found lights instead, great boiling furnaces of energy illuminating the darkness.

And she found worlds, millions of worlds. Every one of them was a sphere or a part of a sphere or a sphere in the making. She could not see that it was so but knew it, all the same. Most dwarfed the Rock, could hold the Rock a million times. And on some of those she could sense minds, selves. Life. Her own mind began to race among the inhabited worlds, visiting in an instant the sum of all Kasstovaal's wide travellings. She could not help but marvel at the sheer profusion of life. Not just sentient life. Lesser organisms, starting from the simplest bacteria and building up through the impossibly bright colours of the vegetable forms that spread relentlessly across the landscape. Then on up into the smallest animals, mindless burrowing things, vigorous but without thought. An explosion of variety as countless millions of animals, countless millions of variations, preyed on each other, passing the life force on up between them. So much life force. There would be more in a single square unit of this universe than ever the Rock would hold.

She thought her mind would never hold such a diversity of life, must explode with the sheer numbers. And then the legions of the sentient began to march before her. Mostly humanoid, as the Beyonders were, but even within that limited form their were a million variations. And these were thinking beings with tales to tell her. Lives and cultures and actions, a tapestry so intricate it would take her a lifetime to unravel it for her people to understand.

She had never dreamed that there could be so much, so many worlds, so many forms, so many different ways to be beautiful and wonderful and wise.

Store it all away, her discipline told her. It is but data and now it is yours to do with what you will. Store it logically as you would any learning. Reorder your mind to make room for it all.

She did so, slotting every fact into its place, making her own pattern. As it took shape, she began to understand the order of it; all the disconnected snippets she had gleaned from her conversations with the Beyonders began to make sense. At last she could see their reality, feel it living all around her. She knew it as well as if she had lived and breathed it for forty years...however long that was.

But she hadn't yet connected fully to Kasstovaal's self. She could feel nothing from him. She had access to all his knowledge and experience but not to him. Something was keeping her out, stopping her from sinking all the way into his perceptions and seeing reality as he did.

She had amassed more knowledge than any one Dweller ever had but it was all only three-dimensional facts. She had to know about him, what all these wonders meant to him. Above all, she had to know why he struggled, why they all struggled, to hold on to their bodies against all reason. She pressed her mind in further, sinking below the surface of the landscape to probe the hidden layers beneath. This new landscape was darker, spotted with more shadows, impossibly black and impenetrable. Mentally she closed her eyes and opened them again.

She felt...cold. It was a sensation she had never felt before; the Rock did not know hot and cold outside the experiments penned up in the laboratories and the Dwellers felt nothing but the constant of the absolute temperature of open space, a temperature comfortable to them.

And yet Te knew what that sensation was and knew that it was nothing to do with ambient temperature.

It was the chill of Kasstovaal's reality. The wondrous colours of the new universe became dull and drear. The brightness and lustre went out of them. Te felt a great sadness boiling up inside her as the beauty of the First Mode ebbed away around her and became...cold. This was how Kasstovaal lived, what he saw.

How can he live like this, Te wondered. With so much to admire, so much to take pleasure in. How could any being see it all this way? Why couldn't he see the wonder of it? Why?

He had known the exquisiteness once. She could feel him lamenting the loss. What had happened?

His mind would not tell her. She could sense the ghost of the answer hiding from her, in the shadows. She wanted to know. Curiosity was the core of her being; her caution was no match for it. She had to know. She probed into the darkness, reached in.

"Tell me," she said, out loud, "tell me why."

"Get out!" Something roared at her out of the darkness. Not Kasstovaal's voice, another's; deep, growling "Go away!"

And the cry thundered in her mind.

She recoiled, wrenching her mind away, but this time the cry followed her, pursuing her like prey. Through it she could hear more words, deep and cold as ice, "I will not let you interfere."

Jeryant saw the air between Kasstovaal and Te distort as though a great heat were being produced by their eyes. Then Te jumped sharply from her seat and seemed to be trying to pull her fingers away from Kasstovaal's head. But she couldn't seem to break the contact.

"I am detecting a psyonic surge," said Ji, urgently, "The link must be severed now. It...."

A violent shock wave erupted from between the linked pair inside the chamber and spread outwards, visibly rippling the air as it went. The observation window cracked as the wave struck it and then burst outwards in a shower of granulating glass. Something like a hurricane roared through the opening into their faces, a violent screaming force that rushed at them like a wind though the air could not be moving.

Jeryant covered his ears. Vo and Ji went rigid, freezing at their controls.

Inside the chamber, Te managed to pull her fingers away from Kasstovaal's forehead. She tried to step away from him but could not. That terrible scream rooted her to the spot.

The air in front of Kasstovaal shimmered, became heavy with matter. And, suddenly, a great, black claw reached out of the empty air and gripped Te around the throat.

Jeryant watched in horror as the taloned hand grew a thick, slimy arm that dripped excess matter to the floor. It grew back towards Kasstovaal, sitting frozen in his own seat, and disappeared around behind him. Then the creature reared its head and roared.

It seemed to rise up out of Kasstovaal, pulling itself free from his body and becoming solid as the matter flowed in to fill up the pattern. Jeryant could see the head, rising by its full length above Kasstovaal's, a bloated black mass of flesh contorted in pure hate. It might have been a human face, perhaps one of a million years past, ridged with excess flesh that pulsated and, in some places, seemed on the verge of melting and dropping off. It bared black fangs as it cried out its triumph and the dark pits that were its eyes, or might not be eyes, glared with incredible venom at Te.

Beyond that, Jeryant could see the upper part of a heavy torso supporting the head. It seemed to be attached to Kasstovaal's back, just below the shoulders and it looked as though Kasstovaal was actually sitting on its lap.

The black arm moved and Te was lifted a foot off the floor and held, the clawed hand beginning, slowly, to squeeze. Te's face creased in pain. She scrabbled vainly at the hand that was crushing her but couldn't break the iron grip.

In the chair, Kasstovaal seemed to snap out of his trance and saw with horrified eyes what was happening, what he was doing or so it seemed. He struggled to rise from the chair but something held him down. He strained his neck around to see where the arm was coming from and stared straight into the face of his own demon, which looked back at him with contempt. His throat locked and he felt his innards turning to water. It was like a hundred of his nightmares. Unable to move, unable to shout, "The monster's coming! The monster's coming for me!"

Jeryant found that he could still move. He reached the control panel in two long strides, took Vo by both arms and shook him hard. "Do something," he bellowed over the screaming wave, "you must know how to stop them."

Vo just stared blankly back at him, frozen into stillness by the creature's force. Ji was the same, though his body was trembling as he fought to regain control.

Kasstovaal found a thread of his voice at last, forcing it into croaking action. "No!" he wheezed, feebly. "Leave her alone."

"Be silent!" The thing grew another arm and hand and clamped it over Kasstovaal's face, holding him down. "I told you not to allow this" it growled, "must I watch you every second. She is a threat. She would interfere. She must not interfere."

The clawed hand squeezed tighter.

Jeryant knew he had to act. He was the only one that could. Frantically, he scanned the room searching for something, anything, he could use against the thing, even if it were only to beat at it and break its hold for an instant.

His eyes lit upon the red crystal, lying innocently on a shelf across the room. Ko's weapon. He rushed across the floor and scooped it up, gripping it tight, not daring to let it fall. He brought it back to the shattered window and held it out in front of him.

Now how, in all the blazing hells, did he make it work? Vo had said something about Ko using mental energy to power it. Oh, well, he had to try. Jeryant furrowed his brow and forced his thoughts outward, concentrating on the red gemstone in his palm.

The blast of power that shot forwards out of the crystal lacked all the precision and focus Ko had been able to employ in using it. It was more like a cannon shot but it found its mark, more by luck than judgement.

The creature howled in pain as the blast hit it, surrounding it with a brief angry aura as the energies tore at it. The grip around Te's neck slackened and she dropped to the floor and lay still.

The creature turned its head, with an effort, and fixed Jeryant with its dark eyes. It swiped in his direction with its free arm but did not seem capable of rising and coming after him. It hissed at him, a liquid, reptilian noise.

Jeryant fired the crystal again, this time achieving a beam though it was thick and ragged and weaved through the air rather than lancing straight at its target. Somehow it managed to strike the creature, though Jeryant never knew how he managed to keep from hitting Kasstovaal with it as well.

The creature screamed out its pain and rage, bringing its hand to its head and writhing to escape the chair and get away from that beam. Slowly its roaring became weaker and then it froze, becoming a statue of stone for a brief instant before crumbling into dust. Then even the dust vanished.

Kasstovaal fell out of the chair and crumpled to the floor. Jeryant twisted the control to unseal the door and rushed in to him. He was unconscious but seemed to be alive as far as he could tell.

Behind him, Jeryant heard footsteps. No doubt Vo and Ji coming in to see what they could do for Te. What a mess.

"Oh, Kass, you fool," he sighed, in exasperation, "what have you done, now?"

25.

"We all felt it," said Oa, quietly. "Every one of us."

Jeryant closed his eyes and brought his fingers to his forehead to try and rub away the vision of thirty thousand Dwellers all frozen in mid-action. "Was anyone hurt?" he asked.

"Ru was in the middle of an exothermic experiment when it happened," said Oa. "He suffered some burns but I have been able to heal him."

"No one else?"

"No."

"I suppose we must be thankful for small mercies."

Jeryant turned and looked again at the two unconscious figures lying on the slabs. Each of them had a long thin green crystal hovering, on its side, a foot or so above them, drifting back and forth along the length of the slab and scanning the occupant from head to foot.

"How about them?" he asked.

Oa consulted the display above Te's slab. A rapid line of figures traced across it, shaded in gentle green which seemed to indicate that nothing was wrong. "Te will recover soon," she said, "I have repaired the structural damage. All that remains is for her to return from unconsciousness."

"How long?"

"It will depend on the healing of her mind. She has received a great mental shock. She is rebuilding now but I cannot tell how long it will take. If she is too long about it, I will summon Ji to reach in and assist her. I do not think it will come to that, though."

"And him?"

Kasstovaal twitched in his sleep, his whole body convulsing and relaxing as though the dreams that racked him gave him pain.

"There is little I can do for him," said Oa. "A few cells were depolarised by the radiation from the crystal but not enough to place him in danger. I have reactivated them now. Other than that, there is no physical damage. He, too, is lost in shock and I know even less about how long his healing should take."

"We can't reprogram our minds like you can," said Jeryant. "We have to rely on nature to do the work, usually."

"Nature?"

"Damn!" How did you explain nature to a race that had more control over matter than nature ever seemed to? "I mean our in-built reparatory systems" he corrected.

"Ah, yes" said Oa. "You explained them to me. A very inefficient system to pin your hopes on."

"You're telling me. I'm a healer, don't forget. I've seen how inadequate to the task it is with my own eyes."

Oa checked the readings over Kasstovaal's slab. "He will do well enough, physically. As for his mind, only Ji can say what damage has been done."

"If he's minded to," said Jeryant, resignedly, "In his place I don't think I'd be over eager to go poking around inside Kass's head right now. Te tried it and look what happened."

"We do not know, for sure, what went wrong," said Oa. "Only Te can tell us that."

"You hope." Jeryant leaned his bulk against the wall and brooded over what he'd seen. All the Dwellers had seen it too, apparently. Clearly none of them had ever felt such a force seize their bodies before and the first impulse of virtually all of them, on regaining their control, had been to ask the Rock what had happened. Natural enough, really. And the Rock, seeing all and remembering all, had shown them. So, now, they all knew what had occurred. What nobody seemed to be offering opinions on at the moment was why or how it had occurred.

"Has anybody ever come across this sort of thing before?" he asked.

"No," Oa shook her head, emphatically. "It has never been known among our people. Only the focused will can create matter and we can all tell that Kasstovaal was not directly willing the creature into existence. It cannot happen from purely unconscious command."

"Cannot?" asked Jeryant. "Or just does not? There is a difference."

Oa hesitated a moment and then nodded. "I take your point," she said. "But even with conscious matter-forming it is not possible to create living matter. Only a birthing can create life. And yet that creature was, quite manifestly, a living entity. A thinking being, though clearly not a rational one. I do not understand how that can be. Nobody does. The veins are alive with questions but no one can furnish the answers."

"I might hazard a guess." said Jeryant.

"Based on what?"

"My knowledge of the human psyche, mainly. From a human point of view, that is. I don't see the mind as you do, nothing more than waves and patterns. I can see it for the complex, heaving thing that it really is, something I'll only ever understand in general terms. Perhaps that's the best way to see it and really understand it. Or it could be that, because we don't understand our minds as you do yours, our minds have become more complicated. They lack the discipline that keeps your minds under control, all the time, so they wander off on random paths and make random connections. Perhaps that makes for a greater complexity of thought."

"It could be so," Oa conceded. "Ji would be better qualified to consider the possibility."

"That I doubt," said Jeryant, flatly. "He's even more used to reducing minds down to mere patterns than the rest of you are. I'm not knocking his skill but all he really does is degrade minds down to a level where they become understandable and, thereby, controllable. It's like the difference between reading a crystal full of data and the experience of gathering the knowledge yourself. It loses something in the processing. Loses its life, you could say."

The illusion of Oa's brow furrowed over that. "It is difficult for me to appreciate what you say," she said, after a while, "I am a Dweller, not a human. I can only see minds as a Dweller does."

"Just take it as read that I have an insight into the mind that Ji doesn't."

"All right. What does your insight tell you about the creature?"

Jeryant got off the stool and started to pace slowly to and fro across the room as though he were delivering a lecture off the top of his head.

"There is a school of thought," he began, "in the field human psychiatry, which claims that the individual facets of the personality exist in the mind as separate entities."

"Facets?" Oa asked.

"It might be more accurate to call them elements, the pieces that make up the whole; the tendency towards kindness or stubbornness or impatience. Pragmatism, compassion; all the pieces that make up a person. It goes some way to explain a condition we call schizophrenia, where a person displays different combinations of personality traits at different times. Humans tend to do that anyway, but to a lesser degree, and call it moods."

"Such things do not define us," said Oa. "We are who we are. Our existence is dictated by our purposes and our individuality is established by our names."

"Those things are just labels," Jeryant countered. "You have your individual traits as well, whether or not you like to admit it to yourselves. They might be suppressed but they are there, all the same."

"You are mistaken."

"No, I'm not. They're obvious enough for me to be able to see them without the benefit of your mental skills. You, for example, chafe at having to approach every problem one orderly step at a time. There's a part of you that just wants to take a chance and make an illogical leap forward because you know in your gut where the orderly steps are going to take you and you deplore wasting time going through the motions. You hide it quite well but I can still see you struggling with it sometimes. Deny it if you can."

"I cannot deny it." Oa regarded him thoughtfully. "This is your insight at work, is it?"

Jeryant gave her his most smug smile. "That's right, my dear."

"All right. I have said already that I would accept it. Go on with your explanation."

"The theory runs something like this," Jeryant went on. "Though the personality facets are separate phenomena within a mind, they do not possess any sentience of their own. The sentience is seen as the central core of the mind, the intelligence. I think it's what you would call the self. That is the main binding force for the personality.

"The individual traits, while not being sentient themselves, can exert an influence on the central self to a greater or lesser degree, depending on the interior and exterior stimuli in force at any given time. The extent of this influence is what dictates a person's mood at that time. For instance, if the tendency to impatience is exerting a particularly strong influence over the self, a person will be snappy and bad-tempered. The tendency towards compassion or charity might counteract it a little, depending on how weak it is by comparison.

"And these influences are not usually constant. Next day the balance of the traits may have changed completely and that same person could be bright and sunny and everybody's friend. Do you follow me so far?"

"I think so," said Oa. "We are not totally devoid of emotions, after all. I know that the elements you describe can grow from them."

"All right, then. Let's suppose that one of those facets becomes powerful enough to develop its own sentience. Or, alternatively, exerts enough influence on the self to be able to steal sentience from it. Would you say that's feasible?"

"I have never known it," said Oa. "But it is possible, I suppose."

"I think that's what's happened to Kass. I think one of his personality facets has grown so powerful that it can think for itself. And with the amplifier and the ability to form matter it can now act for itself as well, to a certain extent. For itself and Kass, apparently. It would have to protect him. It needs him to survive."

"Is it common for such a manifestation to develop among your people?"

"I've never seen it. You hear stories about cases of demonic possession from the religious fraternity and I suppose that comes closest to what we're talking about. But there's no medical record I know of."

"Then why should it happen now?" Oa wondered.

Jeryant said, "We have to take into account the effect your universe has had on his condition. Ours are the first human minds ever to come here. Who knows what side effects the environment might be having on us? The transition from our own universe to yours might have done the trick on its own. Kass did spend a long time as a disembodied mind before Vo picked him up. All that time surrounded by free-floating mental energy. Suppose that dominant personality trait found it could feed on that energy and grow. There would be more than enough energy around it to give it the kick it needed. To develop it into a living thinking creature, separate from Kass. How about it?"

Oa considered, in silence, for some moments. "It is an interesting conjecture," she said, at length. "It would seem to cover the facts. Including, incidentally, the explanation as to how a creature could form living matter for itself to inhabit."

Jeryant stopped his pacing. "Does it? Oh, good! I must admit that point was giving me some trouble. How do you see it fitting?"

"Quite simply. If the creature has direct access into Kasstovaal's mind, and his body, it will have access to the molecular formula for my artificial Bio-flesh. Kasstovaal's body is made of it. All the creature would have to do would be to use his body as a template and extend the molecular pattern outwards from the surface of his body. It would be quite a feat of matter-forming but it is possible."

"And the Bio-flesh is designed specifically for disembodied minds to activate and use," said Jeryant. "Clever."

Oa asked "What personality trait can it be then?"

"It'll be the strongest impulse within Kass. I suppose the strongest in any human, when it comes down to it. Self-preservation. The need to survive."

"I do not understand that."

Jeryant chuckled, without humour. "No, I don't suppose you do. But in our universe it's a drive that can make weak men strong and stupid men wise, when it's put to the test. And I have particular reason to know that it's a drive that is particularly strong inside our friend here."

"Why so?"

"We've been friends for a long time, him and me. Of course, he looks to me for his medical wants. It was him that first got me interested in SMD syndrome. That is Second Modal De-phase syndrome or so I call it. It has other names. Pilot-Captain's disease seems to be the favourite."

"It is a sickness of some kind?"

"Not officially. But I'm convinced that it exists. I've researched it thoroughly and the results are quite conclusive. Not conclusive enough for the authorities, though."

"I do not understand."

Jeryant sighed. "It's complicated. I'll try and explain. Space Operatives in general, and Pilot-Captains like Kass in particular, have a reputation for being antisocial, short-tempered and, generally, bad company. Medically, a very high percentage of them are diagnosed with some form of depression or mental instability after they've been in the field for a few years. After I met Kass and saw how fast he was going in that direction, I decided to do some research on it. I thought there might be a medical reason for it, rather than putting it down to the stresses of the job which is what the authorities said it was."

"Did you find the cause?"

"Oh, yes. Definitely. Quite obvious, when you start looking for it. It's exposure to the Second Mode that does it. Tests have shown that the Second Mode contains radiations, certain wavelengths, which are quite close to the frequencies at which the human brain operates. Prolonged exposure to those radiations tends to cause fluctuations in the brain waves and very prolonged exposure, like the sort you get as a Space Crew member running constant shift cycles, makes those fluctuations permanent. The result is deep depression, paranoia, even instability and suicidal tendencies."

"Surely that couldn't be allowed to continue," Oa protested, "if the damage is so profound."

"That's where you enter the realms of politics and commerce," said Jeryant, sourly. "Two more things that you won't know anything about and count yourself fortunate for it. The syndrome doesn't affect the paying passenger, since passenger compartments are sunk under a lot more shielding than are the crew areas. Besides which, even the most active commercial traveller doesn't clock up a thousandth of the space-time a Space Operative would. So the only people Space Central need to worry about are their own employees whom, they feel, they can treat like dirt with impunity since they pay their wages and can, moreover, prevent anybody else paying them if somebody quits. They have a lot of clout and not all of it is strictly legal. But they're responsible for keeping the space lanes going which, in turn, keeps the inhabited universe going. Not just passengers but supply routes, as well. They could bring most of the inhabited worlds to their knees if the space traffic came to a halt. They know that and so, too, do the governmental bodies that might otherwise have power to regulate their activities. In consequence nobody messes with Space Central, nobody holds them accountable and nobody can effectively stand up to them, the Space crews least of all."

"But," said Oa, "if a cure was found for this condition, their crews would operate more efficiently. Would they not find that desirable?"

"That's what I thought when I compiled my report on the syndrome for the Medical Sub-committee," said Jeryant. "I had a vain hope that they might thank me for it. Should've known better, I suppose. What I actually got was a security team banging on the door in the middle of the night and hauling me off to Space Central in my PJs." He paused and glanced at Oa. "Did I lose you anywhere in there?" he asked.

"If you were saying that it was not a beneficial occurrence" said Oa, "then I did get the point."

"Too right, it wasn't," said Jeryant.

Head of Sector Security Oosterhoff was one of those people who had been bred for intimidation purposes. He wasn't bulky in any way; Jeryant topped him by a head and could have encircled his body with one arm. Indeed, if this had been a street confrontation Jeryant would have pulverised the little creep without breaking a sweat.

But this was not the street. It was a large, cold office furnished one hundred per cent for Spartan functionality and not at all for comfort. Oosterhoff fitted into it perfectly. He was pale and thin. His grey hair, belying the age of his face, was shaved almost back to the scalp and what remained was set hard giving it the appearance of a well-worn wire brush. The lack of hair accentuated the over wide blue eyes in the thin face, which never seemed to blink unless it was that he blinked only when you did, so that you wouldn't know he had. A good trick if you can master it. The mouth was too small, crushed by thinness, and you could tell that if he tried to smile with it, it would do very strange things to his face. The pale grey Security uniform was a snug fit on him and only served to highlight his meagre body, though it was disconcerting just how close it came to matching the colour of the wearer's skin.

He didn't say anything or even move as Jeryant was unceremoniously placed in a chair on the other side of his desk. The guards who had hustled him in stepped back and became two ominous pieces of background. Jeryant was red in the face, not least at being bundled across town in a sleep-suit, barefoot. He had very precise ideas about Space Central, ones he was wont to share with anyone who would drink in his vicinity. It was still dark outside and he was already feeling hungover and all these things taken together made for a very volatile mix inside Bryn Jeryant. He was ready to explode all over somebody and this little shite in the grey suit would do very nicely.

Except. The little man didn't move or say a word. The oversized eyes, in the blanched face, stared straight at him without actually appearing to register him. Jeryant was suddenly gripped by the conviction that he was looking at a corpse in an official uniform and that completely derailed his bluster.

Oosterhoff left him with that illusion for just long enough to be sure of the desired effect. Then he spoke, making Jeryant jump ever so slightly. The voice matched the body, thin, pale and reedy. "Doctor Bryn Jeryant, Space Medical Operative, Level C."

Jeryant pulled himself together. "That's right," he said, hotly, "that's me. Congratulations. It's a relief to know somebody in this place can read. Do you get a prize for getting that right?"

Oosterhoff allowed a few seconds to pass in silence, allowing Jeryant to boil himself out of words. "I have invited you here to discuss your research project into the antisocial behavioural patterns of Operatives in our service."

"How do you...." Jeryant stopped himself. What was the point of asking somebody like this how he knew about Jeryant's research? It didn't matter that he hadn't presented his findings to the committee yet, hadn't even written the report yet, in fact. Instead, he asked "Does this mean I won't need to bother writing a report for you? If you already know about it, I mean. I was going to compile one for the Space Service, in the fullness of time. I suppose I should be flattered that you're taking an interest."

"Oh, we are interested, Doctor Jeryant. We are very interested indeed in the findings you are preparing to publish."

"I should think so," said Jeryant ."The implications are staggering. Have you any idea what this is going to mean for all those medically depressed Space Operatives you keep having to put on the shelf? What it will mean to virtually every spaceman and woman in the Service?"

"We have very clear ideas on what it will mean, Doctor Jeryant," said Oosterhoff. "And that is why you will not be permitted to divulge these findings of yours. Nor will you be permitted to continue this line of research."

Jeryant's mouth dropped open. "Not permitted?" he stammered "What are you saying?"

"I'm saying that, as of this moment, you are being officially warned-off, Doctor Jeryant."

"But...but that's ludicrous. This research could benefit thousands of people. Hundreds of thousands and all of them your employees."

"Nevertheless, Doctor Jeryant, it has been decided that publication of your research into Second Modal De-Phase syndrome would be against the interests of both this Service and the public at large."

"What are you talking about!" Jeryant was almost shouting. "If I can find a cure or a preventative for this syndrome, it's bound to up the efficiency of all your operatives. That's got to be good news for the Service and the public, as well."

"There is no cure, Doctor Jeryant."

Jeryant got to his feet and leaned over the desk to blare directly into the little man's face. He heard two pairs of boots take an approaching step behind him but ignored them. "And how, in the blazing hells, would you know that, sunshine? Got yourself a medical degree suddenly, have you? And will you stop repeating my name in every sentence. I know who I am "

One corner of the small mouth twitched, contorting that whole side of the face for an instant as the thin cheeks adjusted to make room for the motion. "I know there isn't a cure, Doctor Jeryant, because none of your predecessors managed to find one."

Jeryant frowned. "Eh?"

"Sit down please, Doctor Jeryant."

Jeryant growled in his throat. He wasn't sure how he managed it but the little bastard was goading him with his own name. He felt a meaty hand land gently but irresistibly on each shoulder as the guards encouraged him back into his chair.

Oosterhoff reached down behind the desk, as if into a drawer, and produced a text-file pad which he placed on the tabletop. "What makes you think that you are the first to perform this sort of research, Doctor Jeryant?" he asked, coldly.

Jeryant hesitated. It was something he had wondered about, several times, during the work. It seemed such an obvious enquiry to follow, when you sat down and thought about Space Operatives and their reputation. He was one himself, though the syndrome had not affected him, noticeably. The ship's medic was habitually set up somewhere in easy reach of the passengers, under their extra shielding and, besides that, Jeryant's explosively jovial nature was more than a match for any depressive state.

He had checked the medical journal archives and databases on the subject and had found nothing. No work appeared to have been done to establish a cause for the condition. At least, nothing had been published.

Oosterhoff said, "In the three thousand and thirty-five years since Second Modal travel was put into commercial use, Doctor Jeryant, no less that three hundred and sixty-nine medical scientists have pursued this line of enquiry. Some of them were the most eminent practitioners in the field, in their time. Far superior to a third-rate space physician who spends most of his life in an alcoholic haze. None of them were able to find a cure, Doctor Jeryant. Why should we believe that you, of all people, would be capable of succeeding where they failed?"

"I might yet surprise you," Jeryant growled. "Anyhow, medicine has come a long way in three thousand years. I might have the key factor they didn't have."

"That I doubt." Oosterhoff turned the file pad around on the desktop and pushed it towards Jeryant. "Perhaps you would care to read the file yourself, Doctor Jeryant. Compare notes, so to speak." Then he did smile and the whole lower half of his face ballooned outwards to accommodate it. It seemed to draw the extra skin it needed from the upper portion of his face, which seemed to shrink proportionately. The already wide eyes widened still further as the skin pulled away from them. For a moment Jeryant thought they might fall out, not having enough skin left to hold them in place.

Jeryant reached out and took the pad, if only for a distraction from that face. He activated it and skimmed through the contents. There were names he recognised, some of the medical legends he had read about at university, others more recent but well known by their work. Some, even, were still living, he knew. Others, the file made a point of noting, were not so.

It appeared that they had all come to virtually the same conclusions he had and had not been able to make any more positive progress. Jeryant read through a few of the reports from the more prominent names before the text became monotonously familiar and he threw the pad back onto the desk.

Oosterhoff had let his face contract back to normal, thank gods, while Jeryant had been reading and had just sat there watching him in silence while he read. When Jeryant threw down the pad he said, "Apart from those people, and yourself of course, the only scientists who have knowledge of this condition are the special committee formed by this service to periodically review the data and compare it to the latest scientific and medical advances. As I said, Doctor Jeryant, we are very interested in this syndrome and we have taken our own steps to find a solution. The best that are available. No amateurs need apply. And that means you, Doctor Jeryant."

Jeryant bristled. "I'll research what I damn well like. The Universal Medical Charter says I can and should follow any line of research that may benefit the health of any living being. I think that's how the wording goes. And it obliges me to publish whatever I find, successful or not. Legally obliges me, mark you. I've got the Charter backing me up, sunshine. What have you got?"

Oosterhoff steepled his fingers. "Doctor Jeryant, the Charter does not apply to this contingency. As that file will have told you, we have had many opportunities to consider the legalities of banning research into this syndrome. I can assure you that there is now a well-established precedent for not invoking Charter regulations."

"Based on what?" Jeryant demanded.

"Based on the fact that disclosure of this research data will, ultimately, result in several million deaths, Doctor Jeryant."

"What?"

"Do not pretend to be naïve, Doctor Jeryant. Must I spell out for you the consequences of publishing this data? How many people are going to want to enrol into the academy if they know that they will inevitably contract these symptoms? How many of the existing crews are going to want to continue exposing themselves to the Second Mode and, thereby, worsening their condition? How long do you think it would take for all of the universe's space traffic to grind to a halt?"

Jeryant remained silent.

"We of the service have a sacred trust, Doctor Jeryant," Oosterhoff went on, "we are charged with keeping the universe moving. Without us, no planet would receive the supplies that it needs to survive. Whole populations would be stranded. It would not take long for the less self-sufficient planets to start losing people through asphyxiation or starvation or water deprivation or chemical deficiency. The very basics of life would quickly run dry. Millions would lose their lives. Thousands of planets would sink into chaos. We are entrusted with the task of preventing that from happening. Even the administration behind the Charter has come to appreciate the logic of the situation, Doctor Jeryant. Compared to millions of lives and thousands of worlds, what is the health of a few thousand Space Operatives?"

Jeryant gnawed at his lip but said nothing.

"Or, for that matter," Oosterhoff said, "what is one life compared to those millions, Doctor Jeryant?"

Jeryant frowned. "What do you mean?"

Oosterhoff tapped the file pad with a thin finger. "All three hundred and sixty-nine individuals named in this file were warned not to disclose their findings, much as I am now warning you Doctor Jeryant. You may have noticed that some of them met with accidents shortly after they were...advised of the situation. Fatal accidents. Twenty-five of them, to be precise. They were the ones who did not take our advice."

Jeryant's jaw dropped.

"Would you like to meet with an accident, Doctor Jeryant?" Oosterhoff asked, pleasantly. "I have no doubt that something could be arranged."

Jeryant's mouth worked but his voice had deserted him. All he could manage to stammer out was "You...you wouldn't dare."

Oosterhoff flashed his disconcerting smile again. "Would I not, Doctor Jeryant? It has been done before. As I said, there is a precedent."

Jeryant could feel himself going pale. He knew exactly what he thought of Space Central, in general, and, sitting there in front of this little man with his guards, he was coming to realise just how much he really believed what he thought. The thought that Oosterhoff might be bluffing never entered his head for a second.

"Well, Doctor Jeryant?" Oosterhoff leaned back in his seat. Those goggling eyes had not looked away from Jeryant once from the moment he entered.

Jeryant swallowed. "If it's all the same to you, I'll pass."

"Good." Oosterhoff nodded to the guards standing behind Jeryant. "You have more sense than I gave you credit for, Doctor Jeryant. These gentlemen will escort you back to your quarters. If we ever meet again, it will be a very brief encounter. Very brief indeed, Doctor Jeryant." He picked up the file pad. "Now, piss off and don't ever give me cause to have you darken my door again. Not if you know what's good for you."

"And that was that," said Jeryant. "Since then I've only been able to conduct small experiments in secret, not enough to hope for a cure one day. But I persevere. Aside from that, my career took a decided downturn and I had to take work where I could get it. Space Central put me on their 'pain in the arse' list. It's a distinction I've resolved to live up to. Kass is the only other person I've ever told about my findings. He helps me where he can. After all, he has a vested interest."

"He has this De-phase syndrome, does he?" Oa asked.

"He's a prime case, he is. He's prone to extremes of paranoia. It makes him too acutely aware of the dangers of his job and the chances of dying while doing it. I've seen him paralysed by the fear of his own mortality before now. With that much fear of death inside him, can we wonder that his survival instinct has become overdeveloped, even to the point of achieving its own sentience."

"So, if we accept this hypothesis," said Oa, "how do we prevent the creature from manifesting itself again?"

"Well, we don't allow any more Mindsharing, that's for sure," said Jeryant, firmly. "Aside from that, the only thing I can think of is to remove his amplifier for the time being. It'll stop him from doing any more matter-forming but, by the same token, it should stop the creature from doing any as well. Zu can do it for him, if he needs any done for the ship. So can I, for that matter."

"That may not solve the problem," said Oa. "Kasstovaal has been matter-forming for some time now. He may no longer need the amplifier to assist him in doing it."

"Maybe. But taking out the amplifier will, at least, make it more difficult for him and the creature."

"Agreed" said Oa. She walked over to Kasstovaal's slab, leaned down and pressed her fingers into the skin of his forehead around the amplifier crystal. It looked like she was trying to squeeze an enormous pimple. The green crystal seemed to rise up out of the flesh and edges of black plastic became visible on the surface. Then Oa plucked her fingers away and was holding the plastic strip between her fingers, crystal and all.

"It is done" she said, dropping the amplifier on the bench.

"Fine. Beyond that, I suppose, if we put our heads together with Ji we might come up with a way to jam his forming abilities."

"We could always keep him unconscious," said Oa "That is the simplest solution."

"No, that's not an option. We have to leave here, there's no question about that. And we can't do that until he's finished building the ship. I can't do it, nor can I pilot it out of here when it's ready. It's down to him. He needs to be operational."

"Of course. We shall speak to Ji."

"Who knows," Jeryant said, "we may be worrying needlessly. Maybe my sharpshooting with that crystal has destroyed the thing completely." He held out two fingers in the classic gun pose and went "Pow!" under his breath. Then he held them up to his lips and blew down the imaginary barrel.

"Possibly," Oa conceded, "but we have only conjecture to guide us. It is wise for us to take any precautions we can."

"Right." Jeryant turned and wandered over to the two transparent vats that stood, side by side, against one wall. He bent to look more closely at the contents. Each vat contained a familiar figure. One was himself, the other was Kasstovaal, not as they were now but as they had been in their own universe, pink fleshed and repossessed of their body hair amongst other things.

They were Jeryant's creation, with Oa's help. They were made of Bio-flesh, modified and recoloured to resemble human skin. But that was only the outer appearance. It was the internal structure that Jeryant was justly proud of. He had utilised every particle of knowledge he had about the human body and its workings and had replicated every single function within the body; constructing pseudoorganic machines, molecule by molecule, to perform the exact functions of the organs. Even down to the glands, microscopically intricate chemical factories, built to produce the exact enzymes that their natural counterparts would have - more efficiently in many cases. While Kasstovaal had been building his vessel, Jeryant had made these vessels for the two of them. They were his masterpiece, so indistinguishable from the real thing that even a medical scanner would have trouble picking up the difference.

The only real giveaway was the ring of eight green crystals set around the forehead of each, like a coronet. Except these crystals were not attached to a band but were embedded in the flesh.

Eight was the maximum number of amplifiers Ji recommended for any one mind to use. "Anymore than that" he had said, "and you risk positive feedback of energy into the brain. Potentially fatal."

Jeryant had spaced them evenly around the head and had wired them directly into the brain tissue with artificial nerve filaments. Removing them on the other side of the transit would be a question of surgery, but not a major operation. If they wanted to remove them, of course.

Now, Jeryant stared at the circlet around the head with Kasstovaal's old face on it, distorted by the liquid nutrient in the vat that kept the artificial bodies preserved until they were activated.

"The big question" he said, more to himself than to Oa, "is can I risk giving him that much extra amplifier power when we leave?"

"Can you manage to maintain both bodies and the ship on your own?" Oa asked.

"I don't know. Maybe I can. Or maybe even the combined power from both of us won't be enough. There's no way to tell. Common sense would seem to dictate amassing as much power as possible. Better too much than too little. But can we risk what might get out with that much power?"

"I cannot advise you," said Oa. "I have no data either." She thought about it some more. "Of course, if your theory about the creature is correct and it is the embodiment of Kasstovaal's will to survive then surely the creature will do nothing to hinder his return to his own universe. On the contrary, would it not do what it can to assist him in holding his body together through the transit?"

Jeryant nodded. "It might do, at that. In fact, if it can build itself a body, or half a body, from scratch it's probably more capable of holding these bodies together than we are. It might make all the difference, at least for Kass."

Across the room, the monitor over Te's head gave a soft chime. They both turned.

The illusion Jeryant had of Te's body did not endow her with eyelids, in keeping with her own form. It was, therefore, a little difficult for him to tell the exact moment when Te awoke from her trance and how long those pale discs of eyes had been staring at the ceiling. She just raised herself, slowly, into a sitting position and brought fingers to her head as though to make sure it was still there.

Oa went to her and caught the floating crystal out of the air with one hand. "Are you well, Te?"

Te nodded. "I have rebuilt my mind successfully. All is in place. Thank you."

She turned to look over at Kasstovaal on his slab, stirring in his sleep, his head jerking from side to side and his hands clenching and unclenching.

"What of him?" she asked. At the same time an apprehensive wave escaped from her. Jeryant felt it but said nothing. Was it concern for him or fear of him?

"He is recovering," said Oa. "The creature has been neutralised, at least for the time being. Jeryant and I have been discussing steps to prevent a further manifestation."

"He meant me no harm." Te's eyes did not leave Kasstovaal. "He would not." Then, almost inaudibly, she whispered "Such a mind he has. So much life."

"The Mindshare was successful?" Oa asked.

"Oh, yes," said Te. "I gathered so much knowledge from him. So many visions and forms. It will take a long time to document it all."

"It is well, then," said Oa. "It has been decided that there are to be no more such Mindshares with the Beyonders. The risk is too great."

Te still did not turn her eyes away. "I have all I need," she said, simply.

On his slab, Kasstovaal let out a drawn moan. "No!"

Oa consulted the display above him. "His neural activity is increasing. I think he, too, will wake soon."

Suddenly, Kasstovaal screamed out "Keep it away!" and sat bolt upright on the slab, his eyes open but staring straight at nothing. He was breathing hard and fast and seemed to be cowering away from something they could not see.

"Keep it away!" he screamed again, "Get back! Get back!"

Jeryant crossed the room in four long strides, took Kasstovaal by the shoulders and shook him. "Kass!" he roared into the stricken face. "Snap out of it. Now, do you hear me?"

Kasstovaal blinked and his eyes swivelled around him. He made one desperate move to pull away from Jeryant and then his eyes seemed to register who he was. His breathing subsided and he relaxed.

"Jery," he said. Then he swallowed and took the room in properly, took in Oa and Te watching him with consternation.

"I've... made a fool of myself again, haven't I" he said, hesitantly.

"My friend," said Jeryant, patting both of his shoulders simultaneously, "that has to be the most monumental understatement this universe has ever heard."

NINE: RA

26.

The engines burst into life and roared, thunderously, as though to shake the Rock apart. The *Gateway 2* strained at the moorings pinning it to the hangar floor but they were solid rock and held it down firm. The ship was going nowhere this time, which was as well since neither of the two humans were aboard.

They were both watching the spectacle from the safety of the antechamber, though Kasstovaal's eyes were more often turned down towards the figures running across the readout screens.

Zu was there, too, watching with rapt fascination and more than a little awe at the fury he had helped create. Kasstovaal had wondered whether he had lost his helper, after the Mindshare incident. Zu had not shown his face for several days and had made excuses when Kasstovaal had asked after him. He could hardly blame the youngster, he supposed. No one had escaped the effects of the creature's power, Zu included. If he had been nervous about working with Kasstovaal before, he was downright scared of doing so now.

But the lure of the ship had, eventually, become too much for him and the chance to watch a test-firing in progress was more than a match for his fears. Kasstovaal didn't begrudge him his reluctance and allowed the test-firing to continue for somewhat longer than was absolutely necessary to be sure and give him a good show.

Te stood next to him, also watching, though more with detached interest than with the fascination that was leaking off Zu like sweat. To her this was a thing she had seen in Kasstovaal's mind, one of many thousands of identical vessels, jumping vast distances and binding a whole universe of people to one another. It helped her to accept the reality of it, to actually see something from that universe with her own eyes, one real artefact to bind the whole maze of it into reality.

The Mindshare had not scared her away from him. Far from it. She feared the creature, of course, but the intoxication his mind had given her was more potent than her fear. She found herself wanting to be near his mind, to catch any part of that magic that might escape from him. She hung around him easing his troubled soul with calming waves, which he accepted from her gratefully; even managing to return some of them to her from within himself, though clumsily.

The pitch of the roaring rose and fell in time to Kasstovaal's controls and the intensity of the white light burning in the heart of the engine pods. And then both died away with a suddenness that all but one of the spectators hardly expected.

"All right, are they?" Jeryant asked.

"Fine," said Kasstovaal "Almost a perfect run. A bit rough between forty-five and sixty per cent but that looks like a simple resonance problem. Easy enough to fix. We'll need to adjust the baffles, Zu."

He could tell that he'd won Zu back, just by looking at his face. The reawakening of his enthusiasm was making the young Dweller shine.

Just as well. The band of clear plastic Kasstovaal wore around his head was doing the job, Ji had designed it for, most efficiently. He could still send and receive waves but matter-forming was completely impossible while he was wearing it. He would need Zu, if the work was to continue.

"I can attend to it now if you wish, Kass," Zu said, eagerly.

"Not yet," Kasstovaal warned. "The hangar will be hot for a while yet. Give it a few units to cool off."

"And then what?" Jeryant asked.

Kasstovaal counted off on his fingers. "Connect the power and control linkages to the on-board panels, seal up the hull, run the life support tests and, then, that's it. She's ready to fly. We could be out of here in four days, as long as nothing drastic happens." He gestured at his own body. "How about the new...accommodation? How's that coming?"

"They're as ready as they'll ever be," said Jeryant. "But they're not so easy to test as a couple of engines. I've put them through every scan I can think of, and a few I've never heard of before, and they check out okay. But it's going to be a proof-of-the-pudding situation. There's no way around that."

"Then you will soon leave us," said Te. She tried to keep the regret out of her voice but did not quite manage it.

The two humans fell into an uneasy silence. Their own eagerness had carried them along regardless and the realisation that not everyone shared that eagerness was more than a little sobering.

Kasstovaal said, "You know it has to be, Te. The barrier is getting close, now, very close. We can't afford to delay, even if we wanted to."

"I know it." said Te, blankly. "It is not our way to mourn the absence of those who are gone. Indeed, for us it is an event to be celebrated. And yet, I cannot deny that I shall feel the want of your presence among us."

"And we'll miss you," said Jeryant, softly. "Both of us."

A doorway opened from the corridor and Vo entered through it. He had a perceptible spring in his step, an illusion of course, which looked odd on a Dweller body.

"The voids are satisfied," he said, triumphantly, "I have just come from the Voidseer. He has given me the word. I may end my life whenever I please."

Te went to him and embraced him. "Prim, that's wonderful. I knew they would accept you. How could they not."

Zu's radiant enthusiasm went up a notch, even though he didn't have a direct stake in the news.

By stark contrast, the two humans could only find it in themselves to shift uncomfortably and each looked to the other to find something positive to say.

"Yes...er...ahem..." Jeryant stumbled "Congratulations, Vo. A great achievement for you."

Vo raised an arresting hand. "I understand your discomfort, my friends," he said, kindly. "I accept your congratulations with thanks. And be assured that I have what I have wished and worked for. I am satisfied and soon I shall be fulfilled. Take solace from that thought."

"Thanks for that," said Jeryant. "It is difficult to swallow."

Vo said, "The Voidseer has a word for you two, also."

Kasstovaal stiffened, "What was that?"

"Ra requested me to summon you both to his presence," Vo said. "He wishes to speak with you."

"Does he, now?" Kasstovaal growled. His hands unconsciously balled into fists as he said it.

"As soon as you can, he told me," Vo added.

"What can that be about?" Te wondered.

"Question is," said Kasstovaal, "how badly do we want to find out?"

"Well, I'm up for it," said Jeryant, heartily. "One thing you can say about religious pontiffs, they're good for a laugh. I'm sure whatever it is his high-and-mightiness wants to say will be most entertaining."

Te went over to Kasstovaal and tried to look into his face. He looked away.

"You still do not trust the Voidseer's motives, do you," she said. "I can feel it in you. You fear him."

Kasstovaal gritted his teeth. There was no longer anything he could hide from Te, he knew that. But she understood him now. He knew that, too. He could hear her voice carry it, concern not admonishment.

"Yes," he said. "Yes, I do. All the same, I...want to hear what he has to say. He might allay my fears or confirm them. I suppose I should give him the opportunity to do one or the other, just to know which he wants."

"I will come with you," said Te. "I, too, am curious as to his interest. I am sure he will not mind. I have more knowledge of your kind than he has. That may be useful to him."

"Thanks," said Kasstovaal. "That will help. Even so, after what Ko did, I'm minded to take something else with me, as well."

It was a long climb up to the Chamber of Purpose level from the depths of the Rock where the hangar was. It took them all of three hours just to make the ascent, even on the tightest spiral. It was just as well, Jeryant thought, that they didn't get tired anymore. Time and fatigue were not of importance to the Dwellers, which was probably why they hadn't bothered installing elevator tubes throughout the Rock as he would have done.

Eventually they reached the door that led into the Chamber of Purpose and went beyond it to the point where the wall led into the next room, the Voidseer's room. The Rock announced it to them, with what almost sounded like awe in Kasstovaal's mind.

Jeryant stepped up to it, rubbing his hands. "I've been looking forward to this," he said, gleefully. "I've got just the thing for annoying a..."

But he didn't get a chance. A stark, rectangular doorway opened up in front of him.

"Bugger!" Jeryant muttered.

"Never mind, Jery," Kasstovaal murmured, "maybe you'll get him on the way out."

The three of them filed in.

The room was like no other Kasstovaal had seen within the Rock. The walls were not the pure bleached white he had come to expect but had been dulled down to a dark grey as though centuries of filth had been handed down from incumbent to incumbent. In keeping with that illusion, the room was visibly untidy, cluttered with strange pieces of equipment, stacked any old where around the walls; crystals piled up on shelves, unsorted. Benches seemed to have been created at random around the floor space as they were needed and all were covered in the same wild detritus.

Ra stood in the middle of it all, looking out of the empty window, set high in the wall, open to the voids. He did not turn to look at them as they entered. His voice, when he spoke, was deep and forceful. He would have made a good First Voice, Jeryant thought, if he hadn't been called to be Voidseer.

Ra said, "Te, you are not required here. What I will say is for the Beyonders only. Go!"

Te made to protest. "But, Voidseer, I have understanding of them which may..."

Ra turned suddenly, his short cloak flying around him, and glared straight at Te. "I said GO!"

To the two humans, it seemed that he only raised his voice a little. But the force of the wave that went with the word, the sheer malevolent power of it, grabbed hold of Te's mind, spun her around and marched her smartly out of the door and away down the corridor. Kasstovaal saw her face, frozen in stunned shock, as she passed.

She had descended three levels before it wore off and gave her back control. She turned, impulsively, to make her way back but the shock of that mental blow froze her in the act. Instead, she turned and fled.

Ra sealed the doorway and stood regarding the humans stonily. "No others may hear what I have to say," he said, coldly. "That is the law."

"Law?" said Jeryant. "I didn't think Dwellers needed laws. Traditions, possibly, like the one that gives you the final say-so on their fate. But not laws."

"They do not," said Ra. "But the Voidseer follows a different discipline."

"Is that a fact," said Kasstovaal, scornfully.

Ra nodded. "Oh yes. I am the protector of a sacred trust, as all of my predecessors were. Mere tradition, which binds only out of habit, is insufficient to guard what I must guard. I am bound as those that went before me were bound. As Ko would, eventually, have been bound, if he had not acted so rashly."

"Rash is hardly the word I'd have used for what he did," said Jeryant.

"You think not?" Ra almost sneered. "Well, perhaps you will think differently when you hear what I have to tell you. I cannot say these things to my fellow Dwellers but fate has given me an opportunity that none of my predecessors ever had and one that will, probably, be denied to all my successors." He took a step closer to them. "I have this one chance to face my tormentors."

Jeryant frowned. "Do you mean us?" he asked, slowly.

"Yes," Ra hissed, and there was real venom in the word. "My tormentors and the tormentors of my entire race. You!"

His tone stunned the words out of them for several seconds. The glare he contrived to direct at both of them, simultaneously, carried hate in it, the hate that Kasstovaal had felt from him once.

Kasstovaal recovered first. "What are you talking about? We don't torment you or the others. How can we? We've hardly been here long enough to make an impression on your society, let alone do any damage."

"Deception," said Ra, icily. "Such deception." And then he laughed. He actually laughed. A strange enough action from a Dweller; Kasstovaal had only ever heard Te do it the once, out in the mist. But this was not the uplifting sound of joy escaping. This was the laugh of a man faced with something too incredible to believe, the hollow choking of gall.

"It is really true," he said, as the spasm died away. "You really do not know, do you. Or choose not to know, perhaps. It is a terrible irony."

"Know what?" Jeryant demanded. "Get to the point, man. I warn you that I'm losing patience."

"Indeed," said Ra, "I would not wish to deplete your patience or forbearance. Have we not all seen what can happen when a Beyonder loses control?"

Jeryant shut his mouth.

"And while we are on the subject," Ra said to Kasstovaal, "I can assure you that you will not need the crystal you are holding."

Kasstovaal had been fingering the red crystal in his hand, drawing comfort from its presence as he would from a sidearm. He felt it shift in his grip and then it was whipped away from him. He made a grab for it, as it sailed through the air, but it was moving too fast. Ra caught it easily.

"Physical violence will not be necessary here," he said. "Words will suffice." He squeezed his fist around the crystal and it crumbled, easily, into a powder that seeped away through his fingers.

"In truth," he went on, "I had considered keeping my peace and letting you depart in your ignorance. But now your presence here has disrupted the order of the Rock and threatened our very existence. And, as I now know that you are truly ignorant of what you have done, it is perhaps a fitting revenge to inform you of your crime."

"What crime?" Kasstovaal asked.

Ra turned away from them and gazed out of the window again. "You see the voids, do you Beyonders?" he said.

They both looked up at the negative star field staring down at them.

"The Voidseer looks into the voids, it is said," said Ra. "And it is true. It is the foremost skill that is passed from master to apprentice in this place. It takes formidable control but, also, great courage to send one's mind into that darkness and pull it free again. But once the art is mastered, there are things to be seen in that darkness."

He turned his head to look at them over his shoulder. "You know of our purposes, do you not. How they are given to us in the Chamber next to us?"

Kasstovaal nodded. "Te told me."

Ra turned his head back to the window. "The voids hold the purposes. I have felt them there. I can feel it when they are released, transmitted to the Chamber for a young mind to receive them. And I can sense when they are ready to receive the result of the question they once asked, the task they once set. I know when a purpose is truly ended."

"So you say," murmured Jeryant.

Ra snorted, "You do not believe me."

"No, actually, I don't," said Jeryant. "I've heard many people make claims like that. I didn't believe them, either. Not until they could prove it to my satisfaction. None of them could."

"Your disbelief is of no consequence to me," said Ra.

"I didn't think it would be."

"The purposes are only the surface, the smallest fraction of what a Voidseer can see. It is all we can reveal to our people. But there is more, far more and worse. A secret we are pledged to hide from our people lest they despair of their existence. I have looked beyond the purposes, sent my mind deeper into the voids to see the source of them. To know who or what controls our lives."

"Looking the gods in the face," Kasstovaal scoffed. "That's a prize claim. You're not the first to establish your credence with that story."

Ra spun round and fixed him with a glare. "You need not take my word." He held out his hands to the two humans. "See for yourself."

"What do you mean?" Kasstovaal asked.

"Touch my mind," Ra said, simply. "You have that much ability now. Both of you. Come. I invite you to follow the path with me. See what my mind saw."

"No way," said Kasstovaal, vehemently. "Do you think we'd risk that, either of us?"

"Mind cannot lie to mind," said Ra. "If you do not trust my word, it is the only way for you to know the truth. And I have resolved that you shall know."

He closed his outstretched hands and it felt to Kasstovaal as though the fingers closed around and took hold of his mind. He reacted instinctively. His mind flexed to resist the grip and seemed suddenly to jerk free of the restraints that held it to his body. He felt light, too light, as though he'd been set adrift in zero gravity. He felt his body let go as the room fell away beneath him. Something drew him across the room, over Ra's head and towards the open window out into space. He tried to flail out and catch something, to do anything that might control the drift but his mind could find no purchase.

"Are you really moving at all?" Ra's voice, seeming to come from behind him. He wanted to turn and see if the Voidseer was there but he could not even do that.

He plunged through the window and the mists surrounded him once more. It was like it had been on his first awakening, drifting and alone in the vast whiteness. But he was not alone. The back of his mind could feel Ra, a cold malevolence just out of sight behind him. And Jeryant, too, off to one side, a suppressed rage momentarily stunned into silence.

And, he realised suddenly, he wasn't drifting either. He was in motion, not of his own doing. He was being pulled.

"But have you really moved from where you stood?" Ra said, somewhere.

The voids spun before Kasstovaal's vision as he was twisted around, turning him to face directly into the maw of one giant void that took hold of him and began to drag him towards it. He felt panic rising within him as the black mass came at him, drawing him faster and faster as he approached. The thunderous roar of the thing grew around him, vibrating the mist. The force of the motion pressed against him like gravity and he wanted to scream out his fear if only to ease the pressure.

"Your body feels no pressure," said Ra.

Kasstovaal barely heard him. His whole attention was taken up by the impenetrable, roaring darkness that was swallowing up the mist, reaching out and swallowing him. The forward speed increased still further as he plunged into its depths. A terrible cold bit at him on top of the awful force that wanted to crush him to nothing. Some part of his petrified mind found a voice with which to scream. And scream he did. Through the engulfing thunder of the Void, he thought he heard Jeryant screaming also, the merest thread in the noise.

Then the darkness tore open ahead of him and spat him out into....

"Stars!"

He was adrift in Space again. Black Space. The wonderful, familiar emptiness between galaxies. And a hundred thousand stars shone their light on him.

The terrible pressure and noise were gone. There was only the silence, a silence he knew well. He was home.

The stars twisted and moved. The motion began again, drawing him across empty space at impossible speed. A pair of stars drew nearer, grew to suns, a binary system. He slowed and was turned to see the planet that basked in the warmth of those two suns, a green world circled by two great rings, orbiting at ninety degrees to one another. He knew that world. He was sure he did but he couldn't remember the name.

The motion drew him down between the rings and into the atmosphere. Thick clouds parted and revealed to him a panorama of civilisation stretched out beneath him like a map, interlocking fields and settlements dotted here and there by the magnificence of cities, vibrating with life.

And he could feel that life. His heightened mind sensed others like his, millions of his kind thinking their everyday thoughts and dreaming their dreams. Human minds. He was in no doubt, now.

The motion drew him towards the towers of one of the cities. He recognised them as he drew closer. He'd visited them many times. The suns had set over the city and it glowed under its own artificial lights. He was drawn towards one tower, one darkened window left open to the night. He passed through it into the room and hovered over the woman who lay sleeping on a bed within.

He could feel her mind wandering in its dreams, every though randomised. Except for one thread; a cold, primal need that reached clear out of her mind, reached out to grasp him. He felt the cold tendril seize him in an iron grip and drag him down into the sleeping mind, pulling him through the tangle of her dreams and down into her deepest thoughts. There was a void there, a black empty space that tugged at him, longed for him to fill it and complete the picture in her mind. Drawing him gladly in. At last. That's the answer.

"No." Ra's voice thundered around him. "No further. You have gone far enough."

Kasstovaal was dragged backwards. There was a killing moment of intense speed as he was snapped back though the whole journey in an instant. Then he was standing in Ra's room, the Voidseer watching them both, impassively, as he lowered his outstretched hands.

Kasstovaal felt off-balance. The journey had nauseated him but his body told him that he hadn't moved an inch, that he had been nowhere. Jeryant was leaning on one of the scattered benches to support him and rubbing his eyes.

"That was our universe," Kasstovaal breathed. "You took us back to our own universe."

"I have taken you nowhere," Ra said. "I have only shown you what I, myself, saw. Thousands of worlds and quintillions of people living on them. Great spheres of light and heat in place of the voids floating in a space with no mist, only darkness. I saw the forms around the minds that lived and worked there. They were your forms. It was your universe."

"Our universe," whispered Kasstovaal. "The voids lead into our universe? Directly?"

"In a manner of speaking, yes," said Ra. "But no so directly that you could fly your ship into one and find your way back. Though, I admit, it would be an interesting experiment to watch. From a distance, that is."

"How then?" Kasstovaal asked.

"Like all before me, I have followed the trail to its end. I waited until one of my people released his knowledge to the Void and I followed it in. That is another skill the Voidseers have learned, following a package of information, an answer, on its journey. I trailed behind it and saw where it came to rest. I saw the mind that received the answer and accepted it as its own. You saw that mind too, did you not?"

"A mind?" Jeryant asked. "Just one?"

"Yes," said Ra. "One mind out of all those quintillions. A Beyonder's mind. A...human mind."

The two of them fell silent, digesting the meaning of his words.

"You begin to understand," said Ra. "I can sense it. Know this, then. That mind accepted the answer and knew it. It knew what question had been asked because that was the mind that had asked it. That was where the purpose had come from; from the mind of one of your people. It had asked the question and we had provided it with the answer it sought."

"But that's not possible," Jeryant blurted out. "No one in our universe has the power to do that. If we have a question we need answering we have to work it out for ourselves. There's no way round it unless you happen to get...." He suddenly choked on the words he was about to say.

They gurgled, painfully, in his throat as his brain lost control of them, stunned by the realisation that hit him.

Kasstovaal stepped over to him and slammed him on the back. "What, Jery? What is it?"

Jeryant gulped down a huge lump of nothing in his throat and got his voice back. "My gods!" he wheezed. "He's talking about inspiration, isn't he."

"Huh?"

"Think about it, Kass. They way he described it. Needing the answer to something and suddenly getting it without knowing how you worked it out. What would you call that, huh? A flash of inspiration. Weren't we talking about it, not long ago, and saying how much human science has benefited from our ability to do that? Weren't we wondering how we managed it?"

"And the answer is that you did not manage it," said Ra, savagely. "Not through your own direct efforts. We were doing all that work for you. You forced us to solve the scientific problems you could not solve for yourselves. And not only us, of the Rock. All the other worlds where life has come into being are subjugated by you. The Cube world, one hundred thousand units from here, where they ponder philosophy and meaning. The Tubular world at the centre of the universe where music is made. Yes, I know what music is. My mind has visited that world. Inside the tube it is a constant sea of sounds, a cacophony of different notes flooding from one end of the world to the other and back again. And the people stand upon the ledges inside the tube and must listen to the random patterns until they detect a new melody amongst them. Every single world where the people toil for new knowledge or new beauty without knowing why."

"Hang on! Hang on!" Kasstovaal protested, raising his voice to interrupt. "I don't buy this at all. We haven't forced anybody to do anything. Assuming we accept that human minds are the source of the purposes which turn up in the Purpose Chamber; that, somehow, our need for knowledge is leaking through; nobody's making the Dwellers take them on except themselves. Or, possibly, the belief system which you and your predecessors have instilled into them. That's the only compulsion I can see being used to force them to work. All it takes is for a Dweller to say 'No, I won't do it' and that's all. If it's anybody's fault, I'd say it was yours, not ours."

Ra scowled at him. "You do not understand," he said, bitterly. "The purposes you set for us are the least of you crimes. Even, it might be said, the most merciful of them, since the purposes give us a way out of our bondage. Though I, myself, would not sully the pure concept of mercy by associating it with such evil."

"You're right," said Kasstovaal, "I don't understand. What evil? So far all you've told us is that your people have been gullible enough to take on our dirty work for us without being asked. That's none of our doing."

"But it is," Ra shouted, suddenly.

"What?"

"You, of all, should understand," said Ra. "You have touched our minds more than once. You have both seen how a Dweller is born and what horror it has for us. Can it be that you have seen and felt these things and not comprehended their meaning? Have you not sensed the misery of our terrible imprisonment in these..." he gestured down at himself, "...bodies?"

Kasstovaal was silent. He remembered that sorrow. Te had felt it as keenly as the rest of her race and she had shared that with him, once by accident, once by choice. It was a desolation he would not have wished on anyone and would have done anything to relieve her of it, had it been in his power to do so. But she knew of only one way, the way she was taking for herself.

Ra nodded. "I see you have felt it. Well, know this then. A Dweller is brought into existence for one reason and one reason only; to complete a given purpose. It is not a question of creating enough purposes to match the number of Dwellers that live at any one time. Quite the opposite. Dwellers are born to meet the demand of the purposes. The giving of a purpose is not the start but the continuation of the process that will ultimately provide the answer. The Compulsion comes first."

"The Compulsion?" Kasstovaal said. "You don't mean...."

"I do mean it. The Compulsion, also, comes from the voids. From your universe. Think of it, Beyonder. A human mind conceives a problem that must be solved. Why waste time and effort working on it when you can create a ready-made slave to do it all for you? Whether you do it consciously or not is beside the point. A purpose is conceived, so a Dweller must be created to take it on and complete it for you. You send us the Compulsion and force us to capture and imprison more free thoughts to be slave for you and do your bidding. The purpose creates the Dweller who will eventually complete it."

Jeryant said, quietly, "You're saying that our race, humans, created the Dwellers. Every Dweller who has ever lived and is now living."

"The Dwellers, the Rock, the whole of this reality," said Ra. "All created by you to serve your purposes." He snorted. "Perhaps I should lay myself down upon the floor and worship you like gods. Strangely, I do not feel inclined to do so. Having subjugated us and condemned us to a living purgatory, to expect homage from us as well would be adding insult to injury."

Kasstovaal said, "I don't believe it. You're telling us that we have the power to create universes without realising it? Have you any idea how ludicrous that sounds? If it were true, little universes would be popping up all over the place. We'd have destroyed ourselves long before now.

No, my friend, the fabric of creation is not so easily reshaped. We'll never have the sort of power required to do what you suggest."

"You think not," said Ra. "What does it really take to make your dreams into reality? I agree that universes such as your own would be beyond the human mind. But consider the nature of this universe, nothing like your own. What is it? Nothing more than a vast mass of thought-energy programmed to exist in a certain way. All else within the Barrier is created from that basic state."

He touched a finger to the side of his forehead. "What, then, is an idea. Consider that, next. Surely it, also, is a mass of thought-energy keyed to a certain pattern but on a minute scale by comparison, existing inside your mind. How many tiny pockets of thought-energy are you carrying around in your mind, even now? How many minute universes?

"So what would it take to create a full-sized universe like this one? How do you accumulate this much energy, all programmed in the same way? Quite simply, I would say. It just needs many thousands of people to conceive the same idea; an idea which, by its very nature, becomes reality.

"All it would take, I think, would be one human to conceive the idea of a universe made of thought. That would be the seed. If he, then, suggests the concept to a few thousand people then they, too, will have the idea in their minds. They need not consider it as a serious possibility but the idea, once placed in their minds, will never go away. If enough people carry that idea in their minds, the accumulation of thought-energy would be more than sufficient."

"And thought-energy is not confined to the mind. Some of it escapes and becomes free. More than enough, across those thousands of people, to create a small reality, to set up the conditions in which thought-energy is the power. Thought promotes sentience; sentience generates thought. From a small beginning, that mass of thought-energy would multiply and grow, expanding the new reality to the size it now is.

"And then the subjugation begins and the voids begin to open. Desperate human minds, searching for answers, suddenly find a source of labour that they can control. Perhaps all human minds now know, unconsciously, where to come for the answers they cannot calculate alone. Or it could be that only certain minds are capable of reaching in. Whichever it is, the purposes still come. Dwellers are still forced into being. By you. Are you proud of your creation, Beyonders?"

Neither of them answered. It was a question too big to admit of an answer in words.

Ra said, "The Voidseers on every world have known this since the beginning of time. The power to see into the voids inevitably brings us the knowledge. Each of us has been bound never to reveal the truth of it to our fellow Dwellers; every Voidseer enjoins his or her apprentice to keep the secret. The sense in it is clear to see, when the truth is known."

"I don't follow," said Kasstovaal.

"Earlier, you accused me of using my influence to compel my people to work at their purposes. It may be so, to a degree. But what the Voidseer imposes is order and stability. A Dweller knows, by my teachings, that it is his fate to complete a purpose and that he is doomed to remain trapped in his body until he has completed that purpose. That is nothing but the truth. Many have tried, in the past, to gain release from their bondage without the word of the Voidseer. None have succeeded. The voids will not accept half an answer. They became the Lost Ones, stranded in the mists.

"And yet the Dwellers know that there is hope for them. I teach them, also, that they will be released from their bodies, if they only earn the right to be. I can see into the voids and I can sense when the answer will be sufficient. No Dweller has ever been given the word of the Voidseer and not, then, been accepted by the Void. I give them a path to follow, one which will, surely, lead them to what they desire.

"But consider how they would react if they knew the truth as I know it. What would they do if they knew that they were no more than a slave labour force for another race. What would it do to their motivation? Slaves do not work so willingly, even if they are convinced of their reward. And suppose they decided to turn away from their allotted purposes and began to ponder ways of breaking out of their slavery? How much longer would their purgatory be if they were so distracted and what terrible retaliation might they bring down on all of us if they tried?

"That could not be allowed. Far better to continue as we are, fulfilling our purposes and accepting our freedom in return, as our right and due. Logic dictates the wisdom of following the line of least resistance. So we are. So we have always done."

Jeryant said, "All except Ko, that is. This is what he was going on about, wasn't it? When he attacked us."

"Ah yes. Ko." Ra turned back to his window. "A pity about him. Perhaps it was some failing in my teaching of him that has led us to this. Perhaps I let him see the truth too soon, before he was ready to accept it. Perhaps he would never have been ready."

"Our presence can't have helped," Jeryant commented.

"Indeed. Without that, I might have brought him to see reason eventually. But to have two of our tormentors here, now, within reach and vulnerable. The one chance our race might ever have to exact a little of the revenge that is owed us. It was such a temptation. Even I, bound as I am, felt the attraction of it.

"For Ko it was too sore a trial. We both recognised you for what you were, the moment you arrived here. Can you imagine how much it galled us to see how our people welcomed you? How they honoured you?

Ko implored me, he begged me to break the silence the Voidseers have held since the beginning of the Rock and expose you to our people as the architects of our misery. I refused him, of course. I knew that your stay would only be temporary and that when you were gone, all would return to the order that has kept us going for so long. Our people could have continued in blissful ignorance of the insult that had been done to them, never knowing what fools they had made of themselves by venerating their oppressors. You two."

He turned on them again. "How different would your Welcome Ceremony have been if they had known, Beyonders. You may wish to think on that. I choose to believe you when you claim ignorance and innocence of tormenting my people. For my own peace of mind, not yours. It pains me too much to think how you would have laughed at us, in your minds, as we welcomed you with every wave from our selves, had you been conscious of your tyranny."

"I think you contrived to show me, at the time," said Kasstovaal. "I know what I felt from you and it wasn't a hearty welcome."

Ra looked straight at him, seemed to look straight through him. "Good," he said. "At the time, it was as far as my own revenge could go. I would not welcome you, even if my people did."

"I didn't see Ko anywhere on that day," said Kasstovaal. "Or feel him, to my knowledge. I thought everybody was supposed to attend."

"He could not bring himself to attend," said Ra. "Indeed, I advised him to stay away. Who knows what folly he might have committed? More than a negative wave, I think. That much I could sense in his anger. Though even I did not realise how far it would drive him, young fool. He did not see that destroying you would not end our servitude. It would only ensure our own destruction at the hands of the Barrier. Perhaps such an end is to be desired. A final end. But what would come after? We know what happens when our thoughts are freed into the open universe but what if there is no universe to escape into? No mist? He could not see that. To his credit, though, Ko's action need not, necessarily, have jeopardised our peace."

"And how do you work that one out?" asked Jeryant, crossly.

"The outcome for him, if he had succeeded in destroying you, would have been more or less the same as it has been now. He would have been isolated from his purpose for a time until the conscience of the gathering could permit it no longer. There is no worse fate known to us than to be prevented from completing your purpose. They could not have stomached such cruelty for too long a time. He need only have kept his silence and all would have returned to normal.

"As it is, I have placed a block in his mind which will prevent him from speaking what he knows, as he might well be tempted to do now that he has been thwarted."

"And that's why he said nothing at his trial," said Kasstovaal.

"Yes. It grieved me to do it, for I feel his frustration also. It is an even worse humiliation to see our people sympathise with you and move to protect you as the victims of an unprovoked attack. Unprovoked! Did they but know.

"But now they shall never know and that is as it should be. Ko can never tell them; I never shall. And if you are wise, Beyonders, you shall say no word to my people. Feel free to tell your own people, though. Then those, among you, that have compassion may grieve for what they have unwittingly done. A far more satisfying revenge than the deaths of two unimportant Beyonders. I shall be satisfied."

He stopped, watching his words sink in, on their faces. Then he straightened himself, jutted his chin and stared them down, tall and imperious, the prophet of his people facing his demons boldly.

Kasstovaal brought his hands together and clapped a few times in mock applause. "A pretty story," he said, "I'll grant you it fills in all the gaps. But you still haven't offered us any proof of what you say."

"He convinced me," said Jeryant. He sounded a little weary. "There's no denying that trip into the Void he gave us."

"I'm not convinced," said Kasstovaal. "He could have strung that little lot together from our own conversations if he'd listened to them. That wouldn't be hard, either. The Rock sees all, knows all and tells all. Isn't that right, Ra? He could even have tapped into the Mindshare for the pictures. That city we visited is well embedded in my mind; I've been there. It was a good show, I grant you, but it is no proof, Ra."

Ra said, "There is plenty of proof to be found if you look for it, Beyonder. I see no reason to exert myself in seeking it out for you. I know that what I say is the truth. That is all I need. If you need more than my word or my memory, look for yourself."

Kasstovaal snorted. "A clever way out. Quite typical for a priest, in fact."

"I will offer you one thing," said Ra. "Something the voids have shown me in my travels among them."

"More mysticism?"

"You may judge that for yourselves. Ignore it if you wish. It makes no difference to me."

"What is it?"

Ra paused, as though double-checking his memory. Then he said, "We measure our ages in terms of the cycles of the orbits that the voids follow." He pointed out of the window. "You see the configuration of the voids now. One cycle is the amount of time that will pass before they stand in that configuration again."

"All right," said Kasstovaal. "What of it?"

"One such cycle," said Ra, "is equivalent to sixty-seven of your standard days. The voids have shown me this."

"And that's supposed to help?" asked Jeryant.

"Yes," Kasstovaal interrupted him. "It will."

"In which case," said Ra, turning his back on them again as though the window drew him, "you will go, now. I have done what I must and said what I wanted. There is no more. Go and leave us to the fate you have decreed for us. Never return, if you are wise and truly wish us no conscious ill."

A doorway appeared in the wall behind them. It was in the shape of a cross, a symbol still common to hundreds of religions and familiar to both of them.

"Leave me," said Ra and said no more to them.

They left the room, in silence, and the doorway sealed up behind them.

"You managed to get in before he did, then," said Kasstovaal.

"Huh?"

"The doorway, I mean."

Jeryant didn't smile. "I didn't do that," he said. "He did. What do we read from that?"

"That he's a good mind-reader," said Kasstovaal. "It must be clear enough in both of our minds."

"Did you feel him in there, poking around? I didn't."

"Doesn't mean a thing. We, probably, wouldn't feel him doing it, if he's that good. He's still playing with us, that's what it is. As mind games go, it's a good one. I'll give him that."

"If it is a game," said Jeryant. "How about that proof he was talking about. You reckon you know where to find it now?"

"I know where he means for us to look for it," said Kasstovaal. "It's something I've had in mind for a while. And, I admit, if we find what I think he wants us to find, it'll be enough to convince me."

Jeryant looked him the eye. "Even here, I'm no mind-reader," he said. "So tell me. Are you feeling what I'm feeling? Do we both want to find no proof? Do we want it to be a lie?"

The question had a strange effect on Kasstovaal. He felt a sensation he hadn't felt in a long time. He felt his thoughts and feelings turning outwards. For many years his whole being had been turned inwards, scrunched up in a tight protective ball, hoarding his resources to guard himself from the rigours of the outside. He had given so little time to thought about other people so wrapped up was he in his own sufferings. But he felt pity for the Dwellers, compassion. He wanted to reach out and comfort them, if he could do nothing else to relieve their torment. It was Te, and through her all her people, who had found within him a heart to touch. One he had forgotten he had.

"Yes," he said, "I want it not to be true."

27.

The Chamber of Knowledge was virtually empty when they entered it. Voidrise was approaching once again and only a few of the Dwellers seemed able to maintain their control enough to continue working with it so near.

Kasstovaal had refused to go directly there from Ra's quarters. He itched to know the truth as much as Jeryant did but a remnant of his defiance remained and would not allow him to let Ra think that he could still control him, pulling the right strings to send him running here or there as the Voidseer wanted. He would not give Ra that satisfaction. So they had killed some time first.

They had thought to spend some time with Vo, knowing that the time for the suicide he contemplated so joyfully was fast approaching. Neither of them really relished the prospect. They had both watched someone die, Jeryant many times over. But how did you watch somebody go to meet their death so happily, a death done by their own hand and at an appointed time. It was too unnatural for them to grasp. And what did you say to someone in that position? "Everything will be fine," or "Enjoy it. You've earned it"? The human repertoire of platitudes did not cover this sort of thing.

As it was, they were spared the immediate need. Vo was not in his laboratory or his quarters. According to Te, who was closeted in her own room working on her profile of the human universe, Vo would be out and about the Rock tidying up his remaining affairs and saying personal goodbyes to the closer of his acquaintances. Traditionally, she said, it was a process that took a long time and was best started as soon as the Voidseer's word was given.

Instead, the two of them split up to continue their respective work. They both felt the desire to leave more keenly than before, even without testing the truth of Ra's revelations. In human terms, the Dwellers enjoyed a form of paradise. But they, the only two humans who would ever experience it, had found the price to be too high. Disruption, destruction and even death. It was too much.

Both worked but neither gave the work the attention it deserved, lost as they were in their own thoughts. After thirty hours, Jeryant was unable to stand it anymore and stormed into the hangar, demanding that they get on with it now or there would be blood spilled. "...and I don't care what colour it is," he finished.

Kasstovaal had relented and led the way up to the Chamber of Knowledge, a good hour's climb which did nothing to improve their moods. It didn't help that the Dwellers they met en route were, by now, displaying the first signs of the pre-Voidrise tension that they had both come to recognise. Many Voidrises had come and gone during their stay and they could now spot the signs several hours in advance of the event. Fortunate in this case, since neither of them wanted to miss this particular Voidrise. It would take one of their friends away with it and, morbid though it might seem, they did not want to miss the chance to see him off.

They easily found an empty worktable near to the crystals Kasstovaal wanted to consult. He had been planning his strategy for some hours and knew how he would test the information Ra had given them.

Jeryant formed stools for them; the Dwellers seemed to do most of their work standing up.

"I need a sheet of paper and a writing stylus for this," said Kasstovaal. "Would you do the honours? I can't form."

Jeryant stared at him incredulously. "You're not going to use that for your calculations, are you?"

"Sure I am. I've always done my basic calculus on paper."

"There are such things as wrist-computers in our universe," said Jeryant. "That's what most people use, you know. That or stylus-pads for the really old fashioned among us. I've never seen anyone use pen and paper. Outside of a history class, that is."

"I prefer my way. It keeps the brain in practice. You never know when you might have to calculate your way out of something, in my job, and without the benefit of power for computers. Besides, you don't know the first thing about microcircuitry. You couldn't form a wrist-computer if you tried. Not a working one, anyway. Pen and paper will do me just fine."

"Suit yourself, I'm sure," said Jeryant, forming the items on the desk. "Just don't ask me to do any sums. I wouldn't know where to begin."

"You can get the crystals for me."

"Thanks a bunch."

It was a simple matter. Compare the meticulous records of the Dwellers to Kasstovaal's own memory of durations and events, using the conversion factor to bridge the gap between. If it was valid, of course. If it wasn't valid then it might stand up to one of his tests but no more than one and he would soon know if Ra was lying.

He realised that there was one factor he did not have, something so insignificant up to now that he hadn't thought to ask. He didn't actually know what the current date was in Dweller terms. All the crystals were date marked, clearly enough, with a value of normal time units and cycles, presumably in relation to an arbitrary zero point sometime in the distant past. Right now that wasn't a lot of good to him without today's date to compare it against. His previous researches had given him a rough idea but now he needed to be accurate.

He went up to the nearest Dweller, who had not yet started to twitch and was just looking drawn and agitated. He jumped when Kasstovaal spoke to him.

"Sorry to disturb you," said Kasstovaal, politely, "but could you tell me what the current cycle number is? Nobody has ever told me and I need it for my calculations."

"What!" exclaimed the Dweller and then seemed to get a hold of himself. "Oh, yes Beyonder. My apologies. You startled me a little"

"No apologies necessary," said Kasstovaal, "I know how close Voidrise is."

The Dweller let out a little sigh as if contemplating the pleasure of it. "Yes, Voidrise." he said. "But, to answer your question. This is the 22,188th cycle."

"Thanks"

He realised that he should have known that. Te had told him, once, that the Dwellers' recorded history spanned that amount of time and what was more natural than to record the current date on the same basis. Oh well, at least he was sure now.

He started on his piece of paper. One cycle equals sixty-seven days or 0.18356 of a standard year. Jeryant was still searching for the crystals he wanted so he converted the length of the Rock's history while he waited. On that basis the Dwellers had reached the point of recording their history four thousand and seventy-two years ago.

He pondered. That would place their first creation back in the pre-Galactic era. Not too far back, though. Somewhere in the fission power phase, he reckoned, though probably the early part of it. Ra's one inhuman human with the bright idea might even have had a computer to write it down on. Did he really believe that theory? No. Not yet, anyway.

"Hey!" Jeryant called from among the racks.

Kasstovaal looked up. Jeryant was holding out a green crystal and waving it at him.

"This the one you want?"

"I can't tell from here, idiot. They all look the same."

"You're telling me."

"Hold it up to your head," Kasstovaal shouted and then muttered to himself, "If you can find it, that is."

Jeryant placed the crystal against his temple and grabbed hold of the nearest rack to support him as the blast of fresh knowledge made him stagger. "Continuum Disruption," he said. "Is that it?"

"That's the one."

Jeryant brought the crystal over and dropped it on the table. "What's that going to tell you?" he asked. "I thought you already knew this sort of thing inside and out."

"I do," said Kasstovaal, taking the crystal and touching it to his own head. "What's important is the date markings. This crystal should tell me exactly when the two Dwellers, who perfected the theory, released themselves into the voids. If what Ra said is true, it should coincide closely with the date on which Franssart first came up with his Curtain theory."

"And you know when that was, presumably."

"Sure I do. It's ingrained on the inside of my skull. Space Central make a point of celebrating it every year."

"Since they owe their livelihood to this guy, I suppose it's only natural. But which anniversary did we reach last? Can you remember that?"

"I can, actually. It was the 3,050th, exactly halfway through the thirty-first century of the Galactic age. A jubilee year. An easy one to remember."

"I never heard about that," said Jeryant. "You mean to say there was a big celebration going on and I missed it? That's unheard of."

"It wasn't anything to get excited about," said Kasstovaal. "The celebration doesn't usually stretch much outside the higher ranks. A jubilee year just means more people are, politely, encouraged to attend. You would have hated it."

"Don't you believe it. I can liven up any party."

Kasstovaal scanned through the crystal. "Here it is," he said, at last, "both Dwellers died during the 5,571st cycle." He scribbled a few figures on the paper. "That is 16,617 cycles ago."

Jeryant frowned. "Sounds pretty close," he said.

Kasstovaal scribbled some more. They both watched the result unfold.

"3,050.21652 years." Kasstovaal read. "Allow a couple of months since the celebration and that is real, real close."

"Convincing?" Jeryant asked.

"Not yet. It may just be a coincidence. Or Ra might have counted on us testing that one event and adjusted his conversion rate accordingly. I want to try one or two other things."

"You want me to go crystal hunting again, I suppose."

"No, I'll do it myself. I'll be looking for specific elements and I doubt if the Dwellers will call them by the same names we do. I'll have to look for atomic structures that match. You could put this one back for me."

The elemental crystals were on a different level and he had to use the tube to reach them. His slow progress down to the level he wanted clearly got on the nerves of the Dweller female waiting to use the tube after him. Her fists were clenched and she seemed unable to stand still. Voidrise can't be far off now, he thought.

He selected a crystal on Repinnium, a heavy element that was only known to occur naturally in microscopic quantities but could be easily synthesised. One of the facts he'd been able to dredge up out of his memory was that a particular isotope of this element gave off gamma radiation for a period of exactly 39.6 years from the date on which it was synthesised, decaying at an almost constant rate. Exactly why he had been expected to learn that he couldn't remember but the figure stayed with him quite clearly.

The crystal went into the element's properties and synthesis at great length and did, indeed, include an experiment to test the radioactive decay rate of the element within an electromagnetic environment. That, in itself, was suggestive. Since the Dwellers didn't live in an EM environment, the results of such a test would be completely useless to them. But they were relevant in his universe and, apparently, the purpose behind these tests had called specifically for it.

He took the crystal back to his table and scanned it for the figure he wanted: 215.73 cycles. He calculated, 39.6 years, sure enough. One of nature's inviolable constants.

He found another crystal that went into atomic fusion rates, again within an EM environment, and found values and measurements that he recognised from his Stellar Cartography work. They all converted down exactly.

"Find anything?" said Jeryant, leaning over his shoulder to stare at the scribbled lines.

"Enough to prove that the conversion rate is valid," said Kasstovaal.

"Try this one," Jeryant held out a small blue crystal, "I found it over there in the medical section."

"What is it?"

"A treatment for DNA Distortion syndrome. I remember reading about it when I was twelve. They'd just perfected it and were presenting it to the medical subcommittee. That would be...," he furrowed his brow "...forty-one years ago. I remember it because that was when I made up my mind to go into medicine. I started boning up on all the medical journals."

Kasstovaal consulted the crystal, turned the paper over and started writing on the clean side. "Right again," he said. "On the high side of forty-one years."

"Any others we can try?"

Kasstovaal thought. "Got it!" he said and trotted off back to the Elemental section. He returned with a dark grey crystal in his hand. "Centridium alloy," he said, triumphantly. "Including tests on its application as a coating. This should date back to my Pilot-Captain's exam, fourteen years. That ought to clinch it."

They checked.

"Sixteen and a half," said Jeryant. "That's not near enough, is it?"

"I think it is. By the time I found out about it, the treatment was already in commercial sale. Allow for development and all the rigmarole of getting the thumbs up from the shipbuilding companies. I'd say two-and-a-half years was quick work for that lot."

"So you're convinced, are you?"

Kasstovaal nodded. "Pretty much. I wouldn't call it conclusive beyond any doubt, but it's good enough to tip the scales." Absently he began to gather the sheet of paper up in his hand, screwing it up into a ball. "We did this to them, didn't we."

"Ironic, isn't it," Jeryant said. "Not long ago we were wondering if the Dwellers were our gods, with all their power to change the universe. How wrong we were. They are not our gods, we are theirs. Except that they don't know it."

"Gods, you say," Kasstovaal chuckled, hollowly. "Devils, more like. I doubt if they'd worship us, in thanks for the gift of life, if they knew."

"Best not to give ourselves airs, either way," said Jeryant, straightening. "We are, neither of us, divine, if truth be told. Just powerful in our own ways. If there are, really, gods out there somewhere, I think we've just been witness to the latest and greatest of their practical jokes."

"Yeah?" said Kasstovaal. "But who were the victims? Us or the Dwellers?"

"Both," said Jeryant, firmly. "And out of the total population of both our races, only four people know that it's been played. It's probably better that it stays that way."

Kasstovaal looked up at him. "You don't intend telling it to our people, then."

"Not if I can avoid it. What good would it really do."

"True enough."

A male Dweller passed their table stiffly, giving them a curt greeting and not waiting for it to be returned.

"That was Igu, wasn't it?" said Kasstovaal. "The first lost Dweller they brought back."

"Yes. These Bio-forms certainly seem to suit the Dwellers better than us."

"You know," said Kasstovaal, "that's the one big gap in all this reasoning."

"What is?"

"The Bio-forms. And Vo's retrieval crystal. I can't see humans wanting inspiration on either of those things. Not yet anyway. So why were Vo and Oa given those purposes. They must have come from the same source."

Jeryant thought about it. "I suppose it's only common sense to create purposes which keep the Dwellers healthy and functional if you want to keep the answers coming back. And, of course, the answers expected from the lost Dwellers would be a long time delayed by their absence. Perhaps our collective unconscious realised that their work had stopped and took steps to bring them back into operation. It was just lucky for us that they were developing it when we arrived."

"Luck, huh?" said Kasstovaal "Or could it have been design, I wonder."

"What?"

"Suppose the purposes were created specifically for us, to give us a way to survive the transit into this universe?"

"I hardly think that's likely."

"Why not? What would it take? We still don't know if our coming here was accidental or deliberate. If it were a planned mission, there would be lots of people turning the various aspects of it over in their minds. Us included, I should think. It would only take one of them to consider the molecular bondage problem as a possibility and try to work out a solution. And Bingo! Out comes the request for inspiration and couple of relevant purposes are formed."

"But Vo and Oa must have been working on these purposes for years. I doubt if a mission plan would take that long to formulate."

"Like I told you, Jery. The Third Mode theory has been around for a long time. The purposes may stem back to its early beginnings. It might even be that, unconsciously, our mission was planned to coincide with their completion."

From below them a crash echoed up through the galleries of the Chamber. They looked over the edge to see what had happened. The female Dweller Kasstovaal had encountered by the tube was standing, trembling, in the centre of the lowest level, a dropped tray of small crystals spilling its contents at her feet. She didn't bother to pick them up, nor did anyone else move to help her. She turned, stiffly, on her heel and hurried out through the nearest exit wall, not waiting to seal the ragged doorway she had made.

"The natives are getting restless," said Jeryant. "It's nearly time for Voidrise."

Kasstovaal closed his eyes. "Damn it. I've been dreading this."

"You too, huh?" said Jeryant. "Come on. We'd better find Vo before the signal sounds. There won't be any stopping him after that."

They left, pausing only to ask the Rock where Vo was to be found. It told them that he was in Te's room and added in an almost joyful tone that Vo's purpose was at an end and that he would soon depart. Kasstovaal cursed it under his breath.

The wall made no protest to their entry; they had wondered if Vo was saying a private goodbye to Te. And so it appeared when they entered. Vo was holding Te in his arms, the arms they could see, bending to touch his forehead to hers. He was calm and placid, the expression on his face that of a man finally at peace. She shook in his arms, though not with the emotions they might have expected. She was happy, the waves that escaped from her told nothing else. Only the pent-up energies inside her body made her shake as she bade her Prim farewell. It was a picture of true tenderness between them, subdued and understated as were all Dweller emotions and yet more powerful in its purity than they had ever seen between two humans.

Oa was there, also, keeping a quiet vigil over them despite the effort it was clearly costing her.

Their entry did not break the spell and they waited patiently for all that must pass between them to be passed. Finally Vo released Te and the tableau broke. He turned to them.

"Say no words," he said. "Te has shown me what this moment will mean to you. You need not struggle to congratulate or commiserate or say anything against the force of your feelings. I know it will cause you pain. We see this moment differently. It is not an ending but a return to what we once had. We know it. We sense it every time we expend our energies into the Void."

Jeryant said, sombrely, "We don't have your certainty. We wish we did."

"I know it," said Vo. "Perhaps it is I who should be commiserating with you. But this is not a time for commiseration. No ending should be. Think of it as a time to celebrate what I became in this form, what I achieved. It is a time for pride, gratification, not mourning. Use this thought, if you can and be glad, as I am, at this moment."

He went to them and reached up to place one hand on a shoulder of each. "My friends," he said, "for I hope I may call you so. I had thought to be here to see you leave the Rock before me but, as it transpires, my work is done before yours. But I count myself fortunate to have existed at the time you came to the Rock and to have played a part in bringing your knowledge to my people. And still more fortunate to have had a chance to see the wonders of your universe, through Te's mind. My mind is enriched by the experience and because of that my freed thoughts will be so much more wonderful. I thank you for that gift.

"Moreover, I am indebted to you for the contribution you made to my work. You were the first I called from the mists and from that I learned what I needed to bring me to this point. For that service, I am also grateful."

"It's for us to be grateful to you for that," said Jeryant. "Not the other way around. Without you we'd still be stuck out there, helpless. And so would all those Dwellers who have been brought back since. We owe you for that."

Vo nodded. "I accept your thanks. Now is, also, a time for settling debts, closing unfinished matters. The giving and accepting of gratitude, the asking and receiving of forgiveness. All that is done now. I can go to my freedom clean and untroubled."

"Shriven," Kasstovaal muttered to himself.

"Yes," said Vo. "Shriven indeed. And content."

He released their shoulders. "We must go now. We have a long climb to the summit and we must begin in good time, before the signal sounds."

He walked towards the corridor wall but did not immediately open a doorway. Instead, he reached out a hand and pressed the palm against the smooth rock surface.

"Thank you, old friend," he said, softly, "thank you for all you have done."

They did not hear what answer the Rock gave but they could see on Vo's face that it had answered and that answer satisfied him.

He formed a doorway out into the corridor. "Come," he said. "It is time."

He walked out ahead of them. Oa and Te fell in behind him, Kasstovaal and Jeryant trailed at the rear and the small procession climbed the spiral towards the summit.

They had reached the Gallery by the time the signal sounded. The single ringing tone filled the open space from edge to edge, making the few Dwellers still in there jump and throw down their crystals to make, hurriedly, for the exits.

Vo led them across the floor towards the outer walls. He still showed no sign of the agitation that was normal to the rest of his people.

"From here," he said, "we climb outside." He opened a doorway and they followed him out onto the ledge.

This high up the face of the Rock, the ledge curved sharply around the circumference and, Kasstovaal noticed, started to spiral towards the summit. Vo led them upwards. Up here a full circle was no distance at all and it was not long before the upward spiral terminated in a short stairway, leading directly up the last six feet to the summit itself.

It was not pointed, as Kasstovaal had imagined it, but, then, he had only ever seen it from a distance. It was, in fact, a level circular platform, about a yard across, just the right size for one man to stand on.

Vo turned to them. "Here I leave you," he said, simply. "Farewell."

Te and Oa both bowed to him, not deeply, an inclination only. Neither said a word. All that was needed had already been said.

"Goodbye, Vo," said Jeryant. "We shall both remember you."

Kasstovaal said nothing. There was nothing he could add. Then both humans repeated the bow that Oa and Te had performed.

Vo nodded back at them. "So shall I you," he said. Then he turned and mounted the steps, briskly, and within seconds was standing on top of the world. His world, that was no longer his.

Below them, the ledges had filled with the legions of the Dwellers of the Rock. Off in the distance the rumble of the approaching Void began to make itself heard.

Jeryant formed a set of earplugs each for them and they put them in. The spiralling ledge was deserted, except for themselves, Oa and Te. It must be reserved for those bidding farewell to a close comrade or parent. They were able to put a little distance between themselves and the two Dwellers, who were clearly fully absorbed in the task of preparing for their own energy discharges.

Instead of looking outwards, as they had before, the two humans turned to look up at where Vo stood. He, like his fellows, had raised his arms up and out in the supplicant,s pose. The joy that filled his face was a pleasure to see. And even he let go his control, at this final extreme, and sent out waves of happiness and content that burst upon their bodies and washed away the mourning that built up inside them.

The Dwellers on the lowest ledge were beginning to discharge their energy, now. They glanced behind and saw the bloated hulk of the Void boiling up over the lower horizon, rearing up to feed. They had not taken the time, as Kasstovaal had hoped, to study the event since that first time they had seen it. It was no longer as important to them as the battle to escape. But they had watched a few of them. It was too grand a spectacle to ignore for long.

The Void toiled its way up the sky drawing new streams of fire from each ledge as it drew level. Beside them, the bodies of Oa and Te began to glow and they, too, were soon pouring their life energy into the black pit before them.

Vo's body did not react with the rest. He stood there, patiently waiting, and it was not until the lower levels of the Rock had ceased to blaze and gone dark that his body began to glow, building up to a brighter light than any of the other Dwellers had managed. The beam of light he exuded lanced out straight and true, dead into the centre of the Void, unaffected by its pull. It hurt the eyes and the humans had to raise their hands in front of their faces to shade out the brightness of it.

One by one the ledges went dark and the Dwellers all turned to look up the face of the Rock towards the summit where Vo stood, a brief beacon for his people. The light from Oa and Te was the last to fade away and they turned in time to watch as Vo's body began to dissolve, softening at the edges and then, visibly, falling away into the light that engulfed him. To the last second, when his face lost its definition and faded out of existence, he never once lost the expression of joy and contentment. Or was that just the illusion?

Then he was gone. The bubble of energy, where he had stood, gathered itself for one final thrust and shot away out into space, deep into the very heart of the hungry Void. Then there was nothing.

Around and beneath them, the Dwellers began to file away back inside the Rock. Even Te and Oa turned and walked past Kasstovaal and Jeryant, saying no word. The humans let them go.

Jeryant pulled the plugs out of his ears and looked, speculatively, back at the empty platform of the summit.

"Fancy a wake?" he asked, at length.

"I don't expect the Dwellers will be having one," Kasstovaal replied. "It's not their way, is it."

"But it is ours," said Jeryant, firmly. "And what more fitting way do we know to celebrate Vo's life?"

Kasstovaal tossed his earplugs over the ledge and watched them fall away to be engulfed by the mist. Then he gave a short smile. "Why not?" he said. "Vo didn't want us to grieve."

"Good boy." Jeryant draped an arm across his friend's shoulders and led him away. "Let's see if we can find a couple of those amber crystals. Then we can toast him properly. Trust me, you'll love it."

Above them, the Void heaved itself up and away from the Rock. The mists took over again, blurring and then hiding the Void from view.

Voidrise was over. But it would return. It always did. It always must.

TEN: DEPARTURE

28.

"I could use a hand, here," Kasstovaal called over his shoulder. He was leaning in through an inspection hatch into the ship's belly and was trying to insert the plug-end of a cable into a broad socket. Since the cable was twice as thick as his own arm and the plug weighed upward of forty pounds it was proving awkward in the confined space. Not to mention the fact that the cable was carrying enough of a power charge to light up a small town and demanded of him a certain amount of care and respect.

Jeryant did not respond to the call. He was still slumped on a stool next to the workbench, gazing into the heart of his amber crystal as though he were appreciating the quality of a fine wine.

Their private wake had, inevitably, brought them back to the hangar. The atmosphere of contented normality, into which the Dwellers had immediately settled, was not conducive to their mood and unspoken agreement had led them back here to be alone, for a while, with their memories.

Kasstovaal had been the first to get back onto his feet and had resolved to work-off the delicious light-headedness, induced by the crystals, by completing the last connections on the ship's power circuit. The thought that, in his half-drunk state, he might make a serious, if not fatal, mistake never occurred to him. He could do this sort of work in his sleep; inebriation was no challenge.

This cable was becoming one, though, and he didn't have an amplifier to lighten the problem. He shouted back at Jeryant again, "Hello! Paging Doctor Jeryant. You are wanted in reality ASAP."

Jeryant started out of his reverie. "Did you want me?" he asked, innocently.

"Yes. Get your fat arse over here and give me a hand with this."

"How can I refuse such a gracious request." Jeryant bowed and then pointed a finger up under his chin. "I'm sure I'll think of a way if I give it long enough."

"You try it and I'll kick your teeth in. Now get over here or you'll be pushing this ship into space."

Jeryant levered himself, reluctantly, from his stool and sauntered over to the hole in the ship's side. It was a squeeze to get him inside as well but he soon held the thick cable in his arms and, together, they manhandled the plug into place and Kasstovaal tightened the securing bolts to hold it firm. When he was satisfied that it was secure, he gripped the contact lever, set around the rim of the socket, and heaved it round a quarter turn.

There was a sound like a deeply drawn-in breath and the *Gateway 2* came to life. The transparent viewplate of the cockpit lit up as a hundred instruments began to signal their operation. A vibration began to make itself felt in the air immediately around the hull. Kasstovaal bathed in it. It was a sensation he never got tired of, the life force of his ship humming in time with his own.

He gave himself half a minute to enjoy it and then pulled himself free and slid the inspection hatch closed. "Seal that up for me, would you?" he asked Jeryant. "You're the one with the amplifier around here."

Jeryant clicked his tongue, irritably. "This is your revenge for me taking it away from you, isn't it," he grumbled. "You're making me do all the work now, huh."

"That's right."

Jeryant grunted, neutrally, and glared at the hatch. The seam that made it a visible square in the, otherwise, unbroken metal of the hull began to fill in, sealing it out of sight until it vanished completely, leaving no trace in the unblemished surface. As a final flourish, Jeryant signed his name, indenting the letters into the metal.

"Thank you." Kasstovaal turned and made his way around to the airlock, letting himself in to the cockpit.

In here the vibration was all the more potent. He sat down in the pilot's seat and could feel it radiating through his body. The ship felt poised, underneath him, ready to spring. All he had to do was command it and the ship would leap across immeasurable space, rejoicing in its freedom. He laid a hand on the control panel, as though to calm its eagerness. Not yet my friend, he thought. Soon.

Then he started on the controls. He had preprogrammed all the system chips and the displays were already signalling their readiness to accept his commands in letters that he could understand. He ordered the onboard sensors to begin the start up check on all the systems. It would test every component to make sure it was working and would list out any flaws it could find. It was no substitute for the in-depth inspection a human could perform but it was the best a machine could be expected to do. It would take, perhaps, half an hour to test everything and compile the report.

He ran his eyes over the instruments, giving them his own once-over, and then eased himself back outside. Jeryant was leaning, nonchalantly, against the ship's side, waiting for him.

"That's it," he said. "There's nothing more we can do for the present."

"Is she ready to go?" Jeryant asked.

"Should be. We need to wait for the start up report and see if anything needs adjusting. If it comes out okay then we can go any time we're ready."

"Great." Jeryant pushed himself upright. "I suppose we'd better slip into something more comfortable, then, hadn't we."

"What?"

"Our bodies, sunbeam. The new ones. They're ready and waiting for us up in Oa's laboratory."

"You think we ought to transfer over to them now?"

"Might as well. It may take a little while to break them in, so to speak."

"You trust me with all those amplifiers?"

Jeryant folded his arms and leaned back a little, as though to examine Kasstovaal all over from a distance. Then he smiled. "You look pretty calm to me," he said. "How do you feel?"

"I've just been celebrating someone's funeral," said Kasstovaal. "Someone I don't know if I'd have called a friend; I didn't know him long enough for that. But if things had been different, I think I would have."

"We knew him enough to mourn him," said Jeryant. "Isn't that what we've just been doing?"

"True," Kasstovaal agreed. "Even though he didn't want us to."

Jeryant said nothing. The mood was becoming sombre again. He didn't want that.

"On the other hand," said Kasstovaal, more brightly, "if all goes well, we could be flying out of here within the hour. On balance, I feel bloody marvellous."

Jeryant's smile came back. "Won't be sorry to leave, huh?"

"Not much."

"No yearnings for fair maiden?"

Kasstovaal's automatic denial failed to come out. He hadn't allowed himself the time to consider what he felt for Te. Nothing but the building of the ship and his escape had mattered; he had focused his whole being on that, perhaps to avoid facing his feelings. But she had touched him in ways no other woman ever had. Not even...what was her name...Karinda. Yes, that was it. Not even Karinda, who had seen the darkness of his soul through the darkness in his eyes.

Te had reached in further and she truly knew him. She had seen all of him, every dark corner, every clouded thought. His lost hopes, his frustrated dreams, the all-too-brief loves he had felt. She had seen it all and had not shied away from him. She understood him, she accepted what he was without being afraid of it. He had touched her, too, and he knew that it was true. She knew him and could comfort him, shield him from his own demons and make him believe that the universe was not as dark as it appeared. It was all he had ever wanted, someone to know him, to see why he was what he was and to accept it, even to be fond of it.

But he could not stay. If he felt for her so then he owed it to her to leave, to vacate this universe which could not hold him and give her a chance to live out her life and earn her freedom. The freedom that he and his kind had taken away from her.

He said, "I have a part of Te to remember her by. And she has a part of me. That's the best I could hope for under the circumstances. She can't come and I can't stay and that's all there is to it. I have as much as I can have."

"Is it enough, though?" Jeryant asked.

"It will be. It will have to be."

"Good. In that case, I reckon we can risk giving you all that power for a while. Still, we'll keep Te around if we can, just in case you start to get stressed." Jeryant turned and formed doorways out into the corridor. They were large, humanoid-shaped doorways. "If sir would like to step this way," he said, "I'm sure we can find something in his size and to his taste."

Kasstovaal followed him out, anticipation making his extremities tingle. He hadn't realised just how much he was looking forward to having a body that was recognisably his again. The Bio-form didn't bother him like it used to. Time and necessity had resigned him to it. But now he could discard it, change again and become himself, a human.

"Have you worked out how to make the transfer between the two bodies?" he asked, catching up with Jeryant in the corridor.

"I think so. I had a few words with Ji about it. It's more his area than Oa's. He makes it sound fairly simple but...well, we'll see about that. You'll need to have your amplifier re-installed first."

"What for?"

"Ji says it's a question of animating the brain cells in the new body. It's a lot like matter-forming, except that it's not a molecular pattern that's being projected. It's the whole contents of your mind."

Kasstovaal tried to envisage it. What would it be like to be outside his body, either of them, if only for a second? Would he be able to let go or would he instinctively cling on to the brain he was in, keep his mind anchored? What if he let go and never made it to the other brain?

His fears must have shown on his face for Jeryant smiled at him and said, "Sounds daunting, I grant you. But Ji says there's nothing to it. A few of the rescued Dwellers have had to do it when their Bio-forms didn't take properly and they say the sensation is minimal. And over so short a distance it's virtually impossible for anything to go wrong. So, don't worry."

"That's another thing all Doctors say - 'Don't worry!', like 'This won't hurt'."

"Have I ever used it in vain?"

"Often, to my knowledge."
"This time I mean it. Trust me."
"That's another one."
"Shut up."

They walked on, for a while, in silence. Then Kasstovaal asked, "How about you, Jery?"

"What about me?"

"Got anything keeping you here?"

Jeryant gave a short laugh. "Hah! 'Course I have. Quite apart from scientific curiosity, this place is heaven for a materialist like me. Never tire, never get old and anything you want you can just think up for yourself. I used to dream of living in a place like that, lazy bastard that I am. But, no. The price is too high. And I'd eventually get bored. I know I would."

"And Oa?"

Jeryant was silent for a moment and then shrugged. "Me, I'm the original girl-in-every-port man. Love them honestly and leave them amicably. Never regret, always learn. Better and more sincere than most long-term relationships. And more enjoyable for both parties, I find."

They had climbed to the level for Oa's laboratory and were turning into the connecting corridor when something in the air changed. They both felt it. During their time there, they had both become more and more sensitive to the constant background whispers that flowed through the Rock. It was always there, just beyond hearing, and they had come to ignore it, as all familiar noise is eventually ignored. But, just for a second, the whispers went silent and both of them noticed the absence. At the same time the ever-present ambient light, that never seemed to come from any direct source, dimmed perceptibly. Then it brightened again, becoming brighter than it had been before and, at the same moment, the Rock began to scream.

It was not an audible noise, the Rock never made a sound. But it inserted itself into the mind like the words they heard directing them here and there, a cry made up of consternation and more than a little fear, not loud but insistent. It sank into their minds like a needle and seemed to tug at them, trying to pull them in the opposite direction, back to the spiral and down.

"What the hells is that?" shouted Jeryant, putting his hands to his head.

"Don't know. Some sort of alarm, maybe."

"It's alarming, that's for sure," said Jeryant, trying to shake the intrusive noise out of his head. "Whatever it is, it hurts."

Up ahead of them a doorway appeared. Oa and Te hurried through it and ran towards them, actually ran. They had never seen a Dweller running. The implanted illusions made it look unnatural. Their upper bodies remained rigid and they didn't swing their arms in time to the motion of their legs.

"What is it?" Kasstovaal shouted over a sound that wasn't there and the loudness of his voice startled him.

"It is Ko," Oa cried as she ran past them. "Something is wrong." She took the corner hard and disappeared around the curve of the spiral, Te close behind her.

The two humans took off after them, the same thought spurring them into action. They had never tried running in their Bio-forms before; it had never been necessary. It came with surprising ease, especially for Jeryant, who hadn't run anywhere for years. They found that they could keep on accelerating, far beyond the running speed of a normal human, their legs blurring under them as they ran.

It was just as well. They managed to catch up with Oa and Te but had to push for further speed in order to keep up with them. That ungainly motion of theirs was just an illusion; they were making all the speed the humans could and more.

As such they covered the distance, miles of it, in a very few minutes. They slowed gradually, to stop themselves falling over, and neither human felt the least bit winded for the headlong sprint.

The observation window into the cell was flickering with light from within, bright white flashes like lightning. There were a couple of Dwellers there already; the young, brawny Pre-purposers who had been set to guard the prisoner for a time. Oa approached them.

"Ni, what is happening?" she demanded.

"We do not know, Body master," said Ni, slightly the elder of the two. "It began so suddenly. He cried out, screamed in fact, clearly in great pain. Then he began to convulse. We did not know what to do, so we sounded the alarm."

Oa turned her back on him and marched up to the window. The others crowded around her.

Ko was crouched in the middle of the floor, his body screwed up into a tight foetal ball. Only his head strained up and outwards, revealing a face contorted in agony. Tiny fingers of lightning, or what looked like lightning, snaked around his body and struck into the skin with a bright spark that burned the flesh and made it smoke. Ko was shaking with the pain of it and the effort that went into clamping his jaws shut on the screams that wanted to get out was plain to see on his face.

"What's happening to him?" breathed Kasstovaal.

"I do not know," said Oa. "Ni, how long has he been discharging like this?"

"A short time only," Ni said, over her shoulder. "It began soon after the alarm began."

"He appears to be over-energised," said Oa. "Open the door. I must go to him."

"But, Oa," Ni protested. "It was the will of the Gathering that he should not be...."

"I know the will of Gathering, Ni," said Oa, firmly. "I will take responsibility for this. Open the door, now."

Ni nodded and reached for the panel in the wall. Nothing happened, the door remained sealed shut. Ni tried the control again and then ran his hands over the panel, examining it from within. "The control is fused," he said, urgently. "The door will not open."

"Call for technical assistance," Oa ordered. "Quickly."

"Can't you just form a doorway or something?" Kasstovaal asked.

"It will take much time to break through the shielding," said Oa. "I do not know if we have that much time. I have never seen this before. I must examine him."

Jeryant had been concentrating on the prone figure through the window, furrowing his brow in thought. Suddenly his eyes widened. He turned on his heel and pushed past the others to reach Ni who was bending in front of the panel, beginning to open it up for repair.

"The window controls," he snapped. "Where are they?"

Ni looked up, startled. "Window controls?" he stammered.

"The manual controls to open the outside window," Jeryant demanded. "Where?"

Ni pointed to a crystal on the panel's surface. "That one."

"Try it!"

Ni pressed the crystal and all of them craned through the observation window to see what happened. Nothing did.

"The outer window is jammed, too," said Ni. "I do not understand."

"I do." said Jeryant, savagely, "He's done it."

"What?" exclaimed Kasstovaal. "You mean Ko's done this himself?"

"Of course he has," said Jeryant. "Somehow he must have managed to gather up enough forming power to break through the shielding and jam the mechanism."

"But why, for gods' sake?"

"It's obvious, isn't it? He's insulated himself from the Voidrises. Goodness knows how many he's missed by now. I don't suppose anybody thought to check that the window had opened properly each time. They'd all be too busy venting their own energies to worry about him. He's trying to commit suicide."

"Suicide?"

"Yes," insisted Jeryant. "It's like one of us going on hunger strike, only the opposite way round. He's stocked up an overload of energy inside his body. He's trying to kill himself."

"It's impossible," Oa protested. "No Dweller would conceive of such a thing."

"Just like no Dweller would ever think of trying to destroy two visitors, you mean," said Jeryant, firmly. "He's already shown himself capable of one. Now he's going for the other, I tell you."

He could tell that Oa didn't want to believe it but couldn't deny the evidence of her eyes. She hovered, momentarily lost in confusion, and then pulled herself together. She pushed past him and knelt beside Ni. "I will assist you," she said, urgently, "we must open the door."

Kasstovaal came up close to Jeryant's ear so that he could lower his voice and be heard. "He's trying to turn himself into a martyr, isn't he. What the hells does he expect to achieve by that? It's no good being a martyr if nobody knows your cause except yourself."

"I don't know," Jeryant murmured back. "But remember what he threatened. Whatever it is he's doing he must be stopped, for all our sakes."

"YOU'RE TOO LATE!" screamed a voice from behind the glass.

They turned. Oa moved away from the panel to look herself.

Ko was rising, unsteadily, to his feet, energy still coursing and burning all over his skin. As he straightened up, his entire body whited out for a second as an intense pulse of energy enveloped him from head to foot. He cried out in pain as the pulse racked his body and then, as suddenly, let him go. He turned his eyes towards the window and glared at them malevolently. "You cannot stop it," he yelled. "Three Voidrises have come and gone that I have not seen. I have enough now."

His body whited out again as another pulse flashed across it. He moaned.

"Can't you do something." Te pleaded.

"I cannot," said Oa. "We cannot reach him in time. He has locked us out."

Ko drew a sickly smile across his face. "You can do nothing," he growled, "I am fulfilling my purpose. A purpose of my own choosing, not of another's. I will not stand to see my people degraded anymore. I will free my mind. I must. I shall." Another pulse convulsed him.

"What does he say?" Te asked, bewildered. "Who does he think is holding his mind?"

Kasstovaal and Jeryant glanced at each other. Both knew to say nothing.

Ko began to shudder where he stood. The pulses were racking his body every five seconds or so now, and for an instant Kasstovaal saw Ko's body change from the illusion of a humanoid to the reality of his Dweller body. The semiliquid flesh was roiling and throwing up grey foam under the transparent skin, which had split in several places to form oozing wounds. The real body had seven arms; thin, reedy appendages bending through all angles about four elbow joints apiece and without hands. They waved before his eyes in a mad flurry, energy arcing from the stumps where the hands should have grown. The sight sickened him.

Then the illusion cut back in and Ko was a humanoid again. But Kasstovaal could feel that it wouldn't last. The changes to Ko's body were becoming too complicated for his hypnotised mind to turn into visions he would recognise.

Ko seemed to be looking straight at him now, straight into his eyes, as his master had done. Kasstovaal had to blink to shield his eyes from the brightness of the pulses that flashed in front of him.

Ko growled, "I shall have justice. I shall have revenge." He cried out as another pulse hit him. He gathered his last words into a drawn scream. "I SHALL FREE MY MIND."

Then he screamed with the pain as his body whited out completely, becoming a mass of coursing white light and energy, brightening in surges. Kasstovaal and Jeryant shielded their eyes from the light and could just make out Ko's body jumping between forms as the illusions struggled with what they saw. The terrible screams from within the cell assailed their ears.

Something instinctive inside Kasstovaal, something from the Pilot-Captain inside him, made him shout over the noise, "Everybody stand back! Now!"

And then Ko's body exploded. There was a final, blinding flash and a roar of noise. The observation window blew outwards, showering them all with broken glass. Then a wave of energy thundered out of the cell towards them, expanding outwards from the epicentre of the explosion, where Ko no longer stood.

There was nowhere to run, no time. The wave raked across their bodies, stinging the skin with a thousand needle pricks and knowledge exploded into their minds, cold certainty. Then the wave was gone, surging upward into the Rock, spreading out to reach every room and every Dweller. The Rock wall crackled with miniature lightning and then stilled.

High up in his quarters, Ra felt the wave coming but did nothing to shield himself from it. He could have, if he had wished to, but he must know what it held. The wave bubbled up out of the floor and rushed across his body, seeming to jab at him that little bit harder than it had at the other Dwellers. Childish spite, perhaps. But the knowledge it left behind was the same.

Ra sank down to the floor. What would happen now?

"Fool!" he muttered to himself. "Clever, clever fool."

Outside the cell, the silence after the noise had an intensity that made Kasstovaal wonder if he'd gone deaf. The wave had stunned them all, so close to its source, and all six of them fought to regain balance for their bodies.

But they all knew. Kasstovaal knew that they must. He felt the knowledge ram into his mind as the wave struck, knowledge he already had but burning with certainty and resentment for the truth of it. Ko had sent his message in that wave.

They all know now. They know about you and what you are. I have my justice. I have my revenge. My mind is free.

Kasstovaal shook himself. He must get his wits about him. They must get away, now. He looked around for Jeryant. The medic was leaning against the wall, rubbing at his head with both hands.

Kasstovaal strode across and slapped him across the face, twice. "Come on!" he hissed. "We're going. Right now."

Jeryant gaped at him with unfocused eyes. Then they cleared and he nodded, "Yes."

They turned and made off along the corridor, accelerating towards the run that had brought them here. Kasstovaal stole one look behind, before the curve of the wall hid the cell from his view. He looked straight into Te's face, frozen in horrified incredulity, staring straight back at him. It was not the last sight of her he would have wanted, but it would have to be. He wanted to explain. He wanted to go back and beg her forgiveness, seek her understanding. But he could not. He must not. This was how she would remember him, running from his crimes.

Then the curve took her away from him and his soul wept as he ran.

29.

They ran. Neither of them knew what speed they achieved but they kept on accelerating until the walls blurred to either side of them. They rushed past Dwellers in the corridor, all turning to look after them as they passed. They did not stop for them.

Kasstovaal was gripped by the panic born of his fears suddenly coming true, panic that was driving him on. Jeryant had been scooped up in it, in those first confused seconds after the blast. But it had worn off now and he was racing to keep up with his friend and stop him from doing anything stupid, as he looked well in a mind to do.

They did not stop until the reached Oa's laboratory. Gods only knew how Kasstovaal had managed to navigate his way here at that speed, Jeryant thought. They both had to skid along the floor to bring themselves to a full stop; Kasstovaal had not wanted to waste speed in a prolonged deceleration.

Inside their new bodies waited for them, floating in their nutrient tanks.

"Get them ready," Kasstovaal snapped. He was in crisis mode, Jeryant could see; every inch the Pilot-Captain, ready to take the snap decisions and give the orders that would save lives. One perilous step away from panic.

"Slow down, Kass," Jeryant warned. "We can't afford to rush this. We don't need to. Nobody's chasing us and I can't hear any alarms sounding."

Kasstovaal glared at him, seemed to grow a few inches as his emotions swelled him up so that he towered over Jeryant. "They know, Jery," he growled. "We both sensed it. How long is it going to be before that knowledge sinks in? What will happen when it does?"

"I can't tell," said Jeryant, poking him in the chest with a finger. "And neither can you. You're assuming the worst of these people, as usual."

"That's right. I want to be prepared for the worst, whether or not I think that's how they'll act. If I'm wrong then it won't matter; we were going to leave soon anyway."

"All right, then." Jeryant punched a hole in the side of each tank, with his amplifier, allowing the clear liquid to leak out. He didn't bother to form it away but left it, pooling on the floor. "Just don't lose it on me now, okay."

"Anything I can do?"

"You could look around for your amplifier. It might still be in here somewhere."

Kasstovaal searched, trying all the while to keep his frustration in check. It was the worst condition to be searching in; every minute that passed in which he failed to find the thing made his inner rage boil up even further and made him less diligent. He might have stared straight at it a dozen times already without seeing it, so distracted was his mind. If he hadn't found the amplifier when he did, nestling innocently on a shelf, he would soon have been upending whatever furniture would move. He snatched it up, like a prize, and felt the tension subside.

Should he put it in place himself? Could he do it, at all? Could Jeryant, for that matter? Hells, he thought, give it a try.

Tearing the insulating band from around his head, he pressed the plastic strip to his forehead and held it there. He felt it suck onto his skin like a wet leech and quickly drew his hand away as the plastic liquefied. He felt the sharp pressure as the crystal bored into his skin and then there was the sudden disorienting leap of his senses as they reached out further than they were usually able to. He staggered and made a blind grab for the wall to hold himself upright. He didn't quite get the grip he wanted and had slipped to his knees before his perceptions snapped back to normal. He stayed where he was, on the floor, for several seconds while his brain caught up with his senses and then pushed himself back onto his feet.

Better see if it works. He held out his hand and concentrated on forming an orange. He thought he might be out of practice but his mind fell easily into the skill and the orange appeared in his hand with barely an effort.

He vanished it and went back to the tanks. Jeryant had lifted his own other body clear of its tank and was holding it under the arms to stand it on its feet. The skin was steaming as the nutrient evaporated off it, under the force from Jeryant's amplifier.

Kasstovaal went over to his new body and began to do likewise. As he lifted the dead weight in his arms, his own face came up to meet his eyes and he almost dropped it. He had never seen his own face in such detail, all three dimensions plain to view; the tan of the skin, the rise of the cheek bones, the set of the jaw. It might have been like staring into a mirror except that the face in front of him was slack and lifeless, the green eyes staring at nothing. For an uncomfortable moment, his mind insisted that he was looking in a mirror, that this was how he appeared, a lump of dead meat.

He pulled himself together and began to form away the residue of the nutrient, clinging to its skin. It was still an 'It'. He couldn't yet think of it as him.

They dried the bodies off and formed simple one-piece crew coveralls onto them.

"What now?" Kasstovaal asked. "Do we transfer into them and leave the old bodies here?"

"No, no," said Jeryant. "We can't. These bodies need oxygen to operate. We need a pressurised area before we can activate them."

"Best do it in the hangar then," said Kasstovaal, heaving his other self onto his shoulders. "We can use the antechamber as an airlock."

"Right." Jeryant hefted his own corpse and they made their way out.

The corridor immediately outside was deserted. All the better, Kasstovaal thought, though they couldn't hope to go the whole way without meeting somebody. They jogged. Fatigue did not bother them and their strength was dictated only by the force of their will so they could have accelerated to their earlier speed if they had wanted to. But they didn't trust their balance with the extra weight on their shoulders so they kept down to a jogging pace.

Sure enough, they did encounter Dwellers in the corridors. As before, the Dwellers would pause in their stride and stare, strangely, at them, watching them for some seconds after they passed by.

Don't look at them, Kasstovaal told himself. Don't meet their eyes, don't react to their stares. Keep going. Keep going. He repeated it over and over to himself, like a mantra, hoping to hide from them the guilt he could feel inside, guilt he didn't deserve or have any right to.

This time, the distance down to the lower levels seemed to take forever and not merely because of their reduced pace. Kasstovaal wanted to speed up, wanted to run and bugger the risk but that would have been another admission of guilt. His relief was tangible when they finally turned into the corridor and opened the doorway into the antechamber.

They carried the bodies into the hangar proper, and laid them carefully on the floor.

"Check that we sealed the outer door," Kasstovaal said. "We could be here all day if we try and pressurise the entire Rock."

Jeryant looked back through the observation window. "All shut," he confirmed. "Let's get on with it."

They stood, back to back, in the centre of the floor, closed their eyes and concentrated on forming air. A simple enough mixture. Their minds knew what they wanted. They felt a stiff breeze begin to blow against their faces, smelling of mown grass and hot afternoons. Which one of them was being sentimental?

They continued until the breeze stilled around them and the air felt strangely heavy with gas. Kasstovaal squeezed into the *Gateway 2*'s cockpit and consulted the environment sensor.

"Spot on," he said. "Couldn't have done it better with a machine."

Jeryant was crouched over the bodies on the floor. Kasstovaal joined him.

"Just a quick jolt to start the mechanisms," said Jeryant, almost to himself, "and we're ready to rock."

He fixed his forming stare on the facsimile of himself and the green crystal in the centre of his forehead glowed. The inert body on the floor suddenly convulsed as it drew its first deep, shuddering breath of air and then settled down into a steady, natural rhythm. Jeryant re-aimed his thoughts and, soon, both bodies were breathing normally, mindless but alive.

"Right, then." Jeryant blew out his own breath, tinged with nerves. "Now for the proof of the pudding."

Between them, they lifted the other Jeryant onto its feet and Kasstovaal stood back to give his friend room.

Jeryant placed his hands on the other's shoulders. "Now, if I'm right," he said, "it's merely a case of projecting all your thoughts at once. The other brain should absorb them easily." He fell silent, staring hard into his own face. The green amplifier crystal glowed dully.

Then Jeryant's black Bio-form collapsed, its knees gave out and it fell, heavily, against the human body in front of it on its way down. The human Jeryant's arms came up and caught the Bio-form under the shoulders, as it fell, and lowered it gently, almost reverently, down to the floor.

Jeryant, fully human again, turned and gave Kasstovaal his big friendly smile, one that Kasstovaal had not seen for many weeks. A smile on a human face.

"Well, that was easy," said Jeryant. His voice crackled a bit and he cleared his throat a few times.

"How do you feel?" Kasstovaal asked.

Jeryant flexed his limbs and passed his hands over his torso, appreciating his own handiwork. "Better than average," he said. "In fact I don't think I've felt so well in twenty-five years." He beat at his chest. "It's definitely an improvement on the Bio-form."

He bent down to the floor. "Your turn, I think."

Kasstovaal hesitated. Jeryant had made it look easy but.... It would be a moment of death, that brief second in which his mind inhabited no body. Time enough, so they said, for the doorway into the afterlife to open and draw him in if he once lost his way. Did he believe that?

"Come on!" Jeryant urged. "If I can do it, it should be a piece of piss for you. All it takes is one small push. You'll hardly know it's happening. Trust me."

I have to do this, Kasstovaal told himself. It'll be death for real, and for sure, if I don't. I must do it.

He started forward, breaking the hesitation, and was committed. He didn't dare pause again and think about it, in case his resolve failed him. He just let himself act through it.

He hoisted his new body onto its feet, balancing it carefully, and then took a firm hold of its shoulders. He closed his eyes and tried to marshal his thoughts into one, compact package that he could throw across empty air into that other brain.

Help me, he thought within himself, hardly knowing who he was calling to. If you want to save me, both of us, help me across.

He gathered himself, opened his eyes and stared straight into the eyes of the other Kasstovaal, those dead, green eyes. He pushed.

There was a sensation of lightness, like inebriation only increasing moment by moment as the weight of the body fell away. He felt an urge to fight it, to concentrate and think it away like he would a dose of alcohol. Must not resist it, he told himself, must not try to hold on. Must let go.

His vision changed. He was no longer looking into the face of a dead human, but a black, rubbery face that wore his worried eyes. The eyes rolled up into its head and the Bio-form crumpled into his arms. He caught it without thinking, his mind hardly registered the weight.

He had never conceived how good a human body could feel. It was moist, not dry like this thing he held in his arms. The skin did not squeeze into him and restrict his every move. He could feel the hair on his head, feel the muscles that held him upright. He could feel his heart beating. That was what brought it home to him at last, that simple pump and thrust that had been missing from the very core of him.

"I'm...alive," he whispered.

Jeryant came up behind him and clapped him across the shoulders. "You certainly are, sunshine. Feels good, doesn't it."

Kasstovaal's arm muscles began to protest and he laid the inert Bio-form down on the floor with all the reverence Jeryant had shown. It was an ugly, distasteful thing but it had held him safe from death for a while. He owed it respect.

But he could not dwell long over the memorial for his former self. They had to leave. The next task was to put on the flight suits that he had made for them, designed to cope with the cold and vacuum when attached to the supporting helmet. Being fully familiar with his own dimensions, his suit fitted perfectly.

Jeryant's suit turned out to be baggy and he had to matter-form it down to size with much grumbling. Kasstovaal had relied on his memory for the size and he suspected that the Doctor had been downsizing his waistline from the norm while he had the chance to do it the easy way.

"You are leaving us, then," said a voice behind them.

The two humans spun around. Te and Oa stood watching them, just inside the doorway they had made in from the antechamber. The corridor wall was sealed; they had realised about the air pressure.

Kasstovaal took a few paces towards them, holding up his hands defensively. "Don't try to stop us, either of you. We're leaving now. We must. It's for the best." He made to turn away.

"Please wait." There was pleading in Te's voice, almost a sob.

Kasstovaal paused and then turned back to face her. Te seemed to have diminished, her energy stunned and still. She looked very small, very alone.

"Ko has told us all the truth," she said, softly. "I find it difficult to believe and yet we all felt the truth in him."

"The truth as he saw it," said Jeryant. "He blamed us for what has happened. He couldn't accept that we had no conscious control over it."

"Did you know?" Oa's voice was impassive, but only by a detectable effort.

"Not until Ra told us."

Kasstovaal said, "You saw into my mind, Te. You know that I knew nothing of it. You know that I wouldn't have wished it. Tell me that you felt that inside me."

Te hesitated. He could see conflict reflected on the illusion of her face. He went to her and took her in his arms, her face pressed against the newly beating heart. "Tell me you believe me," he begged.

She did not resist him but he felt her quiver in his arms and he knew it could not be the Voidrise this time.

"Tell me one thing," she said, softly. "Can you stop it? Will you?"

Kasstovaal closed his eyes. He wanted to. If he could have put a stop to it, there and then, he would have done it, smashed all the links to his universe and closed all the voids forever. He would, gladly, have given it to her as a gift, no matter what it cost him. But it was out of his reach.

"I don't know," he had to admit. "Truly, I don't know."

She looked up into his face. "Will you try?" she pleaded. "You have so much power within you. Will you not try?"

"I will," said Kasstovaal. He pushed her, gently, away from him and touched the tip of his forefinger to the centre of her forehead. "We have part of each other inside us. I will not forget and I will do all I can."

"I believe you," said Te.

"Will the others?"

"I do not know. Some may but some will not. We shall see. But it is better that you go now."

He withdrew his finger and gestured down at his own body. "What do you think of the real me?" he asked, smiling.

Te took a step away from him and examined his new form from head to foot. "Most peculiar," she said, herself smiling. "But, somehow, it seems to suit you."

"It certainly feels more...me." He glanced over at Oa. "No offence meant."

"None is taken." Oa's voice had softened, no longer needing tight and painful control. "I must admit that I would not have believed that these bodies could work so well, had I not seen it for myself."

"What!" Jeryant exclaimed. "After all my careful tuition, you say that?"

"Some things defy description in mere words," said Oa, with a totally straight face, "and have to be seen to believed."

Jeryant narrowed his eyes. "Are you trying to be funny, woman?"

"I am not sure I understand the meaning of that word, Jeryant."

"You know very well what it means," Jeryant nodded his satisfaction. "I've obviously taught you well."

Oa gave a little bow of acknowledgement and, then, her face hardened into serious lines. "Now you must go, Beyonders," she said. "No more goodbyes. If you can do no more for us, you can give us the chance to continue as we were before. Not free but with a way to freedom. Go. Leave us to our fate."

It was hard to turn away; they had to force their limbs to do it, in defiance of their souls' will. Once done, they did not allow themselves to look back.

They eased themselves through the ship's airlock and Kasstovaal sealed it behind them. In silence, they took their respective seats and strapped themselves in.

"Anything I can assist with?" Jeryant asked.

Kasstovaal let the ship's pulse penetrate his body, brought himself into communion with it. His mind switched into pilot-mode, automatically lining up the procedures he would follow, connecting him to the machine.

"Enjoy the ride," he said, simply.

The thrum of the reaction core rose to his touch and the ship seemed to brace itself for the leap it had been longing to make. Kasstovaal checked the monitor showing the view behind the ship. Oa and Te had retreated to the safety of the antechamber, sealing the doorway behind them. They were visible through the observation window, watching the ship as it readied for take-off. As he looked he saw Te raise one hand in a human gesture of goodbye, as though she knew he would see her at that moment.

He drew his eyes away and flexed his forming power through the array of amplifiers around his head. It came easily, with so much extra power behind it. He created a small hole, to begin with, to allow the air to escape out into the vacuum. Then he opened the hangar fully to the whiteness of Space.

There was a rising tone that filled the cockpit and then the engines fired and pushed the little ship towards the hole. The rock clamps that held it to the floor let go their grip and the ship sprang forward eagerly, lifting itself clear of the floor and plunging out through the hole into the mist. The humans were pressed back into their seats by the thrust and Kasstovaal's heart leapt with his ship. Free, free at last.

Jeryant kept his eyes on the rear-view monitor, watching the Rock fall away behind them. He had never seen the Rock in its entirety before; he had not got around to asking Oa for a trip out on a plate, what with one thing and another. It was an impressive sight. He had seen greater and more imposing mountains on the surfaces of many planets but the sight of the Rock hanging there in Space, proud and unafraid, stood it above its planet-bound contemporaries. He would never see it again and he knew that, wherever he travelled within his own universe, he would never see anything that came near to that sight.

Kasstovaal did not look back but looked out, in front. They were in open Space, clear of the Rock's influence. That was what he wanted. He didn't know which direction he was heading in, the systems had no data to navigate by, but it didn't matter. All he could be reasonably sure of was that he wasn't heading towards the near face of the Barrier. He could not see it in the mists ahead. Even that didn't matter. All he had to do was open a portal in open Space and they would be out of here. He would have to take a chance on what they would encounter when they entered the Second Mode and again when they passed through into the First Mode. But the odds were pretty good; there's a lot of empty Space in both universes. Better than staying here.

He diverted power to the Destabiliser and adjusted the beam focus to a point a safe distance ahead of them. "Ready for transit?" he asked automatically.

"Wait!" Jeryant took him by the wrist to restrain him. "We have to be VERY ready for this transit, sunshine." He tapped his own forehead. "Don't forget that."

He almost had. His brain had been running on its own automatic pilot, the one that could virtually control the ship while he slept, and the amplifiers had all but slipped his mind. A fatal omission, this one time. You didn't make omissions like that if you were in command of a spacecraft. You trained yourself out of them; you didn't let your eagerness or your fears or any other emotions tempt you into cutting corners. You never thought that "Just this once it won't hurt". That was what being a Pilot-Captain was all about. He had known that once. The special circumstances made no difference.

My gods, he thought. Has the De-phase syndrome taken me down that far? I shouldn't be sitting at these controls; I don't deserve to. Did I make a mistake before? Is that what brought us here in the first place?

He still couldn't remember. It might have been so. One mistake that would, indeed, have been fatal for the both of them, had it not been for the Dwellers.

Perhaps it was time, then. Time to surrender his licence and withdraw from active service. Time to take his life off the line.

"Kass!" Jeryant's voice pulled him back from the revelation. These were considerations for later, once they were back in their own reality. They still had a whole universe separating them from it.

"Right." he said "Any advice on how we do this."

"I suppose, to start with, we should make sure our minds are totally familiar with the pattern of our new bodies. Use the amplifiers to get a feel for the pattern. Do it now."

Kasstovaal closed his eyes and concentrated on his body. Through the amplifiers he could feel the life pulsing in every cell, sense the structure that held it together. How strong it was. He had never realised that he had that much strength standing between him and death. It gave him a wonderful feeling of invincibility. He opened his eyes and the feeling stayed with him, swelling his confidence.

"Now what?"

Jeryant shrugged. "When we go through the portal, just concentrate on forming that pattern as hard as you can, I guess. I suppose we'll have to hold it all the way through to the First Mode, to be sure. How long will that take?"

"No more than a few seconds. I'll preprogram the Destabiliser to auto-fire as soon as the ship enters the Second Mode. Ten seconds, at most, for the two transits."

"Fine," said Jeryant. "Apart from that, just pray."

"I can't think of any gods I'd want to pray to, right now."

Jeryant looked at him sidelong. "Who said anything about praying to gods?"

He said no more but Kasstovaal knew what he meant. It wasn't a god that watched over him.

He reached for the controls again. "Ready?"

"Let's do it."

Kasstovaal activated the sequence and the Destabiliser shot a nano-thin beam of energy into the space a few kilometres ahead of them. A pale blue line of light became visible at that spot and began to widen. Then it stopped widening. Lightning began to crackle around the tear and the line spat enormous blue sparks towards the ship. Then the gap snapped shut.

An agonised silence fell inside the cockpit.

After a few moments, Jeryant said, mildly, "Kass! It isn't working."

Kasstovaal just sat there, his jaw slackening.

Jeryant asked, just as mildly, "Why isn't it working, Kass?"

It should have worked. It had to work. He'd tested it, time and again, inside the laboratory, experiments he had done in his own universe, hundreds of time with the same success. It had worked every time. Why not now, just when they needed it most?

"I...don't understand," he muttered.

"Try it again." Jeryant said.

Yes, that was the first step. Kasstovaal reset the sequence and started it a second time. The effect was the same. At the third attempt, one of the sparks reached the ship and bounced off the hull. But the portal remained resolutely closed.

"Is there a fault or something?" Jeryant asked, urgency creeping into his voice.

"No." It had been the first thing Kasstovaal checked when his mind got over its numbness. "The Destabiliser's working perfectly. It must be something else. I don't understand."

Then a thought struck him. "You don't suppose the Dwellers are doing it, do you? Interfering with the beam to try and keep us here?"

"Not likely," said Jeryant. "It's still in their interest for us to leave, no matter what they think of us now. The Barrier will keep closing in on them until we do."

The Barrier. Kasstovaal's mind raced. Could that be the problem? What else had changed around here, after all. "The Barrier's closing in." he said, half to himself.

"You know it is. You discovered it, remember."

"It's closing around the whole universe, squeezing it inwards. Of course! That has to be the reason."

"What does."

"The Barrier still forms a sealed container so there will still be the same amount of spatial matter inside it. The Barrier is compressing that matter into a smaller space, making the fabric of the universe much denser. It's been happening ever since we arrived. It wasn't too advanced when I was doing my lab tests; that's why they worked okay. But now it's reached a point where the fabric is too dense to split apart. We can't make a hole in it big enough to pass through."

"Well isn't it just a case of cranking up the power?" Jeryant asked. "Applying more force?"

"The Destabiliser's at maximum strength. There's no way to up the power any more, even with a second unit."

Jeryant bit his lip. "We'll have to go back to the Rock," he said. "Find some other way."

Kasstovaal felt his mind filling with fear again, the confidence had ebbed out of him. "No!" he snapped. "We can't. Not now."

"What choice do we have?" Jeryant shouted back. "If we can't open the portal, we're still as stuck as we were before. And they're still as doomed as before. There's no other populated world we could reach in time. They must help us."

"No!" Kasstovaal repeated, firmly. "There must be an alternative."

"What?" Jeryant demanded. "What alternative, Kass? Are you proposing that we sit in here and rack our brains for one until the Barrier catches up with us? Or maybe you're thinking of turning us around and crashing us against the Barrier. Getting it over with quick. Well you can count me out of that, sunshine. And yourself. And what are you smiling at?"

Kasstovaal's lips we widening into a grin. "Jery," he said. "You're a genius."

"What? What did I say."

"The Barrier. It's an energy field, right. What's more, it's an energy field whose dimensions are constantly changing as it shrinks. The energy structure will be in a constant state of flux."

"I don't know what you're on about. Try keeping it simple."

"Look, it's like any other force field. It must be. It's at its strongest when it's established at a constant radius. If the radius is changing then the field will be very unstable, constantly having to adjust to the new dimensions."

"So?"

"So the Barrier may be weak enough that we can make a portal in it."

Jeryant stared at him. "You're crazy," he said. "Where the hells would that take us?"

"If we're lucky, it might open onto the Second Mode."

"Or it might just open to the...," Jeryant hesitated for a word, "... outside. Whatever you call it."

"The void between the universes," Kasstovaal said, ominously.

"That's right. You want to end up there, do you?"

"Why not? No other human will ever get a chance to see it. And, who knows, it might be navigable. We could locate the Barrier into our own universe and penetrate that too. It will be unstable, as well, until we return to it. And even if we can't find our way back, it'll still remove us from this universe. It'll save the Dwellers for sure, if not us." He turned his head and looked Jeryant straight in the eye. "What do you say, Jery? Want to see the infinite before you die?"

Jeryant looked back at him. There was no sign of panic, of fear, hardly a single sign of tension. Bouyed up by the new power he had to fight off death, Kasstovaal was calm and rational, at last, and he meant what he said. Jeryant could see that. And there was something in the eyes, a fire of excitement, something Jeryant hadn't seen there in a long time. He beamed. "Hells, why not! Can't think of a better way to go."

The *Gateway 2* banked around hard and its engines thrust it towards the faint blue shimmer that showed fleetingly through the mist. The voids watched them pull away before the mist covered them from sight.

The mist parted and the black wall of the Barrier stood before them. Kasstovaal brought the ship to a stop. Could he really do it, split open a universe? Did he dare?

For his own part, he did. He would remove them from this universe and Te would be safe. He could do that, at least, for her. The mystery out there beckoned him. He wanted to know what was there. Perhaps that was the part of Te that he carried with him, that insatiable thirst for new knowledge. Or perhaps it was part of himself, a long buried part, the wanderer's spirit coming to life and burning again inside him. Wanting to go there.

He did offer one prayer to his invisible mentor and protector, if that was what it was.

You got any objections?

Silence. He took that as a no.

He took the controls again. "Ready?"

"As I'll ever be. You'd better be right about this."

"Okay."

"Or I'll stamp on your head."

"Got it."

The Destabiliser fired. The slit of blue light that appeared in the Barrier's surface was not the mathematical straight line of a normal portal but a ragged crack as might appear in a sheet of glass. But it did open, widening like a horribly twisted mouth, expanding to swallow a ship.

Kasstovaal felt the ship moving under him, though he had not fired the engines to move them forward. The portal was drawing them in, sucking them into its maw.

"This is it," said Jeryant. "Concentrate, Kass. Concentrate for your life."

Kasstovaal was concentrating. He was staring fixedly into the centre of the hole that rushed up to meet them. He could not see the profusion of multicoloured stars that filled the Second Mode. Only blackness, coming fast towards them, engulfing them.

A wave of energy skimmed over the surface of the Barrier, washing over the crack and sealing the portal behind them.

30.

Te was alone. She sat in one of the alcoves in the Chamber of Purpose, waiting silently. It was her time. At last she would know.

Ra had come in person to summon her here, rather than send a message through the Rock's veins as he usually did. Since the Beyonders had left he had become a great deal more solicitous towards his people, one might even say friendly. Te could not help but pity him. His purpose had suddenly become so much more difficult that he might never find a solution for it. His charges had changed from a people resigned to serving a nebulous higher purpose to a people who saw the yoke of slavery under which they toiled. He had to guide them, encourage them along the same path they had travelled for generations, and he no longer knew how.

The Beyonders had changed all their lives, Te's perhaps most of all. But, unlike her fellows, she did not resent the change. Kasstovaal had given her a wonderful gift. He had given her an entire universe full of new wonders to enjoy; millions of worlds, quintillions of people, more new dreams than she could ever experience in her lifetime. As her childhood faded away, the Rock had become dull, nothing but stone, hiding away all the mysteries she had once been able to find. Now she had her own store of wonders.

She still laboured to put it all down in the profile she was creating for her people but there was just so much of it. Besides which, she got the feeling that her people would not be inclined to enjoy it just now. Future Dwellers might, though, when the memory had faded and acceptance had been achieved.

But she would have less time to work on it, now. She would soon have her purpose to concentrate on. She still held out the vain hope that her purpose might be to finish the profile or develop some study in connection with the Beyonders. But that seemed unlikely, now. If the Beyonders created the purposes what need would they have of a study of themselves? No. She would have to work on the profile when she could and be satisfied.

She wondered if they had made it back to their home. She hoped so. She could not wish them ill. She had a part of Kasstovaal inside her. So sad a being, so full of the life he clung on to. That fragment warmed her mind when she touched it, just as his mind had. She would not forget him.

What then would her purpose be? Something normal, she supposed. Now that the Beyonders were gone, normality must eventually reassert itself. The Barrier would eventually cease its inward motion and Ra would find a way to restore the order that had kept the Dwellers going for so long. Te would take her purpose from this chamber and perform it to the utmost of her ability and would, eventually, earn the right to join Vo out among the mists.

Ah Prim, she thought to herself, what would you have made of this?

Then the purpose came to her, not in a great rush or with any ceremony. It just appeared there in her mind, quietly and without fuss. A few short words inserted into her thoughts.

She felt herself go cold. Her body trembled and the wave that escaped from her held dismay and horror as she saw the meaning of it, understood the implications. Knew her task.

"No," she whispered to no one who would hear her. "Not that. Anything but that."

THE END

ABOUT THE AUTHOR

David Mills lives in Orpington, England, immersed in cult television and looking after his pet Dalek (easy to clean up after but a bugger to feed!).

He took up stockbroker back office work in the city of London to pay the rent and ward off the bills but managed to escape from the cage long enough to write this, his first novel, which had been boiling away in his brain for years and had to be let out.

Printed in the United Kingdom
by Lightning Source UK Ltd.
111413UKS00002B/70-72